A LISTENING WIND

NATIVE LITERATURES OF THE AMERICAS SERIES

A LISTENING WIND

NATIVE LITERATURE FROM THE SOUTHEAST

Edited and with an introduction by Marcia Haag

UNIVERSITY OF NEBRASKA PRESS *Lincoln and London*

Manufactured in the United
States of America

Financial support was provided from
the Office of the Vice President for
Research, University of Oklahoma.

Library of Congress
Cataloging-in-Publication Data
Names: Haag, Marcia, 1951– editor.
Title: A listening wind: Native literature
from the Southeast / edited and with
an introduction by Marcia Haag.
Other titles: Native literature
from the Southeast
Description: Lincoln: University of
Nebraska Press, [2016] | Includes
bibliographical references and index.
Identifiers: LCCN 2016007237 (print)
LCCN 2016010583 (ebook)
ISBN 9780803262874 (cloth: alk. paper)
ISBN 9780803295483 (pdf)
Subjects: LCSH: Indians of North
America—Southern States—Folklore.
| Indian mythology—Southern
States. | Tales—Southern States.
Classification: LCC E78.S65 L58
2016 (print) | LCC E78.S65 (ebook)
| DDC 398.2089/97075—dc23
LC record available at http://
lccn.loc.gov/2016007237

Set in Charis by Rachel Gould.
Designed by N. Putens.

CONTENTS

MUSKOGEE (CREEK)

CHICKASAW

CHEROKEE

KOASATI

SMALLER SOUTHEASTERN TRIBES

INTRODUCTION

Marcia Haag

This volume is one in the series of books devoted to Native literatures, inaugurated and edited by Brian Swann. The material here is from the Native peoples of the southeastern portion of the United States. The Southeast groups consist of both related peoples (for example, the large group of Muskogeans) and those whose closest relatives either disappeared or were absorbed by other groups. Hence we find disparate language groups, but at the same time peoples who often share many elements of a common culture, through the spreading of practices such as the cultivation of corn and the ease of trade via the large riverine highways of the Southeast. I cannot define "Southeast" in a way that definitively includes some groups and excludes others. Instead I use my best evaluation of that term, based largely on the cultural groups who were present in the area known as the "Old South" from about 1600 forward and who had not been absorbed or scattered by the time text collection began.

In apprehending the literary traditions of the Southeast peoples, we need to take account of the long shared history of these peoples with European and later American whites, beginning before whites represented as profound a threat as they would prove to be. Europeans introduced cows, chickens, horses, guns, fabrics—things that would become readily incorporated into southeastern native lifestyles, even while the tension over land and European proxy wars made the Natives' control over their own peoples and destinies ever more tenuous.

Some of the tribes were driven to annihilation or absorption within other groups, and their languages were made extinct or virtually so. But others made affiliations with whites, trading with them, joining their military exploits, and adopting much of their material culture. The tribes that survived found themselves living among ever larger populations of white colonists, who intermarried with the Native populations and introduced them to plantation farming and slaveholding.[1]

Mixed-race men were very often leaders in their tribes. Southeastern Native people fought in wars side by side with American or British soldiers. In the Civil War they chose sides; those who sided with Confederates were punished as if they were Americans.

The point is that the societies of Southeast Native peoples have been evolving alongside the eventually dominant white newcomers for hundreds of years. This can be seen in the literature, which makes common reference to that fact; moreover, the influences on their literatures, those of general Southeast, of Europe, and of Africa cannot be completely disentangled, as will be seen.

HOW "LITERATURE"?

Soon after I began this project, it was thrust upon me that my ideas about interesting and valuable pieces written by Native authors might have their cultural and linguistic attractions, but they could not be counted as "literature."[2] Even if we allow that Western concepts of literature can hardly be appropriate here, there remains the problem of how to describe the many artifacts of written Native language; hence we may speak of "texts," "ethnopoetics," "verbal arts," "discourse," "the ethnography of speaking," "rhetorics," "folklore," and probably others. Even the act of writing rather than speaking may be suspect. Compelling arguments have been made to us that the oral tradition in the original language, situated in the true cultural context, is the authentic one, and that written facsimiles of these performances are weak at best and distortions at worst. In H. C. Wolfarts's vivid words, "What is authentic, in any ordinary sense of the term, about reducing a *viva voce* delivery with all its voice qualities, dramatic effects, and gestures, with its knowing and expectant audience, to cold print?"[3] The most successful efforts incorporate as much of the oral performance as possible using techniques especially developed to do so. The work of Dell Hymes is groundbreaking in this regard, as he establishes means of putting the qualities of the performance into written form, what we term *ethnopoetics*.[4] The interpreter-recorder endeavors to capture as much about the sound of the performance as possible, using devices such as capitalization and line breaks that signal voice amplitude and pauses. In some cases a running set of notes in the margin helps the reader to track the narrative, since often the real-life audience knows perfectly well what the story is and does not need much in the way of refreshed references and links to events in the stories.

Even writing itself may lead to the detriment of spoken languages, as Jane Hill instructs us in a sobering indictment, because writing discards the phonetic and prosodic nuances of speech, and privileges the lexical items of one dialect over another, as well as standardizing grammar along the theoretical lines of whichever linguist holds most sway.[5] Worse, it teaches communities of speakers that language preservation is achieved by helping the young to read, learn, and value a standard dialect, the correctness of which can be verified, again because it is written, rather than to speak in natural situations, with the variation attendant upon speech.

Without diminishing in any way the primacy and the glories of performed literature (to coin yet another inadequate term), the simple truth is that Native people have been writing for a long time. Those of us who concentrate on North America often forget that writing was invented in ancient Mesoamerica without reference to European alphabetic systems. (Barbara Tedlock's discussion of the history of texts from this era through Spanish colonialization is highly informative.)[6]

As a consequence of the close proximity, and even the occasional interrelatedness of the Southeast tribes with white Americans, these tribes became aware of writing and its advantages very early on. Indeed, the Choctaws in particular asked to be missionized—this request was eagerly fulfilled—not because they particularly wanted to convert to Christianity but because they wanted to learn to read and write.[7] When the Presbyterian missionary Cyrus Byington came to the Choctaws in 1820 (he would devote the rest of his life to them and their language), he soon developed a roman-based orthography. What is remarkable is that the Choctaws lost no time in learning to write with it. The Cherokees, showing even more alacrity with Sequoyah's marvelous invention of the syllabary, finished in 1821, taught it to each other, even if they did not attend school. The syllabary had and still has enormous symbolic connection to the people. Mooney suggests that the literacy rate among Cherokees was high even a few months after the syllabary's introduction. Certainly by 1828 literacy was high enough to support the first Cherokee newspaper, the *Cherokee Phoenix*, published in New Echota (in present-day Georgia).[8] The Creeks and Seminoles too acquired writing in the early 1830s after having moved to Indian Territory (present day Oklahoma). Again they had invited missionaries to instruct them in literacy, but this story has a less happy ending. Those missionaries were expelled a few years later for preaching, which the Creeks had expressly forbidden. The Creeks eventually settled on a National Alphabet, modified by Loughridge, Robertson, and Robertson from an earlier one. Many Creeks were literate by the end of the nineteenth century.[9]

The fifth of the "Five Civilized Tribes," a term used without irony by many of its members today, the Chickasaws, have an interesting story with respect to writing. Chickasaw is closely related to Choctaw, and many Chickasaws spoke both. The Chickasaws, too, invited missionaries to create schools for them in the early nineteenth century. However, these schools concentrated on agricultural and mechanical skills for boys and the domestic arts for girls, far more than literacy. Most important, the educators did not see their way to learning the Chickasaw language, instead compelling the Chickasaw children to learn to speak and read in English.[10] Hence the Chickasaws did not create their own orthography or even borrow that of the Choctaws. Rather, early Chickasaw texts are written in Choctaw, including even their constitution. That this is so is readily apparent: even though many Chickasaw words are strongly cognate and even identical to Choctaw, the grammatical particles are rather different, such that one who is familiar with both languages knows in a paragraph or so which language is being written.

The Chickasaw Language Revitalization Program (see Hinson, this volume) has tasked itself with the fascinating problem of going back to Chickasaw speaker Zeno McCurtain's early stories, written in Choctaw at the end of the nineteenth century, and translating them into Chickasaw and then again into English.

The Rev. James Humes and his wife Vinnie May created a Chickasaw orthography, published in their dictionary of 1973. Professor Pamela Munro and speaker Catherine Willmond formulated a linguistically based orthography that appears in their 1994 dictionary. The Chickasaw Nation uses both these orthographies in their various undertakings, including language teaching and preservation. Until this point the Chickasaw people had been spelling as they were moved to do and were not especially perturbed by the lack of an official orthography.

But let us return to the problem of literature. It is one thing for people everywhere to apprehend the value of being able to fix speech in time and place, as well as to unburden themselves of the need to recall speech, with its attendant risks. It is another thing to claim that what is written represents literature, rather than other kinds of useful texts, from sets of laws to bookkeeping ledgers. As Arnold Krupat explains, "In the second half of the nineteenth century, the meaning of *literature* shifted away from an emphasis on the form of presentation (writing) toward an emphasis on the content of the presentation (imaginative and affective material)."[11]

Craig Womack, in discussing Native people's "meaningful literary efforts" comments that "it is still a struggle simply to legitimate Native approaches to Native texts, to say that it is OK for Indians to do it their own way."[12]

WHY AND HOW THIS BOOK FOUND ITS SHAPE

This volume is a collection of "Indians doing it their own way." Readers will not fail to notice that each collection is introduced with essays that differ in style and point of view—radically so. For anyone wondering what the editor's instructions to contributors were, those instructions were to think deeply about what this "literature" is for their people, pick out examples, and explain them to people outside their groups.

They were not asked to form essays around some organizing theme (based on some Western lit-crit category): to do that would have been to stanch the flow by creating the distance of criticism, of being watched and judged, of conforming to some template. I fully accept that many readers may be quite comfortable with a template and may prefer that to continually having to recalibrate their brains to new ways of presentation.

My experience in gathering the Koasati (Coushatta) collection perhaps best illustrates the spirit that underlies this book. The Coushattas, who speak the Koasati language, had preserved their culture and language for decades by lying low in rural Louisiana and Texas, reasoning that the less meddling they attracted from the larger culture, the better they could deflect whatever mischief might result from that attention. (See Linda Langley's heartfelt description of this history in her "Koasati (Coushatta) Literature," this volume.) But very recently a new zeitgeist appeared among the people. They told me that they were finished being silent and invisible and felt ready to emerge into the greater world—but only on their own terms. They graciously allowed me to visit them in one of their meetings and present my proposal that they should write a chapter for this book. The meeting was conducted in the Koasati language. I stood quietly to the side. When the participants had discussed the proposal to their satisfaction, they informed me that they would like to write certain stories and memoirs for inclusion. They also required that a photograph of the authors be published, "so that people can see what we look like." (This is the reason that the volume contains a single photograph.)

A Koasati description of a morning walk may not be "artful" in a way that would pass muster as poetry in the Western tradition, but it is highly valued by the community because of the status of the person who wrote it, because it is the first example of this kind of first-person meditation, and because the community is enthusiastically encouraging its youngsters to bring forth this kind of expression. The Coushattas offer us this example not because we might value it but because they do.

What if Native peoples were to make us a gift of their thinking? We would accept it and enjoy it, and expect to understand it eventually, and on its own terms.

WHICH TEXTS?

In preparing this collection of texts, I must refer to Herbert Luthin's wonderful introduction to an earlier volume, *Surviving through the Days,* in which he laments that no collection can get it altogether right, in part because no collection can get it all.[13] In calculating what to keep in and what to leave out, he emphasized one criterion that is equally valid here: the texts must be translations of real stories and other types of oral expression, from the Native language, and verifiably so. In this volume, additionally, actual written texts by Native people are included, when they are available to us; some of these appeared originally in English.

When I began to collect contributions for this book, I believed that *I* would choose the texts, an act that I found quite audacious, no matter how respectfully I might approach the task. But as shown in the case of the Coushattas, I need not have fretted quite so much. Several of the contributors, representing notably the Cherokee and Chickasaw as well as the Coushatta communities, were alive to the idea that they were obligated to offer works that had been ratified by their communities. Contributor Kimberly G. Wieser expresses this quite directly in her essay: "I hope here that I speak in a good way that does not offend people who are fully grounded in their Cherokee identity in all respects." I had long discussions with the other Cherokee contributor, Christopher Teuton, who rejected a number of my offerings, some of them new and unpublished, saying that the author did not have enough status in the community to represent its literature. He was scrupulously attuned to works that had passed muster not with us but with the Cherokees. To have passed muster most often meant that a work had appeared elsewhere.

This careful curating of texts also meant that the Cherokee medicine man Swimmer's famous collection of treatments and encantations was left out, even though readers might well have expected to see it.[14] Precisely because Swimmer's work was part of the traditional medicine, its intention was entirely different from that of texts that entertain, instruct, or remember history, a significant distinction to the Cherokee contributors.

I occasionally experienced disappointment in collecting texts when I had to accept that we could include only the works of those storytellers and authors who chose to share them. I talked to several "owners" of stories who deliberated about contributing them, but who then chose to keep them private, a decision that we must respect.

This book is different from some of the early and famous

anthropological collections, particularly those of Swanton (early twentieth century) and Mooney (Cherokee, late nineteenth and early twentieth century). In these cases particularly, there was an urgency to collect as much Indian memorabilia as possible before the Native people were subsumed into the larger white society, as was fully expected and even encouraged. In the reprint of his introduction, Swanton cheerfully admits to a casual collection style: items were "taken down at various places and from various persons, and for the most part in English . . . part of them recorded directly, while part were written down in the original by an Indian."[15] He continues, "No attempt has been made to separate these stories into classes, but the following general order has been observed." He then creates categories of "myths," "encounters between men and animals," "animals," with a special section on the "Southeastern trickster Rabbit," and finishing with miscellany. A hallmark of the Swanton collection is lack of signs of oral performance; rather, the stories follow a straightforward narrative in a fairly high English register. Still, the stories display no psychological interiority or cultural grounding. This structure characterizes direct translation from the oral tradition—the listeners do not have to be prepped, as it were, as would a larger audience outside the tribal circle.

As editor I made a considered effort to balance traditional with new work, which turned out to be something the contributors were eager to do. All of us have striven to counter the ingrained if unconscious notion that Native cultures are best represented in museums; that real Indians live quaintly on reservations and wear deerskin; that real stories are those created by people long dead. As Craig Womack puts it, less gently, in his complaint that the early twentieth-century story collector John Swanton included "talking animal stories as Creek 'culture'" but . . . "[those] unmarked by sufficient beads and feathers, usually are simply overlooked by Indians and non-Indians alike as authentic Native literature." Swanton himself on at least two occasions deliberately omits stories from his Hitchiti and Natchez collections with the remarks, "the others [stories] are modern tales of trifling value" and "a very modern story told to my informant. It is of little value except for the linguistic material obtained with it."[16] Native people have been creating stories, poems, songs, memoirs, and the like this whole time and are actively creating Native literature as we speak. A good portion of the works in this volume were produced by people who are alive now or are only recently departed. As we might expect, they have been observing the scene right along with everyone else and have incorporated their observations and perspectives into their writings and oral performances. We must not miss an opportunity to shine light on modern work, both for our own pleasure and edification and for the encouragement of the next generation of authors.

THE COLLECTIONS

This book is grouped into seven language-based collections. Five of them include a text that appears in both English and the Native language. Each collection features at least one essayist who is close to the work, either a scholar deeply conversant with a particular literature or a community member; some have both qualifications. Each essayist begins from a unique starting point, without reference to how the other contributors shape their thoughts, creating a montage of approaches.

And yet. Readers will enjoy noting how often the essayists make similar points, coming as they are from completely different perspectives. All the essayists group the texts into various "genres." I left these genres as the essayists named them, even though they sometimes seem to refer to similar categories. We have the Choctaw *Shukha Anumpa* (Animal Stories), the Chickasaw *Shikonno'pa'* (Possum Stories), and the Yuchi Animal Tales. Other collections clearly have traditional stories about animals, but these are placed in other genres. Another theme includes Choctaw Supernatural Legends and Encounters (which are distinct from Prophecies); Yuchi Stories of the Supernatural (which are distinct from Mythical Time Stories); and Cherokee *Ulvsgedi*: Stories of the Wondrous.

An aspect of grouping stories is that some stories "belong" to families or clans. Hence the Chickasaw collection contains *Iksa' Nannano̱li'* (Clan Stories). While humor is a prominent feature in all the collections, and is well discussed in the essays, the Chickasaw collection has an overt genre of *Chokoshpa' Nannano̱li'* (Humor Stories).

Yet another set of genres is that which includes texts based on memoir. We have the Creek Stories of Real People, the Cherokee *Kanoheda*:

Philosophy, History, and Memoir, and the Koasati Modern Stories and Memoirs. One of the most salient developments in Native literature is the departure from folktales toward the artful shaping of memory. Several of the essayists (Hinson, Wieser, Teuton, Linn, and Mould) find the topics of their people's relationships with the past and with the supernatural to warrant special attention. This theme is well worth tracking through the book.

THE ESSAYISTS

In the first collection, folklorist Tom Mould, who has collected Mississippi Choctaw folktales for decades, explains in detail the goals and tools he uses "as a remedy to the inattention often paid to the skill and artistry of storytellers, not just their stories." Some of his collected stories are rendered to reflect their oral performance, so that "we begin to understand how they are heard within a community." Several of the stories are excellent examples of how storytelling is evolving in modern Mississippi. Besides the very intimate views that Mould is able to give us of the stories and their tellers, because he is a professor of folklore he also helps us gain the larger view of how to think about the importance of storytelling in Choctaw or any culture.

Phillip Carroll Morgan brings something unique to this volume. A Choctaw-Chickasaw scholar and specialist in nineteenth-century Native authors, he found and transcribed the handwritten 1830 letter from Choctaw intellectual James L. McDonald to statesman Peter Perkins Pitchlynn. This letter contained his version of a Choctaw tale, "The Spectre and the Hunter: A Legend of the Choctaws," but McDonald also "describes the story styling methods and techniques of a typical Choctaw storyteller of the period." Morgan had been planning to write an article discussing the importance of this document: I acknowledge that I pled with him to let me include it in this volume. The McDonald work is transcendent. Readers will not fail to notice McDonald's high literary register as he situates himself among nineteenth-century white intellectuals. I believe this text may well represent the first known written Choctaw literature and hence provides a perfect reference for the work that follows in the rest of this volume.

The Choctaw collection concludes with my essay on modern Oklahoma Choctaw stories, with four stories that represent a break from the *shukha anumpa* of yesteryear.

Jack B. Martin, a specialist in Muskogean linguistics, has worked for many years collecting and translating a large number of Muskogee texts of all types, in close collaboration with speakers Margaret Mauldin (now deceased) and her daughter Gloria McCarty. In his essay he concentrates on providing details about the authors and the provenances of the stories. He also gives us insights about how the Muskogee language creates stylistic effects using its distinct grammatical structure.

Lokosh (Joshua D. Hinson), director of the Chickasaw Language Revitalization Program, has contributed two essays. In the first he focuses on the history of the Chickasaws, using the seasons as a metaphor for the renaissance of the people from near-extinction to vibrancy. He explains speech and story genres, their uses, and their place in the culture. The second essay, "Interpretation is a Tricky Business," is something remarkable. Hinson describes the process of bringing back Chickasaw stories that had only existed in written form in English, what he calls *re-translation.* Using as an example Glenda Galvan's version of the *shikonno'pa'* "How Poison Came to the Chickasaw and Choctaw," he explains in fascinating detail the problem of shedding English literary tropes and replacing them with the kinds of language structures that are employed in Chickasaw storytelling.

Linguist Mary Linn, a specialist in the Yuchi language, a story collector, and an archivist, gives us an informative history of Yuchi story collection. In her close collaboration with the few remaining speakers of the language, she has had the opportunity to record expert versions of stories from several genres. More important, she is able to share with us the cultural significance of these stories, including the reactions of various audiences to their telling.

Christopher B. Teuton, author and critic, gives us the history of Cherokee literature from the times of Boudinot (in the *Cherokee Phoenix,* 1828–34) as an adaptation to Euro-American institutions, including literacy. He explains that "literary writing began among the Cherokee as a way to explain and defend the people; oral tradition sustained them." Teuton carefully explains the Cherokee genres, not so much in terms of their narrative content but in terms of their relationships to the way the listener is expected to interpret them.

The other Cherokee essayist, Kimberly G. Wieser, takes up the highly relevant and provocative situation of the mixed-blood Indian, the "victims of paper genocide" who cannot "prove" they are tribal members but who are among the most numerous sustainers of Native culture—and who represent the future.

Since the Cherokees are a large tribe with a long history of written as well as oral literature, the Cherokee collection is the largest.

Linguistic anthropologist Linda Langley has lived with the Coushattas for many years (she is married to Coushatta Heritage Department Director Bertney Langley). She grounds her essay in the history of the Coushattas, emphasizing their fierce independence and resilience. Langley's main perspective is the remarkable way in which the tribal members collectively decided to revive the Koasati language. This revitalization effort represents the deepest community involvement, and one of the most successful, of any I have witnessed. Langley describes how this collection was created and edited collectively, with the traditional stories forming the initial work, but how the writers became increasingly interested in the activities of their own lives and the lives of relatives, their own thinking, and their own new writing styles. We are lucky to have this collection, which is the first new material to have been produced by the Coushattas. We are cheering for the birth of a strong new literary movement among a group that was too long silent.

Linguistic anthropologist William Sconzert-Hall lives and works in southern Louisiana, focusing on the smaller tribes in the Gulf region, whether or not they have federal recognition. In his essay he introduces three tribes, the Atakapa-Ishak, the Catawba, and the Houma, by bringing to light their geographical placement, relevant historical details, and discussions of their languages, which are all in different families. This collection is distinct in that each language group also has a spokesperson, a tribal member, who explains the featured stories. Shaman Shawn Papillion of the Atakapa-Ishaks has written up the traditional creation myth, but he also introduces it with his interpretation of it. He compares their myth with those of cultures worldwide and shows how symbols in this myth parallel those of other peoples. Beckee Garris explains the storytelling style of modern Catawbas, along with the impact of those stories on the expected behavior of the youth. MorningDove Verret Hopkins describes the importance and moral force of the animals that appear in the two Houma traditional tales. It is fascinating to compare the Houma story "How Turtle Broke His Shell" with the Chickasaw "Why Turtle Has a Cracked Shell": the style, the details of the narrative, and the emphasis are completely different.

ON TRANSLATION

Every project of this type—presentation of literature from other languages—must grapple with the bugbear of adequate, no, *artful* translation. One volume in this series, *Born in the Blood,* is devoted to precisely that question—it endeavors to help readers gain new respect for the problems of adequately representing the meaning, narrative, characters, cultural underpinnings, sound of the language, sublimities of the grammatical structure, and all the rest.[17] Of course, these problems can only rarely be solved to great satisfaction, but we are not thereby absolved of trying.

A salient point often overlooked when dealing with literature in translation is that the translators themselves are also authors. We find that the storytelling or literary gifts of the translator are those that matter to our audience. Reader of this volume will notice immediately that the styles of the translated stories are quite different, even when the content is somewhat comparable, simply as a consequence of who did the translating. We may forget that the number of speakers of many Native languages has dwindled to very few. When story collectors come around, those speakers are often thrust into the role of performer and storyteller, without regard to their storytelling gifts. We often notice the brevity, flat style, and sometimes loss of narrative integrity of some Native stories (something we have tried to avoid here!) simply because the narrator was perhaps the only one left who knew the outline of a tale and was pressed to relate it.

Another crucial factor, one that is rarely discussed when considering

Native American work, is the influence on all writers of the literary styles of their era. The several stories from the late nineteenth and early twentieth century that were translated by educated Native persons—those who had received extensive schooling and were literate in both English and their native language—have an initial eeriness that comes from being rendered in a high literary register. (Take particular note of J. L. McDonald's story of the specter and the hunter from 1830.) My first instinct on reading these stories was to be suspicious of them—on the mistaken grounds that Native languages could not, and certainly *would* not, have words and clause structures that might count as an elevated register. Native people were not allowed to be hifalutin' in their speech!

For readers who will bear with the linguist in me for a paragraph, I want to point out that words in Native American languages simply have no cognates in English. Many of the languages, taking Choctaw as a typical example, have verbs encompassing several parts that together make very sophisticated meanings, which in turn can be rendered in English in different ways. Equally important, words, especially those that are most basic to the vocabulary, have wide synonymy and extended meanings. To *run after* to *chase*, and to *pursue* differ little in their basic semantics, but they have different senses in usage and in register. Choctaw people may *pursue* as well as *run after* and be perfectly faithful to the language and to the story, especially if the translator wishes to uphold the rhetorical standards of a particular era.

Joshua D. Hinson's essay on translation treating multiple levels of word choice, sentence structure, and story meaning is one of the highlights of this book.

ABOUT UNCLE REMUS

Another direct consequence of the interpenetration of Southeast cultures with that of the white colonists is the exposure of all to African folktales and motifs. This exposure has generated a good deal of scholarship, opinion, and ire and given rise to academic tiffs in an attempt to tease apart what influence the European and African folk traditions might have had on southeastern tales, and the reverse. The issue arises due to the extensive sharing of certain reappearing talking animals, especially the Rabbit, and of story lines that are quite similar, a good example being the sticky doll, the Tar Baby.

Dundes presents the analysis as a stark choice: "The question raised was whether the Negroes borrowed the tales from the Indians or whether the Indians borrowed the tales from the Negroes."[18] Apparently a number of scholars felt the need to come down on one side or the other. The question was attenuated in the Joel Chandler Harris's Uncle Remus tales as primary evidence for an African origin for an appreciable portion of southeastern tales—the large number of animal-based humorous stories. Dundes is one who believed that scrutiny of certain motifs led to the inevitable conclusion that even the rabbit trickster was African. A number of other scholars (Mooney foremost), arguing for the Indians, pointed to the ubiquity of the rabbit trickster motif in a number of languages and in various modifications. Vest is most forceful in his discovery of references to Rabbit, terrapin, the Tar Baby, the briar patch, deer, and the thunder-spirit in a 1728 collection of stories.[19] Those stories are told in Saponi, an extinct Siouan language from Virginia.[20] A version of the Tar Baby was printed in the *Cherokee Phoenix* syllabary in the 1840s, three decades before Harris introduced Uncle Remus in 1876. The Cherokees consider it their story, have a number of versions of it, and count back by generations to its first rendering. In this volume the Cherokee story "The Rabbit and the Image" (Dalala, from Kilpatrick) is fundamentally Cherokee in its characters, language, and emphases.[21]

Overlooked in this debate is the certainty that all peoples know a good story when they hear one and will lose no time in making relevant parts of it their own. I have never heard anyone claim that *West Side Story* is not an American musical because its story line bears a strong resemblance to that of *Romeo and Juliet*. For that matter, Shakespeare's free borrowing of an Italian historical tale does not prevent some of the best-known *English* poetry from emerging from the throats of Italian-named characters.

It remains that the sheer number and variety of Rabbit-based tales in the Southeast through (at least) four language families makes this animal supremely important to Native peoples irrespective of what African slaves made of it or, for that matter, what the people of East

Africa might have thought and told about a Hare. In this volume Tom Mould gives an excellent discussion not only of thematic borrowing but of the documented appropriation and restructuring of specific stories. It is important not to get lost chasing the chimera "authenticity," seeking only strangeness as a definer of what might be uniquely Native American. Rather, it is the changed perception of themes, the emphasis of some kinds of relationships and the diminishment of others, the place of humor, and so many other sublime differences that make these tales Native American.

THOSE WHOSE VOICES ARE FAINTER

In this volume we have the gift of many tales, histories, memoirs, and even songs. All the texts have a Native American author and someone who can discuss and represent them reliably.

We regret that we were simply not able to arrange inclusion of texts and stories that still exist among a number of Southeast tribes and peoples. Too, some peoples lost their tribal identities, their languages, and even their lives before the notion of collecting their ideas and stories was even considered. In those cases we have only the testaments of persons who claim provenance of pieces of the oral tradition.

There are some good general collections of stories including selections from these groups, which although not vetted and attributed to authors in the same way will at least give readers a sense of the oral traditions that remain. Among those easily accessed are Swanton's *Myths and Tales of the Southeastern Indians* and Howard Martin's *Myths and Folktales of the Alabama-Coushatta Indians of Texas.*[22]

NOTES

1. One excellent source that explains the complexity of the Native-European relationship historically is Greg O'Brien's "The Conqueror Meets the Unconquered: Negotiating Cultural Boundaries on the Post-Revolutionary Southern Frontier," in O'Brien, *Pre-Removal Choctaw History: Exploring New Paths* (Norman: University of Oklahoma Press, 2008).
2. I generally refer to the indigenous peoples of the Americas as "Indians," because this is what my close colleagues call themselves and what they

prefer I use. But this is a term that may give offense, or at least give pause, and I would rather not have my writings interrupted by readers' having to process this term. I occasionally use "Indian" in some contexts, but in general I use "Native" and hope that this is acceptable to most readers.

3. Quoted in "Authenticity and *Aggiornamento* in Spoken Texts and Their Critical Edition," in Lisa Philips Valentine and Regna Darnell, *Theorizing the Americanist Tradition* (Toronto: University of Toronto Press, 1999), 122.
4. Dell Hymes, *"In Vain I Tried to Tell You": Essays in Native American Ethnopoetics* (Philadelphia: University of Pennsylvania Press, 1983).
5. Jane Hill, "The Meaning of Writing and Text in a Changing Americanist Tradition," in Valentine and Darnell, *Theorizing the Americanist Tradition.*
6. "Continuities and Renewals in Mayan Literacy and Calendrics," in Valentine and Darnell, *Theorizing the Americanist Tradition.*
7. Clara Sue Kidwell, *Choctaws and Missionaries in Mississippi, 1818–1918* (Norman: University of Oklahoma Press, 1995).
8. James Mooney, *Historical Sketch of the Cherokee* (1900; repr. Chicago: Aldine, 1975); James Mooney, *Myths of the Cherokee*, Nineteenth Annual Report, Bureau of American Ethnology 1897–98, pt. I (Washington DC: U.S. Government Printing Office, 1900).
9. Jack B. Martin, *A Grammar of Creek (Muskogee)* (Lincoln: University of Nebraska Press, 2010), 13.
10. Arrell Gibson, *The Chickasaws* (Norman: University of Oklahoma Press, 1971).
11. Arnold Krupat, *Ethnocriticism* (Berkeley: University of California Press, 1992), 174.
12. Craig Womack, *Red on Red: Native American Literary Separatism* (Minneapolis: University of Minneapolis Press, 1999), 13.
13. Herbert Luthin, *Surviving through the Days: Translations of Native California Stories and Songs, a California Indian Reader* (Berkeley: University of California Press, 2002).
14. *The Swimmer Manuscript: Cherokee Sacred Formulas*, Collected by James Mooney. Bureau of American Ethnology Bulletin 99 (Washington DC: Smithsonian Institution, 1932).
15. John R. Swanton, *Myths and Tales of the Southeastern Indians* (1929; repr. Norman: University of Oklahoma Press, 1995), 1.
16. Craig Womack, quoted in *Totkv Mocvse/New Fire: Creek Folktales by Earnest Gouge*, ed. and trans. Jack B. Martin, Margaret McKane Mauldin, and Juanita McGirt (Norman: University of Oklahoma Press, 2004), x; Swanton, *Myths and Tales*, 117, 266.

17. Brian Swann, *Born in the Blood: On Native American Translation* (Lincoln: University of Nebraska Press, 2011).
18. Alan Dundes, *African Tales among the North American Indians: Mother Wit from the Laughing Barrel* (Englewood Cliffs NJ: Prentice-Hall, 1973), 114–25.
19. Jay Hansford Vest, "From Bobtail to Brer Rabbit: Native American Influences on Uncle Remus," *American Indian Quarterly* 24, no. 1 (2000): 19–43.
20. William Byrd, *William Byrd's Histories of the Dividing Line betwixt Virginia and North Carolina* (1728; repr. New York: Dover Publications, 1967).
21. Dalala, in Jack F. Kilpatrick and Anna G. Kilpatrick, *Friends of Thunder* (Norman: University of Oklahoma Press, 1995).
22. Swanton, *Myths and Tales of the Southeastern Indians*; Howard Martin, *Myths and Folktales of the Alabama-Coushatta Indians of Texas* (Austin: Encino Press, 1977).

A LISTENING WIND

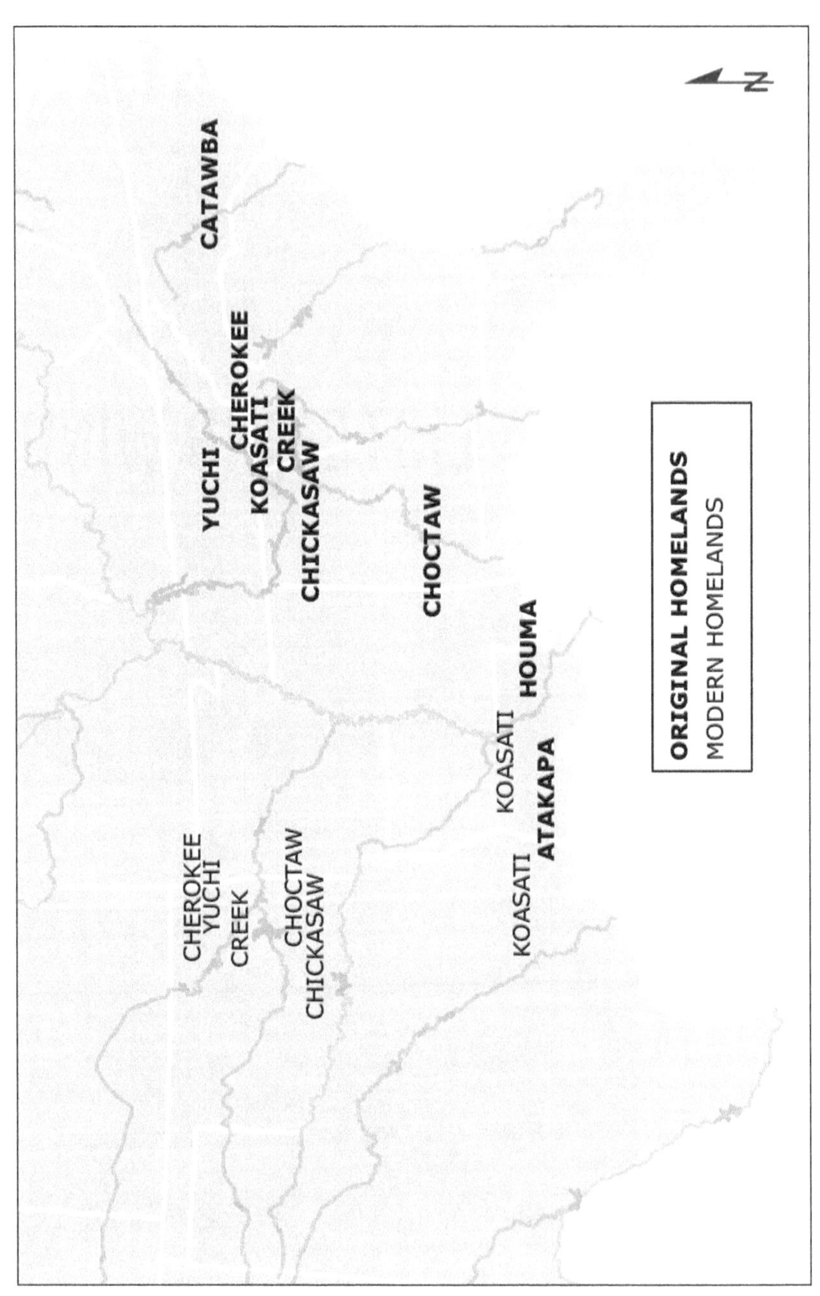

Modern and Traditional Homelands. Cartography by Jeffrey M. Widener, University of Oklahoma.

CHOCTAW

Mississippi Choctaw Oral Literature

Tom Mould

The oral literature of American Indian storytellers can be approached many ways, among them intellectually, aesthetically, emotionally, and socially. Each of these approaches spirals outward exponentially, providing an endless combination of avenues of exploration for scholar and audience alike. There is therefore no single or satisfying answer to the question of how to approach American Indian oral literature. That should not prevent the consideration of the benefits of specific approaches, however. In considering Choctaw storytelling, two approaches appear particularly fruitful, one grounded in the study of genre, the other in performance, both of which serve as correctives to analyses that favor the discrete story over either deep structures or the artistry of the storyteller.

A natural starting place for the study of storytelling is to look at individual stories, trees in a forest of narrative. There is the story about how possum lost the hair on his tail. Or how the Choctaw first received corn. Or how a neighbor encountered the little people one dark night in the woods just behind her house. This is, after all, how we typically encounter any narrative tradition for the first time: through individual stories. But as we listen to more stories, we begin to understand how they are heard within a community: not as isolated performances but as part of a larger tradition with connections that run deep and wide, connecting people as well as themes, plots, and characters. Choctaw oral traditions includes myths and legends of the distant past, more recent historical tales, and prophecies of the future. It also includes humorous animal tales and anecdotes as well as often frightening personal encounters with supernatural beings. Underlying these individual stories is a system—a forest—structured by tone, truth, and time.[1]

Serious stories can be funny, and funny stories can be serious. But Choctaw stories are categorized into genres that make it clear which should be expected. Funny stories are called *shukha anumpa*, literally "hog talk," though "hog wash" is a more accurate translation. Shukha anumpa includes tall tales, humorous anecdotes, and good-natured teasing that gifted speakers can create on the spot. But shukha anumpa also includes what at first glance might seem a wildly incongruous addition: stories about how the bullfrog lost his horns, or how the turtle cracked his shell, stories recognized in other collections as well as by Choctaw storytellers as "animal tales." Uniting the two seemingly disparate types of stories is tone. Both types of stories are funny, where laughter is the immediate goal. But as with most stories, entertainment is rarely the only goal. In shukha anumpa, humor is also used to define and critique social relations—animals stand in for humans, different species stand in for different ethnicities, and the mythic past is drawn into the present.

Neither type of shukha anumpa is valued because it is or is not true. The humorous anecdote one's grandmother tells about being too scared to ride in a car is rarely called into question, just as only the youngest children might ask whether bears really lost their tails because of a time when rabbit tricked bear into freezing it off. Literal truth is irrelevant; the social cohesion that laughter brings and the values that underpin the stories are what matter.

Not so for the myths, legends, histories, and prophecies, all etic terms for emic genres.[2] Nor for the personal experience narratives describing encounters with supernatural beings that continue to live in the Mississippi woods today. These stories describe events where truth is a central aspect of their power and of how they are shared and interpreted. The stories of the origins of the Choctaw and their traditions, legendary Choctaw warriors long past and Choctaw leaders still remembered, and future events on the horizon are all valued as true—affectively, emotionally, ideologically, and for the most part literally. These stories may evoke laughter in a particular detail but, as a whole, are recognized as important and treated respectfully. Such stories can be told by anyone but are expected from elders—members of the community who have gained respect not only through age but through the wisdom they have acquired and for which they shoulder the responsibility for sharing. Some of these stories are personal, creating family histories from personal experience. Others draw from a shared history—stories of how the Choctaw came to live in Mississippi and of great floods and great leaders. This divide between a shared past of long ago and a recent past that encompasses the present suggests the third major axis underlying the generic system of Choctaw storytelling: time. Time transforms the personal encounter into the legend as stories are passed down from family member to family member, elder to youth, as part of the informal process of enculturation. As the events described in a story recede into the past, relevance encourages some stories to be forgotten, others to be transformed, and still others to be maintained rigorously. Those that continue to be told are imbued with the power of tradition and the wisdom of the elders. Narrative structures highlight the divide between the past and the present. Traditionally, storytellers who shared passed-down stories began their stories with *Makato, makato, makato, achili*: "It was said at the time, it was said at the time, it was said at the time, now I say it." Today storytellers more often begin with "They used to say"—less formal, less ritually symbolic, but no less cognizant of the importance of the stories passed down by the elders. Many, especially in the Choctaw community of Conehatta, continue to conclude these stories with the ritual closing, *Makilla*, "That is all."

Opening and closing formulas used in sharing stories help define the larger system of Choctaw storytelling. They are also part of the narrative structure that can be addressed from the broad level of the tale type to the subtle shifts in time and speaker that establish rhythm and authority in a single narrative. In 1928 Antti Aarne and Stith Thompson codified in their book *The Types of the Folktale* what many people had recognized less formally: that stories with similar plot elements are not confined to a single culture but travel, appearing in narrative traditions around the world as recognizable tale types.[3] The result is that when audiences hear the Choctaw story of the Irishman and the horse's egg, or the race between a turtle and turkey, this listener may hear not only a local story but a social history of storytelling across cultures. Visible are those aspects of a narrative tradition that shift from culture to culture. Thanks to geography as well as technology and belief systems, details shift—lakes become swamps, lions become panthers, swords become hatchets, royal balls become village dances—as do narrative structures. One of the best-known examples of narrative adaptation appeared more than forty years before Aarne and Thompson's book, when in 1886 Frank Hamilton Cushing brought three Zuni leaders to the East Coast to meet his benefactors and break bread. One evening the two groups shared stories, with Cushing sharing the Italian folktale of "The Cock and the Mouse." When he returned to New Mexico a year later, he was met with a startling version of the story that had been transformed structurally, thematically, and aesthetically to fit Zuni storytelling conventions and worldview.[4] Similarly, readers of this volume may encounter the Choctaw story "Why Terrapins Never Get Fat" and recognize European versions of the Tortoise and the Hare traceable to ancient Greece. Where the similarity provokes questions of universal trials and truths, divergences suggest cultural variation that reveals unique systems of thought.

However, often lost in these discussions of tale types and motifs, convergences and divergences, are the individual storytellers whose skill and sense of aesthetics shape the stories as much as any larger tribal shifts and norms. In Billy Amos's story about the prophecies his mother used to tell him, audiences encounter a storyteller who artfully tacks back and forth between the past and the present, building suspense until the future of the prophecy is revealed. Estelline Tubby achieves a similar structural feat in her retelling of the prophecy of the Third Removal as she negotiates among the voices of past storytellers—her mother, aunt, and grandmother—the voices of her kinspeople facing the prophesied events, and her own interpretations. Again both art and skill are revealed in the structures of the oral performance of individual storytellers.

Generic boundaries provide some guidelines for storytellers, expectations that they must work within if their audiences are to be expected to understand. But within these boundaries exists great leeway for individual creativity. And the simple existence of generic boundaries, ironically, can allow—perhaps even encourage—those boundaries to be crossed. Harley Vaughn tells a version of the emergence story where instead of the creation of different southeastern Indian tribes, as in most of the Choctaw emergence stories, including Pistonatubbee's, the Creator makes three races of men: black, white, and Choctaw. What begins as a solemn story told as part of the talk of the elders is tweaked so that it falls neatly into shukha anumpa. Such turns to humor are fairly common. The tall tales that Jake York, Lillie Gibson, and Gladys Willis are so proficient in narrating require a frame of credulity that is slowly undermined during the narration, with the lies growing larger and larger until their true identity as shukha anumpa becomes clear. Nellie Billie and Gladys Willis both make similar turns as they recount scary encounters with the supernatural—in both cases, presumed to be *na losa chitto* or "big black thing"—only to suggest alternative interpretations that move the story from one side of the generic axis of Choctaw storytelling to the other.[5]

Such playfulness in Choctaw storytelling is common and extends into verbal acrobatics that may appear solely artistic but that highlight very real linguistic hurdles. In his story about his uncle's dog who spoke Choctaw, Jake York faces a crowd of young boys and girls at a summer camp hosted by the Tribal Language Program. He speaks in Choctaw. To highlight the fact that the dog is speaking Choctaw, Jake might consider shifting between English and Choctaw, especially with a bilingual audience. But the children are at camp to learn Choctaw. So Jake narrates his story with repeated attribution to distinguish the Choctaw words the dog spoke from the Choctaw language of the overall narrated story. Odie Anderson, on the other hand, with no such restrictions, exploits the bilingualism of her peers and herself by shifting between Choctaw and English to create the kind of playful dramatic tension often seen in prophecy: riddling.

Western culture and literature is replete with prophetic riddles—the blind prophet Tiresias in *Oedipus*, the witches in *Macbeth*, and the prophecies of Nostradamus and Mother Shipton, to name a few. The scores of popular books on biblical prophecy make similar moves, reading metaphor out of prophecy and transforming eschatology into playful exercises in creative interpretation. For Odie Anderson and other Choctaw narrators, however, the challenge is linguistic rather than interpretive, as they narrate prophecies that have already been fulfilled.[6] Odie Anderson recounts a prophecy of the coming of cars and interstates. She describes "something with two eyes would be running on it," where "it" refers to the road that she has described as "laid out wide," and "paved"—*Tali yósh patałpáčį.* One of the Choctaw terms for car is *hina ábalíli,* which translates as a runner on the road. Odie has added the "two eyes" description to refer to the car's headlights but borrows the imagery of movement from a literal translation of the Choctaw term itself. While she does not then "reveal" her answer that the elders predicted cars—such a revelation is too obvious—she could, by simply using the English term. This is precisely what she does for interstate, however. She begins by adapting the already descriptive Choctaw terms to describe the new type of road—laid out wide and paved—and then concludes the prophetic narrative by code shifting into English: *Interstate mák makáha ahnilih,* or "I think it is the interstate he was talking about." Even more common is to negotiate this code shifting internally, in a uni-linguistic performance. Judy Billie remembers how her grandparents and her mother used to tell her "they'll have machines, you know, flying like a bird. And we've got the airplane." In Choctaw airplane is *abá píni*—sky boat—or *tali hika*—flying steel. Judy adds the bird but draws on the Choctaw terms to provide some of the obfuscating metaphoric language in order to perform the prophecy as a riddle.[7]

Other language play can be more whimsical, using puns, idioms, and bilingual *in*-competencies for humor. Gladys Willis recounts a story about the legendary Ashman, who hitches a ride with a white man. When the white man asks him his name, he asks for clarification: "What did you say?" spoken as "Whatchasay?"—a common question even today. The white man, perhaps expecting an exotic name, understands his hitchhiker to be named "Whatchasay" and refers to him as such throughout the ride, a Choctaw equivalent of Abbot and Costello's "Who's on First." Lillie Gibson's verbal play in her story "Running Water" also requires linguistic skill in English, although she grew up speaking Choctaw, which reverses the power dynamic between the two women in addition to creating a big laugh for the audience.

The playfulness of Choctaw storytellers moves beyond the narrative text as well. When Henry Williams tells the story of "The Man and the Turkey," he transfers the easy ridicule directed at the story's protagonist to himself, suggesting that his own capabilities would fall far short of those needed to marry well according to tribal custom of the recent past. Such a move makes explicit what most stories inherently do: ask the audience to apply the story to life. Rarely is such application as simplistic as gleaning "the moral of the story." Choctaw stories are typically far more complex, rich, and ambiguous. Stories with etiological endings such as "and that's why the terrapin has no fat," or "and that's why the possum has no hair on his tail," should be understood as the artistic flourishes of a skilled orator rather than the sum total of the message to be conveyed.[8] As the context shifts for when stories are shared, so does meaning. Henry Williams directed the ridicule of his story to himself when it was just the two of us, sitting in his office in the school building in the Choctaw community of Conehatta. But when I saw him a few weeks later at the tribal offices in the community of Pearl River, walking with a fellow tribal councilman from the community of Bogue Chitto, Henry shifted the humor once again. "Remember that guy with the turkey?" he hollered to me, pointing at his fellow councilman. "This is him."

The importance of contextual shifts sits at the heart of the theory that has dominated folklore studies for nearly the past fifty years: performance theory. Oral narratives enter the world not as disembodied texts but as stories situated in very real social contexts, with identifiable storytellers and audiences. Ideally, these stories are recorded in "natural contexts": moments when people would be telling stories whether a folklorist were present or not. But capturing such moments is difficult, especially when the context for the bulk of Choctaw storytelling is informal and casual. Accordingly, most of the stories shared here were recorded in what might be referred to as artificial contexts, during planned conversations at times of the day convenient for the storytellers. Of course, these are real contexts too, embedded in social histories as well. Understanding stories as performances created in specific moments, with specific people, helps explain how and why a story may have been told in a particular way. It would be impossible to capture all the contextual elements that might have played a hand in shaping a particular performance, but the brief descriptions of the situational context I have included with each story is an effort to open up interpretation beyond the narrative text. After all, while some stories are shared as declarations of fact, closed to negotiation from listeners, others are shared as bids for conversation and dialogue. This applies especially to supernatural legends and memorates. Belief is malleable, variable, temporal. When Terry Ben and I sat down in his office in Pearl River where he was serving as superintendent of the Choctaw school system, we both wore a number of hats. Terry was Choctaw and a professional; I was white and still in school. Both of us, however, were from the South and male, which meant he might reasonably expect that I would understand the context of hunting in his story. Both of us were also teachers and committed to various types of inquiry, including scientific inquiry, which meant that both of us might be interested in an experience where science fell short in making sense of what Terry saw. It is perhaps not surprising, then, that Terry narrates his story with rhetorical questions that draw the two of us together in his expressions of doubt. He highlights those moments during his experience when he doubted what he saw, when he assumed it was something else, providing a rational stance that he might expect me to share. "I was sane back then. I'm still sane now," he laughs. Attending to the dialogic nature of storytelling helps us understand how the story is constructed and interpreted in the social act of performance. Sometimes, this "dialogue" is one of expectation, as in Terry's story, where my only verbal contribution was to join him in laughter when he averred his sanity, though one should not discount all the feedback cues that suggested I followed him and believed him—the nods, the smiles of recognition, the attentive gaze. At other times audience responses are far more explicit, as when Cynthia Clegg tells the story of "Pąš Falaya" at the same language camp where Jake York told his story about his uncle's dog, both of which would be considered told in "natural contexts," occurring as they did as part of the natural part of camp activities, irrespective of the presence of a folklorist.

Returning to the question at the beginning of the essay with only slightly more specificity—"How should we approach Mississippi Choctaw oral literature?"—the answer remains that there is no one way, nor even one best way. There are, however, avenues of inquiry that can be usefully employed and that attend to the structures and aesthetics of the narrative text situated within a narrative tradition but constructed by individuals in the act of performance. While it would be folly to approach these stories with a particular interpretive agenda, searching for one particular structure or another on a first read through, it is also folly to assume that one can simply come to a text produced orally rather than for the page, in a culture other than one's own, and expect to appreciate the story fully. Attuning oneself to the areas where individual skill and artistry emerge in culturally specific ways is a generous way to approach narrative, but it is also a rigorous and satisfying one.

NOTES

1. For a more thorough discussion of the axes that underlie Choctaw storytelling, see Tom Mould, *Choctaw Tales* (Jackson: University Press of Mississippi, 2004), 38–60. Thanks are due to the University Press of Mississippi for allowing the reprinting of some of the stories from that book here.
2. Other than the Choctaw term *shukha anumpa* for animal tales and jokes, and the English word *story* used to indicate all narratives and jokes, there are no other consistently used, emic terms for subgenres of Choctaw narrative. However, analysis of Choctaw discourse about stories, and analysis of the narrative tradition, suggest that myth, legend, historical tale, and prophecy all align with emic categories (Mould, *Choctaw Tales,* 45–60).
3. Antti Aarne developed the first tale type index in 1910, published as *Verzeichnis der Marchentypen.* The tale type index best known today, however, is the subsequent collaborative work with Stith Thompson that revised and expanded on Aarne's initial work: Antti Aarne and Stith Thompson, *The Types of the Folktale: A Classification and Bibliography*, 2nd rev. ed. (Helsinki, Finland: Academia Scientarum Fennica, 1961). Their first major attempt to categorize these tale types began with the analysis of narratives primarily in Europe and western Asia. Since then, tale type indices have been developed to extend to other geographical areas as well, including Aboriginal Australia, in Patricia Panyity Waterman, *A Tale-Type Index of Australian Aboriginal Oral Narratives* (Helsinki, Finland: Suomalainen

Tiedeakatemia.1987); the Arab world, in Hasan M. El-Shamy, *Types of the Folktale in the Arab World: A Demographically Oriented Tale-Type Index* (Bloomington: Indiana University Press, 2004); North America and England, in Ernest W. Baughman, *Type and Motif-Index of the Folktales of England and North America* (The Hague: Mouton and Company, 1966); northern East Africa, in Arewa, *A Classification of the Folktales of the Northern East African Cattle Area by Types*, PhD diss., University of California, Berkeley, 1967; and Central Africa, in Lambrecht, *A Tale of Type Index for Central Africa*, PhD diss., University of California, Davis, 1967.

4. For both the Italian version and the Zuni version, see Frank H. Cushing's *Zuni Folk Tales* (1901; repr. Tucson: University of Arizona Press, 1986). For comparative analysis of tale types in different cultures, see any of a number of Alan Dundes's casebooks, including "Cinderella" and "Little Red Riding Hood."
5. Examples of stories from Jake York and Lillie Gibson are included here. For the text of all stories referenced here, see Lillie Gibson's "The Car"; Jake York's "The Trip to Arkansas" and "Tall Stories"; Gladys Willis's "Whatyousay," "Time to Kill Hogs," and "A Big Hog"; and Nellie Billie's "A Black Stump," all in Mould, *Choctaw Tales*.
6. Tom Mould, *Choctaw Prophecy: A Legacy of the Future* (Tuscaloosa: University of Alabama Press, 2003). The shift across generic axes is from the more serious "talk of the elders" to the more humorous *shukha anumpa*.
7. For a more complete discussion of Choctaw prophetic riddling, including an explanation of why Choctaw terms for new technology are so often descriptive, see Tom Mould, "Prophetic Riddling: A Dialogue of Genres in Choctaw Performance," *Journal of American Folklore* 115, nos. 457–58 (2002): 395–421.
8. Ruth Benedict was one of the first to note this use of etiological endings in her *Zuni Mythology* (New York: Columbia University Press, 1935).

Creation Myths

The Choctaw Creation Legend

Isaac Pistonatubbee (1901)
Collected by H. S. Halbert

A very long time ago the first creation of men was in Nanih Waiya. And there they were made. And there they came forth.

The Muscogees first came out of Nanih Waiya, and they then sunned themselves on Nanih Waiya's earthen rampart. And when they got dry, they went to the east. On this side of the Tombigbee, there they rested. And as they were smoking tobacco they dropped some fire.

The Cherokees next came out of Nanih Waiya. And they sunned themselves on the earthen rampart. And when they got dry they went and followed the trail of the elder tribe. And at the place where the Muscogees had stopped and rested, and where they had smoked tobacco, there was fire and the woods were burnt. And the Cherokees could not find the Muscogees' trail, so they got lost and turned aside and went towards the north. And there towards the north they settled and made a people.

And the Chickasaws third came out of Nanih Waiya. And then they sunned themselves on the earthen rampart. And when they got dry they went and followed the Cherokees' trail. And when they got to where the Cherokees had got lost, they turned aside and went on and followed the Cherokees' trail. And when they got to where the Cherokees had settled and made a people, they settled and made a people close to the Cherokees.

And the Choctaws fourth and last came out of Nanih Waiya. And they then sunned themselves on the earthen rampart and when they got dry, they did not go anywhere but settled down in this very land and it is the Choctaws' home.

NOTE

Henry Halbert provides the following contextual information: "Pistonatubbee stated that in his boyhood he had often heard the legend, just as he gave it, from some of the old Choctaw mingoes [chiefs]. While perhaps not apparent in the text, Pistonatubbee stated that the creation of the different tribes all occurred in the same day"; Henry S. Halbert, "The Choctaw Creation Legend," *Publications of the Mississippi Historical Society* 4 (1901): 267–70, quote at 268. Motifs that recur in other versions of this story include losing the trail by accidental fire and drying on the side of the mound. —*Tom Mould*

Creation of Three Races

Harley Vaughn (1996)

Speaking of Nanih Waiya.

You know there's a hole in the ground, like a cave?

The way I've heard it is that, well my dad told me, it's like, when God made man, you know? And God dig this hole, where he would get three kind of races. And the longer he waited, the darker the man got.

That's where this whole cave thing comes in. The way my dad told me was that God would dig the hole in this ground. And he was going to take out three men. About three different colors.

The first one he took out, out of the ground, sooner than he wanted to and set him out in the sun. That man turned white. And he went to the second one, and he waited a little longer, and took him out and set him outside and he turned brown. And the third one, he waited too long, took him out and set him aside and he turned black.

That's where mankind started from—a cave.

NOTE

Harley shared this story May 31, 1996, as he and I were sitting around the kitchen table, having just finished a dinner of fried catfish, buttered cabbage, cornbread, black-eyed peas, and hominy at his home. Harley cooked so his wife Rae was cleaning up; their three young girls, Meagan, Mahliah, and

Breanna, were playing nearby. Rae's mom Caroline Morris had joined us earlier and had mentioned Nanih Waiya; Harley was returning to the topic, taking the opportunity to share a humorous version of the story now that it was just the two of us.—*Tom Mould*

Shukha Anumpa

Why Terrapins Never Get Fat

Olman Comby (1928)
Collected by John R. Swanton

One time Turkey met Terrapin crawling along and asked him how long it would take him to reach a certain place, making fun of him because he was so slow.

Terrapin kept straight on, saying, "I will get there all right."

After Turkey had teased him for some time, he stopped and said, "If you give me time to rest, I will beat you running."

So they agreed upon a date and parted.

Then Terrapin got other terrapins and placed them upon the tops of three hills over which the course lay and one at the goal.

When the time came for the race to start Terrapin placed himself at the starting point and the word was given. Of course Turkey at once left Terrapin behind, but when he neared the first hill he saw what he supposed was the same one just crawling out of sight over the top. He redoubled his speed, but when he had reached the place, the terrapin had concealed himself and presently the Turkey saw another terrapin going over the top of the next hill. The same thing happened at the third, and another terrapin was lying at the finish, which he supposed was his antagonist, and he believed that he had been beaten.

Turkey was now angry with Terrapin for having bested him and told him that the next time he encountered him he was going to cut off his head with an ax.

One day, when Turkey was carrying a sword, he met Terrapin and ran up on him to carry out his threat. Terrapin withdrew his head into the shell so that it could not be cut off, but Turkey slashed at his back until he was nearly dead.

Presently great numbers of ants came that way and Terrapin said to them, "I would give all the fat I have to have my shell completely sewed together." So the ants sewed him together and received his fat in exchange.

That is why terrapins never get fat.

NOTE

From John R. Swanton, "Choctaw Stories from Olman Comby, in English," Smithsonian Institution, National Anthropological Archives, Bureau of American Ethnology Manuscript Collection, 4132-b, Washington DC. The end of this story in which ants sew the terrapin's shell back together is a motif that has been identified in European and African folktales as well under A2312.1.1 "Origin of cracks in tortoise's shell," in Stith Thompson, *Motif-Index of Folk Literature* (Bloomington: Indiana University Press, 1966), and motifs B511.+ "Snail sticks tortoises shell together," and K256.+ "Ant patches shell for tortoise after it has been broken," in Kenneth Clarke, *A Motif-Index of Folktales of Culture-Area V West Africa*, PhD diss., University of Indiana, Bloomington, 1958. See also the Chickasaw story in this volume where gnats sew the turtle back together. —*Tom Mould*

The Dog Who Spoke Choctaw

Jake York (1997)

Recorded and transcribed by Tom Mould and Liasha Alex

When I was seven, my mother took us to Delta City. My uncle lived there and we used to go there. We went to pick cotton. I was the water boy.

When they went to pick cotton, my uncle raised a little puppy. Bounty was his name. My uncle didn't speak English, not very much——not very much English. He spoke Choctaw to this dog.

This dog had a mind of his own.

Mail carrier, white people call it. He brings the mail. He throws the newspaper outside. When he says, “Get the mail,” the dog goes to get the mail. He puts it in his mouth and brings it to him and he says, “Thank you” to him. The dog gives his paws to shake hands when he appreciates him.

“If you are hungry, you have to walk on your hind legs to eat,” he spoke in Choctaw to the dog.

He walks on four, but when he says, “You must walk over to get some,” the dog would get up and walk. Then he would give him biscuit, chicken bones, or other things.

Then he says, “Sit,” and the dog would sit.

When he says, “Lay,” he lays.

When he says, “Sleep,” he closes his eyes.

He was never taught English, but he understood Choctaw.

My uncle never spoke English to the dog but when he said “lay and roll,” he would lay and roll. When you say “eat,” he will stand on his hind leg and walk over. When you say go get the paper, he’ll put it in his mouth and bring it.

This is what I want to tell you. A dog can learn Choctaw.

You can also learn.

NOTE

Tape-recorded from Jake York on June 30, 1997, with the assistance of Choctaw high school student Liasha Alex during afternoon storytelling time at the Choctaw Language Immersion Camp. Jake stood among the children who had all lain down on a wooden platform for quiet time and stories just after lunch. — *Tom Mould*

Running Water

Lillie Gibson (1997)
Recorded by Tom Mould, Glenda Williamson, and Minerva Williamson

Mama got married. Well, our daddy died, and when she married a man, she married one from Conehatta, and so he already had a house. And so we had to move up here.

And we didn't have no way to draw water; we didn't have no running water.

So one day, a nurse, a home health nurse, came to my house, after we moved here, now.

After I got married and we moved over here—when we moved over here, I got married.

And so, she came around and asked, do we have running water.

And I told her, "Yes ma'am. We've got running water; if we run and go get it." [laughter]

NOTE

Tape-recorded from Lillie Gibson on August 5, 1997, with the assistance of Glenda Williamson and Meriva Williamson. Glenda and Meriva are sisters-in-law and introduced me around the Choctaw community of Conehatta, particularly among the elders. Lillie Gibson greeted us warmly in her home decorated with quilts and dolls either made by herself and her family or collected from American Indian peoples from around the country.—*Tom Mould*

The Man and the Turkey

Henry Williams (1997)
Recorded and transcribed by Tom Mould

Grandpa was not that old so he didn't tell us about any stories. He tells us about jokes, you know.

Before, people got married without knowing each other. Parent usually used to make arrangement for these two—couple to get married—especially mamas. Mamas used to talk to the other mama. This guy don't know that he's going to marry this lady. Parent be talking, you know.

Grandpa told me one time, that this guy——I mean, if they're going to marry, they used to look for a good hunter, and good stickball player. Those are persons they used to pick.

And this guy was a lousy ball player and lousy hunter, so nobody picked him. But he likes this girl in that family.

So he finally killed one turkey.

So he went by one morning, carrying that turkey. He goes around and brings that turkey where he kills it at.

Each morning, you know, he had a shotgun. And each morning, he fired that shotgun, carried that same turkey by the house. And the family looked at him, you know, "Oh, this guy finally become a good hunter," you know. "Look at him, carrying turkey."

Next morning, he carried that turkey and goes around and drop it over there, you know.

Third morning, you know, he fired that shotgun again. He carried that same turkey. So they decided to talk to him.

But they found out he had that same turkey all week [laughter].

So this guy got locked out because they found out he had the same turkey [laughter].

"They had flies all over that turkey" [laughter].

I thought that was funny. I don't know how they do it, but families used to find their boys a woman. I guess that was the traditional role of the parent. If this was the same today, I'd die [laughter]. They'd probably take their time finding me a woman [laughter].

NOTE

Tape-recorded from Henry Williams on June 24, 1997. Henry and I sat in his office at the school in Conehatta, escaping the brutal Mississippi heat. Henry shared story after story, virtually all of them humorous, many of them animal tales. —*Tom Mould*

Supernatural Legends and Encounters

The Little Man

Terry Ben (1996)

I was about eleven or twelve, you know, and so forth, and this was the year I got my first gun. My granddad had certain guns, and so forth, and he let me have a single-shot .22 bolt action. I was a big man, all right?

And so he had a couple of hunting dogs and so forth. I remember two. He had real excellent hunting dogs, and there were two.

And this was about maybe November as I remember it. This was on a Saturday afternoon and maybe around maybe five, six o'clock.

Anyway, from the house to the woods it was about maybe half a mile away. So I took my dogs, Chester .22, and some shells in my pocket, and I went on to the woods. And as I crossed the fence into the woods, you know, there were a lot of just, leaves on the ground and so forth. So when you stepped on the leaves it just made all kind of sounds, all right? So I tried not to make any sounds, and I was hunting squirrel.

Anyway, my two dogs were going in front of me, just with their noses up in the air, just going all over like that, you know? I was hunting for squirrel. And of course I had my rifle and so forth, just taking every couple of steps and standing there listening, and so forth like that.

And all of sudden, you know, I heard some thuds.

And I was going into the neighbor's land anyway. He allowed me to hunt on his land anyway. He had cows and all that and so he was probably working—maybe a fence broke down, maybe he's putting some posts into the ground or whatever. Maybe he's digging a ditch, whatever. I thought of that.

So I walked a little bit further, toward the sound, you know. I moved a couple of feet and so forth.

It was beginning to get a little bit dark and so forth. Again, it's in November, you know, and I'd just listen, you know, maybe for some talking and so forth like that. And I didn't hear anything like that. The thud, maybe every, maybe thirty seconds there'd be a big old thud like somebody hitting something into the ground.

And, you know, I'm thankful. You know, even now I've got 20/20 vision. You know, way back then, I still had 20/20 vision. So I had good hearing, and so forth, and even now. So, you know, I understood that.

The dogs were just running all over, about fifteen, twenty yards. They didn't find anything, no rabbit or squirrels, yet. There was no yapping sound yet.

So, I just looked around.

And I saw a big old stump, maybe that high off the ground [indicates about a foot], off to the side you know. I kind of looked real closely—this is maybe about fifty yards away from where I was standing. There was no brush or any other trees—it was sort of a clear path, where I could see real good. And that's where the thud was coming from.

I looked real, real closely, and I saw a little man, facing the other way toward the stump; and he had a little old pick, and he was digging, like that [imitates overhand motion of using a pick ax]. And every whatever, you'd hear a thud. Didn't see the face; he was pointed the other way. He was maybe so tall [gestures about three feet high], about fifty yards ahead of me.

The dogs were approaching that little man but nothing—no yaps, no signs of getting mad or signs of getting scared, nothing. They were just running all over, just, looking for squirrels, rabbits, whatever.

And I just looked at it, and it just——digging away, like that [repeats pick motion]. Definitely I knew that's where it was coming from.

I looked around and I looked around and so forth, and hey, maybe it was kids looking for something, whatever, this that and all that. That's a Saturday night, five or six o'clock at night; it can't be. I don't see no truck, don't see no other dogs around and so forth. You know, "What's this?"

I got my .22 rifle, put the safety off, aimed, right at it at first——

Then all these stories that my granddad told me that came into me. If you mess around with these little guys, you know, they're going to throw something at you, they're going to hit you and you're going to get sick and you're going to die. There's nothing a Choctaw doctor can do about it.

All these stories came back to me. I was not scared at first but I started getting scared.

And it's getting darker. Dogs still around; not even a sign that they knew what was there. Did I imagine them? No. Still, something was in front of me.

So, what I did was, I backtracked, slowly at first. But with every step, just a big old squashing sound against nothing but leaves and all that. And at that point, you know, it didn't matter anyway, you know—I was panicking. There was the fence there. I quickly jumped over the fence, I think. Got my gun and just ran off towards the house.

When I got to the house, just right at nightfall, I told my grandparents about it.

And, you know, "What you saw was that little man." You know, "What did I tell you? You go into the woods and so forth, and you'll see one of these maybe."

And what he told me at that point, may be two things. If I had stuck around there, I might have become a Choctaw doctor. Or there might have been maybe some money there, if I'd stuck around. So they told me.

But he told me that, "Since you ran away and so forth, he will never appear to you again. And since you ran away, whatever was there, you'll never find it again, as such."

The next afternoon, Sunday afternoon, after church, I took my granddad, two dogs, of course a rifle again; and I went to the spot, and I showed him and so forth where the stump was. You know, I couldn't find where that stump was. The stump was not there. I could not find that stump.

To this day, every now and then, you know, when I go by there, I would still look for that stump, but that stump's not there.

So that's one of those believe-it-or-nots, but I actually experienced that firsthand, as such. There was fear, all right?

And I've got 20/20 vision and so forth, and hearing and all that even now. So back then, you know—

And I was sane back then. I'm still sane now [laughter].

So I don't know what it was but I did experience that as such.

NOTE

Tape-recorded from Terry Ben on May 30, 1996, with Rae Nell Vaughn. Rae was the tribal archivist at the time, and her office was in the Choctaw High School building, where Terry was serving as principal. Rae and Terry knew each other well and we settled into comfortable conversation quickly, despite the institutional setting. —*Tom Mould*

Pąš Falaya (Long Hair)

Cynthia Clegg (1997)

Recorded and transcribed by Tom Mould and Liasha Alex

CYNTHIA: This story is about my *hokni*. Do you know what *hokni* means?

CHILDREN: Yes, yes— "grandma."

CYNTHIA: Grandma is *pokni. Pokni.*

CHILDREN: *Pokni.*

CYNTHIA: My *hokni* had died. *Hokni* is "aunt."

She told me. She passed away years ago. And she told me this story when I was little. See, I'm from Tucker and my aunt was from Tucker. So then, she said to me, she had been sick and her *ičǫkašat* was not well. Do you all know what *čǫkaš* is?

CHILDREN: No.

CYNTHIA: *Ičǫkaš* is your heart.

And her heart was not well. And that's what my grandparents died from. They died of a heart attack. So we were scared because she was sick.

So, anyway she lived in this old wood frame house. And the house was like this [motions with her hand]. Door—*okkisa* means "door"—the door stood like this, and the living room was like this. And what was supposed to be the dining room, a table was supposed to stand there, they put her bed there. So that's where she slept. And the door was like this, the wall, and the window was here [she motions with her hands to describe the layout of the house].

From the dining room you could see whoever came over toward the door.

So anyways what she told me was that one night, *ǫbatoh* [it rained]. What is *ǫba*?

CHILDREN: "Rain."

CYNTHIA: *Hilóhatoh* (It was thundering).

What is *hilóha*?

CHILDREN: "Thunder."

CYNTHIA: *Malattatoh* (It was lightning).

CHILDREN: "Lightning."

CYNTHIA: Lightning. It said "Boom."

She was asleep. It was almost dawn.

So then she said she woke up. Then she said something went "boom, boom, boom" at the door. And she said she wondered, "What am I hearing?" Then she laid there.

Someone knocked again. It came to the door.

And it rained hard, it was raining so hard that you just couldn't see good outside.

So she said she sat up, then stood up. And she said it seemed as if someone arrived.

"Who would be so crazy to come out in this rain?" she thought.

Then she went to the window. And there was a curtain on the window, so she quietly opened, like this [pantomimes pulling a curtain to the side], and she looked out.

And at the front door, from the sideways, she said she could see it this way. And she said a tall man was standing there. And he was wearing a black hat, and his hair was long hair.

So when she said *pąš falaya,* I thought she was talking about my grandma's great uncle, because he died long, long time ago. But he was a medicine man and his name was Pąš Falaya.

What is *pąš falaya* in Choctaw?

CHILDREN: "His hair is long."

CYNTHIA: "Long hair," yes.

That's who I thought she was talking about. I wondered was it him who came and revealed himself to her.

But she said that when she looked, with the curtain this way [she pantomimes pulling it aside], he stood there. And when a tall man with a long black coat to his knees, was standing there, when she looked at him in this way, his eyes were like this [Cynthia rolls her eyes back into her head so only the whites show].

Only the whites of his eyes were showing. And it was like this [repeats gesture; kids all scream]. Only the whites of his eyes were showing. He didn't have no pupils.

It was said that when she saw that, she was frightened.

But she wondered, "What will I do?"

She said that when she wondered, "Why is he showing himself to me?" she went back to bed and she was laying there.

She said that the knock stopped and she just fell asleep.

Then when it was morning, she said she didn't tell anyone about it.

It was several days later, she told me about it.

Her son was certainly sick. So it was he who was possibly going to die, she said. Maybe that is the message he is bringing, she said. But, but he never passed away.

It was several months later when it was she who passed away.

And she passed away, she died.

CHILD: How?

CYNTHIA: Her heart, her heart was not good.

CHILD: Who died?

CYNTHIA: My aunt.

After she told me that, when she told me only the whites of his eyes were showing, she said, "I was scared, and I could not go to sleep that night."

So when I see movies today and if it is about ghosts I get scared when I see it.

CHILDREN: Do it again!

CYNTHIA: One last time [she rolls her eyes back into her head and the kids scream].

CHILDREN: Do it again one more time.

CYNTHIA: It was like this [She does it again and the kids scream].

But that's my story and that's a true story, because it was my aunt who told me. That's a true story.

CHILD: That was true?

CYNTHIA: It was a true story.

NOTE

Tape-recorded from Cynthia Clegg on July 27, 1997, with Liasha Alex during afternoon storytelling at the Choctaw Language Immersion Camp. According both to John Swanton in his book *Source material for the Social and Ceremonial Life of the Cherokee Indians* (Washington DC: U.S. Government Printing Office, 1932), 4, and Harold Comby in an interview with the author (1997), the Choctaws' neighbors used to call them *pą̨ši falaya* or "long hairs."—*Tom Mould*

Prophecies

Prophecy of New Inventions and Lost Traditions

Billy Amos (1999)
Recorded by Tom Mould

Indentation in this exchange indicates how Billy Amos negotiates three time periods: the storytelling situation of the present (no indent), life in the past (single indent), and prophecy of the future (double indent).

TOM: And that education in the past, before they had all these schools, who would teach you the old history and the old stories and the old things?

BILLY: That was the old people. Most of them, they die already.
But at that time——some of the things in the future was going to come up. That's how they sit down and explained it.
And some of the things that I saw today and in the past, has come true.
And most of them I haven't seen yet.
But once in a while, they come up.
So it's true.

TOM: And how would that work?

You were saying the other day when we were over at the school——you had talked about a couple of different ones: about, like having water in the house, and the bathroom and TV.

BILLY: Yeah.

Back then, what I was talking about was the sharecropping, that I was talking about.

Same time was,
we didn't have no electricity back then.
Then we have to go and use a toilet outside.
Or we have to tote water from the spring or wells.
And that's how did we used to cooking.

Or maybe we didn't have no electricity on the stove.
We had a fire on the stove.
And we have to build a fire to make it cook.
Everyday.
I don't care if it's hot, you still have to cook, unless you cook outside.
Most of the time, some of them was cooking outside,
Like we do today, cook outside.
And that's how they lived.

> "But," she says, "someday,
> you'll be sitting inside a house,
> and they'll just put on the water
> and the water come in, in the house."
>
> And then electricity.
> "You just flip the button
> and the lights coming on."

We had a lamp to clean back then.
Because I remember going to school,
had to clean that lamp to get study.

Clean it out every night.
Lamp tops, you know; lamp globe in other words.

Kerosene lamp.

And I can't believe that when she said that.
"How can that be?"

    Just put the water on the inside the house and it come on.
    And you got your hot water and cold water.

Well, we have to take a bath,
we have to tote water from the spring or wells
and then pour it in the wash tub, wash pot,
and build a fire to heat it up, warm water to take a bath with.
That's how did we go.

    But like they said was,
    Someday that you could flip the faucet,
    then you're ready to take a shower.
    And in a few minutes,
    you'd be finished taking a shower.

And I can't believe that. How that could be.

And then,
I used to go out to TV——I mean movie.
They had set up the tent; once a week that movie comes out.

And then—I used to be crazy about it—
so I have to go up there at night time, in the evening.
Then I come back and I'm kind of scared coming down the road,
but I go up there every week.

And they had movies come out, chapter continued, movie.
What happens, it goes off, then next week it continues.

And I want to watch the whole chapter, I have to go up there.

She says
"Someday—
—you'll be running around, go up there walking, go see the white people's movie.

But someday
you going to be sitting in your own house, and going to watch them.

You don't have to go out
you just flip that button
and you'd be watching the white people's movies,
pictures in other words.

And I can't believe what she was saying.

But after all that time,
there was——the first to come up was TV,
black and white.
And that's the way it was.

And beyond that,
they got this VCR tape.
What kind of movie you want, you just go to the store and rent it, and clicked it on,
and then you can watch the movies, what you want to see.

But like I said,
I don't know where they got the ideas,
but in the future times that they look ahead of times
and those things was come up.

"And the social dances is going to fade away," she said, "someday."

These are dancing on the weekend, Saturday night, they dance all night long in the ball field.

But they think it's going to be disappeared if they don't watch it.

So is the house dancing.

And today, that's where we at now, if we don't watch it.
So many things has changed.

Only time we have our social dances is go out at some schools and performing, or Choctaw Fair. Stickball game, you see that. But that's the only time. The rest of 'em, when the Fair is over, they done forgot about it. Then the next year time, will be month of time, and here they're trying practicing dancing or stickball.

But at least we still got culture, a little. Some other state, I don't think they have their culture.

NOTES

Tape-recorded from Billy Amos on August 1, 1999. Billy and I sat in his living room in his home in Bogue Chitto talking about the old stories his grandmother and the elders in his community used to tell him. As often, we sat under his arbor outside. In his story, when Billy talks about cooking outdoors and adds, "like we do today," he is referring to my visit earlier that afternoon, when he and two friends were cooking outside under his backyard arbor.—*Tom Mould*

Prophecy of Cars and Changing Values

Odie Mae Anderson (1997, *Choctaw and English*)
Recorded by Tom Mould, Glenda Williamson,
and Meriva Williamson

Well, it was my father and Bike Williamson, the two together, I heard sitting around talking as a child.

But they said, "Even the little road that is laid out here, that road will be laid out wide. It will be paved," they said as they sat.

"How do they know?" I sat wondering.

But then, and something with two eyes would be running on it, I heard him say.

And then——never even imagined there would be houses here. There will be rows of brick houses.

When I heard him say, "And then it will be all paved, other places; it will be paved going side by side," that he had said, I can see.

I think it is the interstate he was talking about. I am thinking, it probably was, as I now think.

And when the brick houses are all built, when the daycare is built, they will just drop the little children off and will continually go. Money will mean more than the children, he used say.

That, I see, is true.

And even though he kept saying, "I am the chief," however, when he said the Choctaws vote "yes", "no"——when they vote and defeat it, the Choctaws will not have a place to live. And then they will not have a place for their bundles.

And when they don't have a home, it will be full of white people, even where it was thought the Choctaws used to live.

Then when they go carrying the bundles they will go to bury the buffalo feces.

They will go eat little frogs.

I used to hear it said.

That has not come about yet.

That's all.

CHOCTAW LANGUAGE VERSION

Akma ąki akoš *Bike Williamson* ittatoklós čįt anǫpolihǫ hąklolihttók siyalla yó.

Hikakǫ makáčih kat "Hína, osi yóš pą bačąya makoš, hínát áwatahóš bačąyáčį. Tali yóš patałpáčį," áčit oklah čįyąh mą.

"Nátit ikkąnaho?" ahnit ąšalittók.

Hitokakǫ anǫti hikmą nánát niškin toklóš áyiłípáčįh áką hąklolittók.

Hikmą anǫti čokkát pa tallayátok ahnih kiyyo mákǫ lokfi nona čokka yóš ittapakkačit talóha tahačįh áčihǫ hąklolimą, "Anǫti hikmą tali patałpo bąnokmą naksika yą talipałpo yóš ittapátáš iyačį," attóką pįsali.

Interstate mák makáha ahnilih. Hittóka ahnit himakak anokfillilih.

Híkmat lokfi nona čokka tobat táhakmą alla čipįta áyášat tobakmą alla čipįta yą pí ǫt bohliča iłkohǫláčįh. Iskalli áš imíšahláčįh alla yą, áhąyattó.

Yammanǫ ąłiką pįsalih.

Hikkat "Anákóš Chief siyá" ahąyattók mákoš, hitok makǫ čahtat "*yes,*" "*no,*" ači vóta ná okla vótat im ayyačikmą, čahtat áyáša ikimikšo kačį ačihhǫ hąklolih bíkattók.

Makokmat ná bonǫta kiya áyášat ikimikšokmat čokkát ikimikšokmą náhollo yóš alóta taháčį čahtat á mąyatok áhnih mákǫ.

Hikmą ná bonǫta šáli ča iłkólikmat yanaš į yałki hoppit iłkóláçįh. Yalǫboši ápat iłkóláčįh áką hąklolih bíkattók.

Manǫ ikǫnokįša.

Makilla.

NOTE

Tape-recorded from Odie Mae Anderson on August 12, 1997, with Glenda Williamson and Meriva Williamson. The thing with two eyes that will be running along the road refers to cars. Bundles can be understood as belongings. In older times, bundles would have been how such personal effects were carried and described.

Readers may find other prophecy accounts in interviews with Viola Johnson, 1974; Annie Tubby, recorded by John G. Wallace, 1977; Estelline Tubby, July 22, 1999; and in Tom Mould, *Choctaw Prophecy: A Legacy to the Future* (Tuscaloosa: University of Alabama Press, 2003).—*Tom Mould*

The Third Removal

Estelline Tubby (1996)
Recorded and transcribed by Tom Mould

Indentation indicates how Estelline Tubby negotiates three different voices: her own (no indent); those of her aunt, mother, and grandmother, who told her the prophecy (single indent); and those of the people in the future reacting to the prophesied events (double indent). When she shifts from narrating the prophecy to sharing a story of how she was inspired to interpret it, those voices also shift: her detached voice describing the experience (no indent), her thoughts in the moment of the experience (single indent), and the voice that came into her mind of what the prophecy meant (double indent).

ESTELLINE: When my aunt came to live with us, well, she know a few of them [stories]. So, well, she teached us, but I didn't, well—I was too young to listen I guess. Well, she tried, but during the night she tried to tell us but we'd go to sleep! And I didn't listen to all of it. And I wish I had today.

TOM: Do you remember what—the kinds of things she was telling you?

ESTELLINE: Yes.

One thing was that our great-grandmother said that
    one day we will have a third removal.
    Here.
And she told that, she said
    why it will be third removal is
    when Indians have good homes, electricity and all of these.
    And then one night—
Well, but I believe that it might be the ending of a world, or ending of time.
I kind of believe it must be that because she said that
    this will not be the removal by Washington or government or whatever.

It will be removal by some person, in a long robes, will be coming at night and tell us that if we—if we stay here we will suffer in days to come.

So we need to be gathering up somewhere in North.

And this will not be the Oklahoma or—or something like that

And then, the children—well, he'll be—they'll be talking to your children because they know more about the English and they understand.

And the children, well—the older person would ask them, said:

"What are they saying to you?"
Said that: "Well if we stay here, we're going to suffer."
And, "They want us to go.
Tonight.
Right now."

But they say:
"Oh, we were born out here.
We will not go.
We will stay and suffer."

But the older boy will say:
"Well, if it's going to be suffering,
I don't want to suffer
so I'm going."

"And all we have to do is pick out a few clothes,
and that's all that we need."
And everybody will say,
"Well, if you go,
we'll go."

And from house to house, everybody will go.

But few will be left, just few will be left, after all night—

[a visitor pulls up in the driveway, briefly interrupting our conversation].

Ahem, and what we was talking about was that removal.
After whenever—
I don't know who is the person that will be here.
And, they will be moving overnight.
Just overnight.

And then, someone will tell the—tell the agency that the Choctaws have moved.
And they'll send a word to Washington.
And that's when the Washington people find out.
And a few of the representatives will come down and look at the houses.

But they have been hearing—seeing and hearing about Choctaws making progress and this and that.
But all in one night, they will be gone.
Again.

TOM: Now, that'll be the third removal, right?
ESTELLINE: Third removal.

To the North.
Where the buffalo used to roam.
That's what they say.

And I—well, I hope I don't live to see it [laughs].
It'd be a lot of work getting up there, I guess [laughs].
[Her story over, we chatted until a lull in the conversation when Estelline looked expectant, as if there was something on her mind.]

But, ahem, anyway. I was talking about that, uh, removal.
Well, I was writing about it.
One day I thought I'd write about it.
And no one was here and I went writing about it.

And I was thinking:
Well we—I guess we'll be hungry when we go.
And there's nothing else we—if we take our clothes, we still going to suffer, look like.
And I keep thinking about it.

And then there was a voice talking to me and said that:
"You read Moses and my people in the wilderness, how they survived."

And so I went to the Bible and read the Scripture all the way down to it.
And it said that the people that Moses took to that wilderness,
these people said:
"Well you come—you bring us here, out to suffer and die.
And you said we were God's people.
But you didn't tell us we going to suffer this much.
We are really getting hungry."

And then, Moses said:
"Well, tomorrow you will be fed."
But they couldn't believe it.
They got on to Moses about it.

They—they didn't have anything to do.
I guess in the wilderness you just go there and stay.

So finally, in the morning, it rained.
And, it was the manna, that came down and fed these people.

And that—that came into my mind while I was thinking about it.

And there was something that they kill and eat and all of that.

And I was thinking—
maybe—the thing that came into my mind, at that time, was the spiritual walk.
It was not just the removal like the other ones.
And maybe that's why the Lord, telling me what they gonna do.
Maybe it was a spiritual walk and we'll be leaving.

NOTE

Tape-recorded from Estelline Tubby on May 31, 1996. This was the first of many taped interviews Estelline and I conducted together. We sat at her kitchen table at her home in Pearl River as she talked. Estelline Tubby recounted this prophecy twice more during interviews on August 5, 1997, and July 22, 1999. Each time, she resituates the story in contexts relevant to recent events in her life.—*Tom Mould*

Where Oral Tradition and Literacy Collide

James L. McDonald's Spectre Essay of 1830

Phillip Carroll Morgan

In the long history of the Choctaws in North America, no dramatic moment or period can much exceed the few months following the *Anumpa Bok Lukfi Hilha*, the Treaty of Dancing Rabbit Creek, signed on September 27–29, 1830. Under the terms of the treaty every Choctaw citizen faced a doubly frightening ultimatum—either pull up lock, stock, and barrel from their ancient homelands and move to Indian Territory, a land largely unfamiliar to most Choctaws in 1830, or stay in Mississippi and become a citizen of that state and of the United States. Two and a half months after tribal leaders signed the treaty, a young full-blood Choctaw intellectual, James Lawrence McDonald, wrote what I call the "Spectre Essay."

When I first discovered his essay, in the form of a beautifully handwritten letter to his Choctaw friend of approximately equal age, Peter Perkins Pitchlynn, I was simply exploring the Pitchlynn Collection in the Western History archives of Bizzell Memorial Library at the University of Oklahoma, looking for nonfiction source material to use for a graduate school term paper in a course on that subject taught by Dr. Robert Warrior.[1] The letter is archived along with other letters to Pitchlynn in the preremoval era, roughly spanning the period between 1824 and 1831. Pitchlynn and his family immigrated to Indian Territory in 1832, and McDonald died tragically in the fall of 1831. The letter and others like it were so fascinating to me that the preremoval writings of Pitchlynn and McDonald later became the central focus of my dissertation study.

McDonald's letter bears interest from several points of view. First, it is politically interesting insofar as it represents the personal communications between two of the most prominent young men in the tribe—Pitchlynn, born to a leadership clan mother and therefore a life of politics, and McDonald, an exceptional student handpicked for an advanced education that resulted in his being the first Choctaw, and perhaps the first American Indian of any tribe, admitted to the practice of law before the courts of the United States.

The distinctiveness of McDonald's Spectre Essay lies chiefly in the quality of the writing and in its almost uncanny foreshadowing of modern critical conversations about American Indian literature—namely the importance of tribal specificity in models for criticizing Native literature.

After receiving what I regard as a high quality, language-based primary education from classically educated missionary teachers during the second decade of the nineteenth century, McDonald continued his education in Philadelphia. Before and after his primary education, Pitchlynn enjoyed tutelage from local scholars in Mississippi, such as Gideon Lincecum, a self-educated doctor, historian, teacher, and naturalist, who remained close with his *protégé* Pitchlynn until he moved from Columbus, Mississippi, to Texas in 1848. In Texas Lincecum gained renown as a naturalist. "He collected plant and animal specimens, corresponded with notable naturalists such as Charles Darwin (sending him forty-eight samples of Texas ants with detailed commentaries), dabbled in geology, recorded weather observations, and tracked drought cycles."[2] Besides what he learned from his tribal elders and from his tutors and neighborhood scholars, Pitchlynn attended two mission schools in Tennessee as a teenager and later completed his education at the University of Nashville.[3]

McDonald's preamble to the Spectre Essay legend appears to be part of an ongoing conversation between him and Pitchlynn regarding the importance of Choctaw language arts traditions as well as the importance of interpreting those traditions firsthand. The exact motive or motives behind the acts of presenting a legend of the Choctaws and then criticizing it in comparison with stories in English are not stated or obvious. The context in which they were written, however, suggests strongly that the young educated leaders were concerned with curricula that Pitchlynn especially would be instrumental in creating while establishing new schools in Indian Territory, following the mass emigration from Mississippi that was set to commence during the next winter, the winter of 1831–32.

Both McDonald and Pitchlynn understood by virtue of their own educational experiences that education always includes a political agenda. Since 1825 both had been intimately involved in Choctaw national politics and well as international politics with the United States and with other tribal nations. Pitchlynn had been elected in 1825 commissioner of the tribal police force, the Choctaw Lighthorse. Earlier in the year 1825, McDonald was called upon to step in and apply his legal education to treaty negotiations in Washington DC as a consequence of the deaths in one season of two of the three veteran Choctaw chiefs. Apuckshunubbee died from a fall at Maysville, Kentucky, in October 1824 during the journey to the treaty meeting, and Pushmataha died on Christmas Eve, 1824, shortly before treaty talks began in early 1825.

The McDonald-Pitchlynn correspondence is in their second language, English, and the seriousness with which the writings were crafted and composed is obvious even in a casual reading of them. Scholars of American literature might rightfully associate McDonald's letter-essay with the period of emergence of American exceptionalism. The term *American exceptionalism* arose after French courtier and author Alexis de Tocqueville published *Democracy in America* in 1835, based on his observations of Americans during his travels in the United States earlier in the 1830s.[4] The articulate Frenchman documented how the innovative social and political experiments based on the ideals of equality and classless liberty and being conducted daily in American life greatly differentiated North America from the courts and communities of Europe and from democratic enterprises elsewhere in the world.

By the year 1830 the Industrial Revolution powered by steamship, railroad, and capital was rapidly unfolding, and nations formerly ruled by kings were gradually transforming into constitutional republics. American Indian cultures were not immune from the challenges of modernity, but neither were they unequipped for change. McDonald, Pitchlynn, and their contemporaries undoubtedly recognized, in a fashion similar to Alexis de Tocqueville, that these movements in the world away from bloodline leadership and toward chartered popular governments were an inevitable outcome of the long march of history.[5] I believe their writing demonstrates that they were embracing the challenges of constitutional government and that they were beginning to create educational materials to supply the school systems in their new republic soon to come into being in Indian Territory.

As bilingual readers and writers themselves, McDonald and Pitchlynn were certainly aware that Euro-American authors with international reputations, such as Washington Irving, William Cullen Bryant, and James Fennimore Cooper, were vigorously embracing their American identities, and the young Choctaw intellectuals predictably and, in the case of McDonald's Spectre Essay, effectively, proclaimed their own ancient traditions in tribal language arts and their readiness to incorporate literacy into what were already robust oral ontological and epistemological traditions.

Pitchlynn, as secretary of the meetings, recorded in English and in the Choctaw language the first written laws of the Choctaws, laws created by sessions of the national council held in the summers of 1826, 1827, and 1828. My great-great grandfather, William Wade, served as a delegate to that council of lawmakers, to which James L. McDonald also served as a delegate. I discovered my great-great grandfather's name unexpectedly, written in an old twine-bound journal, thus learning of his personal relationship to these Choctaw writers on whom I had focused for four years of dissertation research. It was Pitchlynn's journal of those first written laws, and I found it in the spring of 2006 where it lay neatly preserved in an unmarked folder in an archive at the University of Oklahoma.

This example of the twenty-year-old Pitchlynn's bilingual literacy and the important uses to which it was being put illustrate an admirable level of sophistication in the discourse that existed between the two young men leading up to the writing of the Spectre Essay in the late fall of 1830. I assumed that the folder, stored in an archivist's box with Choctaw school ledgers and account books, had just been overlooked, and that the folder had remained unmarked because I was perhaps the first person who had seen it in a century or so who could read the language. Pitchlynn's journal of the council's laws and resolutions comprises 109 pages and is written in Pitchlynn's hand entirely in the Choctaw language, except for the names of delegates such as Pitchlynn, McDonald, my ancestor, and other Choctaws, who were already using their English names on legal forms instead of their tribal names.[6]

Pitchlynn would subsequently chair the council, which drafted the Choctaw Nation's more formal constitution during 1834, immediately following the Choctaws' initial resettlement in Indian Territory. He worked steadily after removal to establish the educational system in the new Choctaw Nation and in 1842 authored tribal legislation that established and funded two permanent male academies and four female seminaries. Pitchlynn served the Choctaws throughout most of his adult life as their delegate to Washington DC was elected principal chief in 1864, and served in that office through the Reconstruction Treaties of 1866.[7]

The reasons why McDonald and Pitchlynn chose the letter form within which to preserve the legend and its comparison to English storytelling styles is not immediately clear. Perhaps they were imitating the popular English literary form of the epistolary novel, although the heyday of that form occurred in the eighteenth century and its popularity was waning in the nineteenth century. My best speculation is that they may have estimated that the transliteration of Choctaw stories with accompanying commentaries in English packaged in the form of letters between tribal scholars might provide a clever form in which to publish the stories and to illustrate their significance in Choctaw thought.

Other letters in the Pitchlynn archives indicate that Pitchlynn and McDonald were acquainted with at least two publishers, Andrew Marschalk and Henry Vose. Marschalk was the publisher of Mississippi's oldest newspaper, the *Mississippi Herald* (and later the *Natchez Gazette*). Vose, whose correspondence with Pitchlynn evidences a close friendship with him and McDonald, was a literary associate of Marschalk's in Natchez and published a small literary magazine there called *The Tablet*.[8] The exact reasons behind the choice of the letter format, nonetheless, appear to have perished with young McDonald less than a year after he wrote the Spectre Essay. I could find no overt explanation for his choice of form in Pitchlynn's sizeable archive of letters, although

McDonald indicates in the first sentence of the letter that he is honoring his promise to Pitchlynn "to reduce to writing the tale I had repeated to you, as illustration of the imaginative powers of our countrymen."

McDonald divided his long letter to Pitchlynn into two sections. The first section, dated December 13, 1830, describes the story styling methods and techniques of a typical Choctaw storyteller of the period. This first section serves, further, as a preamble to the presentation in the second section of the letter, dated December 17, 1830, of "The Spectre and the Hunter: A Legend of the Choctaws."

The legend itself, a horror story, is presented by McDonald as a translation into English of a traditional story told to him by a relatively uneducated and unnamed young Choctaw storyteller, who spoke no English. He declares further that the story reminds him of stories he heard frequently as a boy. McDonald describes to Pitchlynn how as a child he often got together with other Choctaw boys and exchanged stories that they called *shookha noompas*, which means "hog stories."

According to Choctaw scholar D. L. Birchfield, McDonald was sent east at age fourteen on Chief Pushmataha's recommendation to be a ward in the home of Thomas L. McKenney. McKenney, a Quaker and commissioner of Indian Affairs for three successive presidents before he was fired in 1830 by Andrew Jackson for opposing the Indian Removal Act, reports in his memoirs that he placed McDonald first under the tutelage of Rev. James Carnahan, who soon after became president of Princeton College (1823–54). After finishing his language-based classical education with Carnahan, McDonald was sent to Ohio, where he read law in the office of Judge John McLean (who later became a Supreme Court justice). Birchfield, a lawyer himself, credits McDonald with being the first American Indian admitted to the bar and further credits him with "saving the day" for the Choctaws in the treaty negotiations of 1824–25 in Washington.[9]

His very current education in the law enabled him to lead the way in steadfastly resisting costly concessions of Choctaw interests to the United States government. Reflecting on the qualities of his former ward's performance in the 1824–25 treaty negotiations, McKenney said, "I found him so skilled in the business of his mission . . . as to make it more of an up-hill business than I had ever before experienced in negotiating with Indians. I believe Mr. Calhoun thought so too."[10] McKenney is referring to John C. Calhoun, the famous "war hawk" politician from South Carolina, who was secretary of war at the time and vice president–elect to President John Quincy Adams.

As auspicious as James L. McDonald's skills as a young attorney proved to be, he may be more significant as literary critic. His letter-essay, which follows this introduction, may ultimately be his most lasting legacy. He was uniquely situated in the confluence of two great storytelling traditions, Choctaw and English, a brilliant Choctaw intellectual who had received perhaps as good an education as was available to anyone in his day. He is writing at a quintessential moment in Choctaw intellectual history, a member of the first generation of Choctaws to have fully assimilated English literacy as a tool of daily discourse.

McDonald, in his essay of comparative literature, was writing a cool 150 years ahead of the curve in his analysis of the merits of oral tradition compared to those of the new literacy in English.[11] I sense in reading McDonald that he regards oral tradition not as a dead artifact but more as an art in a state of transformation. In the immediate throes of leading the incorporation of literacy into Choctaw discourses, McDonald seems very excited by the transformation going on; certainly he is not perplexed by the end of one tradition and the beginning of another. Though his evaluations tend to romanticize and perhaps overestimate the superiority of Choctaw to English, his essay is neither nostalgic nor defensive.

I am calling the ten-page letter an essay because I think that was his sense of what he was writing. The old legend McDonald presents is by all appearances a direct translation from the Choctaw oral tradition. The commentary and legend serve also as powerful examples of how literacy impacts oral tradition. My first impression as a reader of the legend in its immaculate handwritten and closely edited form was that it has a markedly literate quality. Just the fact that a writer of letters has to accomplish effects in writing that a live storyteller would achieve by gesture, inflection, and other languages of the human body may necessarily result in a transformation of a story that has existed viably only in the memory of tellers, perhaps for centuries.

"The Spectre and the Hunter" is a tale of horror. It is also a cautionary tale, portraying what befalls the great hunter-warrior-athlete Ko-way-hoom-mah (the Red Tiger), a tribal member who "questioned the existence of It-tay-bo-lahs [invisible things] and Nan-ish-ta-hool-ahs [witches], and as to Shil-loops [ghosts] he said he had never seen them—then why should he fear them?–Dangerous it is to trifle with beings that walk unseen among us."[12]

Even though McDonald interrogates beliefs about witchcraft, labeling them absurd and waning superstitions, he explains that the story was told to him during a season of employment at McDonald's home place.[13] The unnamed young Choctaw storyteller has been run out of his hometown, having been accused of witchcraft by a conjurer. The narrator remained in his employment, McDonald relates, until he could earn enough money to buy a good rifle and ammunition and immigrate to the new nation in the western Indian Territory. The inescapable implication here is that Choctaw mythos, and the language forms in which it resides, embodied in people like the young storyteller, are moving West intact with the Nation.

It is my contention that McDonald meant his letter to be an enduring essay with valuable and significant dimensions beyond a demonstration of his personal eloquence. It certainly could be true that the immaculately penned finished copy of the letter that he delivered to Pitchlynn was meant to be a handsome souvenir of their literary conversations, but from my first reading 175 years after it was written, I considered the letter to be an essay on comparative linguistics, comparative literature, and critical commentary regarding the interesting interface of oral traditions with the practices of literacy.

McDonald explains that "The Spectre and the Hunter: A Legend of the Choctaws" was typical of stories he had heard as a child of five or six ("some twenty years since"), when it was the custom of Choctaw boys to assemble together on pleasant summer evenings and tell stories in rotation. "These stories they facetiously styled 'shookha noompas,' or hog stories," he relates, "but the reason why they were so styled, I have now forgotten if I ever knew."[14] He declares that he remembers distinctly a number of these stories, and "compares them with others which I have heard in after years among the white people, and I can truly say that the Indian loses nothing in comparison."[15]

McDonald makes bold, perhaps overly romanticized comparisons regarding Choctaw versus English education, claiming that the average Indian knows much more about the natural sciences and the environment than nine tenths of white people.[16] "There is also, it seems to me," he writes, "much more force and precision in the Choctaw language, than in English."[17]

I will interject the important question here: What was J. L. McDonald's purpose in writing what is essentially a ten-page essay on Choctaw storytelling? Why, for example, is there not a single reference to politics as such in this correspondence between two young and prominent Choctaw political leaders, in a letter crafted within a tense national setting less than three months after the signing of the Treaty of Dancing Rabbit Creek (September 27–28, 1830), which sealed the fate of Choctaw removal from their ancestral homeland? The answer may be that literary criticism is very much a political act. Education is an intensely political process of indoctrination. Literary criticism informs these doctrines, not only in the vital terms of what texts are employed in the literacy-based classroom but also in terms of *how* and *why* these texts are taught.

In framing the story the way he does, McDonald accomplishes three tasks, all essentially literary. First, and perhaps most important, he connects the story being told in the present with the past and with the future of Choctaw artistic, intellectual, and mythic tradition. The young monolingual storyteller's harrowing escape from "his neighborhood" after being accused by a conjurer of witchcraft (a capital offense) rhetorically certifies his placement squarely within the heart of Choctaw mythic tradition.

Furthermore, it places him definitively *outside* English language and other European discourses. "Purchasing a good rifle and ammunition" for his journey to the new nation west of the Mississippi serves to "transport" rhetorically and materially that mythic tradition and its store of story forms, structures, and tropes into the future. McDonald leaves no gaps that would require an imaginative stretch to make this interpretation of rhetorical purpose.

Second, McDonald places *himself*, the critic, within this tightly connected stream of Choctaw intellectual history. He not only cites how mainstream these stories are within the leisure schedule of his family ("this young man frequently entertained us") but also harks back to the December 13 half of the essay, in which he declared the importance of the *shookha noompas* tradition in his own boyhood.

Third, he establishes his essay, essentially a critical analysis of a story-within-a-story, as a work of literature. Webster defines literature as "the class of writings distinguished for beauty of style or expression, as poetry, essays, or history, in distinction from scientific treatises which contain positive knowledge."

McDonald apparently did not intend to leave his readers without a sense of irony, however, in the collisions of oral and lettered stories. On the last page of the Spectre Essay, following the translated legend, he offers a postscript in which he references "a singular story" he once read:

> of one Rip Van Winkle, who went out hunting and, feeling somewhat fatigued, lay down to take a nap. His nap it seems proved to be a long one; for when he awoke, he found his gun covered with mushrooms. I remember having been particularly struck with the "mushroom gun" in my Indian's story—and I think I can safely affirm he had never heard of Rip Van Winkle.

In the end, and perhaps more so in 1830 when Washington Irving's tale was fresh and more popular than today, the reader is presented with a captivatingly literary twist. Striking parallels, in fact exist between "The Spectre and the Hunter" and Irving's short story. In spite of dramatically different settings and characterizations, both are tales of men who wander off alone, except for the companionship of their loyal dogs, experience encounters with supernatural beings, and return home to tell their stories. Both stories, as McDonald points out in his postscript, contain the symbolically rusty, time-worn rifle. Irving frames his tale of "Rip Van Winkle," published in 1819–20 in *The Sketch Book of Sir Geoffrey Crayon, Gent*, as a posthumous "discovery" within the (obviously fictional) writings of Diedrich Knickerbocker.[18] McDonald's oral tradition story is similarly situated within the voice of a shadowy narrator, the unnamed young Choctaw sojourner.

Ultimately, McDonald's highly ironic postscript leaves his essay wide open to a variety of interpretations. Perhaps McDonald's recording of the legend, as told by the young Choctaw outcast, is entirely a fiction—not simply a fiction but a Choctaw revision or parody of Irving's popular "Rip Van Winkle." McDonald immediately deflects this tempting explanation, however, by disavowing the possibility of a direct connection between the two short stories. If not a parody, or an example of Choctaw assimilation of an English language story, then perhaps McDonald is highlighting the humanistic similarities between cautionary tales springing from seemingly diverse cultures. McDonald's allusions to "Rip Van Winkle" remind me of what Acoma poet laureate Simon J. Ortiz observes in his famous essay about the Native nationalistic impulse—how his people had absorbed and transformed Catholic rituals received from the Spanish into their own celebrations and art forms. This "speaks of the creative ability of Indian people," Ortiz writes, "to gather in many forms of the socio-political colonizing force which beset them and to make these forms meaningful in their own terms."[19] Whatever his intent in his references to "Rip Van Winkle," McDonald leaves the nineteenth century reader, or the twenty-first century reader or critic, much to imagine in terms of language, tradition, and literature.

In my ten years of study of nineteenth-century Choctaw and Chickasaw intellectual traditions, no single impression of the period has emerged more dominantly than the sense, inspired by the quality of their writing, that the two correspondents under discussion had received superior educations. This has prompted me to look more intently into the principles of the language-based (Latin and Greek) curricula that were prevalent in that century; what we generally refer to now as a classical education. This was humanities-intensive education (in language, ethics, geography, law, and history) that served in many ways to facilitate the Indians' assimilation of English reading and writing into the older language arts of the oral tradition in tribal culture.

It is an intriguing reality in current Native American writing that poets, novelists, and critics hold so tenaciously to the mythos of their respective tribes. One might regard the tendency to match contemporary literate work zealously with ancient oral forms as an almost universal essence in indigenous writing. Indigenous writers living today, in much the same manner as McDonald and Pitchlynn in their day, cannot ignore the foundational importance of the much older stories springing from this soil, and they seem equally excited about the potentials that reading and writing offer to expand upon those great traditions.

NOTES

1. Peter Perkins Pitchlynn (January 30, 1806–January 17, 1881) was twenty-four years old at the time of McDonald's writings presented here. McDonald's exact birthdate is unknown to me, but their correspondence suggests that they were childhood friends. For chronological reference, they were born during the same decade as Abraham Lincoln.
2. Greg O'Brien, "Gideon Lincecum (1793–1874): Mississippi Pioneer and Man of Many Talents," *Mississippi History Now*, Mississippi Historical Society, 2015, http://mshistory.k12.ms.us/index.php?id=82.
3. W. David Baird, "Peter Perkins Pitchlynn," *American National Biography Online*, accessed March 14, 2015, http://www.anb.org/articles/20/20-007 90.html.
4. "The position of the Americans is therefore quite exceptional, and it may be believed that no democratic people will ever be placed in a similar one. . . . Let us cease, then, to view all democratic nations under the example of the American people" (Alexis de Tocqueville, *Democracy in America, Book Two,* p. 42, accessed April 4, 2015, http://books.google.com/books).
5. "In perusing the pages of our history, we shall scarcely meet with a single great event, in the lapse of seven hundred years, which has not turned to the advantage of equality. . . . If we examine what has happened in France at intervals of fifty years, beginning with the eleventh century, we shall invariably perceive that a twofold revolution has taken place in the state of society. The noble has gone down on the social ladder, and the roturier has gone up; the one descends as the other rises. Every half century brings them nearer to each other, and they will very shortly meet" (de Tocqueville, *Democracy in American, Book Two*, "Introductory Chapter," para. 8).
6. Pitchlynn's handwritten journal record of the Choctaws' first written laws was laboriously and faithfully translated and edited by Choctaw native speaker Henry J. Willis and by University of Oklahoma linguist Dr. Marcia

Haag. It was published in bilingual format, with an introduction by Dr. Clara Sue Kidwell, under the title *A Gathering of Statesmen* (Norman: University of Oklahoma Press, 2013).

7. Baird, "Peter Perkins Pitchlynn."
8. Henry Vose wrote a sincere and personal letter of condolence to Pitchlynn shortly after McDonald's untimely death. Henry Vose, letter to Peter Perkins Pitchlynn, September 1831, box 1, Peter Perkins Pitchlynn Collection, Western History Collections, Bizzell Memorial Library, University of Oklahoma.
9. D. L. Birchfield, *The Oklahoma Basic Intelligence Test* (Greenfield Center NY: Greenfield Review Press, 1998, 165–66). McDonald "saved the day" because he skillfully stepped into negotiations in place of the two great Choctaw chiefs, Pushmataha and Apuckshunubbee, who had died shortly before treaty talks began.
10. Qtd. in Birchfield, *Oklahoma Basic Intelligence Test*, 167.
11. Many volumes of work examining the language arts as they exist in oral traditions compared to how they perform in written traditions sprang up during the 1980s, as exemplified in such important studies as Walter J. Ong, *Orality and Literacy: The Technologizing of the Word* (London: Routledge, 1982).
12. James L. McDonald, letter to Peter Perkins Pitchlynn, December 13 and 17, 1830, 5, handwritten original, box 1, Peter Perkins Pitchlynn Collection, Western History Collections, Bizzell Memorial Library, University of Oklahoma.
13. McDonald, letter to Pitchlynn, 5.
14. McDonald, letter to Pitchlynn, 1.
15. McDonald, letter to Pitchlynn, 1.
16. McDonald, letter to Pitchlynn, 2.
17. McDonald, letter to Pitchlynn, 2.
18. Washington Irving, *The Sketch Book of Sir Geoffrey Crayon, Gent* (London: John Murray, 1820).
19. Simon J. Ortiz, "Towards a National Indian Literature: Cultural Authenticity in Nationalism," *Ethnic Literature and Cultural Nationalism* (special issue), *MELUS* 8, no. 2 (Summer 1981): 8.

Letter to Peter Pitchlynn

J. L. McDonald (1830)
Transcribed by Phillip Carroll Morgan

DECEMBER 13TH, 1830

Esteemed friend:

The promise which I once made you to reduce to writing a tale which I had repeated to you, as illustration of the imaginative powers of our countrymen, had nearly escaped my recollection and I thank you for the hint which has recalled it to mind: For I am confined to the house by the gloomy weather which prevails without, and a little exercise of the pen will be an agreeable relief.

I well remember that it was the custom among the Choctaw boys some twenty years since,—and doubtless, the custom to a certain extent yet survives,—to assemble together of pleasant summer evenings, and tell stories in rotation. These stories they facetiously styled "Shookha noompas," or hog's stories; but the reason why they were so styled, I have now forgotten, if I ever knew.[1] I could not have been more than five or six years of age when in the habit of listening to the "Shookha noompas" of my play fellows, and yet my recollection of some of them is quite distinct. I then knew nothing of civilization. I had seen but few white people,—and these few having mostly adopted the Indian dress and habits, gave me no adequate idea of the "world far off" (as I then believed it to be) of the white people. I can now recall to mind some of those tales of early childhood, and compare them with others which I heard in after years among the white people, and I can truly say that the Indian loses nothing in the comparison. In fact, when we speak of tales adapted to captivate the attention and enlist the feelings of children, I am of the opinion that the Indian has decidedly the advantage. He is in general more familiar with the objects of nature than the white man; and hence can enliven his stories with more apposite and striking illustrations. You have doubtless noticed the superior facility with which an Indian, who is in the habit of roaming the woods, can detect and distinguish objects of sight and sound. You have remarked how readily he can name the different trees of the forest and the almost numberless plants and flowers of the field. You know that not a beast ranges the hills, not a reptile crawls on the plains, which he cannot name. The fowls that sail the air, the birds that warble in the grove, are equally familiar. In his lonely wanderings they become as dear and cherished companions. He has learned all their names, and can describe to you their habits and distinctive histories. Almost every Indian can do this, and nine tenths of white people cannot.

I believe that in tales of high imagination the Indians are deficient; but it is as I conceive, simply for the want of improvement. They have the stamina, if in early life it could be drawn out, cultivated, and polished. There is also, it seems to me, much more force and precision to the Choctaw language, than in the English;—or do I only think so, because it is my mother tongue? It may not be so varied, so rich as the English language; its vocabulary is far from being so copious; but as far as it goes, is it not stronger, more nervous?—Listen to a hunter returned from the chase, or a warrior from the field of battle. The first will describe to you all the arts and wiles which he had used in approaching the game (a deer for instance) with a clearness and distinctness which make you feel as if you had been with him. Even little incidents that had occurred, even to the rustling of a leaf, or the snapping of a dry twig, in his cautious approaches, is thrown in so naturally and with such simplicity in the progress of the story, that if you are a sportsman, it can not fail to rivet your attention. You seem to see the deer as he does; you examine localities; you make your approaches step by step as he does; you become completely identified with the narrator;—in short, you enjoy all the pleasure of the chase, without the fatigue. You may have heard a young hunter giving the stirring details of a bear hunt, and what sportsman would not warm with the tale?—The first cry of the dogs—the rushing of the animal through the tangled underwood—the snapping of cane—the confusion of the flight—the inspiring calls of the hunters—and the death scene when gun after gun is discharged into the head of the bear; according to Indian custom:—is all told with clear connection, and depicted with a vividness, which I should despair of hearing equalled in the English language.

Let us now turn to the warrior. He shall be a warrior in the prime of life—not young, nor yet aged. The lines of thought are on his brow, and he has scars that betoken many a bloody conflict. Imagine him just returned from his war expedition. He is seated, his friends are around him, silent and attentive; not one obtruding a question; but all waiting his pleasure to begin. He has just smoked a pipe, and now adjusts himself for the narration. He tells of the days and nights he travelled before he approached the hunting ground of his enemy. He describes the different objects he sees in his route, the streams he crossed, and his camping places. Here he killed a bear, there a buffalo. He marks on the ground a rude map of the country, to give a better idea of his travels. He describes where he first discovered the trail of his enemy. In such a quarter lay their town; here he concealed himself until he should discover some straggling foe. He describes the rivulet that quenched his thirst and the tree that sheltered him. Not an incident is forgotten; and every incident heightens the interest of his perilous situation. Becoming impatient he sallies forth, and takes a rapid circuit through the heart of his enemy's country. He soon discovers, from unerring indication, that his enemies have discovered his travel, and are on the look out to intercept him. He pauses, views the critical nature of his situation; but not a cowardly thought invades his bosom. He takes his resolution on the instant. He determines to elude his enemies if possible; but if not, he resolves to die like a warrior. His eye is incessantly on the watch, and his ear is bent to catch every sound that floats on the breeze. At length he discovers an Indian. He knows him for a foe by the paint on his face, and his peculiar headdress. Our warrior crouches low, takes a deadly aim, and brings [last page or pages missing from December 13, 1830, installment of the original manuscript].

DECEMBER 17TH, 1830

Esteemed friend:

I resume the task which I left unfinished (or rather untouched) a few days since, in an attempt to prove that our vernacular tongue is more expressive than the English. Should you coincide with me in opinion who shall gainsay our decision? It may indeed be said that the parties interested will generally decide in their own favour. But let the question for the present rest.

Four or five years ago, a young Choctaw of pleasing countenance and modest deportment applied to me for employment. I was struck with his address, and wished to test his habits of industry. He worked with us faithfully during the busy part of the season, and with the avails of his labour, purchased a good rifle and ammunition, and started west of the Mississippi. During his stay with us, I found he was remarkably intelligent for his opportunities. He did not speak a word of English. His father and mother, as he informed me, were both dead; and he had but few near relatives living. He had been charged with witchcraft by a conjurer of his neighborhood—(I am glad this absurd superstition is wearing away among the Choctaws) and had been obliged to fly from the nation to save his life. This young man frequently entertained us with tales during the intervals of labour. He possessed an easy flowing elocution, and from his store of "Shooka noompas" one evening told us the following story, which I will entitle

The Spectre and the Hunter

A LEGEND OF THE CHOCTAWS

No people have been more noted for their courage and their superior skill in every manly exercise than the Choctaws. They are brave warriors, they are successful hunters, and in the Ball play they have had no rivals. Young men now are not what their fathers have been. Old men tell us, that in their day, no man could claim to speak with authority in council who had not faced an enemy. None could claim the smiles of a woman who had not proved his skill in the Ball play; and if he happened to be unsuccessful in hunting, it was vain for him to think of a wife. He became the butt of general ridicule, and the theme of many a jest. Even old women would join in the chorus, and jeeringly invite him to stay at home and mind the pots.

In those days—(it was when our fathers were young)—lived Ko-way-hoom-mah.[2] He was called the Red Tiger for he had the strength and agility of that dreaded animal, and his skill and cunning were equal to his strength. Had he seen battle?—The scalps of six Wa-sha-she attested it.[3] Had he proved himself a dexterous hunter?—old women lifted their children to gaze at him as he passed, and young women hung their heads and blushed as he approached them. In Ball play he had long reigned the unquestioned champion of his district. Kowayhoommah, then, walked the earth fearless of man or beast. He even derided the power of the spirits. He questioned the existence of It-tay-bo-lays and Nan-ish-ta-hool-los, and as to Shi-loops, he said he had never seen them,—then why should he fear them?—Dangerous it is to trifle with beings that walk unseen among us.[4]

Ko-way-hoom-mah once started out on a hunting excursion. He had an excellent rifle, and he carried with him a little cold flour, and some jerked venison. His only companion was a large white dog which attended him in all his rambles. The dog was a cherished favorite, and shared in all his master's privations and successes. He was the social companion of the hunter by day, and his watchful guard by night.

The hunter had travelled far during the day, and as night approached, he took up camp in a spot that bore every indication of an excellent hunting ground. Deer tracks were seen in abundance, turkey were heard clucking in various directions as they retired to their roosting places. Ko-way-hoom-mah kindled a fire, and having shared a portion of his provisions with his dog, he spread his deer skin and blanket by the crackling fire, and mused on the adventures of the day already past, and on the probable success of the ensuing one. It was a bright star-light night; the air was calm, and a slight frost which was falling, rendered the fire comfortable and cheering. His dog lay crouched and slumbering at his feet, and from his stifled cries, seemed dreaming of the chase. Everything seemed to soothe the feelings of our hunter, and to prolong that pleasant train of associations which the beauty of the night and the anticipations of the morrow were calculated to inspire. At length, when his musings were assuming their indefinite and dreamy state which precedes a sounder slumber, he was startled by a distant cry that thrilled on his ear, and roused him into instant watchfulness. He listened with breathless attention, and in a few minutes he again heard the cry—keen—long—and piercing, as that which the Tik-ba-hay-kah gives in the dance preceding the Ball play.[5] The dog gave a low, plaintive, and ominous howl. Ko-way-hoom-mah felt uneasy. Can it be a lost hunter?—was the inquiry which suggested itself. Surely not; for a hunter with his rifle, and flint and steel, feels lost nowhere. What then can it be?—with these reflections, our hunter stepped forth, gathered more fuel, and again replenished his fire. Again came the cry,—keen—long,—and painfully thrilling as before—the voice was evidently approaching;—and again the dog raised a low and mournful howl. Ko-way-hoom-mah then felt the blood curdling to his heart, and folding his blanket around him, he seated himself by the fire and fixed his eye intently in the direction from which he expected the approach of his startling visitor. In a few minutes he heard the approach of footsteps; in another minute, a ghastly shape made its appearance and advanced towards the fire. It seemed to be the figure of a hunter like himself. Its form was tall and gaunt—its features livid and unearthly. A tattered blanket was girded round his waist, and covered his shoulders; and he had what seemed to have been a rifle, the barrel corroded with rust, the stock decayed and rotted, and covered here and there with mushrooms. The spectre advanced to the fire, and seemed to shiver with cold. He stretched forth one hand and then the other to the fire, and as he did so he fixed his hollow and glassy eye on Ko-way-hoom-mah and a slight smile lighted up his livid countenance, but no word did he utter. Ko-way-hoom-mah's sensations may be imagined. He felt his flesh and hair creep, and the blood freezing in his veins; yet with instinctive Indian courtesy, he presented his deer skin as a seat for his grim visitor. The spectre waved his hand and shook his head in refusal. He stepped aside and plucked up a parcel of briers from an adjacent thicket, spread them by the fire, and on this thorny couch he stretched himself and seemed to court repose.

Our hunter was petrified with mingled fear and astonishment. His eyes continued to be riveted on the strange and ghastly being stretched before him, and he was only awakened from this trance of horror by the voice of his faithful dog. "Arise," said the dog, suddenly and supernaturally gifted with speech. "Arise and flee for your life. The spectre now slumbers; should you also slumber you are lost. Arise and flee, while I stay and watch."—Kowayhoommah arose and stole away from the fire. Having advanced a few hundred paces he stopped to listen. All was still silent, and with a beating heart, he continued his stealthy and rapid flight. Again he listened, and again with renewed confidence he pursued his rapid course, until he had gained several miles on his route homewards. Feeling at length a sense of safety, he paused to recover breath on the brow on a lofty hill. The night was still calm and serene. The stars shone above him with steady lustre, and as Kowayhoommah gazed upwards, he breathed freely, and felt every apprehension vanish. Alas! On the instant the distant baying of his dog struck on his ear. With a thrill of general apprehension, he bent his ear to listen, and the appalling cry of his dog now more distinctly audible, convinced him that the spectre must then be in full pursuit. Again he fled with accelerated speed over hill, over plain, through swamps and thickets, until once more he paused by the side of a deep and rapid river. The heavy baying of his dog told him too truly that his fearful pursuer was close at hand. One minute he stood for breath, and then he plunged into the stream. But scarcely had he gained the center, when the spectre appeared on the bank and; plunged in after him, closely followed by the panting dog. Kowayhoommah's apprehensions now amounted to agony. He fancied he saw the hollow and glassy eye balls of his pursuer glaring above the water and that his skeleton hand was already outstretched to grapple with him. With a cry of horror, he was about giving up the struggle for life, and sinking beneath the waves, when his faithful dog, with a fierce yell, seized upon his master's enemy. After a short and desperate struggle, they both sunk, the waters settled over them, and our exhausted hunter reached the shore in safety.

Kowayhoommah became an altered man. He shunned the dance and the Ball play, and his former hilarity gave place to a settled melancholy. In about a year after his strange adventure, he joined a war party against a distant enemy and never returned.

Such, my dear sir, is the substance of the tale as related to me, and as I review what I have written, it seems to me faint and feeble compared with the animated and vivid touches of my Choctaw narrator;—another evidence which I might assign of the superior force of our vernacular, were I not aware that it might be said (perhaps very justly) that I am ignorant of the force and power of the English language, and, therefore, not a competent judge. But let that pass, and in conclusion, believe me to be

Ever sincerely yours
J. L. McDonald

P. P. Pitchlynn
Big Prairie

P.S. By the by, I once read a singular story of one Rip Van Winkle, who went out hunting, and feeling somewhat fatigued, lay down to take a nap. His nap it seems proved a long one; for when he awoke, he found his gun covered with mushrooms. I remember having been particularly struck with the "mushroom gun" in my Indian's story,—and I think I can safely affirm he had never heard of Rip Van Winkle.

NOTES

1. *Shukha anumpa* in standard orthography.
2. *Koi humma* in standard orthography. McDonald changed the spelling of this name several times in his letter. We have left it as he wrote it in the interest of being faithful to the manuscript.
3. *Washashi*, "Osage."
4. *Itiboli* and *nanishtahollo*, words for "phantom"; *Shilup*, "ghost."
5. *Tikba heka*, "leader."

Modern Oklahoma Choctaw Stories

Marcia Haag

Unable to escape the fate of most southeastern peoples, the Choctaws were "removed" in the early 1830s from their homelands in Mississippi to new lands in Indian Territory, along the *Nowa Falaya* (Long Walk). When Indian Territory became a state in 1907, it took the name *Okla Homma* (Red People), taken from a suggestion by Choctaw chief Allen Wright, who died before statehood was achieved.

From then, the Choctaws lived in two major geographical areas: the larger one, which eventually became the Choctaw Nation of Oklahoma, was formed from the exiles, and the smaller was made of those who refused removal and had hidden from the army, reemerging decades later when hostility toward Native people had diminished. The Mississippi Band of Choctaws was federally recognized in 1945.

In my searches for literatures of all kinds among the Choctaws of Oklahoma, I had been struck by the sparseness of what we might call folktales among actual speakers. I had formed a hypothesis that while there were plenty of *shukha anumpa* in the records of Swanton and his ilk, these already seemed to be museum pieces. Oklahoma Choctaw people could refer me to (a few!) stories, such as how the bear got a stumpy tail, and how the tortoise got his splendid shell, and three varieties of creation myth, but these were not the stories anyone was actually telling in company. This state of affairs is in marked contrast to that among the Mississippi Choctaws: see Tom Mould's *Choctaw Tales* for an impressively large collection.[1]

Instead, a very different set of traditions has sprung up, with seemingly little direct relation to the old southeastern motifs, such as Rabbit and the

Trickster, which we have come to expect, and which have been so richly explained by our ethnologists and folklorists.[2] First and foremost, one notices that modern stories are grounded in personal memoir. Many stories are recollections of a storyteller's actual experiences (see Paula Carney's "Boarding School Runaways" and Abe Frazier's "How I Almost Killed a Hog by Scaring It") honed by retelling to audiences of friends and family, with some details perhaps enhanced in favor of the overall impression.

Some storytellers and their tales are so entertaining that they become, if not actual types, at least brands. We are indebted to Tim Tingle, the Choctaw folklorist, for his collections of stories that organically connect their "owners."[3] Among them are the tales of "Aunt Neva," Neva Leon MacAlvain Bryan, a resident of southeastern Oklahoma who has been departed for many years but who lives on as a fixture in the local lore. It may be inferred that just as Winston Churchill has become a default source for pithy quotations that he *should* have uttered, Aunt Neva seems to have gotten into rather more humorous scrapes than are generally allotted to one middle-aged woman. I had the privilege of visiting, on numerous occasions, Aunt Neva's cousin Lois Pugh. At the age of ninety-three Mrs. Pugh, a gifted raconteur, delivered delightful exploits of family members reaching back into the nineteenth century. Apparently the entire family careened from one amusing adventure to the next, at least at storytelling time.

Amusing. The watchword for this kind of Choctaw story is a broad, self-deprecating humor that underscores the not-quite-comfortable place of the Indian in an uncomprehending society. Aunt Neva blows squirrels out of trees and skins them up at the hospital, singularly unladylike behavior, while adolescent girls plot their thwarted escape from boarding school (could there be a more alien place?). The storytellers all exhibit a crucial modesty, an ingenuousness that belies their skills in survival, sometimes even winning on their own terms. Listeners are supposed to have their own sense of how the Indian is placed in situations in which no response can be consonant with either Indian or white culture. Humor inheres in identifying with the one who does not know what everyone else knows, who interprets the world in a way that is out of kilter with the common acceptance of how things work.

This is not to imply that the Choctaws are just a jolly lot. My point is that humor is a deliberate technique in telling a certain kind of story. Mrs. Pugh related much of her life story to me: she overcame a good deal of material deprivation, racial discrimination, and losses as well as successes and deep satisfactions. When she spoke of her life in the manner of simple sharing with a friend, she expressed the full range of emotions, opinions, and grudges that would accompany such disclosures. But when she got ready to tell a *story*, she shifted her position in her easy chair. Her face took on a certain animated expression, and her speech style switched into the easy narrative with illuminating details and editorial comments that characterize her brand of story.

Paralleling their own modesty, the storytellers engage in social leveling. Bringing another person down to size is an attitude that underlies the narratives of modern Choctaw stories. Thus Ma Willard in Bill Nowlin's "The Miracle" takes on and defeats the United States Navy—but in the humblest and most Choctaw of ways. There could be no more culturally satisfying story than one that ratifies the deep Choctaw commitment to equality and consensus by seeing that the haughty get their comeuppance.

"The Miracle" represents another kind of modern Choctaw story, the testimonial to a miracle (Tingle's master's thesis explains this in detail). Again the testimonial is grounded in the storyteller's direct experience and very often describes deliverance from a dire medical event unexplainable by our common understanding.

In a related story type, modern Oklahoma Choctaws also tell numerous stories about encounters with supernatural beings and phenomena, among them the Little People. These are similar to those told by their Mississippi cousins (see Tom Mould's essay). Indeed, the entire southeastern area shares this motif. In this volume are more examples from Yuchi and Cherokee traditions.

In some cases the story passes to someone else who is obliged to find a connection with the original storyteller. (Note Josh Hinson's description of a similar phenomenon in modern Chickasaw stories.) There are certainly at least a few stories that are attributed to a fictive "grandfather."

Tingle's conjecture is that these stories require immediate grounding, and he speculates that many stories will disappear with their tellers.

However, now that a number of the stories have been published, we will see if, even after many of the tellers are deceased, the stories live on as a direct consequence of having been printed. This is the way literature works.

THE STORYTELLERS

Paula Carney and Abe Frazier are fluent Choctaw speakers whose stories and memoirs were recorded as part of a major cultural archiving project, *Chahta Anumpa Holitoblichi*: Honoring the Choctaw Language, conducted by Choctaw Nation of Oklahoma. The Sam Noble Museum of Natural History in Norman, Oklahoma, houses copies of the original recordings and transcriptions of these works. Carney's "Boarding School Runaways" appears as part of an interview conducted by Eveline Steele, a fine Choctaw speaker herself, who often works with linguists to help them understand the structure of the language. Frazier's "How I Almost Killed a Hog by Scaring It" was also recorded by Eveline Steele.

Bill Nowlin is from Texas, a retired school principal who has participated in storytelling workshops and who has an interest in helping others to find their own stories. "The Miracle," recorded and transcribed by Tim Tingle, is reprinted from *Choctaw Language and Culture: Chahta Anumpa*, volume 2.[4]

Lois Pugh, of McAlester, Oklahoma, died in 2007 after a very long life spent in close observation of people and situations. I recorded and transcribed her story "Neva the Hunter" in her living room in 2004. The story is reprinted from *Choctaw Language and Culture: Chahta Anumpa*, volume 2.

NOTES

1. Tom Mould, *Choctaw Tales* (Jackson: University of Mississippi Press, 2004).
2. See the essays in this volume for more details. Another excellent source is Dell Hymes's *In Vain I Tried to Tell You: Essays in Native American Ethnopoetics* (Philadelphia: University of Pennsylvania Press, 1981).
3. Tim Tingle, *Choctaw Oral Literature*, Master's thesis, University of Oklahoma, 2003.
4. Marcia Haag and Henry Willis, *Choctaw Language and Culture: Chahta Anumpa*, 2 vols. (Norman: University of Oklahoma Press, 2001, 2007).

Boarding School Runaways

Paula Carney (2008)
Recorded by Eveline Steele. Transcribed and translated by Dorothy Van Horn. Edited by Marcia Haag.

When I was a child, at first I went to school at home, here at Coalgate. But I didn't go there very long: I was sent to Wheelock Academy. So I stayed and finished there. Then I also went to Chilocco Indian School in Newkirk, Oklahoma, and finished there too.

When I was a young girl at Chilocco Indian School, and I had been there about three years, I had a friend named was Mary Ludlow, and we were both going to run. Before it got almost dark, it re-e-eally did snow. So, even though we don't know why we did it, we finished packing things we were going to take. Even though it was just a few things, it was ours, things we thought were the most important. We finished packing and tying, and put the stuff under our coats.

We stayed at Home Number 5, and we were going to run. So I told her just about what time to meet. I said for her to be at the back.

I am the one who thought of this! [laughter].

What we agreed to take was under the coat. We finished dressing and it was so cold so we covered our heads. We finished doing all this and were going outside. And it turned out that she was ri-i-ght on time! So we left.

As we walked, we didn't say any . . . thing. We didn't tell anyone that we were going to run away [laughter]. And so we started out, but the room was so big we had slip off elsewhere in the hallway. Then when we got outside, we wa-a-lked, but wa-a-y off in the distance stood two big things where anyone could put things in to throw away, and they were large. And as we were walking, we did not see the guard standing there [laughter].

We thought, "What are we going to do?" So I told Mary that I would do the talking and that I would think of something. So we were a-almo-ost there and I told the man, "We came to throw some things away. That's why we came!" Because I said that we had to throw a-a-ll our belongings away! [laughter]. We both finished throwing our things away and then we went back.

So they caught us, but they didn't catch us. So they didn't do anything to us.

This is all [laughter].

How I Almost Killed a Hog by Scaring It

Abe Frazier (2008)

Recorded by Eveline Steele. Transcribed and translated by Dorothy Van Horn. Edited by Marcia Haag.

Okay, I'm going to tell something. I'm going to tell about a time I almost killed a hog by scaring it. This is what I'll tell.

I was young—at that time my age was around twenty, I believe, or twenty-five, somewhere around there. It was summer and I used to go to the creek. It looked like it might rain, so I headed toward home. I was by myself, so I kept going, but it started to rain before I got home.

There was a shed, not very big—it was made of flat metal. Since it was raining I ran to it and went inside. It was raining hard by then, and so I just stood in there. Then I heard a hog saying, "thonk, thonk," from a distance, and he kept coming. So I stepped out the door, and indeed saw him coming.

I stood there thinking, "He's going to come in here!" So I started looking for something to hit him with, but there was nothing, and the floor was a dirt floor. But there was a rusted stovepipe lying there. I stood looking at it, then picked it up and raised it above my head. This is how I stoo-oo-ood there holding it. I was thinking, "I'm going to scare him when he comes in."

I heard him still coming with his "thonk." Just as he was coming in, I hit him ve-e-rry hard in his front side with the stovepipe and yelled real loud. He didn't look like a big hog then: he jumped real high, came down with a thud, and keeled over. When he fell down, he screamed loud like an old woman. He lay there; his feet were trembling—he thought he was running! He was also noisy, which scared me.

I stood there thinking, "If he doesn't hurry and get up, and he has a bad heart, he could die!" I stood there scared, saying, "Get up! Get up!" and finally he stood up. When he saw me he ran out the door saying "thonk, thonk" and ran into the thicket.

I felt better after a while, being scared as I was, and after I dried my tears, I had a good laugh at him.

That's all I'm telling.

Aiisht Ahollo (The Miracle)

Bill Nowlin (2006)
Recorded by Tim Tingle

During World War II, my mother's brother, Hank Brown, was serving on a battleship in the U.S. Navy. In the heat of battle, his left hand was crushed when the breach block of one of the ship's big guns was slammed on it by another sailor. He was shipped back to the veterans' hospital closest to his home, which was in Houston, Texas. His hand was so badly mangled that the doctors decided to cut it off.

When the navy notified his mother of the decision, she took her mother, Ma Willard, to see him. Her hope was to cheer him up, but Ma Willard had a different plan. She was half Choctaw Indian and she had been raised in a time and place where the only medicine was homemade. Uncle Hank was under guard, so Ma Willard got him dressed and the two women ushered him out of the hospital and took him to her house. She left her daughter to sit with Hank and she had her son-in-law drive her into the piney woods of east Texas to gather medicinal plants. She returned home and made a series of poultices that she kept applied to Hank's hand day and night for days.

When the navy doctors found Hank gone, they sent the Shore Patrol to arrest him for desertion. Ma Willard met them at the door and calmly informed them that no grandson of hers ever deserted from any "job-of-work" and that he would be useless to fight the Nazis with one hand.

She said, "When I get him healed up, I'll send'm back to ya. He'll be fit to fight, and he will still have both hands when this fuss is over."

They decided not to challenge her. Some time later, he recovered the use of his hand—with no signs of infection—and the doctors pronounced him fit to return to service. He stayed in the navy for the duration and was given a Purple Heart and an honorable discharge. Another strong-willed woman prevailed.

Neva the Hunter

Lois McAlvain Pugh (2004)
Recorded and transcribed by Marcia Haag

Neva would go deer hunting with her boys. They wouldn't get a deer, but she would. She was a good marksman—I have to tell you about her killing squirrels.

When she was a community health worker, she always carried her .22 rifle in the car with her. She'd take the magazine out and put it down there on the floor. And so once she had to get this little boy, twelve years old, down by Red Oak and take him to Talihina, to have a cast checked on his arm; he had fallen and broken an arm. And so she saw this squirrel running across the road, and so she stops the car, and she says, "Sonny, reach down there very carefully now—don't move fast—and get the magazine for my gun." And he handed it to her, and she slipped it into the gun, rolled the window glass down, and pointed that gun, and shot that squirrel right out of that tree.

And the boy said, "Just wait till I tell my dad. An old woman like you just dead-eyed that squirrel!"

And she took the squirrel over to Talihina—there was a doctor over there at the hospital who wanted every one she could get: he cooked them; he liked them. And so, she went out to where the dump was, and skinned that squirrel, and went to the kitchen and got a pan, put it in there, washed it, took it and said, "This goes to Doctor So-and-So."

MUSKOGEE (CREEK)

Muskogee (Creek) Literature

Jack B. Martin

The southern United States has been home to native peoples for thousands of years. Speakers of Muskogee and other Muskogean languages are generally thought to descend from the Mississippian mound-building societies prospering from about 800 CE to 1500 CE. When Spaniards arrived in the sixteenth century, the Muskogee-speaking peoples lived in small settlements along rivers in what are now Alabama and Georgia. They grew corn, beans, squash, and tobacco, hunted deer and other game, celebrated the arrival of Green Corn each summer, and played stickball. They had a rich oral literature of their own but also traded stories with Europeans and Africans. By the late seventeenth century they had begun to form a confederacy of some forty different groups, including speakers of Koasati, Hitchiti, and Yuchi.[1]

In 1836 the United States forced most of these groups to relocate to Indian Territory, where they established the Muscogee (Creek) Nation. To fend off further encroachment from the United States, many members of the tribe embraced a constitutional form of government, Christian missionaries, schools, and a written form of the language. For forty years, much of the business of the tribe was conducted in Muskogee, leading to a rich literature of laws, newspaper articles, and letters. It is for this reason that the Muscogee (Creek) Nation came to be known as one of the Five Civilized Tribes.

The first efforts to document Muskogee oral literature were made by W. O. Tuggle between 1879 and 1882.[2] John R. Swanton collected stories in Muskogee and in English for his 1929 volume on southeastern myths and tales.[3] Because many Muskogee speakers were literate in Muskogee, he asked Earnest Gouge in 1915 to write out stories in longhand.[4] From 1936 to 1940, Mary R. Haas conducted fieldwork in Eufaula, Oklahoma. At her urging, James Hill wrote out a large number of stories in Muskogee. She retranscribed these phonetically and supplemented them with stories collected by dictation.[5]

The stories in this chapter were chosen to reflect different story types and different periods. What they all have in common is that they are translated from specific manuscripts in Muskogee and thus grounded in specific performances.

THE STORIES

Creation stories are not common in Muskogee, though there are specific stories about the origin of corn and tobacco. "The Story of Corn" presented here was told by Taylor Postoak and collected and translated by Ann Eliza Worcester Robertson in 1882.[6] Postoak was second chief of the Muscogee (Creek) Nation. Robertson, the daughter of Samuel Worcester, was an influential missionary and schoolteacher who supervised much of the translation of the New Testament into Muskogee. The corn origin myth, sometimes referred to as Corn Mother or Corn Lady, is also told by the Cherokees and Florida Seminoles.[7] This version incorporates the Blood Clot Boy theme, in which a boy is born from a clot of blood, and the theme Swanton referred to as the Orphan, in which an old woman educates a boy in hunting and "promulgates a rule constraining some aspect of the hero's behavior that, upon violation, marks an end to his stay with her."[8]

"The Boy Who Turned into a Snake" is a well-known tale with many variants. Swanton includes five English versions, and Gouge (2004) included one Muskogee version. The story is also found among the Florida Seminoles (Jumper 1994). In each version a boy finds a food source in an unusual location (such as eggs in a tree or fish in a stump) and, going against the advice of elders, proceeds to eat it. During the night he turns into a large water snake and then meets one last time with his sad parents. The version presented here was dictated to Mary R. Haas by I. Field in 1937.[9]

"Rabbit Steals Fire" represents a rich vein of Muskogee trickster tales involving Rabbit. In this hero tale recorded by Earnest Gouge in 1915, rabbit travels overseas to bring back fire.[10] He offers to lead a dance by the fire, and while making exaggerated dance movements, scoops up some coals, places them on some tar on his head, and swims back across the water. Two versions of this story are recorded by Swanton (1929) as "The Theft of Fire." Those versions differ in that the fire is stolen from the square ground rather than from overseas.

"Girl Abducted by Lion" was also written by Earnest Gouge in 1915.[11] In this story a girl (or sometimes a boy) is lured into a boat by a lion. The girl eventually escapes but is chased by a chunkey stone (a stone disk) that the lion sends after her. As she flees, she sings a song that her brothers hear. The brothers defeat both the stone and the lion and ascend to become the Seven Little Sisters. A version of this story was collected by Tuggle and reprinted by Swanton. I have heard the same story told by Muskogee-speaking Florida Seminoles. In Muskogee, the word for lion is *este-papv* (literally, "person-eater"). It is possible that this story originally referred to a cannibal rather than a lion, but the term *este-papv* has had the specific meaning of "lion" for Muskogee speakers since the 1870s.[12]

James Hill's autobiography, written for Mary R. Haas in 1939, is included here to represent the very different and powerful genre of life stories.[13] In this moving account Hill describes the utter poverty of his childhood during and after the Civil War in Indian Territory and, two years after Oklahoma statehood, his radical shift from a Muscogee traditionalist to a preacher and politician.

Finally, "Estvmvn Estomen Follatskis" is a beautiful traditional hymn translated here by Gloria M. McCarty. Muskogee hymns are sung as a group and led by a leader. The whole group sings the chorus. Then the leader jumps in early to sing the first line of each verse (not in any particular order). Then the group sings the chorus again, and then another verse. The expression "Momis komakēs" in this song is difficult to translate into English. It can be translated to emphasize effort ("Let us endure," "Let us bear it," "Let us persevere") or to emphasize traditional humility ("Let us be patient").

The Muskogee stories in this collection were all told or written by Muskogee speakers. They were originally translated by a bilingual speaker of Muskogee and English. In some cases a collector transcribed the speech and a free or word-for-word translation. In preparing the materials for this volume, I have made a few changes that could be called "editing" so that the texts would have a broader audience. First, I changed the layout to emphasize the line structure of the original: in most cases a line simply consists of a complete sentence. I have added blank lines to group lines that are closely related. I also made a few changes in punctuation and word choice.

STYLISTIC DEVICES

Muskogee has several stylistic devices that are difficult to translate and that add special meaning to the Muskogee originals. A major difference between Muskogee and English is that where English has just one past tense, Creek has five different past tenses based on distance from the present. Taylor Postoak's "The Story of Corn" begins this way:

Hoktēt	likvtēs,	momet	enhvmkusēt	omvtēs.
woman	lived (Past 5)	and	alone	was (Past 5)

There was a woman, and she was alone.

The suffix *-vtēs* appearing at the end of the second and fifth words is the Past 5 or remote past ending. It is an ending associated with very remote times and is commonly employed in legends. The grammar of English does not normally express these distinctions. To take another example, the first line of "Rabbit Steals Fire" uses two different past tenses:

Cufet	totkv	heckuecet	omvtēs,	mahokvnts.
rabbit	fire	acquired	did (Past 5)	it was said (Past 4)

It's said that Rabbit acquired fire.

Here Past 5 (the remote past) is used for the main events in the story, while Past 4 (distant past) indicates how long it has been since the narrator heard the story. In this case the narrator heard the story long ago, but the events of the story took place long, long ago.

James Hill makes interesting use of tense in his autobiography. Writing at the age of seventy-eight, he uses Past 5 to describe the events of his childhood. Then, when he begins to describe the events of Isparhecher's rebellion, he slips into Past 4 and Past 3 before settling back and resuming the use of Past 5. These are intricacies of Muskogee that simply do not translate well.

A second device that is hard to translate is the very different ways Muskogee and English go about connecting sentences to each other. One pattern used in Muskogee is to start a sentence by repeating the last action of the previous sentence:

Mohmet	hofonofvn	enramet	hēcvtēs.
then	after a long time	uncovered it	looked at it (Past 5)

Then after a long time, she uncovered it and looked at it.

Hēcatet,	catē	rakkēpet	ocen	hēcvtēs.
looking at it	blood	gotten bigger	had	saw (Past 5)

Looking at it, she saw that the blood had gotten bigger.

Here *hēcatet* (looking at it) in the second sentence repeats the action of the first sentence. It thus serves to resume the story once a full stop has been made.

A much more common device, however, is to use the word *momet* (or *mont* or *momen*) to resume the flow.

Momet,	"Naket o haks?"	komet,	catēn	hēcvtēs.
and	what is it?	thinking	blood	looked (Past 5)

"What is it?" she thought, looking at the blood.

Momet	catēn	nekēyicet,	hēcvtēs,
and	blood	moving	looked (Past 5)

And she moved the blood and looked at it.

In the second sentence we have translated *momet* as "and." *Momet* seems to serve in this context as a shorter way to resume the preceding action: "Doing that, she moved the blood and looked at it."

FURTHER READING

A good source on Muscogee (Creek) history and culture is volume 14 of the *Handbook of North American Indians*, containing Willard B. Walker's "Creek Confederacy Before Removal," Pamela Innes's "Creek in the West," and "Mythology and Folklore" by Greg Urban and Jason Baird Jackson.[14] James Howard's *Oklahoma Seminoles: Medicines, Magic, and Religion* provides background information on some of the supernatural characters appearing in stories.[15]

John Swanton's 1929 *Myths and Tales of the Southeastern Indians* is still one of the most important collections of Muscogee and southeastern tales. Bill Grantham (2002) includes stories from many of the same tribes while offering analysis and cultural explanations. Earnest Gouge (2004) provides a collection of twenty-nine stories in Muscogee and facing English. Martin (2011) is a reference grammar. Mary R. Haas and James H. Hill (2015) is the most complete collection of texts.[16]

NOTES

1. Willard B. Walker, "Creek Confederacy before Removal," in *Handbook of North American Indians*, vol. 14: *Southeast* (Washington DC: Smithsonian Institution, 2004).
2. W.O. Tuggle, *Shem, Ham & Japheth: The Papers of W. O. Tuggle . . . 1879–1882*, ed. Eugene Current-Garcia and Dorothy B. Hatfield (Athens: University of Georgia Press, 1973).
3. John R. Swanton, *Myths and Tales of the Southeastern Indians,* Bureau of American Ethnology Bulletin 88 (Washington DC: Smithsonian Institution, U.S. Government Printing Office, 1929).
4. Earnest Gouge, *Totkv Mocvse/New Fire: Creek Folktales*, ed. and trans. Jack B. Martin, Margaret McKane Mauldin, and Juanita McGirt (Norman: University of Oklahoma Press, 2004).
5. Mary R. Haas and James H. Hill, *Creek (Muskogee) Texts*, ed. Jack B. Martin, Margaret McKane Mauldin, and Juanita McGirt (Berkeley: University of California Press, 2015).

6. The citation for the original Robertson manuscript is Ann Eliza Worcestor Robertson, Manuscript 571, National Anthropological Archives, Smithsonian Institution, Washington DC. Robertson reports that she transcribed the story at the request of Pleasant Porter, who was familiar with W. O. Tuggle's work.
7. James Mooney, *Myths of the Cherokee*, Nineteenth Annual Report, Bureau of American Ethnology 1897–98, pt. I (Washington DC: U.S. Government Printing Office, 1900); Betty M. Jumper, *Legends of the Seminoles*, 2nd ed. (Sarasota FL: Pineapple Press, 1994).
8. Greg Urban and Jason Baird Jackson, "Mythology and Folklore," in *Handbook of North American Indians*, vol. 14: *Southeast* (Washington DC: Smithsonian Institution, 2004), 711.
9. Haas and Hill, *Creek (Muskogee) Texts.*
10. The original Muskogee manuscript is Manuscript 4930, National Anthropological Archives, Smithsonian Institution, Washington DC. A translated and edited version appears in Gouge's *Totkv Mocvse/New Fire.*
11. Manuscript 4930, as edited in Gouge, *Totkv Mocvse/New Fire.*
12. In Robertson and Winslett's *Creek Second Reader*, for example, *este-papv* is described as *ponvttv em mekko* (king of the animals) and as living near the Jordan River in the land of the Jews; W. S. Robertson and David Winslett, *Mvskoke Nakcokv Eskerretv Esvhokkolat: Creek Second Reader* (New York: American Tract Society, 1871). The reprinted Tuggle version is in Swanton, *Myths and Tales,* 20–21.
13. Hill's original manuscript is in the Mary R. Haas Papers, American Philosophical Society. Haas's transcription of the text appears in her Creek Notebook XVII: 1–79.
14. Willard B. Walker, "Creek Confederacy Before Removal"; Pamela Innes, "Creek in the West"; and Greg Urban and Jason Baird Jackson, "Mythology and Foklore," all in *Handbook of North American Indians,* vol. 14: *Southeast* (Washington DC: Smithsonian Institution, 2004).
15. James Howard, *Oklahoma Seminoles: Medicines, Magic, and Religion,* Civilization of the American Indian Series 166 (Norman: University of Oklahoma Press, 1984).
16. Bill Grantham, *Creation Myths and Legends of the Creek Indians* (Gainesville: University Press of Florida, 2002); Gouge, *Totkv Mocvse/New Fire*; Haas and Hill, *Creek (Muskogee) Texts*; Jack B. Martin, *A Grammar of Creek (Muskogee)* (Lincoln: University of Nebraska Press, 2011).

Traditional Tales

The Story of Corn (*Vce Nak-onvkuce*)

Taylor Postoak, narrator (1882)
A. E. W. Robertson, collector and
translator. Jack B. Martin, editor.

I am going to tell one of the old people's stories.

There was a woman, and she was alone.
No house was near.
And a mountain stood off in the distance.
And the woman crossed over the mountain.
And returning from that place, she came back to her home.

And she crossed over a tree lying across the road, and saw blood
near her feet.
"What is it?" she thought, looking at the blood.
And she moved the blood and looked at it.
And unable to get rid of it, she took it.

And she arrived back at her home with it.
And she put it in a clay pot and covered it.
Then after a long time, she uncovered it and looked at it.
Looking at it, she saw that the blood had gotten bigger.
And putting it back in, she covered it again.

And again, after a longer time, she uncovered it.
Having uncovered it, she looked at it, and saw that a babe had
been created, that its entire body had been created.
And she put it back in the same thing, into the pot.

And when she looked again, it moved, and had become older, and she took it out.
And it was a little boy.
And she cared for him and he grew to manhood.
And she made a bow for him.
And she said to him, “Kill birds and kill squirrels: they are food,” and he killed them.

And again she said to him, “Kill deer,” and he killed them.
And when he came back from hunting, he found the old woman had a great deal of food that she had made.
When she made that food, there had been nothing, yet now there was a great deal of food.

The young man was very curious to know what she had done.
And the old woman spoke to the young man:
“Do not climb that mountain and look around,” she warned him.
“Why does she warn me?” he wondered.
Then he thought, “When she does not see me, I will climb the mountain and look.”

And he left.
And having climbed the mountain, he looked around on the other side.
And he came back again.

When he looked around on the other side of the mountain, he saw that there was a town and a great many people.
And when he came back, he drew a blanket over his head, and being lonesome, he lay down.

And the old woman knew.
The old woman said, “I think you have come back from what I forbade you to do, from having climbed the mountain, and having looked around.

And so, even though I have cared for you, you may go," she said to him.
And she said, "There is no one in that town who will feed you as I have."

And the old woman spoke:
"I am corn," she said, "I am corn: it is I who have been feeding you.
And in the fall, when it grows cold, you must return.
When you return, you will see that the corn is ripe.
And when you make a container for the corn, you must do it with
 stone," she told him.

"Now where you are going, you will cross water lying just by a town.
And on the other side of that, you must go to a house," she said.
"Now as you are going there, I will give you a plume," she said.
"And I will give you a fife as well," she said.
And she gave him a plume, and she gave him a fife.

And she said to him, "When you go, when you get to the house, you
 will see three women there.
When you get there one woman will say to you, 'Have a seat,' and
 the one that says that to you will be your wife," she said.
"And when she becomes your wife, you must kill fish for her," she said.
"The people in the town you are going to do not know how to kill fish.
You must be helpful to them," she said.

"And when you come back, you and your wife must come together.
And you must both gather the corn.
You must build a stone corn-crib and put it in that.
That is my flesh. I am corn," she said.

And she said, "You must make it the same way that I fed you, and
 eat it. Now go," she said to him.
And sounding the fife, he left.
And she had given him a living plume.
That plume was a jay.

And he left and reached the place where the three women were.
Then, upon reaching it, he saw the three women.
And although the three women saw him, they sat there and did not speak to him right away.

And one said to him, "Have a seat," and after he sat down, the woman sought food for him.
That one at once became his wife.

And the people in that town sought fish, but could not kill them.
And the young man who had come there said to them, "I can kill them for you."
"Search for medicine," he said, "for devil's shoestring."
And he made that into medicine for them and killed fish with it.
And the man was held in great respect.

And when it grew cold, the two went to see the corn, to where the old woman had lived.
And when they got there, they saw the corn was ripe.

Immediately he gathered stones.
And he made a container for the corn there.
And gathering the corn, he put it in.
And he filled the corn container: and taking from it, he would eat it.

And when the corn was gone, they came again to the stone corn-crib.
And when they reached it, birds of various kinds had assembled at the stone corn-crib.
All different kinds of birds had assembled.

And one bird said, "Whoever of you can tear it down, tear it down."
And Owl said, "I will do it," and clawed at the stone corn-crib, but could not tear it down.
And another bird said, "I will do it," but he could not tear it down.

And Eagle also clawed at the stones, but could not break it down.
And Falcon said, "I will do it."
When he clawed at the stones, all the stones fell apart.
When it had fallen apart, all the different kinds of birds devoured the corn.

Then Crow took one ear of corn, flew off with it, and dropped it.
The man saw him with it, chased him, and took the corn from him.
And he came back to his home with only one ear of corn.
And planting that, he produced a great deal.

And all the town's inhabitants became corn planters, and corn became plentiful.
That is why Crow still wants corn, they say.

The Boy Who Turned into a Snake

I. Field (V: 97–111), narrator (1937)
Mary R. Haas, transcriber. Margaret McKane Mauldin and Juanita McGirt, translators. Jack B. Martin, editor.

Hunters once went out. Three people went and made camp. Then they went out hunting. And one of these was a boy who had a father and mother.

Now while they were out hunting, this boy found three eggs. He picked them up and brought them to his camp. Then he ate them.

He had eaten them and was sitting down. Then the other two came back. "I found something like that and ate it," he told them. "You shouldn't have done that," they told him. "It might be something dangerous," they were telling him, and they sat, and it became evening and got dark. "Something might happen," the old people thought, so they watched him.

He was restless that night, and after dark, when it was about midnight, the boy was restless and lay there moving. The two men lay there on the other side watching him as he lay there.

By daylight they saw he was turning into a great snake and was lying there, and they told him, "They said things like that would happen, and you have proven that on yourself." "I am that way, you're right," he told them, and they talked a little while and asked, "What shall we tell your parents?" "I'm going down into that little pond there, so they will see me. But they must call me by my former name," he answered. "When I'm down in that little pond, you two go back, and you must tell my parents," he said.

They went back to their home and told his parents. "Something strange has happened. Your son said, 'If they want to see me, if they call me by name, we will see each other,' and he went down into the water and we came here," they said.

When they told his parents, they said, "You will have to tell us where it was," and they both went, and the parents followed them back.

Then it wasn't the little pond he had gone down into anymore, the water was really hazardous when they reached it. "This is where it was," they told them. Then they called him by name. When they called him a second time, he came up in the middle of the water, it was clear he had become a fine snake, and he came up. They kept calling him till he came, and his parents sat on the edge of the water. Then they kept calling and he came up very close by. "This happened to me and I strayed away and must remain that way, I think, and called you," he told them. His parents thought it was very mysterious, and went back to their home.

They got back, and so it was. They were very old, so they went about crying and crying.

Rabbit Steals Fire

Earnest Gouge (1915)
Margaret McKane Mauldin and Juanita McGirt, translators. Jack B. Martin, editor.

It is said that Rabbit acquired fire. This island had no fire, so there was a meeting to discuss who would be able to get fire. Rabbit said, "I can get it." But they didn't believe in him: "Someone more able should be the one," they said, yet each one said, "I am not able." "I will do it," Rabbit kept saying. So finally they said, "Maybe he can do it."

During this time, fire was overseas. And since fire was badly needed here, Rabbit was put in charge.

Because he meant what he had said, he started off. He ran and ran across the ocean until he had crossed it. Then he came to a house. "Someone we do not know has arrived," they said. "Have a seat," they said, and as he sat, they asked him where he was from. "I come from afar where there is no happiness. I thought there may be some place where people have a little happiness. I enjoy traveling and meeting people in different places, and I thought there may be happiness here somewhere, so that's why I'm here," he said. "You don't say. Well, we're going to a dance, so we'll all go when we get ready," they told him.

Then they asked him, "Might you be a dance leader?" "Oh, that's my specialty," he said. "That's the kind of person we love," they said. "Well, we're ready, so let's go," they said, and he went with them.

They arrived, and as the dance was in full swing, he sat nearby. And the people who had brought him along said: "We have a stranger here who says, 'I'm a leader.' Maybe he would lead," they said. Then he was invited, and he got down and started singing loudly. "This is what you want of me," he said, singing, really exaggerating as he danced. "Let's all help him, as he leads," they said, encouraging him. Almost all the tribal towns helped him as he led, and he thought, "This is what I wanted," and was greatly honored. Even though he was dancing, his mission was to get the fire, but they didn't know this. He made motions, pretending to pick up the fire.

Time passed, and as he said he would, he smeared tar on his hands, picked up the fire, and having more tar smeared on the middle of his head, put a live coal on his head, and started running. They chased him, saying, "He's running away with our fire," but they didn't catch him, and he crossed back over.

Thus he obtained fire, it was said.

Girl Abducted by Lion

Earnest Gouge (1915)
Margaret McKane Mauldin and Juanita McGirt, translators. Jack B. Martin, editor.

There once lived a group of young men. And there was only one girl. And she was the sister of the young men.

Now the river from which they drew water flowed past, and one day the young girl was getting water there. During this time a lion had made puppies out of his testicles, and he went to the place where the girl drew water—it was a river—and put the puppies he had made in a little boat and came down the river to the place where water was drawn.

And the girl saw him. And she took a liking to them. Then the girl said, "May I see your little puppies?" "All right, but you have to climb in the boat and look at them close up, as they usually do," he said.

Then because the girl liked the puppies, she climbed into the boat. And again he said, "They usually get right up to them and look closely," so as she was looking at them, right up close sitting in the boat, she didn't notice that the boat had been given a shove and had gone quite a distance when she looked up.

Then she said, "Dock it for me![1]

I'm getting out and going back." And he said, "I'll dock it for you in the next river bend!" and they continued down the center of the river. And she kept saying, "Dock it for me!"

But he said, "I'll dock it for you! I'll dock it for you over there!" and continued on.

He continued on, and the lion had a den where he lived, so the lion docked the boat below his den. That's how he brought the young girl there. And as the lion had gotten her to his house, he didn't want her to return home.

Now the old lion sat and said, speaking to the young woman he had taken there,

"Make something to eat. Over there in that house is meat. Go cut some of it off and cook it," he said. When he told her this, the young girl went. She got a knife and went. And she went into the house he had meant. And as she entered, she saw a really old lady. Then she spoke to the old lady. And the young girl said, "That old lion said, 'There's meat in that house. Go look for it there and cook it!' he said, and that's why I came in here," she said. Then the old lady said, "He means me! He eats me, so he means me!" she said. As the girl looked, she could see that the old lady had slices cut off of her and looked ragged, so she stood a while and then came out. Then she returned and told the old lion. She told him, "There's nothing out there." As soon as she told him, he said, "There is, too!" and scraping his knives together, he went to where she had seen the little old lady, and as she had said, he trimmed off pieces of meat and came out. Then she cooked it for him. Then they ate.

The lion was going to go out and said, "You stay and fix the acorns!" and left.

And as he left, the young woman went to fix the acorns. And the old lady spoke to her.

She spoke to the young girl, saying, "You must go. You will be tormented. Now when he's through eating me, he plans to eat you, so when you've prepared all the acorns that you're fixing, look for a little green frog and put it in with them, and then go over to the house and leave," the old lady said.

And as she had been told, she went over to the house and left. She was gone when the old lion returned. But he didn't know that the young girl was gone. Because he had left after he had told her to fix the acorns, he thought she was still fixing the acorns.

"Are the acorns ready?" he asked.

"Not-ready-yet!" the frog said, and the lion believed the answer and just lay there.

Then, "Are the acorns ready?" he asked.

"Not-ready-yet!" it said, and kept lying there.

Now again, "Are they ready?" he asked.

"Not-ready-yet!" it said.

"Why is it not ready?" he asked, and the lion, now angry, went down and found it had been a little green frog sitting there talking. When the lion went down, he heard a *Cheek!* and saw it had been the frog sitting down there, and it jumped into the water.

Then the lion was going about really furious, so he got in the water and looked where the frog had jumped in, and found the frog.

Then he took the frog out of the water and mashed it, and he knew that he had lost the young girl, and though he asked, he didn't find out what happened. "I'm sure she is out there somewhere," he said, and having a stone disk, he took it and when he stood it up on a little trail, it just made a rattling sound and fell. He tried all the trails. Then he brought it back to the front of the house and made it go over the house, and then it finally took off.

So as it went, the old lion followed right behind singing, "Stone disk catch up! Stone disk catch up!" and flopped along behind it. Now that stone disk was about to catch up with the girl who had gone away. The girl tried to keep going, but she knew that it was overtaking her and she began to sing.

She sang,

"I won't reach the four ravines where my brothers live below,
For I die,
For I die."

Though her oldest brothers did not hear, there was a younger brother. Now he was outside playing. And he heard her. And he told his brothers, "Our long lost sister is singing." And they said, "Don't say that.

Whatever happened to her is forever," they told him, and he came back out.

And he continued to play outside, and again he heard her singing for sure.

"I said I heard her, and you didn't think it was her, and now she's singing again. So listen!" he said, bothering the brothers several times.

"What is he talking about?" they wondered, and they listened and heard what he had heard, they listened carefully and heard her sing as she used to sing:

"I won't reach the four valleys where my brothers live below, where my brothers live,

For I die,

For I die."

Then they said, "Something's really gone wrong for her."

Now when they could hear her singing close by, they ran and gathered all kinds of clubs and axes, and each had something to hit it with.

Then the little boy ran around asking, "What am I going to use?" but couldn't find anything and went in the kitchen where he found a wooden paddle with a part missing that was wedged into something up high, and he jumped to reach it.

As they had already gone, he ran after them, and finally caught up with the others as they were meeting it.

Then as the stone disk that had chased after her was getting there, they hit it and did everything they knew to do, and yet couldn't stop it. Then as the little boy came up running, a small speckled woodpecker flew by: "Toktus heel, heel! Toktus heel, heel!" it said as it went past, and the boy said, "He says if you hit him in the heel, he'll die!"[2] and he took the broken paddle he had grabbed and hit the thing on the heel and they found that it had been like a mirror. As he hit its heel with the paddle, the thing shattered in a heap.

After this they climbed up in a tree and were sitting there, and the old lion came to where they sat in the tree they had climbed. And coming below them, he said, "I want to climb up there with you." "We climbed up on that grapevine," they said, and as he climbed up, they cut the vine and made him fall, and immediately they went high up.

And they became the Seven Little Sisters, it was said.
So they were people, it was said.

NOTES

1. The Muskogee here is literally, "Lean it for me!"
2. In the Muskogee, this bird cry refers to the ankle rather than the heel.

Stories of Real People

Autobiography of James Hill

James Hill (1939)
Mary R. Haas, collector. Margaret McKane Mauldin and Juanita McGirt, translators. Jack B. Martin, editor.

Where people lived by Greenleaf tribal town there was a store. Before the [Civil] War, a man named Sikomaha operated a store. I was born near that store. And a black lady named me. "Jimmy," she said, and my father's name was Hilly. My father was Sikomaha's sister's son.

I was born in July in the year 1861. At that time the United States, North and South, were engaged in war, and when the war was coming into Indian Territory, the Indians divided. Some men became soldiers for the North, some became soldiers for the South, and the old men, women, elderly women, and small children, some went to the North, and some went to the South, leaving many things in their homes, leaving their livestock, too, they ran.

My mother's eldest brother became a soldier for the South. So they took me toward the South, leaving some of their belongings behind. Many people traveled together, and many people stopped and camped, and my late grandmother, taking one of her sons with her, returned and got the cattle. It was just a few cattle.

It was during the frightful time of war, so thinking there might be Northern soldiers in the area, my father and two other men were appointed to scout around. And leaving the main camp they went far off. Then only two men came back, saying, "When we were in rugged country, Hilly's nose started bleeding, we stopped and stayed there, and he died, and we buried him there," they said. I don't know the land where my father died. But it might be Choctaw country. So my father died before I knew him.

It happened during war time, and I began to understand things that were said, and as time went on, they said, "We live near the Red River": I found that out. It was near Denison, Texas.

We lived in houses close together—Paskofa, Mikkimathla, Talwayahola, Tiwawayhki, Konoyahola—these men lived with their families and we lived there, too. Not too far away there were many houses. We used to live in houses made of logs, ugly little houses. At that time we went suffering. Now rabbit skins were being bought, and young men and even older men hunted rabbits, and killing them, they took the skins and threw away the meat.

At that time, Indians were not to eat rabbit meat, they said, so it was not eaten. For a little over four years, there was no food, there were no clothes, and boys about the age of seventeen and under, we went around naked.

And after the war became peace, we returned to our lands and lived along the edge of the Canadian [River], but still without food, without clothes, for about three years. Pounding ripe corn, making bread, making sofkee [corn soup], too, and going about eating that, they thought, "We have come through starvation." Without even any fat, grease, and such. Only when a cow was butchered did we have meat and beef fat. For a short time meat was available for eating, deer, turkey, and such in abundance, but because there were no bullets, gunpowder, caps, and such, it was a time when we could not kill and eat wild game.

Now they planted cotton on a small piece of land, raised it, gathered it, and removed the seeds by hand, and having obtained a card, spinning wheel, and loom, my late grandmother would draw out the cotton and spin it into rolls when she had a large amount of thread. The loom was located in the house of a man named Taffothlakko, so it was probably a public loom. My late mother would weave with the thread she had made, and when she made a thick material, *tarkv*, they called it, a long shirt was made for me and I wore it.

And we lived about three years next to the Canadian River. They talked of good land for livestock, so we moved. There was a small creek called Shell Creek and we lived in an ugly house they built near that. Also near the old place by Shell Creek is a house I have, and I live there. At the new place where we were living there were no fields, so corn was planted and raised along the Canadian River, too. An old man named Simmatmayi had hogs and my late grandmother traded corn with him for hogs. Those hogs multiplied, and they were butchered when grown, so we began to get pork grease. As the steers grew, we made them into oxen and hitched them, and if corn was being bought somewhere, they'd go sell it and began to buy white flour, coffee, and salt.

And as they sold corn, they began to buy clothing, but even when they bought the thick material, I continued to wear the long shirt. My age was about fourteen years, and about that time, I had learned to read books written in the Muskogee language. No one taught me: I learned by listening while others were being taught. The nearest school was five miles away. And there was no one to encourage me to go to school. My father was gone, and my grandmother didn't want me to go to school, because I had no clothes.

The spring just before I was seventeen, I made a field for myself on two acres of land, planted cotton, and when it was ripe, I picked it and sold it and only then did I begin to wear clothes as others did.

Then within about three years a man named Isparhecher opposed the Muscogee constitution, gathered many of his people, made war against the supporters of the constitution, and divided the Muscogee Nation. All the old full-bloods supported Isparhecher. I was with the supporters of the constitution.

One time many people were in Okmulgee and when a few men were sent out as scouts, Isparhecher's people also had a few scouts about, and they came upon each other and began shooting at each other; those in favor of the constitution ran, the others killed seven men and they all ran. And in Eufaula District, Thomas Polk was the prosecuting attorney, and Sam Smith was the judge, and he said, "The elders opposing the law are against peace." When he gave his lighthorsemen [or sheriffs] authority, only five lighthorsemen had the authority to arrest people, so to help them, he said, "Let ten people join," and included me in the search [i.e., the posse]: "Arrest all of the oldest people in Eufaula

District," he said, and gave us names and we went. So we arrested many old people and kept them and watched over them.

The judge called for a jury, and after meeting and trying them, they said, "Let all these old ones be whipped, according to the law." And after being sentenced, the old people said, "Our lawyer should go and ask the chief for a pardon," and the judge and the prosecuting attorney agreed. "I will wait three days from today until exactly two o'clock," the judge said. So the lawyer went, accompanied by two people, and we guarded the old people that were there. And though many were afraid to guard the old people, they could not do anything. Because they had heard stories from long ago about the old ones, they were afraid.

Now those who had gone to ask for clemency had not returned and as the day and hour were drawing near, those who were to be whipped and those who were to do the whipping, all felt panic at that time. "It is time, but I will wait twenty minutes, and then I will say what is to happen," the judge said, and the fear grew even more. "What's going to happen?" the floggers went around asking one another. And right at the time the judge had set, those seeking clemency returned, and the old ones came and sat before the judge. When the judge was told that the chief had pardoned the old ones, everyone rejoiced. So when the old ones were freed, the judge told them, "Return to your homes. Never again disturb the peace or conduct meetings opposing the law." Thus the judge warned them, and they dispersed. That was about fifty years ago.

Isparhecher's war lasted two years and when peace was declared, it was the year 1882. At that time my age was twenty-one years. And from that year to the year 1910, I went to crazy dances, fiddle dances, drank whisky, ball-games, women's ball-games, and whatever a tribal town did. In good activities I did not favor one tribal town over another, whenever there was something going on and I heard about it, I always went. Even though I was grown, my mother talked to me and I obeyed, and because I knew I must do as told, I was not involved in anything bad.

In the year 1895, in the month of September, the Muscogee Nation held an election according to the constitution, and I was made a representative to the [House of] Kings for Hilabi Canadian.

As time passed, in the year 1899, in the month of September, another election was held, and I was again elected representative to the House of Kings. As elected tribal leaders, our terms ended on March 4, 1906. We were then under the jurisdiction of the United States.

Then in the year 1908 I quit all dancing, ball-playing, and whisky-drinking, and as time passed my thinking changed. I found the faith to live under God's law instead and wanted to be a member of the group called Christians instead. And as Jesus Christ asked to be baptized I went to a Baptist church, Thlewahle Indian Church, and confessed that I believed in the requirement of baptism; in November of the year 1910 a preacher named Sandy Fife baptized me in the name of the father, the son, and the holy ghost, and I became a member with these Christians.

Many churches were established by an organization named the Muscogee, Seminole, and Wichita Baptist Association. At their meeting in the year 1912, the Managing Board appointed seven people, and I was one of them and served for seven years without disruption. And in the year 1915, the church made me head deacon with full credentials. Then in the year 1917, they appointed me exhorter in the church, similar to the work of a preacher, and the church made me a worker.

Time passed, and in the year 1921 on August 28, I was given full authority to preach. Ministers Marsey Harjo, James McCombs, Joe Colbert: these three laid hands on me and prayed, and afterwards, wherever I went, I could preach when asked to tell the word of God to all people. They believed that this authority gave me the power to go and preach. I have been in that work to this day, August 30, 1939,

Jim (James Hill).

Traditional Song

Estvmvn Estomen Follatskis (Wherever, However You Are)

Traditional hymn

Gloria M. McCarty, translator (*Muskogee and English*)

CHORUS: Estvmvn estomen follatskis,
Vm emēkusapatsken,
Vneu cem emēkusvparēs.

CHORUS: Wherever, however you are,
Pray for me,
I will pray for you, too.

Mēkusvpvlkē toyatskat,
Momis komakēs.

O Christians,
Let us persevere.

Erkenvkvlkē toyatskat,
Momis komakēs.

O Preachers
Let us persevere.

Hopuetakē toyatskat,
Momis komakēs.

O Children
Let us persevere.

Puwvntakē toyatskat,
Momis komakēs.

O Sisters,
Let us persevere.

Vkvsamvlkē toyatskat,
Momis komakēs.

O Believers,
Let us persevere.

Pum vpvltakē toyatskat,
Momis komakēs.

O All Our People,
Let us persevere.

CHICKASAW

Chickasaw Oral Literature

Lokosh (Joshua D. Hinson)

The Chickasaw Nation, a federally recognized tribal nation headquartered in Ada, Oklahoma, is a large tribe with a citizenship of more than 65,000 persons. The Chickasaws have a long history of oral literature including public ceremonial speech, medicinal formulas and ceremonial songs, and traditional storytelling. This chapter examines genres of traditional storytelling including creation/origin stories, *shikonnoꞌpaꞌ* (animal tales), clan stories, and humor stories.

A BRIEF HISTORY OF THE CHICKASAW PEOPLE

The Chickasaw people are a Muskogean-speaking people, descending from long-ago Proto-Muskogean ancestors who lived west of the Mississippi River. Our most ancient understanding of our origins begins with the creation of the world, as told by Juanita Byars and retold in this chapter. Tribal narratives recorded in the eighteenth century and oral histories told into the present day tell of ancient and ongoing connections to our other Muskogean-speaking brothers, the Creeks and Seminoles, the Alabamas, the Koasatis, and the Choctaws.

Our origin as a unique people called *Chikashsha* is recorded in a migration story passed from generation to generation for many hundreds of years. Many variants of our ancient migration story continue to be passed down orally, while older versions were documented in written form. British trader James Adair recorded the migration story in the early eighteenth century, writing that "they, and the Choktah, and also the Chokchooma, who in the process of time were forced by war to settle between the two former nations, came together from the west as one family."[1] Later he states that "the Indians have an old tradition, that when they left their own native land, they brought with them a sanctified rod by order of an oracle, which they fixed every night in the ground; and were to remove from place to place on the continent towards the sun-rising, till it budded in one night's time; that they obeyed the sacred mandate, and the miracle took place after they arrived to this side of the Mississippi, on the present land they possess."[2] The most widely known modern interpretation was dictated to Robert Kingsberry by Reverend Jesse J. Humes in 1964, known as "*Ofi' Tohbi' Ishto' micha Itti' Holitto'pa'* (The Big White Dog and the Sacred Pole)." Humes describes in detail the migration of the ancestors of the Chickasaw and the Choctaw from west of the Mississippi River, the split of the two groups into Chickasaw and Choctaw, and the eventual settlement of the Chickasaw in the Tombigbee River valley of northeastern Mississippi.[3]

The Chickasaw have a long and storied history since separating from the Choctaw circa 1450.[4] Today Chickasaw tribal history is conceptualized in four seasons. Summer, the start of the Chickasaw New Year marked by the Green Corn Ceremony, is understood as encompassing the lives of Chickasaw ancestors pre-contact. In this time our lifeways and language were fully intact and strong. Fall, marked by the closing of the ceremonial grounds and preparation of food for the long winter, is understood as encompassing the challenging years of the eighteenth century, when the Chickasaw were hard pressed on all sides by the French and French-allied Choctaw, losing hundreds of our people to warfare and disease. From the Yamasee War beginning in 1715 through the defensive consolidation at Old Town in present-day Tupelo, Mississippi, to the flight of eighty Chickasaws to the Savannah River near present-day Augusta, Georgia, circa 1720, the Chickasaws declined to a population of as low as 1,600 individuals by 1760.[5] Winter, marked by hunger months of limited food and long nights filled with tribal stories, is today understood to encompass the horrors of Removal to Indian Territory beginning in 1837, the struggles of reestablishing our nation in these new lands, the losses of the Civil War, and the heartbreak of allotment, as our tribal government was for all intents and purposes terminated and our tribal lands broken up into individual allotments. Winter continues into the lean years of the early to mid-twentieth century, as we struggled to survive without a functioning government, limited financial resources, and a population increasingly forced to leave traditional communities in order to find work. Spring, traditionally marked by the return of ball play, dances, and the first growth of wild onions, is today understood to encompass our present Chickasaw cultural and political renaissance since the election of Governor Bill Anoatubby in 1987. With the advent of Indian gaming under the Indian Gaming Regulatory Act (Public Law 100–497-Oct. 17, 1988 100th Congress Sec. 2701) the Chickasaw Nation has flourished. Gaming dollars reinvested into essential services have changed the quality of life for the Chickasaw people for the better, with dramatically expanded programs and services.

The Chickasaw Nation has also undergone a cultural revitalization since the mid-1990s. Ceremonial and social dancing traditions were revitalized at the Kali-homma' stomp grounds located east of Ada, Oklahoma. Simultaneously, community-based plans for a cultural center began, culminating in the opening of the Chickasaw Cultural Center in 2010. The Chickasaw Press was founded in 2016, devoted to publishing books on Chickasaw topics, from language texts to history, cookbooks, and children's literature. Chickasaw citizens are returning to their ancestral roots, taking up bow making and archery, pursuing traditional foodways, and participating in language learning programs; and some living outside our service area are increasingly returning home to live in the Chickasaw Nation. The state of our nation is strong.

BRIEF HISTORY OF THE CHICKASAW LANGUAGE

Chickasaw is a member of the Muskogean language family, a family composed of Chickasaw, Choctaw, Alabama, Koasati, Hitchiti, Mikasuki, Creek, and Seminole. Chickasaw and Choctaw are classified as members of the western branch of the Muskogean language family.[6] This view is the most generally accepted view of the branches of the Muskogean language family, attributed to Munro.[7]

The Chickasaw language was the dominant language of the Chickasaw people prior to and following Removal. Multilingualism was common throughout the Southeast, with some Chickasaws conversational in Chickasaw, Choctaw, related languages like Alabama and Creek, and the Mobilian trade language. A small minority of Chickasaws spoke English in the late eighteenth and early nineteenth centuries, and far fewer were literate. Some limited language attrition began to occur in the nineteenth century, particularly among Chickasaws of mixed ancestry who attended tribal boarding schools. As an influx of non-Indians came to overwhelm the Chickasaw in their own nation, English became increasingly dominant, first as a language of trade and later as a language of daily communication.

A conservative core of Chickasaws, largely living in intact tribal communities in Oklahoma, maintained the language as a medium of daily spoken communication into the twentieth century. A broad range of factors contributed to steeper language attrition at mid-century, including increasing out-marriage to non-Indians, intertribal marriages without a shared language beyond English, service in World War II, the Bureau of Indian Affairs relocation program, and the federal Indian boarding school system. In the early part of the twentieth century there were thousands of speakers of Chickasaw, living for the most part in the Chickasaw Nation. This number would begin to decline as natural transmission in the home ceased in the 1930s and 1940s.

Chickasaw is now spoken as a native language by fewer than fifty persons nationwide. There is one speaker in California and one in Tennessee, with the remainder living in the Chickasaw Nation tribal boundaries. The youngest native speaker was born in 1948, while the oldest speakers were born in the 1920s. There are several hundred passive bilinguals, persons who understand but do not actively speak Chickasaw, living in Oklahoma. A small core of conversational second language learners reside in the Chickasaw Nation at present, numbering no more than eight to ten.

The Chickasaw Nation tribal government, under the leadership of Governor Bill Anoatubby, has taken language loss very seriously. Beginning with the founding of the Chickasaw Language Revitalization Program in 2007, dedicated language revitalization efforts are at the forefront of the Chickasaw Nation's cultural revitalization initiatives. In

2009 a dedicated tribal language program was founded. The program offers a wide array of enrichment and immersion activities, ensuring that Chickasaw people, no matter where they live, have access to their heritage language. At the core of all the work the program does is the Chickasaw Language Committee. Composed of twenty-five native speakers, this advisory committee assists in directing all aspects of program development, among them new word creation, Chickasaw language publications including a Chickasaw prayer book (2012), public signage, and direction on language usage.

CHICKASAW ORAL LITERATURE

The Chickasaws have long traditions of tribal oratory, as do other related Muskogean tribes in the Southeast. One genre of oral literature was the public ceremonial speech. *Minko'* (chiefs) and clan leaders ruled not by force but rather by artfully crafted public speeches designed to convince fellow tribal members that their line of reasoning was correct. In a similar vein, ceremonial ground leaders, in a manner similar to later Chickasaw preachers, offered hortative ceremonial speeches instructing the people on how they ought to be conducting their lives and what bad behavior to avoid. In the ancient past tribal religious leaders called *hopayi'* (prophets) offered ritual instruction in a related ceremonial speech genre called "the beloved speech."

Tribal medicine people called *alikchi'* also possessed a type of ritual speech. Their medicinal formulas were spoken over plants while gathering them, in preparation of medicine, and in application of medicine on persons who were physically and spiritually afflicted. This speech genre was also extended into song, as many medicinal formulas and speeches were sung over the ill. Songs in the genre called *pishofa* were performed for an ill person in conjunction with a ritual meal of corn and pork, along with a series of dances. The medicinal speeches and songs are unknown today, the last Chickasaw doctors having passed away in the 1970s.

Another genre of tribal oratory was traditional storytelling. These stories were often told by elders or parents to children, or among adults in settings where groups of people gathered, often in the winter time in large communal houses or the town big house. These stories cover a broad range of topics and had diverse motivations, from moral instruction to simple humor. These types of stories are pervasive throughout the Southeast (see collections assembled by Mooney, Swanton, Tuggle, and Gouge).[8] Traditional storytelling continues in earnest in the present day, whether in English or Chickasaw.

TRADITIONAL STORYTELLING GENRES

Chikashsha Naaikbi' Anoli' (Creation-Origin Stories)

Creation-origin stories are a genre in which Chickasaw storytellers related their understanding of the creation of the earth, the origins of the Chickasaw people, and the origins of related tribes of people. Included in this genre are the tribal migration stories. The story retold here related to the creation of the entire world, and appears in other contexts including a version enfolded with a world flood story. These stories are marked by a certain straightforwardness, a matter-of-factness that accompanies true stories. Unlike other story genres, many of which are understood to be fanciful at their core, creation stories, including the tribal migration stories, are true. These stories are told without the hear-say evidential markers and third person attributions seen in other story genres. This particular world creation story was told by the late Juanita Byars, a full blood Chickasaw born and raised near Tishomingo, Oklahoma.

Shikonno'pa' (Possum Stories)

Shikonno'pa' or "possum stories" are animal tales from long ago, when it was said that animals and humans could talk together. These stories feature an often mischievous, vain, or conceited animal like *Chokfi'* (Rabbit), *Choklhihili'* (Possum), or *Loksi'* (Turtle). These animals get into a variety of troubles, and though not overly didactic, the stories impart a certain moral instruction. Some possum stories offer explanations for natural phenomena, including why possum grins, why turtle has a cracked shell, or how the alligator came to have rough skin. Still others describe how essential elements like fire, medicine, or corn came to the people. Some speakers consider these stories to be creation stories of a sort, rather than actual *shikonno'pa'*. Included in this collection is a classic possum story, "Why Turtle Has a Cracked Shell," as told by Weldon Fulsom, one of the youngest native speakers of Chickasaw. Weldon's father Roy Fulsom knew an astonishing range of *shikonno'pa'*, of which Weldon recalls a dozen or more. This version tells of the misdeeds of a thieving Turtle who attempted to steal potatoes from a family of skunks, with dire and lasting consequences.

Iksa' Nannanoli' (Clan Stories)

Clan stories are a subgenre of traditional narratives dealing with general knowledge and characteristics of clans and house groups and true stories about things that happened to members of a particular house group. A number of clan stories were collected for anthropologist John Swanton by Chickasaw tribal member Zeno McCurtain in the 1910s and translated and published in Swanton's "Social and Religious Beliefs and Usages of the Chickasaw Indians."[9] This story involves a member of the *Kowimilhlha' Iksa'* (Wildcat Clan), who encountered a *Lhofa'* (Bigfoot or Sasquatch) while on a hunting trip.[10]

Chokoshpa' Nannanoli' (Humor Stories)

Humor stories are a vital subgenre of traditional storytelling. These humor stories are a mixture of true stories that are retold again and again because they are truly funny, fanciful stories with elements of truth, and stories that are completely created for the amusement of the teller and audience, having no basis in fact. The story here, retold by Jerry Imotichey, was first told by the late John Puller, a former resident of Madill, Oklahoma, a Chickasaw veteran and a well-known storyteller. Almost any traditionalist from the southern part of the nation will know a John Puller story. This story is based on a group of buzzards and a crow that John saw on the road to Madill, with a fair dose of *loshka* (lying) included.

These stories are but a small sampling of the rich and vital tradition of Chickasaw storytelling and oral literature. Stories are an essential and vital part of tribal identity, so much so that even with language loss and cultural attrition, the stories have remained a vital part of cultural life. Contemporary storytellers including Glenda Galvan, Stephanie Scott, and Lorie Robbins share creation, origin, tribal history, and *shikonno'pa'* stories with contemporary audiences in English. Our native speakers continue to talk with each other the way they always have, relating humorous stories of days gone by and sharing the happenings of the present. Even now, second language learners are learning and retelling the old stories, while creating new stories of their own.

NOTES

1. James Adair, *History of American Indians* (Tuscaloosa: University of Alabama Press, 2005), 34; John R. Swanton, "The Social and Religious Beliefs and Usages of the Chickasaw Indians," in *The History of the American Indians*, ed. Kathryn E. Holland Braund (Tuscaloosa: University of Alabama Press, 2009), 174. The three tribes are, respectively, the Chickasaw, Choctaw, and Shakchihomma', also spelled Chakchiuma. Joshua D. Hinson, To'li' Chikashsha Inaafokha: Chickasaw Stickball Regalia, MS, 2007, 32.
2. Adair, *History*, 195 footnote; Swanton, "Social and Religious Beliefs," 174; Hinson MS, 32.
3. Rev. Jesse J. Humes, "Ofi' Tohbi' Ishto' micha Itti' Holitto'pa' (The Big White Dog and the Sacred Pole)," MS, ed. Robert Kingsberry, 1964.
4. George Aaron Broadwell, "Reconstructing Proto-Muskogean Language and Prehistory: Preliminary Results," 1992, http://www.albany.edu/anthro/fac/broadwell/flora.pdf.
5. Robert A. Brightman and Pamela S. Wallace, "Chickasaw," in *Handbook of North American Indians*, vol. 14: *Southeast*, ed. William P. Sturtevant and Raymond D. Fogelson (Washington DC: Smithsonian Institution), 491; J. Johnson, "The Chickasaws," in *Indians of the Greater Southeast: Historical Archeology and Ethnohistory*, ed. B. G. McEwan, 85–121 (Gainesville: University Press of Florida, 2000). An untitled manuscript dated 2005 is in the Chickasaw Nation Tribal Library.
6. Broadwell, "Reconstructing Proto-Muskogean Language."
7. Pamela Munro, ed., *Muskogean Linguistics*, UCLA Occasional Papers in Linguistics no. 6 (Los Angeles: University of California, Department of Linguistics, 1987); Pamela Munro, "The Muskogean II Prefixes and Their Significance," *International Journal of American Linguistics* 59, no. 4 (1993): 374–404; Catherine Willmond, *Chikashshanompaat Holisso Toba'chi:*

Chickasaw: An Analytical Dictionary (Norman: University of Oklahoma Press, 1994); Catherine Willmond, *Let's Speak Chickasaw: Chikashshanompa' Kilanompoli* (Norman: University of Oklahoma Press, 2009).

8. James Mooney, *Myths of the Cherokee*, Nineteenth Annual Report, Bureau of American Ethnology 1897–98, pt. I (Washington DC: U.S. Government Printing Office, 1900); John R. Swanton, *Early History of the Creek Indians and Their Neighbors*, Bureau of American Ethnology Bulletin no. 73 (Washington DC: Government Printing Office, 1922); John R. Swanton, "Social Organization and the Social Usages of the Indians of the Creek Confederacy," in Forty-Second Annual Report of the Bureau of American Ethnology for the Years 1924–1925, 279–325 (Washington DC: Government Printing Office, 1928); John R. Swanton, *Myths and Tales of the Southeastern Indians*, Bureau of American Ethnology Bulletin 88 (Washington DC: Smithsonian Institution, U.S. Government Printing Office, 1929); W.O. Tuggle, *Shem, Ham & Japheth: The Papers of W. O. Tuggle . . . 1879–1882*, ed. Eugene Current-Garcia and Dorothy B. Hatfield (Athens: University of Georgia Press, 1973); Earnest Gouge, *Totkv Mocvse/New Fire: Creek Folktales*, ed. and trans. Jack B. Martin, Margaret McKane Mauldin, and Juanita McGirt (Norman: University of Oklahoma Press, 2004).
9. John R. Swanton, "Social and Religious Beliefs and Usages of the Chickasaw Indians," in *Forty-Fourth Annual Report of the Bureau of American Ethnology* (Washington DC: Government Printing Office, 1928).
10. *Lhǫfa'* is a nominalized form of the verb *lhǫffi*, meaning "to skin." In this form it refers to the creature known to tear the skin off his victims. Traditionally children were discouraged from saying his name out loud, lest it call attention to the child.

Chikashsha Naaikbi' Ano̱li'

Creation-Origin Stories

Chikashsha Naaikbi' Ano̱li'

(Chickasaw Creation Story)

Juanita Byars (1995, *Chickasaw and English*)

[In this text, each Chickasaw language sentence is followed by its English translation.]

Chikashsha alhi haat Aba' Bínni'lika' hooyimmi bíyyi'kachattook, yammako̱ nanna oshta aba' aa-ashako̱ i̱holiito'pattook.

The Chickasaws have always believed in He Who Sits On High, who was composed of four sacred elements from above.

Nanna oshta yammat, hashi', hoshonti, shotik bosholli', micha aba' yaakni' micha intannap aba' pílla bínni'lika' i̱holhchifokat Aba' Bínni'li': Aba' Binni'likat hattak mó̱ma̱ shinok shobolli' aaikbi tahlihma̱ ishki' yaakni' hochifottook.

These four things were the sun, the clouds, the clear sky, and sitting in the middle of heaven, he who is called Aba' Binni'li', He Who Sits on High. Aba' Binni'li' made all the people from dust and when he was finished he named the dust mother earth.

Shakchi'koot lokfi' chakissama̱ oka' nota' pílla aa-ayo'wacha yaakni' ikbittooko̱ himmaka' yaakni'ma̱ ishki' hochifottook.

It was the Crayfish that gathered sticky mud from under the waters and made the land now called mother earth.

Lokfi' Ihayyita'ma̱ ishto' tanahli tahamako̱ yaakni' ishki' hochifottook.
He piled up the mass of wet dirt called mother earth.

Yaakni' latassa'ma̱ pisahmat ikanhi'cho, haatoko̱ Fala Ishto'ko̱ onchaba' micha yaakni' hayaka' ikbi apilaanaka̱ imasilhha. Aba' Bínni'li' kashapaka̱ Chikashsha milínkakat hashittook lowak ishto' holítto'pa' aba' pílla aalowak ishto' holítto'pa'. Okloshi' ilayyoka mó̱ma̱ aa-áyya'shaka̱ imattook.

Crayfish saw the flatness of the earth and did not like it, so he asked Raven to help in the creation of mountains and valleys. The part of Aba' Binni'li' closest to the Chickasaws was the sun, the great holy fire that burns on high. In all the different towns were places where a great holy fire burned after it was given to them.

How the Day and Night Were Divided

Traditional

Translated by the Chickasaw Language Committee (2012)

They say a long time ago the animals had a meeting. They used to talk together, just like people do today. Bear was in charge.

All the animals were going to decide how to divide the day from the night.

Some animals liked the day best.

Some animals liked the night better.

They talked and talked together, just like people do. So then Ground Squirrel stood and said to them: Look at Raccoon's tail. It is divided evenly, black and gray. I think that we ought to divide the day and the night like that.

The animals liked the Ground Squirrel's idea the best and all were happy. They divided the day and the night evenly, just like Raccoon's tail.

Bear was really mad and jealous.

So Bear, being very jealous of Ground Squirrel, scratched his back. So today that's why all the ground squirrels have striped backs, so they say.

That's it.

Shikonno'pa'

Possum Stories

Katihmit Loksi' Hakshopat Bosholli

(Why Turtle Has a Cracked Shell)

Weldon Fulsom (2011)
Translated by Weldon Fulsom with Lokosh (Joshua D. Hinson)

So Skunk's children were at their house and Turtle arrived. He said to Skunk's children, "Where has your mother gone?" Skunk's children said, "She's gone digging potatoes."

Turtle said, "These potatoes she's digging, when she gets back with them put them under the bed for me. I'll return and get them, eat them, and then slide under the bed."

So then Skunk's mother returned and her child said to her, "This person with red eyes came here." Skunk's mother said to him, "It might have been Turtle."

He told her what Turtle had said, about how to slide the potatoes under the bed after she brought them, so that he might eat them.

Skunk's mother went and got a hatchet and then began trailing Turtle. She caught up with Turtle, and cut him with the hatchet—cut him all to pieces. The mother skunk just left him there.

Turtle lay there for a while, calling to the gnats, "Eat all my fat and then sew my shell back up." After that the gnats sewed him up and left. Then the turtle got up and went. I believe that's why Turtle's shell is the way it is.

Iksa' Nannanoli'

Clan Stories

Kowimilhlha' Hattakat Lhofa' Ittafama

(Wildcat Man Meets the Bigfoot)

Zeno McCurtain (1921)
Collected by John Swanton

Once a number of men belonging to this clan went hunting and camped a considerable distance from home. Afterward they scattered to see what they could find but remained within call of one another, having made an agreement that if anything happened to one of them he should shout for help. But one of them ventured farther than he was aware and got a long distance off. Presently he got tired and sat down to rest, but while he was there a lhofa' came up and said, "What are you doing here? You are intruding upon my land and had better get up and return to your own place." But the Indian believed himself to be strong enough for any situation, so he sat still without speaking. Presently the lhofa' ordered him off again and added, "If you do not get up and go away I will tie you up and carry you to my place." "You may do so, if you can," the man replied, and upon this the lhofa' seized him. At first it seemed as if the man were the stronger of the two and he was able to throw the lhofa' down, but the latter smelled so bad that it was too much for his antagonist, and the lhofa' overcame him, hung him up in a tree and went away.

The man hung there all night, and when he did not make his appearance at camp the other hunters began a search for him, and when they found him, cut the grapevine by which he was fastened so that he fell to the ground. They asked him what had treated him in this manner but he would not speak and they thought he might have seen a ghost or something of that sort. Some time later, however, he came to himself and related what had happened. Afterward, although he was very fond of hunting and knew that he would be successful, he would not venture out unless someone were with him.

Chokoshpa' Nannan<u>o</u>li'

(Humor Stories)

Fala Shiiki Táwwa'a, or Falat Ibichchal<u>a</u> Inkaniya

(Crow and the Buzzard, or Crow Loses His Nose)

John Puller, retold by Jerry Imotichey (2011)

One time John was going along to Mill Creek. So he was getting on to Mill Creek, going along the road between Ravia and Mill Creek, in that direction. So near Mill Creek he saw a bunch of buzzards, so he said.

And so he went along and saw something dead there in the road, he said.

So a group of buzzards was together there, circling around.

So of all these buzzards that were there, one would come down and would land and then go back up in the sky, and not too long after that John saw Crow arrive, flying around.

Crow was circling, flying going along, going and landing and standing on that dead thing, and beginning to eat it. The buzzards saw this.

So this is what was happening—Crow was just biting away on the dead thing, while from up above the buzzards were really staring at him.

So after a little while, one buzzard became angry at Crow for eating his dead meat, and came down, so John said.

So the buzzard kept flying and coming in, and just as Crow was about to really take a bite, the buzzard hit him on the head, causing his beak to strike the hard road, and breaking his beak off. It was ruined, and Crow didn't have a beak anymore.

Well, Crow didn't like not having a beak.

So he was just standing there, looking around to see if anyone saw what happened, with the buzzards there, he was embarrassed.

So he was standing there and then took off flying, and the buzzards came down to stand on the dead thing lying there.

The Crow went high into the air, flying with one wing while covering himself with the other one, so that no one would be able to see him. Flying with one wing, he flew around there, flying in circles, so John said.

Oral Narratives Pose Interpretative Challenges

Interpretation Is a Tricky Business

Reviewing Glenda Galvan's Kati̱hsht Itti̱sh Oppolo'at Okla Alhiha' Imalattook *(How Poison Came to the Chickasaw and Choctaw, 2011)*

Lokosh (Joshua D. Hinson)

We use the word *interpretation*, rather than *translation*, quite purposefully. When these stories were retold in English, things changed somewhat, and they change when we go back to the original Chickasaw language. Interpreters have to be careful about keeping the important parts intact and bringing back some of the richness that gets lost in translation.

These are not literal, word-for-word translations from English to Chickasaw. Such translations would be unintelligible to a native speaker of Chickasaw. Instead, what we have strived to do is put the Chickasaw stories, retold in English, back into a Chickasaw form that reflects the conventions of Chickasaw oral tradition. We've tried to give them a voice that sounds like how the old folks, *kamassa*, would've said them. We hope you enjoy them.

—J. Ellis, J. Imotichey, and colleagues, 2011

WHY INTERPRETATION? THE ROLE OF TRANSLATION IN LANGUAGE REVITALIZATION

Were the Chickasaw language still healthy, we would have no significant need for translation of pedagogical, archival, or other types of materials. If the language were still with our families, coming from the mouths of babes, we would have no immediate concern for our language status. If we had more than fifty fluent speakers of our language left, we would have no need for revitalization work. The fact is, these are just glimpses of what our communities used to look like, where everyone could speak their language. They are also what Chickasaw language revitalizationists hope for, the reason that we do this work.

A significant part of this work is taken up with translation and interpretation activities. Overt knowledge of the two codes—one native, and one foreign, Chickasaw and English—is a prerequisite for revitalization work. We mediate between the two in our work, as all translators do, struggling for *close* when what we want is *perfection.*

Translation-interpretation is an integral part of the efforts of any revitalization-focused program. Whether enrichment or immersion focused, programs require materials, and materials creation demands talented translators. The Chickasaw Language Revitalization Program early identified the need for enrichment materials and programs designed to bring the language back into prominence in the Chickasaw community, to convince a new generation of tribal members that language is a critical and valuable part of their world—a process of commodification for salvation.

In this essay I examine the interpretation process for *How Poison Came to the Chickasaw and Choctaw*, a traditional Chickasaw narrative.[1] I trace its origins in Chickasaw oral traditions, the process of its Chickasaw language telling through Minnie Ayakatubby, its English reinterpretation by her son, its retelling and transformation to the written word by her granddaughter Glenda Galvan, and its reinterpretation into Chickasaw by JoAnn Ellis and Jerry Imotichey.

GLENDA GALVAN, CHOLA HOMMAˈ IKSAˈ

Glenda Galvan is a Chickasaw tribal citizen, and a descendent of the *Chola Hommaˈ Iksaˈ* (Red Fox Clan). She was born at Olney, Coal County, Oklahoma, in 1954.

"Minnie Ayakatubby, my grandmother, was of the Fox clan and she told a number of old stories to her son and to my dad who then told them to me. They were told in our language until dad and my grandpa told them to us in English—sometimes in our language so we could hear it, I guess. I like to 'bring the stories to life' for the audiences so I seldom tell a story the same way—ever! Even when I use a story from Swanton or another source, as I tell it in front of an audience, I 'change it up' to make it 'mine.' I always remind them these stories were first told in our first language and now in English which is why the books are very important."[2]

The Red Fox Clan, like other Chickasaw clans, had specific origin stories associated with their clan, as well as more widely shared *shikonno'pa'*. Zeno McCurtain recorded the Red Fox Clan origin story for John Swanton during his Oklahoma fieldwork, circa 1920, and Swanton published it in 1928. The story relates the founding of the clan, when a hunter encountered a fox sleeping in a cave during a hunt. Seeing that the fox appeared to be red all over, the hunter called him Red Fox, and after that the hunter's descendants were known by that clan name.

In contrast to ancestral storytelling practices, where any member of a family, house, or clan group could tell stories (though certainly some were more skilled orators than others), contemporary Chickasaw storytelling has become more ritualized and formalized. Glenda Galvan was appointed as the Chickasaw Nation's first official storyteller and continues to hold that office. At a later date Glenda took on Lorie Robbins as her apprentice, and passed on her repertoire, including ancestral clan stories, *shikonno'pa'*, and stories adapted by Glenda from other southeastern tribal groups. In recent years Stephanie Scott has taken on a more public role as a storyteller. All three are now considered official tribal storytellers. This is not to say that informal storytelling does not persist in Chickasaw families, but with the decline in native speakers, traditional storytelling practices have been fading in the last few decades.

In 2011 the Chickasaw Press published *Chikasha Stories*, volume 1: *Shared Spirit*. Written by Glenda Galvan, illustrated by Jeannie Barbour, and with Chickasaw interpretations by JoAnn Ellis, Jerry Imotichey, John P. Dyson, PhD, and this author, *Shared Spirit* marks the first occasion for tribal oral narratives to be presented bilingually, in written form, for a general audience. Several aspects of this text are noteworthy: former Chickasaw language-medium stories are now presented in English, with Chickasaw reinterpretations, former oral stories are now committed to text, and former tribal stories are now accessible, in both forms, to non-Chickasaws.

KATI̱HSHT ITTI̱SH OPPOLO'AT OKLA ALHIHA' IMALATTOOK

How Poison Came to the Chickasaw and Choctaw is a *shikonno'pa'* or "possum story," a genre of Chickasaw oral narrative. *Shikonno'pa'* are animal stories that often center on a trickster animal like *Chokfi'* (Rabbit), *Choklhihili'* (Possum), or *Loksi'* (Turtle). These stories impart moral instruction, often through the examples of bad behavior or poor choices by the animals. Still other types of *shikonno'pa'* explain some sort of natural phenomenon—why Turtle has a cracked shell, why Possum grins, or in the present case, how poison came into the world when a poison vine distributed its poison to animals in need of it, including the rattlesnake, wasp, bumblebee, and copperhead. The vine, divested of all its poison, became the water lily.

Glenda was certainly conscious of this genre and the implied moral instruction that these stories imparted: "I later learned some of the stories we were being told were version[s] of Swanton; sometimes ours were longer—sometimes shorter but the basic characters and outcome were the same. The poison story was one such story—we had been told this story (and one other one) from the time we were very young—we supposed to keep us away from the ponds on our dairy (without supervision). The version we were told growing up was longer and had several more characters but basically it's the same story because of the outcome."[3]

REINTERPRETATION PROCESS

The process of reinterpreting these former Chickasaw language stories back into Chickasaw was complicated, inasmuch as their transformation from Chickasaw *shikonno'pa'* to English children's stories was complicated too. The original Chickasaw narrative existed only in the minds of speakers, who passed the stories with their implicit moral instruction from generation to generation. The specifics of the story varied from family to family, speaker to speaker. Using standard conventions of Chickasaw storytelling, individual speakers offered their variations on a theme to their audiences.

This oral tradition was passed to Glenda Galvan's father, who was a passive bilingual, understanding Chickasaw but not speaking it fluently. He learned the poison story and others from his mother Minnie Ayakatubby. Given that his own children were not speakers of Chickasaw, he retold the stories in English, changing and embellishing the narrative to suit his English-speaking audience, while remaining true to the fundamental structure of the story. In like manner, Glenda took these stories, some exclusively Chickasaw, others shared with other tribes, and still others borrowed from related tribes, and using the conventions of English storytelling, created her own elaborated versions of Minnie Ayakatubby's stories. These versions, much like her grandmother's and her father's, were fluid, with shifting details around a core narrative. It was only when they were committed to paper and published as a collection in *Shared Spirit* that they were made permanent, fixed, immutable in their details. From these fixed, written versions the interpreters worked to create Chickasaw versions that were simultaneously faithful to Chickasaw narrative conventions and to Glenda's elaborated versions.

REINTERPRETING HOW POISON CAME TO THE CHICKASAW AND CHOCTAW

As interpreters we had to grapple with particular problems in the languages—retaining the core narrative structure, reinvigorating the Chickasaw with narrative elements that are essential to the *shikonnoꞌpaꞌ* genre, and remaining largely faithful to the Galvan version.

Given that we did not have an original Chickasaw language medium recording of *How Poison Came to the Chickasaw and Choctaw*, we looked to other traditional *shikonnoꞌpaꞌ* for guidance on how to craft the new Chickasaw version of the story. All traditional stories, *shikonnoꞌpaꞌ* in particular, follow certain formulae that are consistent throughout the subgenres of Chickasaw oral narratives.

One primary feature is the traditional opening phrase structure, a phrase that encompasses the general meaning of 'a long time ago':

hopaakikaashhookano
'long ago'
chiiki pillaꞌ áyya'shakaash
'long ago'
mishaꞌ píllakaash
'long ago'

An additional feature is phrase repetition of significant elements. Unlike English storytelling, which uses elaborate tone and pitch variation for emphasizing important subjects, Chickasaw oral narratives rephrase and repeat elements that are of the most importance:

> . . . Shiiki yammat aachihmat, "Abooha aashachakla mó̱maka̱ pillaꞌ okshittat hashtáyyahna kanookya ikpiꞌsokmako̱ imalikchilaꞌni," aꞌshna, abooha choꞌma̱ aashachakla yamma̱ okshittat táyyahna abooha okshitat tahna Shiiki yammat Chokfi yamma̱ imalikchi.
>
> . . . and Buzzard said, "If you just close up all the cracks in the house so that no one can see, I can doctor him," he said, and they closed up all those cracks that were in the house, they closed the house all up, and Buzzard doctored Rabbit.[4]

In the case of Rabbit and Buzzard, the critical element is the Buzzard's desire to have all the gaps in the log house sealed up—completely sealed—so that Buzzard, under the pretense of doctoring the ill Rabbit, can kill and eat him without alerting bystanders. Three clauses with repeated narrative details reinforce this important point for the listener.

Chickasaw, like the other Muskogean languages, tracks the subject of related clauses, indicating whether the subject of one clause is the same as or different than in a following clause, a phenomenon called switch-reference.

> Koloꞌfa**na** impállammi**cha** tíꞌwa**na** kaniyaꞌma**t** imalikchaꞌni**ka̱** hoyo**kat** áyyaꞌsha.
>
> He [Rabbit] was wounded, and he had it so bad that he was lying down, so they were looking for someone to doctor him.

In the first clause Rabbit is the subject. The first switch-reference marker **+na** generally indicates a different subject, and in this case the information is being backgrounded to the final clause *hoyokat áyya'sha*, but the following marker +**cha** indicates that the wounded subject is the same as the subject of the verb meaning 'to have it bad' and the subsequent verb 'be lying down'. The third marker **+na** signals that the subject has changed, in this case to unknown third persons who are looking for someone to doctor the wounded Rabbit. The switch-reference marker **+ka** tells the listener that the ones doing the looking are not the ones who will be doing the doctoring. The final switch-reference marker **+kat** signals that the third person subject is the same as that referred to by the final verb, meaning 'to be in a place' (of three or more persons).[5]

At the level of discourse, Chickasaw switch-reference shows reference functions across both sentence and paragraph boundaries, in effect serving as "traffic signals to tell the hearer whether to expect a change in participants or whether the participant relations will remain the same."[6] This elaborate system of both phrase and discourse level reference tracking is used extensively in Chickasaw oral production, of which oral narratives play a significant part. Chickasaw discourse markers include

haatokoot (same subject) / *haatok<u>o</u>* (different subject)
'so, therefore'
naalhchohmit (same subject) / *naalhchohm<u>a</u>* (different subject)
'being that way'
yahmikmat (same subject) / *yahmikm<u>a</u>* (different subject)
'be doing'

Finally, Chickasaw oral narratives generally feature a standardized closing phrase (southeastern storytellers were also known to spit at the closing of a story):

yammak illa
'that's it, that's all'
yammak illa aashli
'that's all I have to say'

In interpreting from Chickasaw to English, Glenda's father consciously manipulated the language devices of the original, keeping essential aspects while making subtle changes to ensure that it was in fact, a "good" story in English. Glenda did much the same, modifying her father's story for dramatic and other desired effects, in response to both what constituted a good English language story at the time and the narrative requirements from the Chickasaw original. Being a step removed from the Chickasaw, I would posit that the cultural expectations of English storytelling, stylistically anyway, could have become dominant, but in fact the final product is much more of a hybrid. In the same manner as Chickasaw oral narratives, English oral narratives have stylistic devices that conform to a specific cultural expectation of what makes a good story.

Like those in Chickasaw, English stories have standard opening phrases that occur again and again in oral literature, devices that position the story in the remote past:

Once upon a time
Long ago
A long time ago
Long, long ago

In the case of the English version of *How Poison Came to the Chickasaw and Choctaw*, we have two framing devices: one deriving from the Chickasaw tradition that positions the story during a time when animals could speak to each other, and an additional time reference that is more in keeping with English narrative devices:

> From when animals and humans could talk with one another, there comes a story of how poison came to our people. Long, long ago . . . [7]

In contrast to the Chickasaw, where phrase reduplication is used to emphasize important aspects of the narrative, Galvan uses elaboration of story details, particularly the extensive use of adjectives, to highlight particular portions of the narrative and to give the reader a richer, fuller mental image:

> A **certain** Vine lived along the edge, and he loved to hear the **joyful, happy** voices of the people, particularly the children as they laughed and played in the water.[8]

Galvan also gives additional details at the phrasal level, to flesh out what may have seemed to her father a very skeletal story. At a later point in the story the animals come seeking poison from the Vine and offer elaborate explanations for why they need it, elaborations that would surely be missing in the original. Whereas Galvan's audience expects a full reading, with clear motivations for actions, our ancestral Chickasaws would have taken it at face value that an animal now known to be poisonous would have had some legitimate reason for acquiring the poison in the remote past.

Galvan also extensively uses proper nouns to track actors and patterns of behavior, whereas Chickasaw can rely on its extensive switch-reference system to track the actors in a given phrase or narrative passage. In the first two paragraphs alone the proper noun Vine is used six times, whereas in the Chickasaw interpretation the proper noun *Alba Balalli'* is used only four times. A traditional *shikonno'pa'* would likely have used the proper noun much less. The hybrid form of the new Chickasaw version adheres to the English more closely, given the interpreter's insistence on faithfulness to the source document.

Having extensive use of adjectives and elaboration of story details to emphasize the crucial aspects of the narrative, Galvan dispenses with the phrasal repetition of the *shikonno'pa'* genre. This type of repetition would likely be considered somewhat strange by an English audience. Consider again the English interpretation of the Rabbit and Buzzard story, where the cracks in the house are referenced no fewer than three times. While a perfectly good English interpretation of the Chickasaw story, it rings strange to English ears:

> . . . and Buzzard said, "If you just **close up all the cracks** in the house so that no one can see, I can doctor him," he said, and they **closed up all those cracks** that were in the house, **they closed the house all up**, and Buzzard doctored Rabbit.[9]

When JoAnn Ellis and Jerry Imotichey approached this text, they confronted the English text as it was but viewed it through the eyes of native speakers—speakers who have the demands of traditional *shikonno'pa'* deeply set in their minds. What they produced was neither a stilted, awkward literal translation of the English into Chickasaw nor a true, unaffected *shikonno'pa'*. Instead, the final interpretation was somewhere in between. Inasmuch as our ancestors occupied the middle ground between the heavens and the underworld, this story lives between its original form as *shikonno'pa'* and its transformation into an English language children's story.

One signal of this place, or even a certain tension between the two, is found in the title itself. Good English titles like *How Poison Came to the Chickasaw and Choctaw* are actually posed in the form of a question when interpreted in a Chickasaw way: *Katihsht Ittish Oppolo'at Okla Alhiha' Imalattook* is actually a question. In its most literal translation the title is "how (infinitive) medicine bad people come.to.remote past tense?" The only alternative to an English title of this type is a statement, something like *Ittish Oppolo'at Okla Alhiha' Imalattook,* "medicine bad people come.to.remote past tense," glossed as "Poison Came to the People." This simple declarative statement was a suitable alternative, but the speakers felt a sense of obligation to the English text, instead opting for the question form.

We can also see some of this hybridity or tension through comparison between Galvan's English text and a more literal English translation of Ellis and Imotichey's Chickasaw version. This first selection is the opening passage from Galvan, with the English to Chickasaw interpretation following in italics:

> From when the animals and humans could talk with one another, there comes a story of how poison came to our people. Long, long ago, the Chickasaw would come to the water, sometimes to bathe, to wash their clothes, or maybe just to play in the water.
>
> *Long ago, the people enjoyed swimming all the time, they say.*
>
> A certain Vine lived along the edge, and he loved to hear the joyful,

happy voices of the people, particularly the children as they laughed and played in the water. However, many times when they happened to touch this Vine, they would get sick or sometimes even die.

So a Vine grew there, near to the river. It was that way but if the people touched this vine they were sickened and sometimes died, they say.

This made Vine very sad, but because he had no way of letting the people know about the dangerous poison, the humans kept getting sick and dying. Finally, Vine decided to pray to Aba' Bínni'li' (The Great Spirit) about how he could give some of his poison away.

So the Vine was sad and prayed to the Great Spirit, asking how its bad medicine might be gifted [to another] they say.

Immediately the reader gets a sense of the contrasting story styles, the elaborate details of the Galvan version against the sparer English-Chickasaw version. The later version retains many defining characteristics of the *shikonno'pa'*, preserving much of what makes the genre distinctive. The stock opening phrase *long ago* is preserved, with a scene-setting statement that establishes the subject of the story without unnecessary detail. The repeated *they say* is a hearsay marker, an evidential statement telling the listener that the storyteller is not reporting a firsthand experience but a long-ago tale to which that no one living could attest. The intricacies of the discourse markers are lost to the English—*so, therefore, it was that way*, and the like. The information conveyed by the Chickasaw markers cannot be interpreted easily and naturally into English. An additional compromise in the English-Chickasaw version is seen in the use of *Great Spirit* rather than the traditional *Aba' Bínni'li'* (He Who Sits On High.) This was the translator's choice, keeping with the English original. Finally, the English-Chickasaw version literally interprets poison (*bad medicine*), while the poison itself is not given away by Vine but gifted to another, suggesting that for the Chickasaw speaker the poison, albeit dangerous or "bad," has some useful purpose for its recipients.

These are but a few highlighted instances of the different foci of the parallel stories where the Galvan rendering contrasts strongly with the Chickasaw interpretation, as seen through the lens of the English-Chickasaw interpretation. These stories derive from the same source with a common thread running throughout but, as we have seen, are demonstrably different. Each attempts to describe how poison came into the world, through an act of gifting by sentient plants and animals, with the guidance of a supreme being. The audience—the recipients of each story—themselves differ. The original oral *shikonno'pa'*, in its native language form, was for the instruction and entertainment of a native audience. In its second incarnation as an English translation of the original, it was told for the young grandchildren and children of native speakers, children who did not themselves speak Chickasaw. The third incarnation was Glenda Galvan's English interpretation of her father's own English interpretation, told for the entertainment of both native and non-native audiences. The fourth version was a retranslation by native speakers, back into Chickasaw, for the benefit of both the Chickasaw community and non-native patrons of the Chickasaw Press as well as second language learners of Chickasaw. The fifth version, an English reinterpretation of the Chickasaw translation, is here presented for the benefit of the reader as well as our second language learner community. Ultimately, two of these communities are the primary focus for ongoing revitalization efforts and revitalization-focused interpretation and translation work: the Chickasaw community as a whole, both at home in Oklahoma and in the worldwide Chickasaw diaspora, and most especially our small but growing community of second language learners. The ultimate goal, of course, is a community of newly proficient speakers and their children, who, having learned the language from birth, will no longer have need of English translations-interpretations. We continue to do this work for, and in expectation of, these future generations.

NOTES

1. The title of the story, "Katihsht Ittish Oppolo'at Okla Alhiha' Imalattook," literally means "How Poison Came to the People," but in the version published by Chickasaw Nation Press, *okla alhiha'* (people) is translated using Chickasaw and Choctaw, so we are using that translation here.

2. G. Galvan, email to author, December 14, 2012. The epigraph opening the present essay is drawn from another of the same title in a volume edited by Galvan: J. Ellis, J. Imotichey, J. Dyson, and J. Hinson, "Translation Is a Tricky Business," in G. Galvan, *Chikasha Stories*, vol. 1: *Shared Spirit* (Ada, OK: Chickasaw Press, 2011).
3. Galvan, email to author. Swanton is John R. Swanton, ethnographer, who recorded Chickasaw clan narratives with Chickasaw interpreter Zeno McCurtain, which were published in John R. Swanton, "Social and Religious Beliefs and Usages of the Chickasaw Indians," *Forty-Fourth Annual Report of the Bureau of American Ethnology* (Washington DC: Government Printing Office, 1928).
4. P. Munro and C. Willmond, *Let's Speak Chickasaw: Chikashshanompa' Kilanompoli'* (Norman: University of Oklahoma Press, 2008), 291–93, 332.
5. Quote from Munro and Willmond, *Let's Speak Chickasaw,* 291–93, 332; marker discussion from P. Munro and C. Willmond, *Chikashshanompaat Holisso Toba'chi: Chickasaw, An Analytical Dictionary* (Norman: University of Oklahoma Press, 1994), 45.
6. D. Payne, "Switch-Reference in Chickasaw," in *Studies of Switch-Reference*, ed. Pamela Munro, 89–118, UCLA Papers in Syntax no. 8 (Los Angeles: UCLA, 1980).
7. Galvan, *Chikasha Stories,* 1:78.
8. Galvan, *Chikasha Stories,* 1:79.
9. Munro and Willmond, *Let's Speak Chickasaw,* 291–93, 332. See also James Mooney, *James Mooney's History, Myths, and Sacred Formulas of the Cherokees: Containing the Full Texts of the Myths of the Cherokee (1900) and the Sacred Formulas of the Cherokees (1891) as Published by the Bureau of American Ethnology: with a New Biographical Introduction, James Mooney and the Eastern Cherokees* (Fairview NC: Bright Mountain Books, 1992); John R. Swanton, *Myths and Tales of the Southeastern Indians,* Bureau of American Ethnology Bulletin 88 (Washington DC: Smithsonian Institution, U.S. Government Printing Office, 1929); W.O. Tuggle, *Shem, Ham & Japheth: The Papers of W. O. Tuggle . . . 1879–1882,* ed. Eugene Current-Garcia and Dorothy B. Hatfield (Athens: University of Georgia Press, 1973); Earnest Gouge, *Totkv Mocvse/New Fire: Creek Folktales,* ed. and trans. Jack B. Martin, Margaret McKane Mauldin, and Juanita McGirt (Norman: University of Oklahoma Press, 2004).

YUCHI

Yuchi Stories

Mary S. Linn

The Yuchi, also spelled Euchee, are a small but vibrant tribe. They are located within the boundaries of the Muscogee (Creek) Nation in east-central Oklahoma. Their original homeland was in the southeastern United States, and along with other tribes and tribal towns affiliated with the Creek Confederacy, the Yuchi were forcibly removed to Indian Territory in the early nineteenth century. Once there, they regrouped in familiar tribal towns along the Arkansas River and its tributaries, around what is now Tulsa, Oklahoma, and to the west and south.[1]

Unlike their Muscogee Creek neighbors (see Martin, this volume), the Yuchi did not adopt a constitutional form of government or respond at first to missionary efforts in Indian Territory. The Euchee Mission Boarding School in Sapulpa, Oklahoma, was founded in 1894 by the Presbyterian Mission and then was run by Muskogee Nation from 1897 until 1907. Noah Gregory, a Yuchi man, was the first superintendent. Although the early Presbyterian boarding school was probably conducted in Yuchi, a writing system did not take root. Pickett United Methodist Church was founded in 1901, and the services were held in Yuchi until the mid-1980s. However, church records were kept in English, in pre-printed church ledgers provided by the Methodist Conference. These three avenues of government, school, and church often led to writing systems but not with the Yuchi. Subsequently, Yuchi people themselves did not write down tales and narratives until the Euchee Class of Sapulpa began writing and producing materials in the language, including animal tales and personal narratives, in the early 1990s.[2]

Folklorist Jeremiah Curtin was the first person known to collect Yuchi texts.[3] For a month after New Year in 1883 Curtin lived with Sam Brown and his wife just south of Wialaka Mission, a location that is now part of Bixby, Oklahoma. If he wrote down the stories in the Yuchi language, these versions do not survive.[4] Only English versions can be found today. During work for the Euchee Dictionary Project in 2006, Maggie Cumpsey Marsey, Josephine Barnett Keith, Josephine Wildcat Bigler, Maxine Wildcat Barnett, and I looked at these texts, originally for ideas of missing vocabulary.[5] However, the elders found several of the texts to their liking, and so they translated these back into Yuchi. From these new Yuchi stories we also created a more modern English translation while trying to keep the feel of the Yuchi narrative.

In 1885 linguist Albert Gatschet collected the first narratives in the Yuchi language, also at Wialaka Mission. He published the creation story and published it in English in 1893.[6] And then in 1904 ethnologist Frank Speck collected more than thirty-five sacred narratives (myths), legends, animal tales, and beliefs and practices with Ekilarne Cahwee, Washington Holder, and Joe Allen from around Kellyville and Bristow, Oklahoma. While the Yuchi versions are difficult to use (and not all of them are in Yuchi), the depth and scope of the collection of myths (sacred narratives), legends, tales, and historical and personal narratives is significant.

Günter Wagner's *Yuchi Tales* (1931) is still the most monumental effort to record Yuchi oral literature.[7] Wagner worked in the summer of 1928 through the winter of 1929 while he was a doctoral student of Franz Boas. He worked with several storytellers varying by region, age, and gender. He wrote down fifty-four stories in Yuchi and then transcribed and translated them. The collection includes sacred narratives, legends, and animal tales, and the life story of Maxey Simms, which he broke into seventeen chapters. The Yuchi texts suffer from some inconsistencies, yet the body of knowledge about the scope of oral narrative forms, belief systems, and the Yuchi language is not diminished and stands as a testament to Yuchi oral traditions and to the expert Yuchi storytellers Maxey Simms, George Clinton, Sally Clinton, Ida Clinton (Riley), and Andy Johnson, who worked with Wagner to record their knowledge.

Lewis Ballard compiled a noteworthy collection in the mid-1970s.[8] He and Addie George, a Yuchi teacher and historian, visited many of the last monolingual and predominantly Yuchi speakers. The recordings of these visits contain both elicited and spontaneous storytelling events, including three Rabbit stories expertly told by Waxin Tiger (Linn and Jackson 2004) and several other animal stories told by Lochar Greene.[9] The conversations are also sprinkled with process texts, personal narratives, and historical narratives. Other linguists who recorded smaller collections of narratives include Haas (1940), Wolfe (1951), Crawford (1970–73), and Linn (2001).[10]

Here I have included narratives from a variety of storytellers and collectors over all time periods. I have tried to emphasize stories that reflect the continuity of Yuchi oral traditions even as their telling may have shifted to English or to a new context for telling. Some of the narratives have been reintroduced into oral tradition through community cultural and language revitalization efforts. It is not clear yet to what extent these will be retold and passed on. I have chosen a few on the basis of their being relevant to current cultural practices or interests today. An example of my decision process is that I have left out the widely published Creation Myth. Jackson includes Newman Littlebear referring to episodes in the Creation Myth during speeches at Polecat Ceremonial Ground, but I have not found it either to be in the memory of elders today or to appear as central as other narratives to Yuchi culture and ceremonial practice today.[11] On the other hand, personal stories of the supernatural, which were rarely collected, are the most frequent genre told today, along with prayers and personal narratives. In all cases I have chosen stories that were originally in Yuchi or, in the case of the Curtin texts, are from the retranslated versions.

MYTHICAL TIME STORIES

Jackson ends *Yuchi Folklore: Cultural Expression in a Southeastern Native American Community* with a chapter dedicated to the continuity of the Monster Lizard, or in Yuchi *sothl'ẽdash'ẽchathla* (red-mouthed lizard), in oral tradition and through the Lizard Dance at Yuchi ceremonial grounds (180–204).[12] He recounts a telling of the Monster Lizard sacred narrative as told to him by Jimmie Skeeter and the symbolic retelling every year in the Lizard Dance. The narrative reinforces the power of the Yuchi and their medicine as the Yuchi are able to defeat the Monster Lizard. Like Jackson, I have been privileged with a spontaneous telling of this narrative told to me in a ceremonial context, and talk about the Lizard is still very much alive among the ceremonial grounds Yuchi. In order to complement this narrative, I am presenting two other tales of Yuchi men unexpectedly finding, fighting, or tricking and finally overcoming *sothl'ẽdash'ẽchathla*. These two tales are not directly connected to the medicine and ceremonial practice but are representative of southeastern stories of human encounters with *sothl'ẽdash'ẽchathla*.[13] They are still exciting tales of hunting and bravery.

Curtin, Speck, and Wagner all collected the story of Wind and Iron. With varying degrees of detail, they all have basically the same plot and motifs. The sons of Wind (*Hoda*) go out into the world (they leave or are sent), and they do not come back. He goes to search for them, but since Wind has no body, he clothes himself in various reptiles and amphibians to take form. In addition, he takes what was apparently necessary for life and comfort, such as his ammunition bag (or a side bag), his pipe and tobacco and flint (or matches), and a chair. He comes to a river and sees a white bird (crow or rooster), and a mysterious man comes out to take him across. In Curtin's version, Wind had instructed the sons not to take help from the man. Wind remains clean by refusing all aid from him. Finally, as they sit and smoke together, the smoke from Wind's tobacco–"the most powerful of all snakes" (Speck) or the mythical tie snake (Wagner)–kills the man. He falls to the floor with a loud noise, and it is revealed that the man was Iron (*Sene*). His wife is outside, and she instructs Wind how to get his sons back. The Curtin version ends immediately after the sons are released, but the Speck and Wagner stories tell how the boys were changed from their contact with Iron. In Speck they are changed into specific animals, the wolf, crow, raven, and dog. These versions also end with Wind prophesying his return.

In presenting the story of Wind, I used Maxey Simms's version (from Wagner). I did not add any elements from the other versions. However, I retranslated some of the Yuchi based on a more complete picture from all the stories combined and from discussions during the Euchee Dictionary Project's work retranslating Curtin's version. The story does not appear to be in oral tradition or in the memory of elders today. Yet in this current age of Batman and Iron Man, ordinary men who cloak themselves in power to achieve good, Wind is the ultimate Yuchi superhero.

ANIMAL TALES

Animal stories, called *dē'ēlā* in Yuchi, provide the audience with a moral or lesson, and often the trickster Rabbit shows us how something came to be by revealing the nature of our animal cousins and therefore our own nature. The lessons are never directly stated in Yuchi storytelling tradition, and some of the animal stories and the original humor seem opaque to modern Yuchi. Out of the rich tradition of animal stories in Yuchi, and found abundantly throughout the Southeast, two are presented here.

"The First Woman to Leave a Lazy Husband" was collected by Jeremiah Curtin. Animal stories take place in the time when animals talked. This story is unusual in that it takes place in a mythical time when talking animals and humans lived together but has the lesson and subtle humor of an animal story. A woman has taken a dove and then a mockingbird as a husband, but she makes both leave when she discovers that they are lazy. Finally she marries a lizard, who is a hard worker. The woman is Yuchi as retranslated by the Euchee Dictionary Project. They use pronoun *sā-*, which refers only to Yuchi females; to achieve this distinction in English, the woman's brother, who appears in the story before the woman, is translated rather bluntly as "a Yuchi man." The husbands are referred to with the pronoun *wā*—used for any living creature that is non-Yuchi.

The Dictionary Project women had never heard this story before reading Curtin's manuscript, and they were immediately drawn to it. It was the first Curtin story that they wanted to translate back into Yuchi, and they took it with them to language classes. The story has reentered Yuchi knowledge through them. The story's lesson about appropriate male and female expectations and roles is clear enough, but the attributes given to the different types of men to whom young women are amused them the most. Young women, they felt, are always attracted to the "cooing" types and the flashy mockingbird types, but the hardworking yet more modest lizards get overlooked. There is also subtle adult humor in the timing of her kicking out the first two husbands, found in the lines "they went back into the house" and "(he) stayed all night." Jackson includes the original Curtin translation with a discussion of gender roles in contemporary Yuchi society.[14]

"Rabbit and Turkeys" is a masterpiece of Yuchi animal stories and storytelling. This trickster tale was told by Ida Clinton Riley, who as a young girl worked with linguist Günter Wagner and whose stories appear in *Yuchi Tales*. She clearly had more. Close to the end of her long life, Yuchi language activist Gregory Bigler would visit her, and he recorded this tale. Bigler, with Maggie Marsey and the Euchee Language Class of Sapulpa, transcribed and translated it.[15] Even in her frail voice, she commands the audience with her storytelling up to the end, with what is in effect a punch line. At church gatherings, on feast days, and at home, the more traditional Yuchi women still eat last. I have often heard the bitterly humorous last line of this narrative quoted by female Yuchi speakers to other women at such occasions, with the response of much giggling and laughter even by non-Yuchi speakers.

Other Yuchi animal trickster tales can be found in Linn and Jackson 2004 (revised and reprinted in Jackson's *Yuchi Folklore* in 2013). Outside storytelling or teaching events created for language camps and classes, I have never heard a Yuchi animal tale being told in full. However, the genre is reemerging. The teachers and students involved in the Yuchi/Euchee Language Project have been setting the stories as skits, which the students perform for the Yuchi community and wider audiences. Stories such as "Rabbit and Giant" and "Race between Turtle and Wolf" are given new life in this way.

STORIES OF THE SUPERNATURAL

Scancarelli describes Cherokee stories of personal experiences with the supernatural as an important verbal art form and an important factor in affirming cultural beliefs in the presence of supernatural forces in daily life.[16] Stories of the supernatural may be chance interactions with

Little People, encounters with the forces of bad medicine, and the presence of those from the spirit world making themselves known through strange lights, noises, and other sensory stimuli.[17] This genre is clearly represented in Yuchi daily life. For example, Josephine Wildcat Bigler tells of the night that a favorite aunt passed away. She was not in Oklahoma with her at the time of her death. She recalls sitting quietly at home when her teacup on the side table rattled all by itself and almost fell off. She knew then that her aunt had passed and that she had been there in the room with her. William Cahwee would tell of sitting on the porch as a young boy and watching a strange light make its way down the hillside. No one ever came to the house, and they never heard of anyone in the woods that night.

As reported by Scancarelli for Cherokee, these stories in Yuchi are not told to inspire fear, as ghost stories in English are supposed to do. Instead, they confirm long-held beliefs in the interaction between this world of the living and the after world and engender respect for powers that humans do not understand and control. In these stories the speaker always reacts calmly, even in intense or seemingly life-threatening situations. Not having fear, overcoming fear, or not showing fear is in part how the living should interact appropriately with the supernatural. Having personal interaction with the supernatural is part of being Yuchi, and telling these stories reaffirms connections between family, community, and the supernatural world.

As with other personal narratives, stories of the supernatural often become part of a person's repertoire. They are told many times over a lifetime, always to intent listeners. Even those not prone to talking about themselves often have a story about the supernatural to contribute. Personal stories are enduring to the individual and to Yuchi culture. These narratives are told in Yuchi, and unlike other genres, they have survived the shift to English as well. Thus I have found that personal stories of the supernatural are the most abundant uniquely indigenous genre in Yuchi culture today.

Jeremiah Curtin collected supernatural stories in Yuchi. He titled his typed version of the stories "Yutci Beliefs," and handwritten on the top of the page he notes in parentheses "Modern."[18] I have renamed them Spirit Stories here to give a better indication of the content. The Euchee Dictionary Project women and I do not believe that what Curtin recorded were modern beliefs for the nineteenth century but that they are told today just as they were told many hundreds to thousands of years before Curtin arrived. His account is extremely important because, unusual for its time, Curtin recorded not only the supernatural stories themselves but the storytelling event in which they occurred. One can imagine the people sitting around the small, breezy cabin after dinner that cold winter night. Sam Brown's cabin sat near the bank of the Arkansas River, close to Wialaka Mission, where a produce center in Bixby, Oklahoma, sits today. Curtin states in his manuscript that the talk "turned on spirits," exactly as it does today after a meal when people are sitting around. The guests at the Browns' home pass around turns and tell about an encounter with a spirit, and when more such storytelling goes on for a while, the conversation finally drifts into how people are supposed to behave when a loved one passes, and how customs, though known, are not being kept correctly today. This scene could be transplanted exactly as it is from 1883 to today. The enduring nature of the stories and the storytelling event itself suggest that interactions between human and supernatural had been worthy of retelling long before this account.

NOTES

1. For an overview of the Yuchi see J. B. Jackson, "Yuchi," in *Handbook of North American Indians,* vol. 14: *Southeast,* ed. Raymond D. Fogelson, 415–428 (Washington DC: Smithsonian Institution, 2004.).
2. G. Bigler and M. Marsey, *Yuchi-haw Go-wa-da-na, Material from a Yuchi Language Class* (Sapulpa OK: Sapulpa Indian Community of the Muscogee, 1991).
3. J. Curtin, Yutci Myths (1884), Manuscript no. 1293, National Anthropological Archives, Smithsonian Institution, Washington DC.
4. Sam Brown spoke both Yuchi and English. In his journals Curtin wrote about learning the Yuchi language from Brown, but given his short stay, Curtin may never have written the stories in Yuchi, especially the Spirit Stories, as the journal indicates that this was collected the first night that Curtin arrived. J. Curtin, *Memoirs of Jeremiah Curtin,* ed. Joseph Schafer (Madison: Wisconsin State Historical Society, 1940), 327.

5. The Euchee (Yuchi) Dictionary Project was funded by NSF Documenting Endangered Languages grant.
6. A. Gatschet, "Some Mythic Stories of the Yuchi Indians," *American Anthropologist*, 6, no. 3 (1893): 279–82.
7. G. Wagner, *Yuchi Tales*, Publications of the American Ethnological Society 13, ed. F. Boas (New York: G.E. Stechert and Company, 1931; repr. New York: AMS Press, 1974).
8. W. L. Ballard, 1970–75, Yuchi transcriptions and recording from Ballard.
9. For the Waxin Tiger stories see M. Linn and J. Jackson, "Trickster in Transition: Changing Contexts for Yuchi Tales," in *Voices from Four Directions*, ed. Brian Swann, 368–82 (Lincoln: University of Nebraska Press, 2004), reprinted in J. Jackson, *Yuchi Folklore: Cultural Expression in a Southeastern Native American Community* (Norman: University of Oklahoma Press (2013), 44–56.
10. M. Haas, 1940. Brief notes on Yuchi, American Philosophical Society Library, Philadelphia; H. Wolff, "Yuchi Text with Analysis," *International Journal of American Linguistics* 17 (1951): 48–53; J. Crawford, Field Notebooks, 1970–73, American Philosophical Society Library, Philadelphia; M. Linn, *A Grammar of Euchee (Yuchi)*, PhD diss., University of Kansas, 2001.
11. J. Jackson, *Yuchi Ceremonial Life: Performance, Meaning, and Tradition in a Contemporary American Indian Community*, Studies in the Anthropology of North American Indians Series (Lincoln: University of Nebraska Press, 2003).
12. Jackson, *Yuchi Folklore*.
13. See J. Swanton, *Myths and Tales of the Southeastern United States*, Bureau of American Ethnology Bulletin 88 (Washington DC: Government Printing Office, 1929); J. Kilpatrick and A. Kilpatrick, *Friends of Thunder: Folktales of the Oklahoma Cherokees* (Dallas: Southern Methodist University Press, 1964); Jackson, *Yuchi Ceremonial Life;* Jackson, *Yuchi Folklore*, 227.
14. Jackson, *Yuchi Folklore*, 86–99.
15. Bigler and Marsey, *Yuchi-haw Go-wa-da-na.*
16. J. Scancarelli, "Cherokee Stories of the Supernatural," *Kansas Working Papers in Linguistics* 21 (1996): 143–58.
17. For Cherokee and Choctaw stories of Little People see Kilpatrick and Kilpatrick, *Friends of Thunder*, and T. Mould, *Choctaw Tales* (Jackson: University of Mississippi Press, 2004).
18. Curtin spelled the name of the tribe *Yutci.*

Mythical Time Stories

The Red-Mouthed Lizard and the Hunters

Maxey Simms, narrator (1928)
Günter Wagner, collector and transcriber. Mary S. Linn, editor.

A long time ago, some people gathered together and agreed to round up a bear. They went out, and while they were hunting, they found a hollow tree with the bark scratched off where something must have climbed it often. They made a fire around the tree and watched for the bear to come out so they could kill it. One of them climbed up with a big burning coal. He threw in the coal and when it fell in, the thing came out. It looked out of the hollow tree, but it was not the right animal.

It was a red-mouthed lizard.

When the people they saw it, they ran off. The lizard came down and ran after them.

The one who had thrown the fire in was still sitting on a limb. He moved a little out of the way. The lizard followed the people who had run off. He could hear shooting, and then a call for help. And then it was silent.

It was not long before the lizard brought one of them back in his mouth and threw him in the hollow tree. At once he went back, and not long after that, somebody shot, called for help, and then immediately the lizard caught him and brought him back to the hollow tree and threw him in. The lizard picked off all the people this way.

The man who had climbed the tree was still up there. He did not know what he could do to escape. The lizard did not see him. Every once in a while the lizard would climb down to hunt, then came back and go in the tree again. It would climb down, but he did not find another person. A very long time passed and then the lizard went down again to hunt, and when he did not find anybody, he went back into the hollow tree. Then even more time passed, and he went down to hunt again. So now, the man on the limb thought he could get very far before the lizard came out again. Finally, the lizard went down to hunt, and just when he went into the hollow tree again, the man climbed down and ran off.

He went along for a long time. And then he heard the lizard coming. He did not know what to do. While he was running, the tiger came up and stood there.

"What are you doing here?" the tiger asked.

"We were many people, but something fierce killed all of them. I am the only one left, and I am running because he is after me," he said.

"You go over there and watch. I will fight him," the tiger said.

The lizard got there, and he and the tiger fought. The tiger said to the lizard, "Shoot me!" he said.

The lizard threw sparks of fire at him, and the tiger threw sparks of fire back at him. In this way they shot at each other. The tiger was defeated. The lizard killed him and ran back with him.

The man ran on. He could hear the lizard coming back. Just then there was an opossum, and when the man got up to him, the possum said, "I will fight the lizard. Go over there and watch," he said.

"You cannot do anything," the man thought.

The lizard was coming, and just as soon as the possum saw him, he shook himself. The man saw the possum grow bigger, and he had faith in him. But when the lizard got there, the possum at once fell down and pretended to be dead. The lizard took him and went back with him.

The man ran on. This time when he heard the lizard coming, he did not have any hope. While he was running, he met the polecat. "Something fierce is running after me," he said. "He killed the others, and I alone am left.

"You go over there and watch. I will do it," said the polecat.

Then the polecat shook himself, hit the ground and grew big. The lizard got there and ran after him with his mouth open. The polecat ran away. While he was being chased, the polecat suddenly ran backwards and shot into the lizard's mouth. The lizard got dizzy, and when he fell down, the polecat ran up close to him and shot into his mouth and also into his nostrils. In this way, the polecat killed him, they said.

The polecat helped the man very much and saved him. And so the man, whom the polecat helped, should not eat him they said. But the polecat tastes very good, and so they used to eat him anyway.

Afterwards, they went back to where the man had thrown the coal into the hollow tree. When they got there, they cut the tree down. The people that the lizard had killed were in there, and so they took them out. Young lizards were in the tree, and those they also killed.

How the Yuchi Kill the Red-Mouthed Lizard

Andy Johnson, narrator (1928)

Günter Wagner, collector and transcriber. Mary S. Linn, editor.

When the earth was just made, there was plenty of game, and fierce beings were also plentiful. Four sons went hunting.[1] Two of them were left to watch the road together. There was a very dark pine woods, and in this grove, there was a very tall pine tree with eagle feathers lying underneath it. One of the young men wanted to get the feathers, but when he realized it was the nest of a red-mouthed lizard, he immediately ran away.

The next young man went up to the tree, close to the eagle feathers. The red-mouthed lizard came out of his nest and crowed "*Stistihę!*" Then he jumped out and ran after him.

The young man had not run very far when the lizard reached him and caught him. The lizard took him by this side and put him in his nest.

Then, the lizard went after the other young man, but he had set fire to the underbrush. He jumped through the fire and escaped.

When he got back to where his relatives were camping, he reported what had happened. They all fled back to their town.

When they got there, they gathered at their Big House to make their medicine.[2] They appointed one of the old men to make medicine, and they appointed four young men to kill the big red-mouthed lizard. The old man made medicine for this purpose. When they left, the old man carried only an axe, and the young men each carried a bow and four arrows with points to help them.

The old man led them as they went to the red-mouthed lizard's nest. When they got near, he instructed the young men, telling them that they should shoot at the lizard's throat since there a point could pierce him.

Then the old man climbed up to the tree and pounded on it. He pounded four times. The lizard came out and went to the top of the tree. And then they shot him right in the throat, and he fell back into the tree. The old man chopped into the tree and cut it down. There were young lizards inside, and he pounded them all to death. He gathered their bodies together and burned them all.

Of the young man whom the lizard had killed, only his bones were left. They picked them all up, put them in a sack, and brought them back to their Big House. Then all his kinfolk gathered there and put his bones in a box and buried them.

NOTES

1. Wagner translated this "four Yuchi men" (*Yuchi Tales*, 238–43). The text in Yuchi reads literally "the-Yuchi-people four sons." Later in the text, one of the men runs to their relatives' camp. So I have translated the four as being sons from a family hunting camp. This also brings the story into alignment with the setting in the Monster Lizard sacred narrative (Jackson, *Yuchi Folklore,* 183). Yet another interpretation, given that is it set in mythological time, could be that the Yuchi people chose four young men to hunt for the tribe, thus representing sons of the tribe.
2. Big House is an older term for the ceremonial grounds. It is still used metaphorically today to refer to the clean ground, or sacred area, of the ceremonial grounds.

Wind and Iron

Maxey Simms, narrator (1928)
Günter Wagner, collector. Translated by Mary S. Linn (2013).

The wind sent his young boys across the world to see the earth.[1] He himself had no arms and no legs, and was just lying there, so he sent his youngsters off. One after the other, he sent them away, and every time he had sent one, the young man did not come back. The youngsters all kept going, and not even one came back. And then Wind said, "What can be so fierce that every time I send one of my sons, he never comes back? I will go and see."

And so he made himself and his clothes ready to go. Turtles were his shoes, a softshell turtle was his side bag, and his side bag strings were rattlesnakes. A diamond-back rattlesnake was his belt. Black ratsnakes were his leggings. His pipe was a bullfrog, his tobacco the tie snake, his matches a glass lizard, and his pipestem a spotted snake.[2] An alligator was his chair. And then he left. He wanted to find out why his sons did not come home, and so he went across the world.

While he was going, he came to a river. On the other side of it there was a house with a white rooster standing there and watching the road. Right after he saw the wind, he ran back, got on top of the house and crowed. Right then a man came out, got into a boat and came over.

"Stay there, and I will come across with a boat and you can get in!" the man called.

But Wind did not stop, and when the man got there with the boat, again he said, "Get in my boat!"

Wind answered, "Be it so, I got my own boat," and he walked cross on top of the water.

And when he got to the house, he set a chair before Wind and said, "Though it only be a chair, please sit on it!"

"Be it so, I got my own chair." Then Wind threw down the alligator. He just stretched himself, and then sat down on it.

The man set a pipe before him and said, "Sir, if only you would take my pipe and smoke my tobacco."

"Be it so, I got my own pipe," he said. He took out the bullfrog and for a pipestem, he pulled out the spotted snake and stuck it in the frog.

"Sir, if only you would smoke my tobacco."

"Be it so, I got my own tobacco," he said and he took out the tie snake and put it in the mouth of the bullfrog.

"You can use my matches," he said.

"Be it so, I got my own matches." The glass lizard was his match.

Wind lighted the glass lizard, and the tobacco also lighted. He drew the tobacco in, and when the smoke spread, the snakes got mad and jumped about. When the man whose house this was saw this, he said, "You are a very powerful person, it is true."

But Wind answered him, "Be it so, you will get to know me."

While they were sitting there talking, Wind said, "Every time I sent my youngsters around the world, they did not come back."

"They are here, but they never think of you now they are here," the man answered.

While Wind was sitting there and smoking the tobacco, the man smelled the smoke. He fell over, making a loud rattling noise. It was Iron who fell over.

His wife was out in the yard pounding corn, and Wind asked her, "Where did he send the youngsters?"

When she answered, "He threw them in the water over yonder," he asked, "Which direction did he say they would return from?"

She answered, "He said to cut down that tree over there and let it fall into the water, then they will come back."

"Well then, cut down the tree and let it fall into the water," he said. And the woman chopped the tree. When it fell into the water, the young people that Iron had thrown in appeared right away on the surface. They came to the bank, but they were not the same as they were before. Wind made them again, and sent them far and wide.

Then Wind cut up the tree that the woman had chopped down, built a fire and threw the wood into the fire until it was blazing high. The he caught the woman and threw her into the fire. Every time she got out, he threw her back in again until she was very small. Then he made a rat out of her.

And then Wind said, "I will be lying in the water right here, but some day, I will go back cross the world. I will sweep all over the world." Then he lay down again.

And so someday, the wind will come out and sweep across the land, so they used to say.

NOTES

Wagner gives the title "Wind seeks his lost sons and kills the Iron Monster" (*Yuchi Tales*, 76–81). I have chosen Curtin's simpler and more suspenseful "Wind and Iron."—*Mary S. Linn*

1. Maxey Simms uses the word *goyathlēnā* (more accurately *go'yathlēnā,* which Wagner consistently transcribed as 'youngster.' Both other versions and Wagner's title use 'sons.' The Yuchi word can mean both 'young man' and 'young person of either sex,' although when specifically referring to a young woman, the form *wæ'yathlēnā* is used. Therefore I have translated the words as 'his sons' while using 'youngsters' periodically for variation.
2. The glass lizard is a species of legless lizard that 'breaks' in defense when it is handled. The Yuchi direct translation is 'breaking snake.' The 'spotted snake' translation comes from Curtin, as neither Wagner nor Speck knew the name of this snake in English, and speakers do not recognize the species Simms names.

Animal Tales

The First Woman to Leave a Lazy Husband

Narrator unknown (1883). Jeremiah Curtin, collector.
Maggie Cumpsey Marsey, Josephine Barnett Keith, Josephine Wildcat Bigler, Maxine Wildcat Barnett, and Mary S. Linn, editors, 2006.

A long time ago, there was a Yuchi man and a pigeon. The pigeon married the man's sister. After the pigeon was married, he went off into the field to work, but he sat on the stump of a dead tree cooing. The woman cooked dinner and went out into the field to call her husband and found him sitting on the tree just cooing.

He went back into the house with her that evening, but he wasn't good for work, and at last the woman left him.

Her next husband was a mockingbird. He went into the field to work, too. The woman got dinner and went into the field to call him. She found him singing all sorts of songs. He hadn't done a bit of work.

He went home to dinner, stayed all day and all night, but she found he wasn't a worker. And so she turned him out.

Her third husband was a lizard. He went into the field. She heard no noise.

All was quiet.

At noon, she went out to call him and found him hard at work, cutting down each blade of grass.

He was a good worker, and the woman was satisfied. They lived happily.

This was the first woman who wouldn't live with a lazy husband.

Rabbit and Turkeys

Ida Clinton Riley, narrator (1990, *Yuchi and English*)

Gregory Bigler, collector and translator. Mary S. Linn, editor.

Rabbit was in a sack rolling down a hill, just laughing. Turkeys were going by. They heard the rabbit laughing. They came to the edge of the hill to see what Rabbit was doing. Rabbit saw the turkeys. He asked if they would like to try. He got back into the sack, and rolled down the hill again. He asked the turkeys again if they wanted to try. They said they would, except one. Finally, he changed his mind, and he got into the sack. Rabbit tied it up, and he rolled it down the hill once or twice. Then he threw the sack over his shoulder and carried it home.

He put the sack in the corncrib and told his wife not to open it.

His wife said, "I wonder what he has inside? I am going to see."

She opened the crib door, and when she did, all the turkeys scattered. She managed to catch one by the leg. "I caught a leg!" she cried.

"I told you not to open the door!" Rabbit said. "Don't just say you caught a leg, make some hot water! We will kill the turkey and eat it. I have asked my friends to eat with us. They are bashful. When they get here, you have to wait outside."

So she set the table. Then she went outside.

Rabbit was talking and walking around the table making noise. He ate out of each of the plates, piling the bones beside them. Then he told her, "They are all gone now, you can come in!"

"They ate up the turkey, all that is left is the bones. You can just suck on the bones!"

YUCHI LANGUAGE VERSION WITH ENGLISH CORRESPONDENCES

Shach'wanā ba du'ā s'œba 'yadā wābēthlo.

A Rabbit was in a sack rolling down a hill.

Dakā wāk'œchyachya.

Just laughing.

Wācha'œ gāwāgā jẽfa.

Turkeys were going by.

Shachw'anũhnũh wāk'œk'œ yõch'œ.

They heard Rabbit laughing.

S'œba dādahā ayõgœ Shach'wanāwānũh gala k'œthlœ'ẽ wāthla gēwā'nā.

They came to the edge of the hill to see what Rabbit was doing.

Wācha'œwānũh Shach'wanā wā'nā.

Rabbit saw the turkeys.

Wādēdāsuh wāyu'nẽ'nẽ wātœ yõ'œnā.

He asked them if they would like to try.

Bachē tēlā wāthla.

He got back in the sack.

Dāpulā yœdœ wābēthlo.

And rolled down the hill.

Dāpulā wācha'œ wānũh yo'œnā wāyu'nẽ'nẽ wātœ dēchē.

He asked the Turkeys again if they wanted to try.

Gā'ẽ wāthla dālœ wāgwa hēt'ālā hœgā'ẽ wāthla dẽ.

They said they would, except one.

K'ẽshta'ẽdā wākyũhnā k'ayõthlœ.

Finally he changed his mind.

Bachē dē wāthla.

He got in the sack.

Shach'wanā bachē yũhkwœ hẽdā sahalā nāha'e yœdœ yõbēthlo.

Rabbit tied it up and he rolled it down the hill once or twice.

Bachē wādēt'ẽ dawāpa hẽdā gēlā wāk'ũhthla.

Then he threw the sack over his shoulder and carried it home.

Bachē dodada dē'yũhdẽ hẽdā wāk'at'õnũh nẽk'ayũhta yõgwa

He put the sack in the corn crib and told his wife not to open it.

Wāk'atõnũ ogwa, "Wēgœ badēchē wāha?"

His wife said, "I wonder what he has inside?"

"Dē'nẽ," wāgwa.

"I am going to see," she said.

"Dodada." Yudash'ē koyõta.

"I'm going to go see." She opened the crib door.

Kosēotahā wācha'œ wānũh hēlā gālā gāwāstunũh.

When she did, all the Turkeys scattered.

Hēt'ālā wādāha sēohālẽ.

She managed to catch one by the leg.

"Wādā'ā dohũhlā," sāgwa.

She said, "I caught a leg!"

Shach'wanā ogwa, "Ēdashēfa nẽkoyũhta asogwajẽ.

Rabbit said, "I told you not to open the door.

Nẽgodā'ālā dohālẽ hõgwa.

Don't just say you caught a leg.

Dzāshahē k'ũh.

Make some hot water.

Wācha'œonũh wā'ũht'wa hẽdā wā'ũhthlœ.

We will kill the Turkey and eat it.

Dēk'adēnāhẽnũh go'a ha õdzāthlœ dẽchē hõdo'œnẽjẽ.

I have asked some friends to eat with us.

Nẽhã thlēhā thlahā wāsha yosh'ẽ hõdā'a b'ẽwã."

When they get here, you have to wait outside because they are bashful."

Yastadagothlœnāchē shẽshē sāthla.

She set the table.

Hẽdā thlahā sēothlajẽ.

Then she went outside.

Shachw'anõnũh wā'wādā yastadagothlœnāchē yulā'adā dakā chœchœhẽ wānũh.

Rabbit was talking and walking around the table making noise.

Dadanā dēt'œgā dēwāthlœ, wāsh'ẽha k'œlā wāk'wẽ dāshœ'ẽ.

He ate out of each plate, piling the bones beside them.

"Gādā yudēguhnũh hõfādā," hẽhõgwa.

He told her, "They are gone now, you can come in.

Wācha'œwānũh hēlā hõlaha wāsh'ẽ halā howẽ.
They ate up the Turkey, all that is left is the bones.
Wāsh'ẽ halādā nedzā yodudu hātāgũh!"
Just suck the juice out of the bones!"

Stories of the Supernatural

Spirit Stories

Mr. and Mrs. Sam Brown and another unknown narrator (1883).
Jeremiah Curtin, collector. Translated by Mary S. Linn (2013).

One evening at the house of Mr. Brown, a half-Yuchi and treasurer of Creek Nation, the conversation turned on spirits. There were present at the time Mr. and Mrs. Brown, an old man who had the reputation of being a great medicine man, and a Yuchi policeman.[1]

The policeman said, "One time I was going home in the night and something seized the reins of my horse so he couldn't move forward. We had buried a man late that evening. It was rainy and foggy. I lived ten miles from the place where the man was buried, and the people there wanted me to stay all night, but I thought I would go home. After I had gone about two miles, the horse stopped suddenly and backed up with me. My body grew cold, and my hair stood up on my head. I drew out my pistol and at that instant, my horse pulled away from what was holding him and ran away with me.

"When I go through a graveyard, I carry a knife and they don't bother me. A good many people have a song to drive the spirits away."

The old man answered, saying, "I have medicine and a song I drive the spirits away with. When this medicine is in my pocket, the spirits cannot touch me." He showed a piece of sassafras root about an inch long.

Mr. Brown then began, "My wife's uncle died, and one year later I lost a child. We wanted to move the uncle's body to a new burying place. I went over to the place to see about the removal, and as I rode along near the fence enclosing the ground, I saw a man walking by the fence. I thought it was the uncle, and I said to the man I was with, 'Do you see that man?' He couldn't see anyone. The old man was dressed in the same kind of clothes as those he wore just before his death. He soon disappeared, vanished as I was looking at him. The body had been brought over the road to the burial ground, and this shows that the spirit was following the body."

Mrs. Brown added that she thought a good man's spirit will come back to his friends.

Then the policeman said, "Formerly, when a person died, all the people in the neighborhood remained quietly in their houses for four days. No work of any kind was done. Of late, this has changed. Old people used to think of the dead a long time and would not comb their hair. When they were cooking the last food for the dead man, on the third evening after his death, the favorite horse was bridled and tied near the grave so the spirit could ride. Some keep up the custom of cooking for the dead. Others don't."

NOTES

The original title is "Yutci Spiritualism (Modern)"—*Mary S. Linn*

1. Curtin's translation is "wizard." In his journal he writes that Mr. Brown had invited an "old man reputed to be wise" (Curtin, *Memoirs,* 327).

CHEROKEE

Cherokee Literature

Christopher B. Teuton

In the prospectus for the *Cherokee Phoenix*, published in October 1827, Cherokee writer and editor Elias Boudinot outlined the lofty goals for this first American Indian newspaper.[1] The biweekly periodical published in both English and Cherokee would present:

> The laws and public documents of the Nation.
> Account of the manners and customs of the Cherokees, and their progress in Education, Religion and the arts of civilized life; . . .
> The principal interesting news of the day.
> Miscellaneous articles, calculated to promote Literature, Civilization, and Religion among the Cherokees.

From 1828 to 1834 the *Cherokee Phoenix* served the Cherokee in the ways Boudinot lists, demonstrating both to the Cherokee Nation and to the many subscribers of the newspaper outside it that the Cherokee were a people on the rise. Boudinot, like others of his day, held that "Literature, Civilization, and Religion" develop hand in hand. Thus while the *Cherokee Phoenix* was a source of news, it was also a living symbol of the literate, Christian—in other words, "civilized"—nature of Cherokee society.

For the class of Cherokees like Boudinot who had been educated by Christian missionaries, and for other Western-educated Americans at the time, human societies were understood to exist in a hierarchy with "savages" at the bottom and the "civilized" on top. As historian Theda Perdue explains, "'Savages' hunted for a living, relied on frequently brutal customs for their law, worshiped nature or idols, and lacked a written language." Civilized people, on the other hand, had "farms, republican governments, Christian churches, and systems of writing." For those labeled as "savage," as were the Cherokee and other Native Americans at the time, there was hope: "Because of a common humanity, men and their societies could progress, and even the most 'primitive' society could become 'civilized.'"[2] In 1827 the Cherokee were eager to demonstrate they were indeed civilized. Although they had been at peace with the United States since 1800, the ravages of the colonial period continued. European diseases such as smallpox had decimated Cherokee communities several times since the seventeenth century. They had suffered sustained incursions into their homelands, which led to decades of armed conflicts and outright wars with the British and Americans. By 1827 the Cherokee had signed twenty-seven treaties, almost all of which ceded land to Great Britain and then the United States. Though reduced to a fraction of its original size, Cherokee Nation territory was still lusted after by colonists. The ready excuse used by Americans that Native peoples such as the Cherokee did not "improve" their lands by deforesting and cultivating them was often used as a justification for inciting conflicts or rationalizing further conquest. In spite of this history, by 1827 the Cherokee were prosperous, among the wealthiest people in the Southeast.

The Cherokee had adapted. They had come to understand that their best protection as a people lay in embracing certain forms of Euro-American acculturation. By the first third of the nineteenth century the Cherokee Nation had adopted a model of government and constitution modeled on the U.S. government and Constitution. The Cherokee Nation had incorporated capitalism and agrarianism into its economy, and embraced Western education, and many of its members had become Christian. Literacy, both in the Sequoyan script of the Cherokee language and in English, became a cornerstone of Cherokee society. Emblematized by the *Cherokee Phoenix* newspaper, literacy for Cherokee nationalists like Elias Boudinot held out the hope that the Cherokee Nation would be able to continue to prosper and exist independently, without further attacks on its land base or people. Of course, that was not to happen, and the Cherokee were forcibly relocated to Indian Territory in what is now Oklahoma, ethnically cleansed from their southeastern homelands due to the Removal policy of the United States.

I begin this introduction to Cherokee literature with Elias Boudinot and the *Cherokee Phoenix* in order to highlight how Cherokee literature, literacy, and even oral storytelling should be approached with consideration of the politicized contexts in which these cultural constructs are written, recorded, and told. Boudinot was a fluent Cherokee speaker; he undoubtedly grew up with Cherokee oral tradition. However, what he referred to as "Literature" would not include oral traditional stories but written works conforming to a Euro-American aesthetic. Beginning with Boudinot's era, Cherokee society as a whole has valued Western education and literacy in particular. Since the nineteenth century Cherokee writers in English have been numerous and influential. The first Native American novel, *The Life and Adventures of Joaquin Murieta*, was published by John Rollin Ridge in California in 1854. John Milton Oskison, Lynn Riggs, Will Rogers, Wilson Rawls, N. Scott Momaday, Louis Owens, Robert J. Conley, Wilma Mankiller, Sequoyah Guess—and many, many more writers of literary art—have shaped not only Cherokee letters but Native American and American literature as a whole. If one embraces a more expansive definition of the literary to include letters and newspaper material, Cherokee literature becomes vast and inclusive of writings in Sequoyan as well as English.

What we mean by literacy and literature is culturally contextual and changes over time. For Boudinot and other writers of the nineteenth century, stories that arose out of Cherokee folklore and worldview would not conform to the image of the people that they wanted to project in order to defend the Cherokee Nation from further political incursions. The result is that there are few examples of Cherokee oral tradition until the publication of ethnologist James Mooney's *Myths of the Cherokee*, recorded among the Eastern Band of Cherokee Indians in Western North Carolina and published in 1900. Nevertheless, though those stories were rarely published, Cherokees maintained their oral stories and teachings, passing them along from generation to generation as a way to share Cherokee values and knowledge. Cherokee literature, then, includes both the written and the oral, writing that arises out of a context of colonialism, and stories that are rooted in a people's relationship to place. Literary writing began among the Cherokee as a way to explain and defend the people; oral tradition sustained them.

The story of Cherokee oral tradition begins in their relationships with their homelands. Cherokees have lived for thousands of years farming and hunting in the mountains and river valleys of what is now western North Carolina, northern Georgia, northern South Carolina, northeastern Alabama, and Tennessee. Since the time of Removal in 1838–39, Cherokee people and governments have also been in what is now Oklahoma. All this time, Cherokees have been learning about the world they inhabit. They study the ways the animals interact. They learn about the plants. They consider the earth, waters, weather, and seasons. They remember where they come from and they reflect on the teachings they know. I phrase this description in the present tense because Cherokees continue to have relationships with their homelands and to reflect on the histories that have been shaped within them. From Elias Boudinot's time until today, Cherokees share that knowledge with one another through orally told stories and teachings.

Cherokee peoplehood is maintained through language and literacy, and we can be thankful that the terms and ideas used to understand Cherokee writing and stories have changed considerably since Boudinot's time. We Cherokee no longer need to proclaim to the educated our equality as civilized people, and consequently, we need not be as wary to publish our oral traditional stories, teachings, and customs that are appropriate to share publicly. Like other Native peoples, until recently the Cherokee were almost exclusively studied, explained, and written about in books by non-Cherokees. Today Cherokee scholars, storytellers, and writers are publishing their own books and offering insights, experiences, and knowledge that had not previously been considered.

The selections that follow would normally be classified in genres such as "oral tradition," "memoir," and "autobiography," all of which arise out of Western literary and scholarly tradition and have their unique characteristics. The selections come from a variety of sources separated by time, place, and method of collection and recording. Some were written rather than told and recorded. Some of the stories are told by speakers of Cherokee, some are not. All are presented in English. And while study of their formal diversity might be interesting, the form of these selections is not as instructive as considering what unifies them as samples of Cherokee literature. In order to answer this question, we need to frame the selections within a Cherokee linguistic and cultural context.

When I was working with my elders on *Cherokee Stories of the Turtle Island Liars' Club*, from which several of the stories in this section are excerpted, I was taught that the stories themselves are not what matters most; more important are the values that they teach and the relationships that in their telling and sharing they weave. What matters is the *sgadug*, the community, that the stories and teachings serve. While diverse in form, all these selections of Cherokee literature arise out of a context that is decidedly grounded in Cherokee experience, community, and worldview. In order to understand how stories serve the *sgadug*, one needs to have a conception of how stories and storytelling function within a Cherokee context.

Galgoga, which literally means "he or she is lying," is the Cherokee term for "storytelling." When people are "lying," or telling stories as expressed within the Cherokee language, it means that they are using a verb form expressing that they are recounting information they did not actually witness. Stories about the Ancient Time when animals could talk, or about the Cherokee migration—both of which the teller could not have witnessed—are all potentially *galgogv*—"lies." Anything one recounts as true but did not actually witness could be a lie, and that epistemological tension is highlighted, even celebrated, in the word *galgoga*. Every time a *galgogv'i* (liar) tells a *galgogv*, the teller is putting his or her credibility on the line. The question is, what is truth and what is a lie? When listening to or reading these types of stories in Cherokee, in order to gauge the veracity of the story one must depend not only upon one's estimation of the speaker but upon the context of the telling. Why was the story told at a certain time? Who was it for? What does it mean to the listener? These are the types of questions that listeners will consider in silence as they hear a *galgogv*. The term for personal story in the Cherokee language is simply *kanoheda*, or "that which is discussed/told." Unlike *galgoga*, *kanoheda* is taken as factual because speakers would use a verb form indicating they witnessed an event. *Kanoheda* is a suitable term for a personal story as it simply relates that something has been told to a person.

Framing the stories that follow as either *galgogv* or *kanoheda* presents them in a Cherokee cultural context, worldview, and particular register for veracity that lends itself to a specific interpretive approach. As the writer Thomas King suggests, the power of a particular literature is not in its themes—family, home, jealousy, fear, etc.—which are often universal, but "in the way meaning is refracted by cosmology, the way understanding is shaped by cultural paradigms."[3] The stories collected here present but a series of snapshots of Cherokee experience as expressed in oral and written forms of *galgogv* and *kanoheda*, but here are some general themes and ideas to consider in each section.

GALGOGV'I: NEW AND OLD LIES

As you read these stories, consider the relationships they explore, the values they teach, and your experience reading them. While the original contexts for sharing the stories have changed with this presentation of them, key cultural aspects remain. Most of these stories take place in the Ancient Time when animals could talk, before their natures hardened and they became the creatures we know today. In reflecting on these stories that continue to be told from the Smoky Mountains to Oklahoma and beyond, it is up to us as listeners and readers to discern their truths, their lies, and to reflect on the methods we use to make these decisions.

ULVSGEDI: STORIES OF THE WONDROUS

Encounters with the spirit world, the uncanny, and the seemingly inexplicable are worthy of careful thought. The stories in this section were once experienced and shared within particular contexts, each of which would have been worthy of deep consideration as they presented teachings. Even within a Cherokee communal context today, stories of the wondrous, *ulvsgedi*, are presented with little to no context or explanation; either one is aware of the deeper implications of the experience and story for having the cultural knowledge to understand why a spirit or ghost would reveal itself, for example, or one is not. It is clear, however, that stories of the wondrous remind us that existence is larger, more complex, and more alive than how we often imagine it in our quotidian lives.

KANOHEDA: PHILOSOPHY, HISTORY, AND MEMOIR

The oral and written histories in this section chart the connections between the individual and communal in Cherokee life. In "The Language and the Fire" Hastings Shade articulates what many Cherokees think: there are key facets of Cherokee life that must be maintained in order for the People to continue. But as the stories by Harry Oosahwee, Wilma Mankiller, Freeman Owle, and Sequoyah Guess demonstrate, Cherokees have traveled great distances—literally and figuratively—since they first came together as a people. In these ancient and modern stories about movement, change, and continuity, one may discern some of the key concerns of contemporary Cherokee communities. Among these concerns are the importance of the retention and revitalization of the Cherokee language, which is currently endangered; the cultivation of relationships with and in our homelands; and the cultural desire to account for changes in contemporary Cherokee community by considering stories of past movements. In this way, a story—*kanoheda*—provides teachings.

FURTHER READING

For more about Cherokee oral literature, see the texts from which these selections have been drawn: *Cherokee Stories of the Turtle Island Liars' Club*, by Christopher B. Teuton with Hastings Shade, Sammy Still, Sequoyah Guess, and Woody Hansen; *Living Stories of the Cherokee*, edited by Barbara Duncan; and *Friends of Thunder: Folktales of the Oklahoma Cherokee*, by Jack F. and Anna G. Kilpatrick. In addition, James Mooney's *Myths of the Cherokee* remains a crucial source of Cherokee oral tradition. For Cherokee literary history, see *Literacy and Intellectual Life in the Cherokee Nation, 1820–1906*, by James W. Parins, and *Our Fire Survives the Storm: A Cherokee Literary History*, by Daniel Heath Justice.[4]

NOTES

1. Theda Perdue, ed., *Cherokee Editor: The Writings of Elias Boudinot* (Athens: University of Georgia Press, 1996), 15.
2. Perdue, *Cherokee Editor*, 13.
3. Thomas King, *The Truth about Stories: A Native Narrative* (Minneapolis: University of Minnesota Press, 2005), 112.
4. James W. Parins, *Literacy and Intellectual Life in the Cherokee Nation, 1820–1906* (Norman: University of Oklahoma Press, 2013); Daniel Heath Justice, *Our Fire Survives the Storm: A Cherokee Literary History* (Minneapolis: University of Minnesota Press, 2006). The texts from which selections are drawn are cited where pertinent in this volume.

Galgogv'i

New and Old Lies

The Rabbit and the Image

Dalala (1961)
Collected by Jack F. Kilpatrick and Anna G. Kilpatrick

The Maneaters were going to dig a well.[1] There had been no rain, and it was very dry.

The Rabbit came up and asked, "What are all of you doing?"

"We are digging a well for water. Help us, and we can all use it," he was told.

"No. I can find water whenever I need it. You see, I can find mine in the dew."

When he refused [their request], they told him, "All right, when we find our water, don't you be stealing it."

The Rabbit said, "All right, I'll find mine in the dew."

Then the Rabbit left, but that very night he came and got [some of] their water. They found out that they had lost some water, and they said, "We'll assume that the Rabbit did it." And then the following night they lost some more water.

Well, they set a trap for him [the Rabbit]. They set up something in the shape of a person, very sticky. Even if you accidentally touched it, you would be stuck fast to it.

When on the third night the Rabbit came to get some more water, he saw the image standing there. The Rabbit said to it, "Who are you? Move out of the way!"

He kept saying this to the image. The image remained silent.

"Aren't you going to answer me?' he [the Rabbit] said, and hit it [the image] with his fist. The Rabbit became stuck to the image.

Well, he tried to get loose, but he couldn't, and he kept saying, "Let me go! Let me go!" Then he hit the image with his other fist, and that became stuck. Now both arms were stuck.

Well, the next morning when the Maneaters came, they found the Rabbit hanging to the image. They took him off [the image] and said, "We're going to kill him, aren't we?"

"Yes, I'd be glad if you'd kill me," said the Rabbit.

The Maneaters decided not to kill him since he said that he would like to be killed. Then the Maneaters said, "Let's throw him in that huge pile of brush."

The Rabbit said, "I'd like that even better."

"Well, then," they said, "let's just whip him with switches."

Then the Rabbit said, "I'd like that even better."

Then the Maneaters said, "Let's throw him in that dense briar patch."

The Rabbit howled and cried.

So they swung him by his arms over to the briar patch. When they threw him into the briar patch, he whooped and ran away from them [laughs].

That's all I know of that.

NOTE

1. Maneaters are generally a Muskogean, not an Iroquoian, mythological catlike beast.

Rabbit and Possum Look for Wives

Sequoyah Guess (2010)

Collected by Christopher B. Teuton

Rabbit and Possum, they were like best friends.
They grew up together.
From time to time that they were little bitty babies,
they grew up playing together.

They'd stay over at one another's house and everything else.
Sleep over.
And they'd play out in the woods all the time.
And Rabbit, he found out at an early age that he like to play tricks on people.
On anybody.
And old Possum, on the other hand,
he liked everybody.
He was always trying to be helpful.
Wanting to help.
And that's the way they grew up.

But just like you,
just like me,
just like everybody in this world,
Rabbit and Possum,
they kept getting older . . .
and older . . .
and older . . .
and older . . .
until they were really,
really,
old.

Well Rabbit and Possum, you know, like I said, they were friends.
They were best buds, you know.
And so, as they grew older,
while they were growing up,
Rabbit kept getting smarter because he'd always get into fixes and everything.
Among Cherokee stories, Rabbit is always a trickster;
he's always getting into trouble.
And so that's how he grew up.
So by the time he was really old,
he was really, really smart.

On the other hand, Possum,
while he was growing up, like I said,
he's always wanting to be helpful and everything else.
So he started learning medicine.
And when a Keetoowah or Cherokee man,
an Indian man, learns medicine they call him a "medicine man."
If a woman learns medicine, an Indian woman learns medicine,
    they call her a
        "medicine woman."
And since Possum learned medicine
the other animals,
they always called him
        Medicine Possum.

So anyway,
        they got really, really old.
Now, out by where they lived there was this big old shade tree.
And they'd sit under there every day.
And every once in a while they'd go to sleep
while they were watching others going in and out of the village.

Well this one day
        while they were sitting under the tree,
        dozing in the summer sun,
        Rabbit jumped up,
        looked down at Possum and said,
        "Possum!
        You know, I was thinking . . .
        I was barely able to get out of bed this morning."
And old Possum looked at him and said,
        "Yeah, I know what you mean.
        I was barely able to cook my breakfast."
Well old Rabbit said,
"Possum! You know, I was thinking . . .
maybe it's time we got married."

And old Possum said, "Huhn?!'
And old Rabbit said,
"Not to each other!
We need to find us some wives."
And so Possum thought that was a really good idea.
And so they went into the village where they lived
and they started asking everybody they saw,
"Will you marry me?"
"Will you marry me?"
"Will you marry me?"
"Will you marry me?"
But everybody they asked said no.
Like one said,
"Don't be silly, you're a possum and I'm a squirrel. That's not gonna work!"
Another one said,
"You're stupid! You're a Rabbit and I'm a Bear! Just go away."
And so they couldn't find any wives in their hometown.

And so they went back outside, you know,
and sat under the tree.
And old Possum, he was kind of a crybaby type.
He was sitting under there saying,
"Uhh. Nobody likes us.
We're never gonna find any wives."
And remember old Rabbit,
he's always thinking he's smart.
And so after a little bit, he jumped up and said,
"Possum! You know I was thinking . . .
maybe if we go to the next town,
maybe we'll find us some wives there!"
And so Possum thought that was a really neat idea.
And so they started heading to the next town.
And there were cars going up and down that road
and they were dodging.

And old Rabbit, you know, he's quick.
So he wouldn't get hit.
But old Possum, he's kind of slow,
So a car was coming at him
and he couldn't move fast enough and he got hit and got splattered out!
But . . . remember . . .
he's a medicine Possum!
So he fixed himself up
and they took off again.
Well they got halfway to the next town and old Rabbit took off!
Took off running.
Left old Possum just barely going.

Well Rabbit, he got to the next town in no time at all
and he got all of the animals together.
And he jumped up on this big old rock and he said,
"I have a message from the Chief.
The Chief said that he wants everybody in this town
to get married right now!"
And boy howdy, everybody started grabbing each other
and taking off and getting married.
It didn't matter what they were.
A squirrel grabbed a duck and took off and got married.
A coyote grabbed an eagle and took off and got married.
Even a dog grabbed a cat and took off and got married.
That one didn't last long, though, 'cause they were always fighting.

But even old Rabbit, he found himself a cute little bunny and got married.

Well here comes Possum.
Finally made it to the village.
And he started asking everybody,

"Will you marry me?"
"Will you marry me?"
But everybody he asked said no.
Why?
Because they were already married!
Well, he couldn't find no wife there in that village
so he found himself a big old shade tree outside of town
and he was sitting under there,
"Uhhh. Nobody likes me!
Even Rabbit found himself a wife but nobody likes *mee*!"

Well old Rabbit heard
old Possum crying and he kind of felt sorry
that he had played this mean trick on him.
And so he went out there and sat next to old Possum
and after a little bit he jumped up and said,
"Possum! You know I was thinking . . .
maybe if we go to the next town,
maybe we'll find you a wife there."
And Possum though that was a really, really great idea.
So they got out on the road again,
and again they were dodging cars and everything else.
Possum still slow and he got hit and got splattered out again.
But again, he fixed himself up
and they took off.
Well they got halfway to the next town and Rabbit
took off running!
Left old Possum just barely going.
Now Rabbit, when he got to the next town
he got all the animals together again.
He jumped up on this big old stump and he said,
"I have a message from the Chief!
The Chief said that this is one of the laziest towns he's ever
seen
and he wants everybody to start fighting.

Right now!"
And boy howdy everybody took to fighting, right then and there.
It didn't matter what was going on.
Two of 'em ganged up on one and three on one.
Just throwing sticks and stones and everything.
And even some of 'em knew that hii*yah*! stuff.
It was awful!

Everybody in town fighting.
And old Rabbit, he didn't want to get beat up
so he ran out of there real quick.

Now here comes Possum.
Finally made it to the village.
Well, when he got there he saw these animals
rolling around in the dirt and he thought to himself,
"Oh boy! I'll be able to find me a wife here.
There's a party going on here."
And so he went up to the first animals and he said,
"Will you m . . ."
But before he could finish, somebody yelled out,
"Look! There's Possum! Get him!"
And everybody jumped on Possum and started whupping the tar out of him. Everybody taking turns kicking him and hitting him and everything else.
Biting and scratching.
And old Possum didn't know what was going on.
He was just laying on the ground going,
"Ewh! Ach! Ihh! Ah!"
After a while he thought to himself,
"I gotta think of something or they're gonna kill me."
After a while he got real stiff.
And when somebody would hit him he'd just roll over.
When somebody else would kick him,
he'd just roll over.

Finally somebody noticed that he wasn't making any noise or moving around anymore.

And they said,
    "We KILLED him! Oh no! We killed the Medicine Possum!
And everybody started crying and
right when they were crying the hardest,
old Possum jumped up and ran out of that village
and never went back again.
And there's a trick that we learn from Possum that day.
And that is,
    Playing Possum,
    or playing dead.
But you know what?
Gramma said that Possum never did find himself a wife.
He's still looking to this very day.
You know how you can tell that he's still looking for a wife?
When you're going down the road somewhere,
you see him splattered out on the road.
He's headed for the next town to find himself a wife!
At least that's what Gramma said.

How the Possum Lost His Beautiful Tail

Kathi Smith Littlejohn (1998)

Let's hear another one.
Anybody want to hear another one?
What does a possum look like?
Do you think possums are very pretty?
Possums are not very pretty animals if you ask me,
    but did you know

a long time ago
that the possum had the most beautiful tail
of all animals?
It was long and thick and beautiful,
and he was so proud of his tail.
Did you know that he was so proud of that tail
that all he did was comb his tail?
He'd comb it,
and he'd braid it,
and he'd put ribbons in it,
and the other animals didn't like that.
They'd say,
"Possum, come and help me today."
"Oh no. I've got to wash my tail."
And they'd say,
"Well, possum, how are you today?"
And he'd swish around,
and he'd stick that old tail in their face
and say,
"Me and my tail are just fine, thank you very much."
Well, they didn't like that.
It wasn't nice.
And so
the possum was so conceited and thinking about his tail,
he never once thought that the fox had a pretty tail,
that the other animals had pretty tails.
He didn't care.
But they decided that they were gonna get rid of his tail.
And they knew
that he wanted to be the lead dancer,
so they wouldn't let him
'cause his tail would get in the way.
But this time
they said,
"You can be the lead dancer."

And sure enough
he was so excited
he went over to the cricket,
and he said, "I want you to fix my tail."
'Cause cricket was the barber to all the animals.
And he combed his hair,
and he hummed a little song,
until possum fell asleep.
And when he fell asleep,
cricket cut off every hair on his tail,
made it so ugly and naked.
Eogh.
Then to hide it,
he tied it up in a ribbon,
and when possum saw that he said,
"What have you done?"
He said,
"Oh, I have made a beautiful tail hair design.
Don't take the ribbon off until you're dancing.
Then everyone will love it."
Well, possum was there the next morning,
and they started,
and he was the lead dancer,
and he stepped out and started dancing,
and he reached back and took that ribbon off,
and sure enough
everybody pointed at his tail.
Oh, he loved it,
he danced so hard,
he'd throw that old tail around,
and then,
he saw that
they were laughing and pointing at his tail,
and he thought,
"Laughing? They aren't supposed to be laughing at my tail."

And he looked back over his shoulder,
        and he saw that naked, bony-looking tail.
He was so embarrassed, guess what he did?
He rolled over and played like he was dead.
And even today,
        that's what possums will do,
        they'll roll over and play like they're dead.
And that's how the possum lost his beautiful,
        beautiful tail.

Thunder and the *Uk'ten'*

Siquanid' (1961)
Collected by Jack F. Kilpatrick and Anna G. Kilpatrick

This is the story of when an Uk'ten and Thunder had a fight.[1] Some people tell it a little different. When I hear other people tell it, sometimes it [their version] seems better. This one I know is a little bit similar, and others have told it before. The older men used to tell this one. This one tells about how the Uk'ten' and Thunder found each other.

In olden times there were two boys. They used to hunt all the time with bows and arrows. Sometimes they killed birds and squirrels, sometimes rabbits and many smaller animals.

Once the two boys were walking in a deep valley where it was very rugged and rocky. As they were walking among big rocky crags, they found a large snake lying upon a rock. This snake was large enough to eat squirrels. This snake was very lean and hungry. He told the boys to stop, that he wanted to ask them something.

"I'm very hungry," he said to them, "Would you find me some food? I'll eat birds or squirrels. When I become strong again, you can use me, or I'll help you in whatever you are doing in any way that I can for as long as we live."

So the boys decided to help him. The very next morning they brought him birds and squirrels. They brought him food many times, and he was growing stronger and larger.

Several days later they came by and brought him more squirrels, and this time the snake was huge. Then the boys forgot about him for a while; but then one day they remembered him.

"Let's go by and see him," they said, "and take him some more birds and squirrels."

When they arrived where the snake was, they called him, and he came out of the rocks. This time he was enormous, and he had grown horns. As he was coming out when they called him, they saw lightning-like sparks before they saw his horns. They gave him his squirrels and birds.

The boys said to him, "You certainly are enormous now! You have grown up!"

The snake said, "Yes, but remember: we are to be friends always." (The snake was duping them because he really wanted to kill them soon.)

The next morning they came nearby. As they entered the valley, they heard some blasts in the valley. After several blasts, the blasts became fainter.

The boys said, "Someone is in trouble over there! Let's hurry and get over there! That's where the snake lives." So they hurried over there.

Soon they saw the snake. This snake that they had fed had coiled himself around something. He and Thunder were fighting. He had enveloped Thunder in his coils. The snake was wound about Thunder so tightly that Thunder could make only faint blasts. Thunder could barely move.

"Boys! My nephews!" said Thunder. "This snake that is coiled around me is very fierce and kills people. If you can, do something to kill him! Shoot him in the seventh spot. He'll die instantly!"

The Uk'ten' cried out, "Don't! Don't! Kill Thunder instead! The Thunder is fiercer. His blasts will kill you," said the Uk'ten'. (You see, this snake that these boys fed grew up to be an Uk'ten'.)

The boys were undecided what to do.

"Don't you do it! You boys are my grandchildren, and I am your helper! I always help you! This huge snake that said he would help you was only tricking you. He wanted to kill you. So shoot him on the seventh spot!" said Thunder.

So the boys believed it, and with the Uk'ten' crying, he was shot on the seventh spot. The Uk'ten' fell over, and Thunder was again free.

When Thunder was free, he said to the boys, "Go back in the direction from where you came. On your way build seven fires; build them as you go. You see, the fumes from the Uk'ten' will be stopped by the first fire so that you may have time to build the second fire which then will hold the fumes long enough for you to build the third fire. By the time you build the seventh one, you will be safe—and I will be working for you while you are on your way.

"You can always depend on me. While we live on earth or until the world ends, we must protect and help each other," said Thunder. "I am the Ruler of all the fierce things in the world," said Thunder.

So the boys believed it, and they did as they were told to do. They went down into the valley and escaped—so said the very old that lived long ago.

These boys began feeding the small snake, and it grew to be a huge one. There was a small river; there was a deep place in it. That's where he [the snake] was seen after he grew up. He had large horns then, and his horns were shiny and bright; his scales were dazzlingly bright. The boys had devoted a lot of time to feeding him, and he had nearly killed Thunder.

But the boys decided to believe Thunder. That's why Thunder is with us as long as we live. God made it that way: that Lightning-and-Thunder and human beings should live together. Thunder is not dangerous. Some people say that he is. It leads us to believe that they do not think about God when they say such things.

Since we have learned all these things, to invoke the name of Thunder is very useful, and that is the reason that he has helped us. If it hadn't been for that, if they had decided to allow the big snake to live, if there were Uk'ten' all over the world, we wouldn't be living—for instance, we [those present] wouldn't be living.

That's all.

NOTE

1. *Uk'ten'*, spelled in various ways, refers to the Cherokee great mythical keen-sighted serpent.

How the White Man Was Made

Hastings Shade (2010)

Just like, the other night I was watching the news about the weather. Wind storms and tornados coming through here.

And they tell the story from a long time ago about how the white man was made from the foam of the water. That's how he was made.

We were formed from the earth, or dirt, as we call it. But, it says wind was pushing this foam around one day all over the water, you know?

Once it finally pushed it up against the bank. And when it got to the bank it touched something solid and became man.

Immediately when he became man he wanted to own the land because he thought the wind pushed him around. So, since then, when the white man sees land he wants to own it.

The first thing he does is put up "KEEP OUT" signs and fences. He doesn't want anyone else on the land that he has and he's afraid he might have to go back to the water again.

But, you know, we can never own anything. One of these days it will belong to somebody else or it will fall down. It's never mine. I can use it while I'm here.

But I was listening to the weather and it said the wind velocity, wind direction, wind rotation, all that.

And I thought: "The wind is still pushing them."

They kept saying if high winds are coming toward you get out of the way. But we as Indians, when the wind comes toward us we move it. We tell it to go. We don't run from it. We respect it, but we move it. So it don't push us around. It pushes the non-Indian around. If you ever listen to the weather, you'll hear wind velocity, wind rotation, wind direction, all that. Wind gusts. But we as Native Americans, we talk to it. We don't run from it, we talk to it.

Ulvsgedi

Stories of the Wondrous

The Owl at the Window

Hastings Shade (2010)

Not too long ago, about the time they started to build new Indian homes, there was a family that qualified for a new home. The new home was to be built about a half a mile from their old house. Once the new home was completed and the family had moved in, the two boys of the family would sometimes go back to the old homeplace to stay all night.

One night they had planned to spend the night at the old place and invited their cousin to go with them. They had bought some bread and wieners so they could snack that night. But as they were walking toward the old place that evening they had to pass by their uncle's place. As they walked by he told them, "I wouldn't go there tonight if I were you boys. It's not a good night to be there." The kids listened to him but went on anyway.

As it began to get dark they had brought a radio and they turned it on and the oldest boy had brought a .22 rifle and five shells with him. As it got darker, they heard an owl outside. Their father had put hail screens on the window because it was stronger than regular screen wire and the squares in it were bigger but not big enough to let flies in. The owl got closer to the house and got louder. The boys turned up the radio.

Soon the owl was right outside the window and they could hear it over the radio even though the radio was turned up as loud as it would go. Finally, one of the boys said, "I'm going to run it off." So he went out but once he got outside he found he couldn't run the night bird off. He went back in the old house and told the older boy he couldn't run the owl off.

"I'll go out there and shoot it," the older boy said. He picked up the gun and walked out. As he was stepping out the door he loaded the rifle with a shell. When he got out there, the owl was sitting on one of the low limbs of the tree that stood in the yard. He took aim and pulled the trigger but the firing pin only made a snapping sound. The oldest boy thought the .22 bullet was no good so he took out another shell and loaded the rifle again. It did the same thing. He tried all five shells and they all wouldn't fire so he felt around on the ground and found a piece of wood lying near his feet. He picked it up and threw it at the owl. With that, the owl finally flew off. The boy walked back into the old house and told the other two boys, "Well, I ran him off."

Just about that time they heard something hit the screen and they looked and saw talons hanging on the screen. One of the boys grabbed something and threw it at the window. When the object bounced off the screen the owl flew off. The boys turned and started to get ready to lie down. Suddenly, they heard the noise at the window once again and when they looked they saw fingers sticking through the screen where the talons were before.

They ran out of the house, leaving everything there. As they were running back home they had to pass by their uncle's house and he was sitting on his porch, laughing at them as they ran by.

The next day, about noon time, the boys gathered up their courage and went back after their stuff. When the oldest one picked up his .22 rifle, he said he was going to try the shells again. When he did, they all went off as he tried each one. They all stared at each other as one of the boys asked if the other two had noticed something strange about one of the fingers that had been sticking through the screen the night before.

"One of the fingers was half gone," one of them said, and they remembered one of the fingers on their uncle's hand had been cut off. Half of it was missing!

Did their uncle try to scare them? Who knows. But they never went back to stay all night again.

Crossing Safely

Sammy Still (2010)

One day my oldest daughter, wife, and I had traveled to a town about fifty miles away. My daughter had to attend an event so we went with her as chaperones. The event began around 7:00 in the evening. We were provided with a nice dinner, listened to speakers, and then my daughter was introduced and she did her presentation. She is a very fine musician; she played a flute when she was in grade school band and throughout her high school years, traveling with her school band and competing in individual music competitions. Along the way she had learned to play an Indian wooden flute and she was known in our area as a wonderful flutist. So she would be asked to come and entertain at conferences and special events.

Well this one particular evening as we were traveling back home, we took a short cut, driving on a rural paved road. We had just driven through a small community town and by this old lime-mining plant. It was a straightaway for about a mile, and with all the lime being mined there was dustings of white lime along the road. It looked like snow on the trees and roadway.

As we drove down the straightaway, I had my headlights on bright and could see over one hundred feet in front of us. I noticed a huge object by the side of the road. I thought it was a huge stone but as I stared at the object it began moving. My wife and daughter also noticed that object and my wife said, "Do you see that? What is it?" As we drive closer we noticed that the huge object was a large raccoon. But (now this is where the story becomes a little unbelievable, but true) as we drive up to the raccoon, the animal stops in the middle of the rural road. I slow down to a stop to avoid hitting the animal. My wife says to me, "What is this raccoon *doing*?" I tell her that I probably blinded the poor thing with our headlights and the raccoon cannot see.

To our amazement, the raccoon raises its front paw, telling us to stop. I think to myself, "What the heck! What is this raccoon doing?" Then all of a sudden three little baby raccoons come running behind her, crossing the road to the other side. My wife, daughter, and I looked at each other with amazement. After the three baby raccoons safely crossed the road, the mother raccoon lowered her paw and looked our way and it sure looked as though she gave us a wink and went her way with her babies. We all looked at each other and began laughing, telling each other that no one would believe this. We continued home and never told anyone for a long time. When I finally decided to tell our friends about this incident, they just laughed and told me that it was a great story. And to this day they still don't believe me. But honestly, it's a true story!

Santeetlah Ghost Story

Edna Chekelelee (1998)

I was born
        back in Santleetlah, where Joyce Kilmer is now.
And we used to walk
        from there to school to Snowbird,
        and we walked about fourteen mile round-trip.
Anyway, a long walk,
        and sometimes we'd be barefooted
        even in wintertime.
Sometimes we didn't have good clothes to wear.
Now we are lucky that we got clothes flying all over the place.
And they're abusing our clothes,
        and I feel sorry for the good clothes that's in trash cans—
        we wish we had that whenever we was growing up.
But this is a ghost story.
Somebody had passed away,
        and my daddy said we had to go set up,
        'cause they believed in setting up all night;

when somebody died,
one of their relatives,
they'd set up all night long,
they wouldn't sleep.
So he said, "We're going to have to go."
So we left.
I think it was right around eight o'clock in the evening.
When we got the news, it was seven,
so it was eight o'clock, probably, when we got ready to go.
So we crossed the river,
and we had big rocks that we jumped over
to get across,
and so we crossed over,
and we started climbing up the hill.
And nothing but laurel bush and moonlight,
that's all we could see,
going up the trail.
So we walked the trail, and I was behind my mother,
and she was walking in front of me,
and then I grabbed her skirt and hang on to it
'Cause I used to listen to the old people
sit out on the porch;
they leaned back on their chairs
and they spit their tobacco wa-a-ay out.
And when they spit tobacco,
then
they was ready to tell stories.
So I would listen.
They would tell some ghost stories,
and there was one ghost story I was always afraid of,
and thought, sure enough, there must be ghosts.
So we was walking on the trail,
and as we walked up
I heard something going like this: [whistling sound].
And I said,

"Daddy, what is it?"
And he said,
"Oh, don't worry about it, everything's okay."
And I keep hearing it getting closer.
I said,
"Daddy, it's getting closer, what is it?"
It would go like [rhythmic whistle],
like that,
so it must have been a-breathing,
that sound that I heard.
Anyway, I got close to my mother, and I closed my eyes,
and I kept hearing something behind me.
Then I got between my mother and dad,
in the middle,
and I closed my eyes tighter.
And then finally I peeped a little bit,
and I saw something white behind me.
And as we walked up, Daddy said,
"Everything's going to be all right.
Don't get scared.
You don't ever get scared.
If you don't get scared, everything'll be okay."
So—I couldn't help but shake.
But I thought I would just keep walking.
Finally Daddy said,
"Okay, everybody stop.
Get back up on the side.
Let that thing go through
in front of us."
I said,
"What is it?"
He said,
"Oh, that's okay, I'll take care of it."
So we stood back on the side,
on a bank,

and I kept hearing
chomping on the leaves,
and it would go
[heavy breathing] like that.
And I peeped,
opened my eyes like that,
and I saw nothing but a
sheer
white
cloth
looked like a clinging curtain,
and it didn't have no head,
no shape over the head,
all I saw was the shoulders.
So he was standing right on the side,
and Daddy said,
"All right."
He said,
"You've scared my children enough,"
said, "I just about know who you are,"
said, "go on ahead and step ahead,
I don't care about you."
Said,
"Go on ahead, and step ahead.
You're not going to hurt my children,
And I'm not going to hurt you.
Just go on by, we made room for you to go by."
And all at once we heard a little bit,
and it just chompin' up the leaves.
All at once I closed my eyes again,
and I kept hearing—
and I just shook.
Finally I opened my eyes
a little bit like that,
and here he was going up in the air—

no feet,
and all I could see was sheer cloth
climbing up the laurel bushes like that.
And finally just went on
through the laurel bushes,
and it faded away.
And Daddy said,
"He's gone, he left us alone, so don't worry about it.
Don't ever get scared, everything'll be okay."
So ever since then I felt much better about being in the dark.
I'm still afraid of the dark [laughs].
But just remember, if you're not afraid,
a ghost can't hurt you.
If you get afraid and panic,
you might run over a cliff or fall and hurt yourself.
But if you're not afraid,
a ghost can't hurt you.

The Little People and the *Nunnehi*

Robert Bushyhead (1998)

Now the Little People.
This really happened
through the aid of the medicine man,
and some of the leaders of the tribe
would get together,
and they would learn these things.
And if anyone wanted to employ the Little People—
in Cherokee "Nunnehi"—
they're not born, they don't die, Nunnehi—
They're like spirits,
and they could implore them to come,

and there are some who have seen them.
Now you can't see them
unless they want you to see them.
And if you see them,
there's something going to happen
whether good or bad,
either way.
Now we have some younger people,
that Dakota, she saw them
when her mother died.
Now when her mother Maggie died—
those who employed them,
they talked to them before they died, that:
"If I should die you go back to your home,"
and they do.
And in this case,
the mother must have employed some,
and her daughter says
when she died,
they saw this little man walk out
and down the hall, and left.
And my mother even told me this,
about the Nunnehi.
And "immortals: is what I'm saying now,
they're immortals."
And she said that her mother told her one day,
said,
"Let's go over and see our neighbor,"
who was an older woman, and
"Let's go see her, she's bad off,"
see.
And whenever they arrived,
She told my mother, said,
"Sit here on the porch."
They had a high porch, see.

She sat on the porch with her feet hanging down.
She said,
        "That woman's not going to last long,"
        and went back in.
And she was sitting out there.
And it wasn't a very,
        but a few moments
        when she heard people screaming and crying,
        and she knew the lady had died.
        And as she set there,
        of course the lights from the lamp shone out into the yard,
        and she saw a little man
        walk out from under the front porch
        and go on out,
        went halfway across the yard
        and turned around,
        and went back at the house,
        and turned and vanished into the yard.
        She had talked to that immortal,
        and he left.
        Now there are those who have some of this,
        but don't have time to tell of it all to me,
        and they died.
        There's a place in Whittier where my uncle lives.
        Now I know he had them,
        because there were too many evidences to say otherwise.
        For instance,
        he and I went to visit his sister across the hill,
        and we sat there and talked with them
        till around midnight,
        and then we went up the hill,
                up to the edge of the hill,
                to the ridge,
        and followed the ridge, and then on down to his house.
And we were sitting at the edge of the fields,

and he said,
"Let's sit down here a while and talk."
And we had not been sitting there very long,
until we'd seen a wall of fire
come up across from the other side of the mountain,
and it traveled at treetop height
all the way down to the creek.
And it turned and went down toward his sister's house,
and then went to the spring,
and it rose back up again
and followed the same track back over the mountain.
And he said,
"Hmm, what does that mean?"
And about that time,
you know how you can take a rock
and make it fling, "ktum,"
we heard that sound,
and it hit a tree right next to us.
And he just laughed.
He said,
"I guess we'll just have to go."
He said they always do that,
meaning the Little People,
I guess they go look for him
whenever he's away.
And we went back home—
and the trail led around to the back of his cabin—
so he had to go to the back and walk around to the front.
And just when we stepped off to the corner of the house
we heard that same sound,
and it [makes smacking sound with hands]
hit a tree right next to us.
And he just laughed.
He said,
"They are coming with us, but don't worry about it."

And then we talked a few minutes,
    and I told him I guess I better go,
    I guess the time was to go.
And I lived about two houses away from there.
He told me, days later,
    he said,
    "Did you see anybody when you left here the other night?"
I said,
    "No, in fact I ran from the house all the way home,
    and I didn't see anybody."
And he said there was someone who was walking slowly,
    and someone was haunting him—
    so that remains—
    whatever.
And so I think they are real,
    they are there.
And like I said,
    if you don't have time to talk to them,
    they'll see that,
    and nobody had better not go there
    because they would raise a fuss.
For instance,
    my oldest boy
    and my next-to-the-oldest boy
    went to this place,
    I guess more or less to experiment.
And they knew that he had had them,
    and they had heard everything when they were growing up.
Well, this time,
    before they arrived to the location
    they heard somebody,
    like dipping water out of a spring into a bucket,
    they could hear that noise.
But they went on and on,
    and just before they arrived,

before the house had been located,
they heard these same sounds,
drops in a bucket.
And oh, they ran from that place.
And my oldest boy said,
"I thought I could run fast,
but Richard passed me" [laughs].
And just incidences like that.
And Lucy Armortain in the Big Cove area said she saw one.
And this one did not have any clothes on,
the others I mentioned had clothes on.
This one did not have a stitch of clothing on him
and was lying on a limb that went over a river.
And he was lying there,
but she could never explain why
or, you know.
So there are evidences,
and you can hear them make noises,
in different ways, walking and, you know.
They are not mischievous.
They are protectors.

The Spirit of an Ancestor

Hastings Shade (2010)

As a young boy growing up along the banks of the Illinois River, I fished and swam in its waters during the summer, and I hunted and trapped along its banks in the winter. In time, as I grew older and began to venture farther up and down the banks of the river I decided I would go up the river and float back down, fish and camp along its banks at night.

I had traveled up and down the river banks many times and thought I knew every one that lives or had lived along its banks.

I picked out a place about seven miles from where we lived and figured it would take me about three days to get back to our place. I asked Dad if he would take me and the flat-bottom johnboat that he and I had built, and about how long it would take to get back, and he agreed.

The place I had picked out was right below one of the bridges that crossed the river. As we put the boat into the river and had loaded all the things I thought I would need, he said, "I'll look for you in a couple days." As he drove off, he said, "If you see a stranger and if he's hungry, feed him."

I watched him as he drove off down the road. This wouldn't be the first time I had spent the night on the river alone. I had camped on its banks many times. I pushed the boat into the river and got in. I was glad Mom had packed me something for the supper the first night. Tomorrow I would have to find food on my own.

There are many strange sounds at night when you are alone. Some I could identify, others I had heard but didn't know what they were: a bird, insect, or an animal. Maybe even a frog. There was one sound that night similar to something I had heard before. It was in a language much like the Cherokee language spoken by the people that came to fish and swim in the river.

I understood and spoke the language. The language I heard that night was Cherokee, but it was spoken in a dialect that I couldn't understand. Only the Creator could understand what was being said. I remember my grandpa saying, "If you hear something that you don't understand, the Creator knows what is being said."

Soon, they began to sing. As I listened to the songs, I knew they were being sung by someone a lot older than anyone I knew. They were more like chants. I listened to the songs, never understanding what they were saying but knowing that very few people had heard what I was hearing. I finally went to sleep and was awakened by the birds as they began to look for something to eat, reminding me I, too, was hungry.

I got my pole and put my line and hook on it without a sinker. Dad used to say, "The only thing a sinker is good for is to get you hung up." So I never use a sinker. Dad called it "drift fishing." I caught me a medium-sized crawdad, hooked him through the tail and threw it out where the water was swift. In about two minutes I had me my breakfast: a fat smallmouth bass.

I built me a fire, cleaned the fish, and sliced me up a potato that I had brought along just for this purpose. If you have never eaten fresh caught fish and fried potatoes along a creek or a river, you are missing out on some of the best eating that you can have. Along with a good cup of coffee, you just can't beat it. So I made some coffee.

After I had eaten my breakfast and cleaned up my mess it was about seven thirty. I thought, "If I'm going to make it home by tomorrow evening I better get started."

So off I went, letting the current take me down the river. Every now and then I would use one of the oars to straighten the boat and head it in the right direction. I would fish the headwaters where it was swift and ran into a deep pool. Sometimes I would catch a good-sized "lineside," as we called the largemouth bass, and even a channel cat every now and then. Once I hooked something that broke my line after it had pulled me and the boat around for a while in one of the deep places along the river. Probably a big flat-head catfish, I thought. As I replaced the line on my pole I noticed that it was getting late. It was time to look for a place to camp.

I found a place and pulled the boat onto the gravel bar. It was time to catch me some supper. I found a good spot and didn't take long before I had a couple of bass and a nice-sized channel cat. I cleaned what I had caught and got ready to build me a fire to cook them on. I heard this voice that startled me; I wasn't expecting anyone along this stretch of the river. "You wouldn't mind sharing your supper, would you?" he asked. At first, I couldn't see him real good with him standing in the late-evening shadows. As he stepped from the shadows, I looked at him and a calm feeling came over me. I knew he could be trusted. I said, "Sure, come on," and began to build a fire. "Wait," he said, "I got a better idea. Let's go to my house and cook them. I just live across the field, not very far. Just tie your boat right there; no one will bother it."

When we got to his house it was real neat. A wood stove sat in the corner and a small table and a couple chairs in the middle of the room "You don't need much when you live alone," he said.

By the time I got the fish battered and the potatoes peeled and sliced he had a fire going. We had two skillets with grease in them on the stove, one for the fish and one for the potatoes.

"Got any coffee?" he asked.

"Sure," I said, "let me get it." I poured water into this gallon can I carried to make coffee in and soon it was boiling away.

We sat at the table after we had eaten and drank our coffee. I don't know how long we talked into the night. He told me many things about the past and what might happen in the future. As I sat and listened to him talk I could almost picture what he was telling me.

When I told him what I had heard the first night I was on the river, he kind of smiled and said, "Oh that was just the Little People. They still know the Ancient Language; that is what you heard. Sometimes I go up there and dance with them. Their grounds is right below where you camped. It's been there for a long time." He said, "I remember when they first came there." It never dawned on me to ask him how long ago that was. I just listened.

He fixed me a pallet on the floor and I lay down and listened as he told me things that no mortal human being should know. I never asked him how he learned all of this. He even told me the name of the girl that I was going to marry. She and her family hadn't even moved into the area yet.

I never asked him how he knew these things. I just listened. Sometime in the night I fell asleep. When I woke up the next morning, I was the only one there. The old man was already gone. I looked for him but never saw him again. We never told each other our names, but he knew mine.

I didn't eat breakfast that morning. I wasn't even hungry, still full from the night before.

As I drifted down the river I kept wondering about the things he had told me. Everything seemed so peaceful as I went down the river.

It was late afternoon when I got to the place where I would leave my boat and go across the field to the house. As I approached the house, Mom came to the back door. Her first words were, "My, you look like you grew up these last two nights. Did you have a good time? Nothing didn't scare you?"

"No," I said, "nothing." I never mentioned the old man to her.

When Dad came home that evening, he said, "Let's go get your boat. It's going to rain tonight. If it floods you'll lose your boat and we'll have to build another one."

As we rode across the field he said, "Well, did you feed anyone?"

"Funny you should ask," I said. "I ate supper with an old man. You know where the big elm trees are? He lives across the field from there. I shared my fish, potatoes, and coffee with him."

"Did he talk like he hadn't had anyone to talk to for a long while?" he asked.

"Yes, he did," I said, "He also told me a lot of things. Do you know him?"

"I only met him once when I was young and floated the river like you did," Dad said.

"Did you spend the night with him?" I asked.

"Yes I did. He told me many things."

"Like what?" I asked.

"What is the old man's name, Dad?"

He said, "I don't know. He died when your Grandpa was young." He then told me, "Don't look for the house where you stayed the night, because it isn't there. Someone burned it down right after the old man died."

I fished and floated the river many times after that, but I never looked for the house. Sometimes when I come by there I look across the field. I know there is nothing there, but I still think, "Maybe . . ." But I know better.

I did look for the Little People's stomp ground. All I found was a place where the grass was beat down in a round circle that looked like someone or something had stomped it down. Again, *maybe*. Maybe I was at the right place.

As the elders say, "The spirit never dies." The old ones, the ones that have gone on before, will always be with us. Sometimes they come and try to tell us something, but we have forgotten how to listen. Then again, maybe someday they will talk to me again.

Kanoheda

Philosophy, History, and Memoir

The Language and the Fire

Sequoyah Guess, Hastings Shade, Woody Hansen, and Christopher B. Teuton, narrator (2010)

"There is a legend," Hastings said, "that as long as we speak to the fire in Cherokee it will not go out, and as long as the terrapins sing around the fire we will have the fire for our use. When the language is gone, the fire will be gone. And so will the Cherokees. That is why the terrapin shells are used for the shackles the women wear while they are stomp dancing; this is how the terrapin sings."

The flame that Doyunisi gave us as a gift of the Creator has burned continuously since ancient times. Called the eternal flame, the fire was brought over from the Cherokee homelands in the east when we were removed to Indian Territory. It is a sacred fire, a living embodiment of Creator. It is watched over and maintained to this day.

The Cherokee language that we speak is another gift of the Creator. It is said that the ancient language Cherokees spoke transformed through the course of the long migration from the south to where we are today. The language we speak today is the fourth language we've spoken.

Hastings, Sequoyah, Woody, and I talked about the connections between the fire and the language, and about the perpetuation of Cherokee peoplehood:

"The focal point, rightly, is the *language*," Hastings said emphatically. "Because, we lose the language we lose the fire. The Jews have already lost their fire. There was only two entities, and that was the Native people or indigenous people and the Jews that had fire at one time. They have done something that put their fire out; I don't know what it was."

"And to me that fire was the Ark of the Covenant," Woody offered.

"Yeah. It was a direct gift from the Creator. It wasn't something that we thought of, it wasn't something . . ."

"Or a gift from somebody else. But, from above!" Woody said.

"The Creator. And it took a, it took a little spider to get it for us; it didn't take the biggest animal. It took the smallest," Hastings said.

"And just like the story of David slaying the lion," Woody said.

"I've seen that fire," I said. "I've seen it rain and the fire would not go out."

"Mmhm. Yeah," Hastings said and smiled. "Yeah, once you start the fire at the stomp grounds . . . I don't care how much rain, it won't go out. People don't realize that."

"That's the prayer, you know," Woody offered.

"I've seen the water go right around it. Flood right around it," I said.

"Yeah."

After a moment, Hastings said, "But if you start a fire at the grounds . . . I don't care if it rains, it won't go out. Because it's been called up. I mean, somebody's, 'Where's the fire at?' It's there, I mean, it's *there*." He laughed. "You can't see it, I can't see it, but when you call it up it's there."

"The fire is *alive*. It's an entity in itself," Sequoyah said.

"If you could see it. It's just like them four directions. It's burning this way," Hastings said, and made a weaving gesture with his hand. "If we could actually see it with these eyes. But they have certain ones—the fire starters—that they've doctored. They can go out there and, just like you and I sitting here, next thing you know they got a fire. You don't see 'em doing this or that with it. Pretty soon that fire's burning."

"They don't have to fan it," Sequoyah added. "They don't have to keep feeding it wood and stuff. But that fire, like I said, it's alive and it knows what it's doing. I mean, it has a mind of its own. At the grounds, of course you know this, you're not supposed to be drinking or using drugs when you're at the grounds. But if there's somebody there doing that the fire will tell, will point him out. That this person isn't supposed to be there. And, it knows what it's doing and I say it's got a mind of its own. Was that last weekend when we was at the lake?" Sequoyah asked Woody.

"Mmhm."

"We couldn't get the fire going. I mean, this was just a regular campfire. We had a bunch of coals, but the fire just wouldn't start, you know?"

"And, finally it kind of started just enough. Just a little bit. And, there was a couple little boys there. It kept them busy all night long. So that fire knew what it was doing. If those boys didn't have that fire to keep on feeding and trying to get it going, they would have got bored right away. 'Cause there was just a bunch of grownups there."

"Who knows what they would have gotten into," I said.

"Hmm," Woody nodded, then laughed.

"So that fire *knew* what it was doing," Sequoyah said.

"Well, they might have burned themselves if it was a flaming fire," Woody added.

"Yeah, a big flaming fire. 'Cause it was kind of windy," Sequoyah said.

"A long time ago they would evaluate you by what kind of fire you started," Hastings said. "If you were smart, not lazy, and you build a fire it'd happen quick. If you were lazy it takes that fire a little while to . . ."

"You know, I was lazy that night 'cause I'm the usual fire starter in our family at gatherings like that," Woody said. "And I just attributed it to being lazy, because I broke my first rule of thumb. Which is to start small. Well, to pray about it and walk around it first. And I didn't! I had my former wife there and my present wife there and my kids and other people, you know, and it's just like, 'Let's hurry up. It's getting dark.' And didn't start small," he said and laughed. "And boy it bothered me for three or four days. I kept telling Joyce, 'I can't believe I did that.' But then again, you know, the fact of those little boys."

"Yeah," Sequoyah agreed.

"And I said as we were sitting around, fanning it, I said, 'I'm glad we have young men to help at least keep this going.' So it did have a good thing about it."

"Yeah," Sequoyah agreed.

"There's people that can build fire that tall," Hastings put his hand waist high, "that fire will be cold."

"Mmhm," Sequoyah agreed.

"There's people that can build fire, be like that," Hastings placed his hand shin high, "and you can have all the heat you want."

"Yeah, even at the house, if there's just a couple of coals in my wood stove I can get it going without paper," Woody said. "And I've always been that way."

A Cherokee Vision of Eloh'

An Excerpt

Sakiya Sanders (1896)
Translated by Wesley Proctor. Edited by Howard L. Meredith and Virginia E. Milan.

When we lived beyond the great waters there were twelve clans belonging to the Cherokee tribe . . . back in the old country in which we lived, the country was subject to great floods. So in the course of time we held a council and decided to build a store reaching to heaven. The Cherokees said that when the house was built and the floods came the tribe would just leave the earth and go to heaven . . . we commenced to build the great structure and when it was towering into one of the highest heavens, the great powers destroyed the apex, cutting it down to about half of its height. But as the tribe was fully determined to build to heaven for safety, they were not discouraged but commenced to repair the damage done by the gods. Finally they completed the lofty structure and considered themselves safe from the floods . . . after it was completed, the gods destroyed the high part again. Then the tribe held another council and concluded to move out of the floody country and hunt one more dry and suitable to their liking. So they journeyed for many days and years and finally came to a country that had a good climate and was suitable for raising corn and other plenty upon which the tribe subsisted. Other red tribes or clans to the Cherokee began to come also from the old country. The emigration continued for many years, never knowing that they crossed the great waters. In the course of time the old pathway which had been traveled by the clans was cut by the submergence of a portion of the land into the deep sea. This path can be traced to this day by the broken boulders. This was of no surprise to the clans as they were used to the workings of the floods.

[The Eloh', the history of the Cherokees, describes the formation of a government and a religion in a time of prosperity in the new country. After many years two separate groups of warriors "crossed the great waters," necessitating furious but successful warfare with the use of clubs.]

Then the Cherokees trained their young men for war and all the clans were notified of the fact . . . when the warriors came again across the waters they were fully prepared to meet them again. These warriors came by the thousands and thousands but they had, in the meantime, knowing also that they had to resort to some other scheme besides depending upon their war clubs, fell upon the idea of using poison in their wars with the terrible invader. Then they sent some great warriors out to kill the great and terrible seven rayed serpent and get its poison, which they did and placed the liquid poison in simblings.[1]

At the close of the seven years the dark and terrible warriors crossed over like locusts in numbers, with boats and loaded with poison and arms, thousands and thousands.

When the enemy arrived, the Cherokees and all their clans came in with their war clubs and the simblings filled with *oocatene* poison . . . running near the lines of the enemy.[2] They shook their gourds of poison and spilling the poison near them they kept on one after another, whooping as they went. The Cherokees sat at right angles to the first run and decoyed the enemy to follow. When the invader came to where the poison was they fainted and fell down. The Cherokees then came up and slaughtered them by the thousands and thousands. This defeat discouraged the dark invader and the war from that source ceased. The Cherokees then lived for ages in peace. And a knowledge of the war with the dark invader became in the course of time only a story.

Then it happened, while the Cherokee tribe thus lived in their new country, that strange white canoes appeared on the broad expanse of great waters.

The clans gathered on the shore in wonder and astonishment at the arrival in their waters of these strange vessels. These white canoes hovered in sight for several days as though not confident that they would be received with welcome by the tribe. The clans, thinking they were beings from heaven, began to beckon to them to come to the shore.

[The Eloh' describes the great hospitality with which the Cherokees treated the white newcomers.]

Then these strangers made known their desire and willingness to remain with the native Cherokee clans, if they were allowed to purchase a small piece of ground upon which to camp and sleep. They made known to the tribe that they only needed a small piece of land about the size of a bull hide. This modest request was freely granted to the strangers and sold to them for a trifling consideration. The supposed heavenly strangers then cut one of the ox hides which they had brought with them into a small string which they stretched around a square enclosing several hundred square yards. This they claimed to be in accordance with the purchase agreement to which the tribe finally agreed, saying at the same time that they had been deceived. Other purchases of land were made for which a consideration was always given by the white heavenly strangers, after the cession of which the tribe always acknowledged that they had been deceived.

Then the tribe finally came to the conclusion that this white stranger was from the opposite pole of the heavens and put on his white skin for the purpose of deceiving. Then the Cherokee tribe began to destroy the white invader; as in the case of the dark invader they saved some to report what great warriors the Cherokees were. But the white invader began to use firearms against them and the Cherokee tribe was driven back farther and farther.

[The Eloh' tells how the Cherokees became discouraged. The *oocateni* had become extinct so they could no longer use their poison. The wise men conducted a great council, trying to restore the ancient half-sphere temple. But the force of the temple, the original fire, had been allowed to become extinguished, and the wise men could no longer draw its strength. The Eloh' ends with a prophecy.]

The race will, according to the oracle of the stone of truth containing the image, be driven to the seashore, where they will cross the waters, landing in the old country from when they came, will find the five lost clans, become reunited into twelve clans, into one people again, will become a great nation known as the Eshelokee of the half-sphere temple of light.

NOTES

1. A species of summer squash.
2. A different spelling for Uk'ten', the mythical serpent.

The Cherokee Migration Story

Sequoyah Guess (2010)

Ilvhiyujigesv
In the great forever that was.
        Our people lived
        on land
        that was surrounded by water
        you couldn't drink.
And the people
        thrived
        on this land.
The different families
of the people
which later became known as clans,
they all had different jobs
that they were to do.
Like, one family
did all the planting and growing.

Another might have been in charge of
the games, like marbles, stickball.
Another family might have been in charge of medicine
for everybody.
And then there was a clan that was in charge of medicine only for
children.
And then there was the architects, or the builders.
There was a clan that kept the fire.
A clan that were, like scribes.
There were the messengers.
Of course, the warriors.
And then there was the knowledgeable clan, I guess you'd say.
Unanti.
Which later on got mixed and they started calling 'em Kutanis.
And then there was the . . . there was four more.
There were fourteen families altogether.

All of the things that the people done,
it was great.
I mean, there was none that
rivaled what the people knew,
and how to grow things,
and how to build things,
and everything, everything was
the best on this island.

The architects, they built cities.
They built great cities
with temples that reached to the sky,
and pavilions that went on for miles.

And the farmers, they grew so much that
hunger wasn't known with the people.
And it wasn't tolerated.
If anybody needed food they could just

go out into the fields and pick whatever they wanted,
and leave the rest for whoever else wanted some.

The medicine was so great that
hardly anybody ever got sick.
And if anybody did, the medicine
was so great that they all were healed.

The knowledgeable ones,
the Unanti,
they were the greatest seers of that time.
And, one day,
the seers, they,
they looked into the future and saw
something that was gonna happen
years from then.
And so they got together,
they got all the families together and
told 'em to do the best they could and
get everything ready for
in seven years there was going to be something that,
something big, cataclysmic was going to happen.

But the architects, they went
to the architects, the builders,
they told 'em,
we need you to build us
seven vessels, that will not sink in the water.
And so the architects, they started working on these vessels.
And, according to the legend,
it took 'em seven years to build seven vessels.
But when they were done,
the vessels that they had created
were more like works of art,
rather than just ships or boats.

The railings and everything else,
they were covered with copper and brass,
and shiny material.
And each vessel just
gleamed inside.
And each vessel also had
huge sails.
And on the sails were written
the fourteen families.

In seven years,
the Unanti got together again,
and they knew that the time was getting close,
where this great disaster was going to happen.
And so they started getting the best
out of each family.
They recruited the best out of each family.
And when they had done this,
when they had gotten the best builders,
the best farmers, the best medicine people,
the best game keepers, the best fire keepers,
all these things,
when they had gotten the best ones out of
each family,
they put 'em on these boats
and sent 'em in different ways.
Different directions.

And when they were gone it wasn't
too long after the boats left
that the ground started shaking.

And, the legend says that
the mountains that were on that land,
they exploded and started spewing forth fire.

The water that surrounded the land,
it started flooding in.
And the earth
        cracked.
Earth spewed out of the cracks.
And the legend says that
in one day over half the people
that was on the land, on the Mother Land,
died because of these different things that was going on.
Those that were left were running to the Unanti
and telling 'em, "*Save us.*"
And the Unanti said,
"There is a way that we know
to get off of this land and go
to a bridge between the great waters."
And about that time,
the water just kind of flowed back
and it showed this rock bridge
going across from the land that the people were on
to another, greater land.
And so, one by one,
the families got together and started crossing the rock bridge.
Of course, the warriors went first,
to make sure everything was clear.
Not dangerous.
And then, after them, were the scribes.
And then after them were the messengers.
And so forth, until the last one were the builders.
And it's said that the builders
stopped when they got across to the big land,
they stopped on a big mountain,
and they looked back at the Mother Land
and watched it go under water.
And . . . everybody cried.
There was a great cry that went out

because we had lost the Mother Land.
And, from there on,
the Unanti said we must go toward the
blue direction, which is the cold direction.
North.
And so, the people started walking towards
the blue.
And, every once in a while they would
stop
and rest.
And when they would stop and rest,
the builders, of course,
being builders,
would start building again.
And they would build temples and everything else.
And then the Unanti would say,
"It's time to go now,"
and the majority of the people would leave,
but there were still some that would stay
in the cities that the builders had built.
And this happened several times,
until they came to a river.
They crossed the river,
but on the other side of this river,
was land that was scarce of water.
And on this side of the river,
they saw animals that had humps on their backs.
And these they killed for food and clothing.
And the people kept going,
and they crossed the land that was scarce of water.
And they crossed another river.
And on the other side of this river
was land that kind of reminded them of the Mother Land
that had gone under.
And some of the people wanted to stay,

but the Unanti said we had to keep on going,
so they kept on going.
They kept walking towards the blue, or the north direction.
And one day it started raining
and then the rain turned white.
But they kept on walking, and walking, and walking, until
they came on a white mountain.
    A white mountain that moved.
Here again, the Unanti said,
"We got to turn toward where the sun comes up.
    Toward the yellow direction."
And so that's the way they started going.
And they came upon land again
that reminded them a lot like the Mother Land that they had lost.
And all the people wanted to stay there
because it felt like home.
And some people started to
settle down,
but the Unanti said,
"No, we can't stay here. This is a land of sorrow.
    The land cries up to us."
They said, "We got to keep on going."
And so, even though a lot of the people didn't want to,
they packed up and kept on going
toward where the sun comes up.

They kept on walking until they came upon another river.
    And, this river they called the "Long Man"
because it was so wide and so long.
They were barely able to cross this river,
and when they got to the other side of this river,
they came upon people
who were mound builders.
And they built great mounds
and they were really good at it.

But they, uh, shared secrets
or shared knowledge with our architects,
to where they built even greater mounds after that.

And then one day, something happened.
A prominent person,
        of our people
was found dead.
And . . .
they noticed she had no
        blood.
And the people started wondering what happened.
And then they realized that these mound builders
        were cannibals.
And they sacrificed humans.
And with this prominent person being found dead,
and everything pointed to these mound builders
being the ones that killed her,
our people had a great war with them.
And they, well, you might say they wiped 'em out,
but there were still some that were left
and they had married into our people.
But most of the others were killed.
After this happened,
the people,
the Unanti said, "We must keep on going."
So they kept on going towards
where the sun came up.
And, during this time,
as they walked toward where the sun came up,
the Unanti started becoming really, really . . .
        great in their own eyes.
They thought nothing could harm them.
They thought they held power over the people,
which they did because everybody was scared of 'em

because they were, back then, the most powerful
medicine clan there was.

As this time went along,
from the time the Mother Land went under water
to this time,
the original language was lost.
And the writing that we had back then was lost, too.
And the only ones that remembered anything about it was the Unanti.
And that was one of the reasons why they thought
they held such great power over the people.

One day, there was a man named Nicotani
who kidnapped the War Chief's son's wife.
The War Chief's daughter-in-law.
Nicotani wanted her for his own.
And, uh, the War Chief's son retaliated.
And a lot of the rest of the people,
they joined in, and they
massacred the Kutani clan, or the Unanti.
And from then on there hasn't been
another clan that was totally devoted to religion,
or the leaders of our medicine.
But during this time, also, a lot of the
other clans joined together.
The smaller clans joined the bigger clans.
Like, the panther and the bear, they became
the wildcat clan.
They all became one clan.
The raven and the pigeon clans became one.
There were a lot of other clans that came together
and made one bigger clan.
So by the time we reached
a land that reminded us so much of the
Mother Land that had been left so many years before,

the people decided this is where we are going to stay.
And the legend says that this is where we were
when the Europeans came over.

And also it ends by saying that
at that time
when we reached the new land that we were supposed to be at,
there were so many of our people
that we covered most of the eastern seaboard.
But over the years, of course that number dwindled,
and dwindled, and dwindled.
But, that is the migration story.

The Trail of Tears

Freeman Owle (1998)

I found that out as I was growing up,
and my parents began to tell me this story of the Trail of Tears.
And you look at me and you say,
"Well, he's probably as much Scots-Irish as I am."
Yes, I am.
But I am Ooguku tsikayi Tsalagi ashkaya.
My name is Owle, and I live in Birdtown,
and I happened to grow up on the reservation.
Sort of like a little story that Marsha was reading to our daughter last night
about the zebra.
Says, "Are you white with black stripes or black with white stripes?"
Are you Scots-Irish with Indian, or Indian with Scots-Irish?
I don't know, I really don't.

All I know is I'm different from anyone who's ever lived,
and different than anyone who ever will.
And my fingerprints are different, so I must be special.
They told me that
my family was, in 1838, in a log cabin near Murphy, North Carolina.
And all of a sudden,
someone was banging on the door
early that morning.
And they opened up the door and they looked out,
and fifty Georgia soldiers were standing in the yard.
They said,
"Come out of the cabin."
And when my great-grandfather—
I'll just call him grandfather—
did,
they burned the cabin to the ground.
He and his wife and small baby were taken to Murphy, North Carolina,
put into a stockade,
stayed there for six weeks.
There was no roof, only a line of poles
encircling the stockade.
They say that
the mud was deep,
there wasn't much food,
no one had anything to cover themselves with,
but the baby survived because the mother was feeding it.
Early one morning,
on that October morning
when the frost was heavy
and the ground was frozen hard enough for wagons to travel,
General Winfield Scott began to march the people out of this fort.
So he marched them across the frozen ground
and across the Santeetlah Mountains

into Tennessee.
There was a woman by the name of Martha Ross,
Scots-Irish and Cherokee.
She had a beautiful coat,
and she began to look, late that night,
and the rain was coming down, and it was cold,
and she heard a baby crying,
She went to the sound of the baby and found the child
very cold
and wet—
it had pneumonia.
She covered the child with her coat,
and two days later she died of pneumonia herself.
It is people like this
who have made contributions to the Cherokee society.
It is people like the people of North Carolina
who allowed those people living in North Carolina to remain there.
The history is written,
the history says
that North Carolina did not remove its Cherokees.
They were called the Oconaluftee Cherokees.
And you go see *Unto These Hills*, it doesn't mention this.
But they didn't make them leave.
The other fifteen thousand began to march on toward Oklahoma.
When they got to the Mississippi, they asked my grandfather
if he would count the Cherokees who crossed the river.
And he said
"Yes, I will."
But he told his wife in Cherokee,
"Go hide in the cane brake and take the baby with you.
And I will tell them you're here.
And we'll go back home."
So he counted the Cherokees as they crossed the flatboat across the Mississippi,

and he told the soldiers,
"All the Cherokees are accounted for."
And they said,
"Are you sure?
Go back to the river and check again."
And this is what he wanted,
and he goes back to the river,
and he looks into the bushes and the brush,
and all of a sudden he leaps into the water.
They come running behind, and they shoot many times into the water.
They look into the black, swirling waters of the Mississippi,
and this Cherokee doesn't surface.
So—for a long time.
And they gave him up as being dead.
He's breathing through a reed all this time.
And after he gives the soldiers time enough to go away,
he comes up and he swims back across the Mississippi.
He looks for his wife on the other side,
and—she heard the gunshots.
She ran
with the baby in her arms,
she would run all night long,
and then find a briar patch to sleep in in the daytime,
or a farmer's haystack.
Took her several weeks to get back home,
but she came on back to the old burned-out cabin site
because that's all she knew as home.
She waited there week after week,
and her husband didn't return.
She went down to the village,
to the Scots-Irish settlers,
and they gladly gave her food.
And they were feeding those Cherokees
that were hiding in the mountains.

If the North Carolina people had been caught by the Georgia guard
handing out food to the Cherokees,
they too would have lost their land and been put in prison
as Cherokee sympathizers.
But the Scots-Irish people were feeding her
one morning, a year later,
when she heard a noise up on the hill,
and she looked and there was someone coming.
And so she ran and hid with her baby.
And after a while it was her husband
coming out of the woods.
They were reunited,
and we still live
in a little place where they came and rebought with their own money
called Birdtown.
And the reason they were able to rebuy it was:
there was a wagon train coming through here,
and it had a little baby on it—
a little white child
who was very sick.
And the parents were smart enough to say,
"If we go on with this child, it's going to die."
And they said—
Have you ever heard the term, "Give it to the Indians"?
They gave the child to the Indians.
Chief Yonaguska made the child better.
His name was William Holland Thomas.
Will Thomas was already a citizen of the United States,
and the Cherokees could go and buy up land
and put it in this child's name
by the thousands of acres,
and we are still here.
But in the early 1920s
my grandfather, Solomon Owle,

was living in this little place called Birdtown
and paying his taxes to Swain County,
and I think was a good citizen.
The federal government looked down and said,
"This can't be.
This bunch of savages are not supposed to be able to take care of themselves."
And they came down and took the deeds away from these people
and set up what they called the Qualla Indian Boundary.
They couldn't call it a reservation
because a reservation is land that is given to the Indians,
and the Indians are forced upon it.
This land was bought back
under Will Thomas's name—
see, it's not a reservation
it's a little different.
You know I came here tonight to tell you
that the Cherokee people don't really hold any hatred
or animosity in their heart
for those things that happened in the past.
We can take our hats off to the past,
but as one great gentleman said,
"We should take our shirts off to the future."
The reason the Cherokee people survived
is because they loved their neighbors
and were good neighbors.
The Cherokees of today
still welcome even all the visitors in the '41 Chevys
and the '40 Ford coupes
and the bears and everything—
they were glad to see the tourists come.
And we're glad to see the tourists come, even today.

Mankiller

A Chief and Her People

Wilma Mankiller and Michael Wallis (2000)

[The Mankiller family has moved from Oklahoma to San Francisco through a federal policy of relocating Indian people to urban areas. Excerpted from Mankiller and Wallis, *Mankiller: A Chief and Her People* (New York: St. Martin's Press, 1999), chapter 7: "Child of the Sixties."]

My family's relocation experience in San Francisco was disturbing in many ways. But in retrospect, our ordeal was not nearly as harsh or painful as the problems encountered by the Cherokee people who had been forced to take the Trail of Tears in the late 1830s. At least we did not have to walk hundreds of miles through snow and sleet. We did not worry about getting bayoneted or shot by some soldier or bushwhacker. Our relocation was voluntary and not by federal mandate. There were some parallels, however. For instance, even after we had settled down in our two-family flat in the Potrero District, we still felt as alienated as our ancestors must have felt when they finally arrived in those unfamiliar surroundings that became their new home. Despite the decades that separated us, we shared a feeling of detachment with the Cherokees who had come before us.

I know that many native people who turned up in San Francisco as part of the BIA's removal program in the 1950s considered California to be the land of new beginnings. At least that was their hope. They wanted to believe the promotional literature that spoke of good jobs and happy homes waiting for those who had relocated. I was only a youngster, but I did not accept the government propaganda. Instead, I was convinced that my parents had made the wrong decision when they bought the BIA's bill of goods.

At first, nothing about the city was very appealing. The overt discrimination we encountered is what got to me the most. It became obvious that ethnic intolerance was a fact of life in California, even in the urbane and sophisticated world of San Francisco. Not only did African and Hispanic Americans feel the sting of racism, so did Native Americans.

I recall an incident that drove home for me the concept of racial bias. Soon after we moved to California, a woman came up to my mother and told her straight out that we were all "nigger children." Then she called my mother a "nigger lover." The woman said those things because of my father's dark complexion. Mother was outraged by that repulsive word of contempt. Prompted by blind hatred and ignorance, it was intended to inflict pain. It must have stung like a hard slap on the face. My soft-spoken mother was so distraught by such a blatant display of malice that she jumped the woman!

Most of the time, however, people who had a problem with our being different did not say what they thought about us to our faces. They made snide remarks behind our backs. It was then that we found out the place where we lived was hardly exempt from racial prejudice.

[. . .]

Some of the questions I am asked most frequently today include what happened to native people, such as those in California? Why do native people have so many problems? How is it that they ended up facing high unemployment, low educational attainment, low self-esteem, and problems with alcohol abuse? I answer that all one needs to do is look at our history. History clearly shows all the external factors that have played a part in our people being where we are today.

Regardless of all the problems Native Americans faced, they became the fastest-growing minority group in California in the twentieth century. This took place without their reaping much of California's extraordinary affluence. From fewer than sixteen thousand in 1900, at least forty thousand native people lived in the state by 1960, just a few years after my family arrived. Some sources claim that the 1960 population count could have been as high as seventy-five thousand, because census takers did not identify as Indians all native persons who were using Anglo or Hispanic surnames. Only a small percentage of those native people lived on reservation or *rancherias*; most had homes in the Los Angeles or San Francisco areas.

Several factors account for the dramatic rise in the Indian population in California, especially since World War II. First of all, native people were starting to be treated a little better. Numerous social and economic troubles remained, but an awakening of consciousness began among some whites in the late 1920s and continued to gain momentum. About the time our family moved west, California was attempting to abolish barriers separating Indians from non-Indians in terms of education, welfare assistance, and other public services. The substantial Indian immigration from Oklahoma, the Dakotas, and the Southwest throughout the postwar years helped to boost the Native American population in California. The BIA's removal program accounted for a great many Native American individuals and families moving to California, including the Charley Mankiller brood, direct from Mankiller Flats in Oklahoma.

Nonetheless, our troubles did not disappear, even though the old days of exterminating Indians had ceased and California's Native American population was increasing. There were still problems to solve and predicaments to face. Besides the poverty and prejudice we encountered, I was continually struggling with the adjustment to a big city that seemed so foreign and cold to me.

The San Francisco I experienced as a young girl in the late 1950s and early 1960s was not the sophisticated city of palatial Nob Hill mansions, picturesque cable cars, fancy restaurants, and elegant hotels. My family did not lunch amid the tourists at Fisherman's Wharf or dine at Trader Vic's. We did not meet friends to watch from the Crown Room high atop the Fairmont Hotel as the mists rolled in on the bay. Folks who did those things were on a much higher rung of the economic and social ladder than we were. Our family was more familiar—and comfortable—with the crowd that shopped for bargains at Goodwill or St. Vincent de Paul. We ate simple meals at home, wore hand-me-down clothes, and got by from paycheck to paycheck. Our family's meager budget could not handle any nonessentials or luxuries.

After we had lived in San Francisco for a little more than a year, my father, with help from my older brother Don's salary contributions, was able to scrape together enough money for a down payment on a small house. So we left the crowded flat in the Potrero Hill District and moved into a new home in Daly City, just south of San Francisco on the southern peninsula in San Mateo County. Daly City had come into being as a result of the earthquake and fire of 1906, when many San Franciscans fled to John Daly's dairy ranch. It grew into a residential area that mushroomed during the boom years after World War II, when it became one of California's fifty most populous communities.

Our new residence looked as if it had come straight out of a cookie-cutter mold. There were three small bedrooms, a full basement, and not many frills. My sisters and I shared bunk beds. I would describe it as modest, just like the hundreds of other ticky-tacky houses in endless rows that climbed up and down the landlocked hills flanked by the Pacific Ocean and San Francisco Bay.

For our family as a whole, the move to Daly City was a good one. It represented a marked improvement over our first dwelling. We were moving up in the world. At about that same time, my father started to become active at the San Francisco Indian Center, where we met and spent time with other native people living in the area. That had a positive impact on the family. But for me, nothing had changed. I still loathed being in California, and I particularly despised school.

I was uncomfortable. I felt stigmatized. I continually found myself alienated from the other students, who mostly treated me as though I had come from outer space. I was insecure, and the least little remark or glance would leave me mortified. That was especially true whenever people had to teach me something basic or elementary, such as how to use a telephone. I was convinced that they must think it odd to be teaching an eleven- or twelve-year-old how to pick up a phone, listen for a tone, and then dial a number.

In Daly City, I was getting ready to enter the seventh grade. The thought of that depressed me a great deal. That meant having to meet more new kids. Not only did I speak differently than they did, but I had an unfamiliar name that the others ridiculed. We were teased unmercifully about our Oklahoma accents. My sister Linda and I still read out loud to each other every night to lose our accents. Like most young people everywhere, we wanted to belong.

Also, there were changes going on inside me that I could not account for, and that troubled me very much. I was experiencing all the problems girls face when approaching the beginning of womanhood. I was afraid and did not know what to do. Besides having to deal with the internal changes, I was also growing like a weed and had almost reached my full adult height. People thought I was much older than twelve. I hated what was happening. I hated my body. I hated school. I hated the teachers. I hated the other students. Most of all, I hated the city.

I did not hate my parents or the rest of my family. I always loved them very much. But it was a time of great confusion for me. I was silently crying out for attention, but nobody heard me. My dad was constantly busy trying to make a living and, at the same time, deal with his own frustrations and confusion about city life in California. My mother was doing her best to help all of us with our problems while she kept us fed and clothed. Then on top of everything, my oldest brother, Don, announced that he was going to get married. He had met a nice young Choctaw woman named LaVena at the Indian Center. They had fallen in love. Everyone was very happy about the news, but there were long discussions about Don leaving home with his bride and how that loss of income would affect the rest of the family.

With so much going on, I felt like nobody had any time for me. I felt there was not one single person I could confide in or turn to who truly understood me. My self-esteem was at rock bottom. That is when I decided to escape from all of it. I would run away from home. At the time, that seemed my best and only option.

I ran off to Grandma Sitton, who lived at Riverbank. She was an independent woman. I had gotten to know her better since our move to the West Coast, and I liked her very much. I thought perhaps my grandmother would understand and comfort me and help with my problems. Also, I liked Riverbank because Oklahoma families who had come out during the Dust Bowl period were living in the area. I felt more comfortable around them.

My younger sister Linda and I had stashed away a little bit of money saved from baby-sitting jobs we had gotten through meeting other families at the Indian Center. We did not have much, but it was enough to buy a bus ticket. Of course, as soon as I got to her house, my grandma called my folks and said, "Pearl's here, you better come get her." My parents were upset—very upset—and my dad drove out and took me back. But that did not end it. That first time was just the start of a pattern of behavior that lasted until I became a teenager.

I waited a little while, and then I ran away a second time and went straight to my grandmother's house. My parents and I went through the same routine. But I did not stop. I did it again. Once more, my dad drove to Riverbank and took me back to Daly City. One time my sister Linda ran away, too. She took off for somewhere on her own. I am not sure where she went. My folks found her and brought her home. But I kept running away. Every single time, I went to Grandma Sitton's. Over a year or so, I guess I ran away from home at least five times, maybe more.

My parents could not control me. Eventually, they decided that I had become incorrigible. They saw that I truly did not want to live in the city. I wanted no part of it. So they gave in and let me stay with my grandmother. By then, she had outlived another husband. She sold her home and gave the money to her son and his wife—my Uncle Floyd Sitton and Aunt Frauline. They had moved to California after Uncle Floyd's return from World War II and his discharge from the service. He used the money my grandmother gave them to buy a dairy ranch north of Riverbank, near the town of Escalon. In exchange for helping them buy their "dream place," Grandma Sitton moved in with my uncle and aunt and their four children, Tommy, Mary Louise, and twins about my age, Eddie and Teddie.

I was preparing to begin the eighth grade when I joined my grandmother and the other Sitton relatives at their ranch. The agreement was for me to stay with them for one year. Ultimately, it turned out to be a very positive experience, but at first there were difficulties. There was a fair amount of conflict between my cousins and me, but they finally got used to my living there. Our problems sprang not from my Native American blood, but from a rivalry between the four of them and me. In a nutshell, we were all competitive kids. We were pure country, too, and that meant we would not run from a fight. When I arrived, it took only the slightest agitation to provoke me. I was highly sensitive and self-conscious.

One time in particular, I recall, several of us were walking back from the fields following Uncle Floyd. My cousin Teddie kept taunting and teasing me until I could not take any more. When he pulled my hair again, I whirled around and punched him in the jaw so hard that he dropped to the ground. I got into trouble over that incident, and there was some talk about shipping me back home to the city. That finally passed. I settled down, and the teasing stopped. The conflict faded. My life seemed to improve.

I began to gain some confidence. As I felt better about myself, I felt better about others. My grandmother deserves much of the credit. Even though she was strict, she was never judgmental. At a very critical point in my life, she helped me learn to accept myself and to confront my problems.

School even seemed more palatable. When I moved to the farm, I did not have one single friend my age at school. I relied on my tough demeanor to protect myself, and I found that this really turned off people. My cousins had told all the other kids at the small community school we attended that my parents had sent me to live with them because they could not handle me. That was not a good way for me to begin. During lunch and recess, I was usually by myself. Although I got off to a bumpy start, I had made some friends and had developed a routine by the close of the school year. I got along better with my cousins and enjoyed the work on the farm.

All in all, the year I spent on the dairy farm was just what I needed. I slept in the same bed with my grandmother, and we all got up every day at 5:00 a.m. to milk the cows and take care of chores. My main job was to help keep the barn clean. Besides the dairy cows, my uncle and aunt had some pigs and a horse. There was a big vegetable garden. I even helped my Aunt Frauline deliver a calf during a difficult birth. The hard work and fresh air at the farm were so good. We also found time to explore the fields and swim in the creeks.

During our year together, my grandmother helped shape much of my adolescent thinking. I spent much of my time with her, and never considered a single moment wasted. Although she was small, only about four feet ten inches tall, she was solidly built. She also was opinionated, outspoken, tough, and very independent. She was deeply religious and sang from her hymnbook every day. Her favorite song was "Rock of Ages." My grandmother also loved to garden, raise chickens, and pick peaches. Grandmother Sitton and my father—two of the people I most admired as a young woman—valued hard work. I believe it was their examples more than anything else that contributed to my own work ethic.

I continued to visit the farm every summer during my high school years. Some of my brothers and sisters usually came too, and we would help tend the crops or pick fruit to earn money for new school clothes. We worked alongside some white people in the fields, and my mistrust of whites certainly did not apply to them. The people whom some Californians derisively called Okies or Arkies were great friends—hardworking people, close to the land, and quick to share what little they had with others who had even less. The farm work was demanding, but those were summers of freedom. We swam in the canals, went to drive-in movies, and sipped cherry Cokes or limeades at the local Dairy Queen. Sometimes we headed to the nearby town of Modesto to cruise the streets. Later, Modesto was the setting for *American Graffiti*, the film about teenage life in small-town America directed by George Lucas, a native son.

I looked forward to those visits with my grandmother. After I was married, I still went to see her. I would sit on her lap, and we teased each other and laughed. Full of spirit and energy, my grandmother married her third and last husband when she was in her eighties. During their courtship, she had me dye her hair black because she believed it would make her look her best. I obliged. Later, I helped her get all prettied up before they went to Reno, Nevada, for a quick wedding. Pearl Halady Sitton never stopped enjoying life. She canned vegetables and fruit, kept chickens, worked in the garden, and sang those hymns until shortly before she died. I am inspired whenever I think about her and all those good times we had.

At the end of the year I spent with my mother's family, I returned to the Bay Area, but not to our house in Daly City. My family no longer lived there. While I was gone, my brother Don and his girlfriend, LaVena, had married. LaVena got a job with the telephone company, and Don went to work for Pacific Gas and Electric. They set up housekeeping at their own place not far from Candlestick Park. As was expected, the loss of Don's income meant my parents were forced to make budgetary adjustments. That meant giving up the house in Daly City. I came home to a more affordable residence my father had found for us, in southeastern San Francisco on a spit of land projecting into the bay. It was a place known as Hunter's Point.

Named for Robert E. Hunter, a forty-niner from the last century who had planned to create a city on the site, Hunter's Point eventually had become the home of a huge U.S. Navy shipyard and dry docks. It flourished during World War II and continued to thrive for some years afterward when a severe housing shortage occurred. Ironically, Japanese-Americans returned to the Bay area after their long confinement in Dillon Myer's camps only to find that black workers, attracted by plenty of jobs at the shipyards and defense plants, had moved into the "Little Tokyos" of the city. But thousands of black families also occupied the housing built on tidelands adjoining the shipyard at Hunter's Point. Many of those black families had migrated from Oklahoma, Texas, and other states that whites also had fled during the Dust Bowl years.

Hunter's Point may sound like the name of an affluent residential development where polo players and stockbrokers lived, but it was far from that. The only thing fancy about it was the name. Shipyard employees and hourly wage earners made their homes there. Although the shipyard did not close until 1974, jobs started to become more and more scarce in the 1960s. The workers who resided at Hunter's Point fell into financial difficulties, and the housing area became little more than a ghetto.

We found a few Native Americans living at Hunter's Point, including another Cherokee family. They had come to California from Locust Grove, an old Cherokee Nation town in eastern Oklahoma and the home of the late Willard Stone, the wood sculptor whose claim of Cherokee ancestry recently created a great deal of controversy. That other Cherokee family at Hunter's Point was also part of the relocation program masterminded by the BIA.

At Hunter's Point, my perceptions of the world around me began to take shape. Most police, teachers, political leaders, and others in positions of power and authority were whites. There were a few white people living at Hunter's Point, perhaps a few Asians, and several Samoan families. Regardless of the ethnic sprinkling, Hunter's Point was primarily a community of black families. Black culture had a profound impact on my development. When the rest of America was listening to Pat Boone, the Beach Boys, or Elvis, my friends and I listened to Etta James, Dinah Washington, Sarah Vaughan, B.B. King, and others. I talked endlessly with my best friends, Johnnie Lee and LaVada, about things which girls our age were obsessed with—music, boys, parents, and growing up. We sometimes put on makeup, fixed our hair, played records, and danced, pretending we were at a party far away from Hunter's Point. Even today, more than thirty years later, the sisterly company of black women is especially enjoyable to me.

My mother also became good friends with people from different backgrounds. She developed a close relationship with a Filipina woman who lived next door. This neighborhood of diverse cultures was where we remained for several years. Those outside our community called our new home "Harlem West."

We lived in one of the typical little houses, but to everyone's amazement, it had a surprisingly pleasant interior. The rooms were small, but the house had two stories and was not as tiny as some of the other places we had lived. More important, there was not a rat in sight. The kitchen and bathroom were satisfactory, and the wooden floors were in fairly decent shape.

Outside was another story. There was a great deal of animosity between the black youths and Samoan youths of Hunter's Point. Sometimes it seemed like a war zone when rival gangs clashed on the streets. Now and then there were enormous battles. Upstairs, in the bedroom I shared with my sister Linda, we could gaze out the window at the beauty of the sky and water, or we could lower our eyes to the streets where the gangs fought furiously.

I was taught invaluable lessons on those mean streets. They were part of our continuing education in the world of urban poverty and violence.

In many ways, Hunter's Point appeared to be like everywhere else we had been, yet it was also a very different world. Most of the differences,

I found, were a matter of perception. I learned that in the "hood," there is a constant fight against racial prejudice. There is a struggle to keep the children off the streets and away from drugs. This takes place in an environment of overwhelming frustration among many diverse people who are alienated from the rest of America in many ways other than by simple geography. Living there was really like one long, hot, boring, lazy afternoon—nothing to do, no place to go, and no promise of anything better in the future.

I will not forget the time I was choking on something, and I became so distraught that my father called an ambulance. It was late at night, and when my father gave our address to the person on the telephone, he was told that no ambulance would come to Hunter's Point after sundown. My father finally cleared my throat and I was fine. We never discussed what would have happened to me if he had not been successful. Another time, I recall a police car driving around our neighborhood. When the officers stopped to make a call and left their car unattended, every window was shattered. That was standard procedure. All of the police, across the board, were considered to be "the enemy." They were never looked upon as concerned individuals who could help. Hunter's Point was like a "no man's land" that was constantly under siege.

Living in Hunter's Point also gave me an insight into cultures I otherwise might not have ever known. In 1991, when I saw the film *Boyz N the Hood,* I was struck by how familiar the families in the film seemed to me, even though more than thirty years had passed since I had lived in a similar place.

Whenever I hear or read about inner-city crime, drugs, and gangs, I filter it through my own experiences at Hunter's Point. Although communities such as Hunter's Point have tremendous problems, they also have strengths that few outsiders ever recognize or acknowledge. The women are especially strong. Each day, they face daunting problems, as they struggle just to survive. They are mothers not only of their own children but of the entire community. Poverty is not just a word to describe a social condition, it is the hard reality of everyday life. It takes a certain tenacity, a toughness, to continue on when there is an ever-present worry about whether the old car will work, and if it does, whether there will be gas money; digging through piles of old clothes at St. Vincent de Paul's to find clothing for the children to wear to school without being ridiculed, wondering if there will be enough to eat. But always, there is hope that the children will receive a good education and have a better life.

By the time we moved to Hunter's Point, in 1960, my father had left the rope factory and was working as a longshoreman on the docks. He began to augment his income by playing poker. People used to come to our house for big poker games that lasted well into the night. Before they left, my dad usually had picked up a little money. He had a lot of confidence. That was important. Some of those who played cards with him were men he worked with, but many were other native people he had met at the San Francisco Indian Center.

Located upstairs in an old frame building on Sixteenth Street on the edge of the very rough and tough Mission District, the Indian Center became a sanctuary for me. It was my safe place for many years. At last, the mythical Rabbit had finally found a hollow stump the Wolves were not able to penetrate.

In many ways, the Indian Center became even more important to me than the junior high and various high schools I attended. During my teen years, I transferred from an inner-city school dominated by violence to another public high school with a predominantly Asian student body, because it offered a calmer atmosphere. However, changing schools did not help me very much. I had made some headway in gaining self-esteem, but like many teens, I remained unsettled as far as goals, with no sense of direction. I was not sure what I wanted to do once I finished school and had to make my own way in the world. But a moody and self-absorbed teenager could count on one thing—at the end of the day, everything seemed brighter at the Indian Center. For me, it became an oasis where I could share my feelings and frustrations with kids from similar backgrounds.

There was something at the center for everyone. It was a safe place to go, even if we only wanted to hang out or watch television. For the younger children, the center provided socialization with other native people through organized events such as picnics and supervised outings.

Older kids went there for dances, sports programs, and an occasional chance to work behind the snack bar to earn a little money. Adults played bingo, took part in intertribal powwows and, most important, discussed pertinent issues and concerns with other BIA relocatees from all across the country. We would jump on a city bus and head for the Indian Center the way some kids today flock to shopping malls.

The Indian Center was important to everyone in my family, including my father. Always a determined person who stuck to his principles, even if they turned out to be lost causes, Dad ultimately quit working as a longshoreman to become a shop steward and union organizer with a spice company based in San Francisco. Besides his union activities, he also became more involved with projects at the Indian Center. For instance, when the question arose about the need for a free health clinic for Indians living in the Bay area, he rallied the forces at the Indian Center to get behind the issue. In an effort to heighten public awareness, he appeared on a television panel discussion about the urban clinic. Perhaps at that time, he influenced my life in ways I could not imagine then.

When he believed in something, he worked around the clock to get the job done. He was always dragging home somebody he had met, someone who was down on his luck and needed a meal and a place to stay. It was a tight fit, but we made room. My dad never gave up on people. I think my father's tenacity is a characteristic I inherited. Once I set my mind to do something, I never give up. I was raised in a household where no one ever said to me, "You can't do this because you're a woman, Indian, or poor." No one told me there were limitations. Of course, I would not have listened to them if they had tried.

The exception would have been my father. I always listened to him, even if I did not agree with what he had to say. From the time I was a little girl, we discussed all the topics of the day. Our very best debates concerned politics. Sometimes those conversations would get a bit heated. After my political awakening as a teenager, I became aligned with the party of Franklin Roosevelt, Harry Truman, and a rising young star of the sixties—John F. Kennedy. My father, on the other hand, was a registered Republican, which was not unusual among older members of the Five Tribes, especially the Cherokees. Folks who know our people's past can usually figure out why so many of the older Cherokees belonged to the Republican Party. The story goes that a historian once asked an Oklahoma Cherokee why so few of the old-timers became Democrats. The Cherokee supposedly replied, "Do you think we would help the party that damned ol' Andy Jackson belonged to?" For the elders, the choice was obvious—Republicans were the lesser of two evils.

Despite our political differences, my father and I enjoyed our discussions, and especially our time spent at the Indian Center. Throughout the sixties, my entire family considered the Indian Center to be a stronghold. At the center, we could talk to other native people about shared problems and frustrations. Many families we met there were like us. They had come to the realization that the BIA's promises were empty. We all seemed to have reached that same terrible conclusion—the government's relocation program was a disaster that robbed us of our vitality and sense of place. That is why the Indian Center was so immensely important. It was always there for us. It was a constant. During the turmoil and anguish of the 1960s, it was where we turned.

In 1960, when my brother Robert was killed, we went to the Indian Center for solace. Bob was only twenty years old when he died. He had joined the National Guard, boxed a little bit, and worked at various odd jobs. He did not seem to have any real plans. My dad wanted him to settle down and find steady employment. But Bob was restless. He and his pal, Louie Cole, a quarter Choctaw, decided to leave the city. Louie was nineteen, and I thought of him as my first real boyfriend. He and my brother took off one morning, intent on making money for a grubstake. Then they planned to go off on their great adventure and discover the rest of the country.

Bob and Louie had been gone for two or three weeks and were up the coast in Washington State when they found work as apple pickers. The boys lived in sharecroppers' cabins near the orchards. When they got up early in the morning, it was still cold and dark outside, so they would start a fire in a wood stove using a little kerosene to get the flames going. One morning, my brother was still groggy with sleep when he lit the fire. Instead of the kerosene, he mistakenly picked up a can of gasoline. The cabin exploded in flames. The door was locked with a dead bolt, so by the time the boys got outside, they were severely burned. Louie was burned over much of his body, but Bob was in far worse condition.

My parents, my brother Don and my oldest sister, Frieda, who still lived in Oklahoma, went to Washington to be with Bob. The doctor told them that if Bob lived for seven days, he would probably survive. Among Cherokees, the number seven is considered sacred. We have seven clans, our sacred fire is kindled from seven types of wood, and there are seven directions—north, south, east, west, up, down, and "where one is at." We thought maybe the seven days would bring luck to Bob.

Attractive and charming, Bob always had been the best looking of all of us. He was tall and athletic, a happy-go-lucky type. I looked up to my big brother Don, but for my carefree role model, I had Bob. I think all of us wondered what his life would be like if he survived. It was clear that he would never be the same.

When it seemed that there was a slim chance Bob might pull through, my father, who had to return to his job, left my mother in Washington to stay with Bob through his long recovery. But as it turned out, Bob could not be saved. He lived for seven days and no more. On the seventh day, he died. I am not so sure the number failed him.

When they brought him home to California, he was buried at Oakdale, a community on the Stanislaus River not far from my grandmother's place. Bob's death stunned all of us. It left me in a state of shock. I cannot remember who told me that Bob had died. Probably it was one of my older sisters. All I know is, I just stood there and screamed. I screamed as loud as I could, hoping that my screams would drown out those awful words I did not want to hear. I was fifteen years old, and the loss of Bob was the closest I had ever been to death up to that point.

My parents, of course, were devastated. The loss of a child is the worst kind of death experience. You never expect to outlive your offspring. But after that tragic event, something very good happened to our family. My mother, who was forty years old, became pregnant the same month my brother Bob died. Everyone was quite surprised. Nine months later, my brother William was born. No one can take someone else's place, but after losing Bob as we had, all of us were happy when Bill arrived.

Louie Cole remained hospitalized in Washington for several months before he was allowed to return to California. He lived near Riverbank, where I had first met him when I stayed with my grandmother. We stayed in touch after he came home to recover, but we were never girlfriend and boyfriend again. Every so often, we wrote to each other, and then finally that stopped.

Many years later, long after I had come home to Oklahoma and had become involved in tribal politics, Louie came to visit me. He had been married several times, and he still collected disability because of the injuries he had received in that fire so many years before. I was not totally comfortable seeing Louie again. There was something brooding about him, and he wanted only to focus on the past, especially the bad times. About a year after his visit, I received a letter from Louie's mother informing me that he had been shot and killed by one of his former wives during a quarrel.

Louie was my first boyfriend, but it was not as if I had a whole string of them. In fact, I was basically shy with boys. However, I did meet several young men at the Indian Center who interested me. One of them was Ray Billy. I was about sixteen when I started to date him. He was Pomo, a California tribe, and was a little older than I was. He had his own apartment. I dated him for about a year. My dad liked him, and that counted for something. Occasionally, Ray got the use of a car, and he would come to our house at Hunter's Point and ask my dad if he could take me for a ride. Other times, my dad let us go for rides in our family car. Everyone liked Ray. He was a gentleman—most of the time.

He was also crafty, and I had to watch my step. One night we were down on the beach. I was getting cold, so he suggested that we go to his place to get a jacket and warm up. It was a classic trick, and I almost fell for it! When we got to his apartment, he said he was tired and we ought to rest on his bed for a while. I came to my senses. I put my foot down and would not cooperate. He thought I was stupid for reacting as I did. A short time later, he dropped me for a girl who had just been crowned Miss Indian San Francisco, or some such title. Ray and I did not see each other again. I was hurt by his treatment, but I pulled through. I learned that most first crushes—even second or third crushes—can be survived.

Friends and family helped me mend my broken heart and get over

Ray Billy. Our music was also a big help. My girlfriends and I listened to rock and roll and to soul music. "Hit the Road, Jack" and "I Found My Thrill on Blueberry Hill" were popular then. We listened to two soul stations, KDIA and KSAN. We dreamed of the time we would be out of school and free.

Most of the time, I was only going through the motions of attending classes. I was never much of a scholar, and I do not have many memories from my years in high school. Those I do have are not of much consequence. My grades ranged from A to F, depending on the subject and my level of interest. Science and math were my downfalls, but I had an affinity for English and literature courses. None of my teachers left enough impact for me even to remember their names. I was not much of a joiner. I did not go in for glee club or the yearbook staff or sports or any of the organizations except Junior Achievement. I did participate in that for a while, and I liked it.

Mostly, I went to the Indian Center. That is still my best teenage memory. Much more was going on at the center besides Ping-Pong games and dance parties. It was the early 1960s, and change was in the air. A person could almost touch it. During that time, many people, including my friends and siblings and I, were aware of the currents of restlessness. The new decade promised to be a time of momentous social movements and open rebellion. There would be sweeping legislation and great achievements, as well as devastating war and senseless tragedies.

Even before the 1960s, the entire Bay area had become a magnet for artists and rebels who were ready and willing to act as the merchants of change. Now a new generation was getting its voice, testing its wings. I was part of that generation. San Francisco was the place to be. We were ready to proceed with the decade and with our lives.

Who Is Cherokee?

Harry Oosahwee (Adawi Donowelani, 2010)

I grew up in a fairly remote Cherokee community in a small two-room house. We were pretty isolated from the mainstream society during this time. Therefore, we were able to maintain close relations to our extended families and maintain a large part of our culture as well as our language. I believe this isolation was by choice: we did not want to be bothered by the white people or the mixed bloods. We wanted to live the life of a Cherokee community: what we had for substance came from the land, creeks, and wild game. We also raised our own hogs, chickens, and cows. Although we did go into town every now and then. We mostly stayed around our communities. On occasion we would visit other communities when there was something going on like a stomp dance, gospel singing or a birthday celebration and there was always a big hog fry during these occasions.

When I was growing up I can remember people having dances around their homes. I can even remember in the earlier fifties when we had the Cherokee Holidays in downtown Tahlequah. The elders would build a fire and have a stomp dance on the front southwest corner of the courthouse building. Back then there were several stomp grounds one could attend. There were Baptist churches near most Cherokee communities where everything was done in the Cherokee language. People would go to a stomp dance on Friday and Saturday nights and be in church on Sunday. This was not unusual when I was growing up. But, there were Cherokees who still had the belief that either you were a traditional stomp ground person or a Christian person.

During some of the meetings, when it was at my grandfather's place, he would butcher two or three hogs at a time and people from different communities and families from those communities would stay for several days afterwards for fellowship. Then when they were getting ready to leave Grandfather would always give them fresh hog meat to take home. This was a common practice with our family.

Grandfather would also talk to us when he took us fishing. Sometimes I would listen and sometimes I would just hear but not listen. And today I wish I had listened more because he talked about a lot of things to come and things he had experienced during his lifetime. One of the things he would tell me is to get the white man's education because he knew I was resisting school and that I might quit. The one thing I remember was that I needed to get a good understanding of the *yoneg*'s language.[1] I needed to understand how he thinks, how he talks, and how he understands his world because it is different. He said that the white man now owns the earth. He has taken everything that was good for our people except our language. He has taken our laws, our medicine, our schools, our land, and if you go into town he owns every store—not one Cherokee owns anything.

He said don't just learn about him, but learn to understand him. He said one can learn something but may not understand it. He said there is a difference in learning something and understanding something. Then he would say this is the only way you are going to be able to survive the changes taking place here on earth.

This was about the time I saw a real shift taking place in our language. It was changing from a predominantly Cherokee-speaking community to a predominantly English-speaking community. This was about the time some of our neighbors in the nearby communities were getting electricity and we would go over on weekends and watch the TV until it went off the air. At the same time most families started to own their own automobiles, making our communities more mobile. It was about this time that my generation was getting real proficient in speaking English and using it more and more to communicate with our friends and in school. We began to bring English into our homes and teaching it to our younger siblings so they did not have to be punished like we were for speaking Cherokee. We were losing more of our elders who spoke only Cherokee, so the younger children who were born after the mid-fifties did not have the opportunity to experience the opportunities we had being surrounded by Cherokee-only speakers. Therefore some of our younger siblings did not learn to speak as fluently and that, I feel, was the real beginning a rapid decline in our Cherokee language usage as a primary means of communication in our communities and that has led us to where we are today with our language loss.

When I first went to college I had no idea what I had got into. I really had no idea how to enroll or that I had to have any paperwork to be accepted into school. All I knew was the coach at Bacone College had told me he needed Indian ball players and said that I had a pretty good arm and a good stick and if I came to his school I had a very good chance to play ball. And I could get some "Indian Money" to pay for my school. I later learned the Indian Money he was talking about was the Bureau of Indian Affairs (BIA) Higher Education Scholarship. I did not know anything like this existed for native students.

In high school we never got any information about scholarships or how to enroll or any information concerning college, but our part-time counselor, who was the superintendent's wife, told me that I would never make it in college because of my high school grades, and my attendance records indicated I was not college material, according to her. She told me the best thing I could do for myself was to learn a trade or join the military.

I knew that Bacone College was known as an Indian college. I first knew about the college when we first went to the Muskogee State Fair, and I could see the light inside Bacone College Chapel steeple from a distance. For years that was the first thing you saw when you came from the north or east into Muskogee, and when I first saw the steeple I asked what that was, and my mom and dad said it was an Indian college. I must have been in fifth grade then.

So in the fall of 1968 I arrived at Bacone College, where my parents dropped me off and left. I went into the largest building on campus and told the person at the desk that I was here to go to school. She asked me my name, where I was from, and if I had been accepted into school, and if I had a dorm room assigned me. I told the lady what the coach had told me about coming here. She was sad to tell me that the coach had got a new job and now they had a new coach.

The school did enroll me. They took me to the Federal Building in Muskogee and had me fill out my papers for the BIA scholarship and some other papers at the school. I was assigned to one of the dorm rooms on campus but had to stay in the gym for about two weeks while the school finished a brand new dorm for women.

This was the first time I met young Indian people, brown people who were thinking like me. Smart Indian young people with ideas that were not your normal mundane ideas. These young people were talking about changes in Indian Country—radical ideas—and it felt good to be around these young people. They were Indians: young people from all over the United States. Up to that point I had met only two other young people, one about my age and the other a little older, who had radical ideas or ideas that did not set well with the established tribal leaders.

After I got enrolled in college I did play some baseball but got more involved in the social and political aspects of college so my stay at Bacone was short-lived. I was suspended from school at the end of the first semester and the little voice in my head said maybe the old high school counselor was right; I may not be college material. Shortly thereafter, during the spring, I was called upon to work for Uncle Sam, drafted into the United States Army, and that was an experience in itself.

After completing my work for Uncle Sam I was more mature and better focused. I went back to Bacone College and cleaned up my old records and graduated from Bacone and got involved with the American Indian Movement (AIM).

Like many young people I got involved with the AIM Movement. My mother told me years later that they were concerned with my safety and were afraid I was changing too much. My dad especially did not like it. He thought AIM was just wasting time and nothing would come out of it. He once told my mother that if he ever saw my face on TV with AIM, she was to tell me not to come home or he would shoot me. You have to understand Dad. Dad was a patriotic man; he was loyal to America. He bled red, white, and blue. He was a highly decorated WWII war veteran, serving with the 15th Air Corps based in Italy, so he did not always agree with what he called my antics. But, years later, he said, "One has to do what one believes." He said he understood why I got involved. I knew during his early days he was also involved with social issues concerning our living conditions in northeastern Oklahoma and our rights as Cherokee people.

I bounced around different parts of Indian Country for a while and eventually graduated from Northeastern State University. All along the way, I saw how society still remained the same—it did not change because I had a college degree. Society still saw the Native as a novelty, a savage, something less than human. Natives were portrayed and stereotyped in a negative light and it is still the same today. For example, as I write this I can drive to Stilwell, Oklahoma, about thirty miles east of Tahlequah and find "Tommy Tommy Hawk," the local high school mascot with his oversized head, big nose, big eyes, with long black braids and wearing fake buckskin. Nothing like a real person or a Cherokee person. Although some progress has been made in Indian Country, not much has changed.

NOTE

1. *Yoneg* is a shortened version of *ayonega,* "white person" and *yonega,* "English language."

Who Is Cherokee?

Federal Recognition, Culture, and Rhetorical Sovereignty

Kimberly G. Wieser

In the title of preceding story, Harry Oosahwee asks what may appear to be an easy question: "Who is Cherokee?" The answer is not as obvious as it seems. While Oosahwee never answers that question directly, his answer is implied, as I have suggested elsewhere, and is common in American Indian discourse when people are making what might be a controversial statement. Oosahwee firmly believes in his answer to this question, but he wants to be as polite as possible about staking his claim. For Oosahwee, to be Cherokee is to be a full-blood Cherokee speaker immersed in Cherokee family, community, lifeways, and culture. He speaks of the years of his upbringing:

> We were pretty isolated from the mainstream society during this time. Therefore, we were able to maintain close relations to our extended families and maintain a large part of our culture as well as our language. I believe this isolation was by choice: we did not want to be bothered by the white people or the mixed bloods. We wanted to live the life of a Cherokee Community: what we had for substance came from the land, creeks, and wild game. We also raised our own hogs, chickens, and cows. Although we did go into town every now and then. We mostly stayed around our communities. On occasion we would visit other communities when there was something going on like a stomp dance, gospel singing or a birthday celebration and there was always a big hog fry during these occasions.

This answer—to be truly Cherokee, one must be a full-blood Cherokee speaker immersed in Cherokee family, community, lifeways, and culture—might not sit well with a lot of people. For one thing, many of the citizens of the three federally recognized Cherokee nations—the Cherokee Nation of Oklahoma (CNO), the United Ketoowah Band of Cherokee Indians (UKB), and the Eastern Band of Cherokee Indians (ECB)—fall outside Oosahwee's definition. While all citizens of these nations descend from ancestors whose lands at the time of contact were in North Carolina, northern South Carolina, Georgia, Tennessee, Virginia, and Alabama, "blood quantum" varies. CNO, in fact, has no blood quantum requirement. All that is required for citizenship is that one has an ancestor listed on the 1903 Dawes Roll. UKB and ECB require one-quarter Cherokee ancestry. Fluent Cherokee speakers are few and far between. Moreover, the diaspora caused by Andrew Jackson's removal of many Cherokees to Indian Territory during the Trail of Tears and further diaspora caused by urbanization and the Relocation Era of the mid-twentieth century spread Cherokee citizens all over the country. Not all citizens grew up in or live in Cherokee communities. Today, Cherokee citizens have diverse lifestyles and reside in many locales. However, they remain Cherokee, otherwise known as *Tsalagi* or *Anikituwah*—the People of Kituwah, the People of the Place That God Made.

Certainly, all those thousands and thousands of people who have

Cherokee descent, who claim a long-ago mythical Cherokee "princess" for a grandmother, or who are members of groups not federally recognized—some of which are more like social clubs or hobbyist associations, and many of which have no connection to traditional Cherokee culture or communities—would fall outside what Oosahwee defines as Cherokee. While some of these people have documentable Cherokee ancestors, some are victims of what Geary Hobson (Cherokee/Quawpaw) calls "paper genocide"; that is, they may have Cherokee ancestry but no proof of that in records.[1] They are not legally Cherokee; that is, a citizen of one of the three federally recognized tribes. Others claiming to be Cherokee may actually have ancestry from other tribes that is lost in the oral history of their families and has been handed down falsely as Cherokee. In the introduction to *The People Who Stayed Behind: Southeastern Indian Writing After the Removal*, Hobson writes of these people, detribalized by the Southern Diaspora, southern people who are tribal descendants of mostly white or mostly black heritage and culture or who were "paper victims" of genocide, a practice Hobson shows to have been widespread: "genocide by administrative or clerical fiat occurred through . . . such methods used by government officials, and later, sometimes by anthropologists and linguists as well." Hobson asks: "What other agents and agencies of disappearance still exist in the Southeast, and are still at work denying identity and sovereignty to indigenous peoples and their descendants?"[2] But there are also people out there claiming to be Cherokee who may have no American Indian ancestry at all, causing quite a bit of consternation for those clearly as identifiable as Cherokee. Hobson continues:

> While it has become commonplace to regard stories of Cherokee grandmothers and great-grandmothers with suspicion (and sometimes even ridicule), given that Cherokees were, and still are, the largest tribal group in and from the American South, the Cherokees are indeed likely the tribe of origination for many modern-day white or black claimants to Southeastern Indian heritage. Furthermore, "Cherokee" often functions as a catch-all designation, since an individual asserting such ties might in actuality be descended from one of the many

> tribes that comprise the Muscogee, or Creek, tribe, or may be from the Natchez or any of the many smaller groups . . . that merged into larger groups. Many families throughout the South have cherished the passed-down stories of Cherokee grandmothers, at first revealing their ancestry with great fear and reluctance, and nowadays with pride and openness.
>
> . . . Federal census reports since 1970 reveal that most black people currently living in the South and who trace their roots at least three generations in the region have some degree of Indian blood. Among white people, the percentage of Indian blood is smaller, though in certain rural areas it is higher.[3]

While this may seem confusing or unimportant to non-Cherokees, for a number of years CNO and ECB have considered this to be a serious problem. Some claiming to be Cherokee have misrepresented to the outside world not only themselves but also what it means to be Cherokee or of Cherokee descent. Some incidents of this have been so offensive that CNO and ECB issued a joint resolution: "BE IT FURTHER RESOLVED that any individual who is not a member of a federally recognized Cherokee tribe, in academia or otherwise, is hereby discouraged from claiming to speak as a Cherokee, or on behalf of Cherokee citizens, or using claims of Cherokee heritage to advance his or her career or credentials."[4]

As a person of distant Cherokee ancestry, I have searched for more than twenty years for documentation. I feel I must add a disclaimer to this introduction. My forebears are alleged by some genealogies to include Ata'gul-kalu (Attakullakulla) and his wife, a Paint Clan woman; their daughter and Black Fox; and Martha Sherill, born in Cherokee, North Carolina, in 1766, on my mother's father's side of my family; and others who I was taught in my own family's oral history were and who I believe were Cherokee—Reeds, Bryants, Littlefields, and Nances, on my father's mother's side of the family. I did not grow up in a Cherokee community. I hardly speak any Cherokee. Though I go to stomp dances and attend and participate in other ceremonies, both southeastern and intertribal, I am not a member of a Cherokee ceremonial ground. Though I grew up in a matriarchal household led by my grandmother and her sisters and learned to cook traditional southeastern Indian foods like chicken and dumplings and cornbread, and learned to pick berries, muscadine grapes, poke salad, and such, I did not grow up with any oral traditions other than those belonging to my immediate family for just a few generations back. My words here are not based on knowledge I gained growing up. My knowledge has been gained through study and scholarship. I hope here that I speak in a good way that does not offend people who are fully grounded in their Cherokee identity in all respects.

Several longer collections of Cherokee stories have been gathered over the years by scholars, notably by James Mooney (1890s), Jack and Anna Kilpatrick (1960s), and by the education director of the Museum of the Cherokee in Cherokee, North Carolina, Barbara Duncan (1990s). Most recently, American Indian literature scholar and CNO citizen Christopher Teuton worked with noted storytellers Woody Hansen, Sammy Still, Sequoyah Guess, and the late Hastings Shade, all citizens of CNO or UKB, to create *The Cherokee Stories of the Turtle Island Liar's Club* (2012).[5] While written collections, as Teuton says of Mooney's work, can provide "a glimpse of Cherokee culture and beliefs," the oral tradition is alive and well through the work of these storytellers and others such as Gayle Ross, Choogie Kingfisher, Robert Lewis, Kathi Littlejohn, and Bo Taylor. The Hastings Shade Memorial Storytelling is held in Tahlequah each year, but Cherokee stories are told in many venues throughout the world—in none, however, more notably than in the everyday lives of Cherokee people and families.

Among the tellers of the stories in this present collection are some of the most authoritative Cherokee voices anyone could have chosen. These stories demonstrate Cherokee values, Cherokee epistemology and logic, and Cherokee ontology, cosmology, and metaphysics as recognized by those with the most authority in Cherokee culture: elders, ceremonial people, and storytellers with culturally centered traditional upbringings. This is rhetorical sovereignty in action. Cherokee people utilize the power of words in both oral and written form to keep on being Cherokee despite all challenge and change. Only the sovereign collective of the Anikituwah's recognition can gift words with any kind of authenticity we can consider valid. If a story does not come from the People to the People or on behalf of the People with cultural endorsement, rights, and responsibilities in a way that is recognizably Cherokee, that story is simply the words of an individual human being. It is not Cherokee.

The Cherokee stories in this portion of the book are divided into three sections. The first is "*Galgogv'i*: New and Old Lies." These stories fall under the category of what anthropologists and others might call "myth." I prefer to avoid that term. "Myth" is simply a word for other people's sacred stories in which the speaker does not believe. "Thunder and the Uk'ten'," as recorded by the Kilpatricks, is one of the old, foundational Cherokee stories. These stories are key to understanding a traditional Cherokee worldview. They are as true to traditional Cherokee people as the Garden of Eden and Shadrach, Meshach, and Abednego are to Jews and Christians—unless you consider Bible stories to be part of the Judeo-Christian mythos. Though it may be of later origin, Hastings Shade's telling of "How the White Man Was Made" is no less a part of the Cherokee worldview. Whether or not these stories are true with a lower case *t*, they are True, from a Cherokee perspective, with a capital *T*—they encapsulate philosophical truths and cultural differences, wisdom necessary for Cherokee people to survive as Cherokee.

"The Rabbit and the Image," recorded by the Kilpatricks, is what many scholars would call a "trickster" story. It focuses on the antics of Jistu (Rabbit), the best-known Cherokee trickster—though certainly other characters, like Possum, can act as tricksters as well, as these stories demonstrate. Readers may notice the commonality with the Uncle Remus stories that Marcia Haag mentions in her introduction to this volume. Whatever the academic jury has to say on the subject of Jistu stories, for traditional Cherokee people, these stories are Cherokee, just as the Rabbit stories of other southeastern tribes, such as Chukfi stories of Choctaws and Chickasaws, are intrinsically part of those cultures. Rabbit stories simultaneously entertain with humor and teach life lessons regarding human nature. Jistu, like the Cherokee people, is a survivor. While Jistu certainly does not act like a good neighbor and is not meant to be a moral example, the stories about him do celebrate his mental acuity and his charm, two of Rabbit's intrinsic traits that help him to survive as—well, *as* Rabbit. He outsmarts the giant cats known as Maneaters by stealing their water during the drought rather than working for it . . . and he gets away with it, too. The story told by Sequoyah Guess of how Rabbit and Possum went looking for wives is also a Jistu story. Though the story collected by the Kilpatricks indicates that the storyteller laughed, suggesting that the telling is humorous, there is nothing funny to readers today in the text itself. As it is recorded here, Guess's story is funny. As Guess tells it in person, the story is hilarious. Though Guess always stays as close as possible to his grandma's tellings of traditional stories, his tellings are contemporized because they are living. His style of storytelling builds in both dramatic vocalizations and suspense, drawing in the audience. The version here, first published in *Cherokee Stories of the Turtle Island Liar's Club*, tries to capture those with transcription in the style of Dennis Tedlock and Dell Hyme's ethnopoetics that Haag discusses earlier. As editor of that volume, Teuton utilized both this "oral poetic method of transcription" and prose, depending upon which of these he and the storyteller felt was appropriate for a particular story. As Teuton put it, "Some storytellers, such as Sequoyah Guess, have an oral performative style that lends itself to this form of transcription."[6] Here, this method is rendered well, making the written record as vivid and lifelike as possible, immersing the reader in the story. As we learn both why possums are often seen on the sides of highways rather smashed up and why possum is prone to playing dead in order to avoid *really* dying, we are also entertained by both his friend Rabbit's tricking him and his own tricking of the fighting townspeople. The next trickster story, "How the Possum Lost His Beautiful Tail," told by Kathi Smith Littlejohn, is a little more direct in its teaching of a life lesson—if one is conceited, one's peers are going to have a tendency to try to bring one back to earth, so to speak. In this tail-tale, also contemporized and dramatized, all the other animals play a trick on the vain and beautiful possum, also teaching the story of why this creature plays dead—this time, out of embarrassment.

The second section, "*Ulvsgedi*: Stories of the Wondrous," involves what many people have labeled as the "supernatural." It is important to note, however, that for American Indian people, what outsiders might consider supernatural is simply natural—such occurrences are a part of life. There is nothing mystical about them—they just *are*. Moreover, as Mary Linn mentions in her introduction to Yuchi stories elsewhere in this volume, Scancarelli claims that Cherokee stories of what non-Indians call "supernatural" experiences are "an important verbal art form and an important factor in affirming cultural beliefs in the presence of supernatural forces in daily life."[7] Linn notes that these stories may involve "Little People . . . the forces of bad medicine, and the presence of those from the spirit world." While I would agree, I suggest that a shift in semantics from the academic to the colloquial reflects a more Cherokee perspective on exactly how natural what non-Indians consider supernatural is seen to be by traditional Indian people of various tribes today. Certainly in daily life, aside from more formal storytelling, people do tell stories of coming across *Yunwi Tsunsdi'* (Cherokee for "Little People," commonly known in eastern Oklahoma as LPs); of the symptoms of being "witched" by those who use medicine in a bad way; or of running into ghosts or other spirits or critters who dwell in the woods or are hidden by the dark, such as a local Bigfoot or two, which some say are the same as *Tsul 'Kalu* from traditional stories. These stories are not only entertaining as they relay experiences that are frightening or at least exciting; they also relay crucial information on how respectfully, wisely, and safely someone else handled an encounter with the supernatural.

It is not surprising, then, that several stories in the present volume reflect this. "The Owl at the Window," "Crossing Safely," "Santeetlah Ghost Story," "The Little People and the Nunnehi," and "The Spirit of an Ancestor" show that encounters of this kind are not only within living memory of Cherokee people; they still occur.

The final section, "*Kanoheda*: Philosophy, History, and Memoir," contains several types of "tellings." "The Language and the Fire" is a straightforward explanation by Hastings Shade of the relationship between two aspects of Cherokee life that are crucial both to identity and to the continuance of the Cherokee people. Cherokee people, by one definition, one of the most traditional definitions, are "people of one fire." This fire was brought by Doyunisi (Water Spider) and, as Hastings says, was a gift of the Creator and "has burned continuously since ancient times." This fire was brought to each of the stomp dance ceremonial grounds. The ceremonies performed there include music made by the singing of men's voices accompanied by sound of the terrapin shell shakers on the women's legs. As long as the ceremonies continue, as long as the language is spoken to Fire, life as Cherokee people will endure.

Other stories included in this section—the excerpt from "A Cherokee Vision of Eloh'," told by Sakiya Sanders in 1896, and "The Cherokee Migration Story," told by Sequoyah Guess, are the same kind of old, foundational Cherokee story as "Thunder and the Uk'ten'" from the first section. "The Trail of Tears," told by Freeman Owle, tells more recent history and explains aspects of Cherokee life such as mixed ancestry and how Indian Removal affected the ancestors of those who live today in Oklahoma, as well as those in North Carolina, explaining how federal recognition of the Eastern Band came about. The story that precedes Harry Oosahwee's "Who Is Cherokee?" is an excerpt from the late CNO chief Wilma Mankiller's facilitated autobiography and shows how Cherokee identity survives even the Relocation Era, when the U.S. government sent Indian people from many, many tribes to cities in an attempt to urbanize and assimilate them and ultimately do away with the trust relationship, Section 8 of the U.S. Constitution.

While these written recordings of the oral tradition can never replace the living words of the people, while they may give only "a glimpse of Cherokee culture and beliefs," I do believe that readers will enjoy them immensely. And perhaps for some, with no chance to go home as Teuton did to learn from elders and storytellers, this collection can help people understand just a bit of what their distant Cherokee ancestors believed, help them understand just a tiny portion more what it means to be Cherokee, what it means to be Anikituwah, and how those who ended up in Indian Territory and those who stayed behind continue to be so.

NOTES

1. In his classes at the University of Oklahoma, Dr. Hobson has further outlined his paradigm of what constitutes an "Indian" that he lays out in the introduction to *The People Who Stayed*. He suggests that there are four categories that make up Indian identity—legal, social, cultural, and genetic. Geary Hobson, Janet McAdams, and Kathryn Walkiewicz, *The People Who Stayed: Southeastern Indian Writing After Removal* (Norman: University of Oklahoma Press, 2010).
2. Hobson et al., *People Who Stayed*, 1.
3. Hobson et al., *People Who Stayed*, 8.
4. The first version I saw of this document was listed as Joint Council of the Cherokee Nation and the Eastern Band of Cherokee Indians, Resolution #14-08, "A Resolution Opposed to Fabricated Cherokee 'Tribes' and 'Indians,'" Catoosa, Oklahoma, April 9, 2008.
5. Christopher B. Teuton, with Hastings Shade, Sammy Still, Sequoyah Guess, and Woody Hansen, *Cherokee Stories of the Turtle Island Liar's Club* (Chapel Hill: University of North Carolina Press, 2012). The earlier works are James Mooney, *Myths of the Cherokee*, Nineteenth Annual Report, Bureau of American Ethnology 1897–98, pt. I (Washington DC: U.S. Government Printing Office, 1900); Jack F. Kilpatrick and Anna G. Kilpatrick, *Friends of Thunder: Folktales of the Oklahoma Cherokees* (1964; repr. Norman: University of Oklahoma Press, 1995); and Barbara Duncan, ed., *Living Stories of the Cherokee* (Chapel Hill: University of North Carolina Press, 1998).
6. Teuton et al., *Cherokee Stories*, 10.
7. J. Scancarelli, "Cherokee Stories of the Supernatural," *Kansas Working Papers in Linguistics* 21 (1996): 143–58.

KOASATI

Koasati (Coushatta) Literature

Linda Langley

THE COUSHATTA TRIBE OF LOUISIANA

The Coushatta Tribe of Louisiana has been located in the piney woods of southwest Louisiana for almost 150 years. After the Spanish explorer Hernando DeSoto encountered a Coushatta community on an island in the Tennessee River in 1540, the Coushattas relocated several times to avoid European encroachment. By the 1700s the Coushattas had resettled near the confluence of the Coosa and Tallapoosa rivers in Alabama and became part of the powerful Muskogean-speaking Creek Confederacy while maintaining their own culture and language. Following the 1795 Treaty of San Lorenzo the influential Coushatta chiefs Stilapihkachatta (Red Shoes) and Pahimikko (Grass Chief) led a group of nearly one thousand Coushattas westward to establish villages in the neutral territory between French, Spanish, American, and Mexican territories. Using existing homestead laws, approximately three hundred Coushattas ultimately settled in the 1880s at Bayou Blue north of Elton, Louisiana, where they were finally re-recognized as a tribe by the secretary of the interior in June 1973.

The Coushatta are recognized for their strong sense of community and self-determination, qualities gained from years of struggle and numerous relocations. Tribal elders adopted the saying, "The Struggle Has Made Us Stronger" and eked out a living by farming, working for the local timber company, and making long-leaf pine needle baskets, which have since become prized collectables. When offered the "opportunity" to join other tribes on reservations in Oklahoma, the Coushatta chiefs politely refused and used existing homestead laws to purchase their own land. When the BIA refused to provide their children with educational assistance, the Coushatta families contributed lumber and nails and built their own school. They lived in Louisiana for nearly a century without the state or federal government paying much attention or offering support to the community. Even now researchers find Coushatta historical documents filed under "Creek," "Choctaw," and "Cherokee" in such illustrious repositories as the National Archives.[1] This pseudo-invisibility never seemed to bother older tribal members, who just laughed and said, "We know who we are. We don't need anyone else to tell us who we are."

Life in the community changed dramatically when the tribe opened Coushatta Casino Resort in 1995. The business enterprise grew to be one of the largest private employers in the state of Louisiana, significantly impacting the economy in the tribe and surrounding communities. Along with the economic growth and prosperity, the tribe began to see a worrying trend of Native language loss as more families had multiple computers, televisions, and toys that continually streamed the English language into their homes. Where once Koasati was spoken everywhere in the community—at the gas station, convenience store, Laundromat, community meetings, tribal events, and ball games—it slowly became relegated to gatherings of elders. Today the youngest native Koasati speaker who speaks the language in daily conversation is twenty-five, and less than one-third of the more than nine hundred enrolled members identify themselves as fluent in Koasati.[2]

THE KOASATI LANGUAGE PROJECT

In the summer of 2006 we began developing a plan to reverse the trend of Koasati language loss. After my husband, Bertney Langley, director of the Coushatta Heritage Department, and I received training in language documentation at the University of Arizona's American Indian Language Development Institute, the tribal council approved our plan and held a community meeting to solicit volunteers to work on the project.[3] More than thirty volunteers signed up to work on the language project at that first meeting, and the Koasati Language Project was born. The first meeting of the Koasati Language Committee was held in June 2007;

over the course of a weekend workshop, tribal members discussed the relative merits of adopting a spelling system for Koasati (which had never previously been done in the community), developed a practical orthography, and developed ideas for various products in Koasati, including bumper stickers, T-shirts, coloring books, and refrigerator magnets. There was never any discussion of payment or other incentives for committee members; to this day no one on the committee has asked for compensation for their time.

In almost seven years of sometimes difficult and tedious language documentation work, meetings of the Koasati Language Committee have remained upbeat gatherings, well attended, full of laughter, and always accompanied by delicious home-cooked meals prepared by committee members. Even when differences of opinion arise over such issues as pronunciation or translation, members have agreed to disagree and move on rather than allow meetings to become bogged down or contentious. The supportive, altruistic attitude of the committee is facilitated by a common understanding at the core of all its activities, which is that the Koasati Language Project was conceived, initiated, and run by the Coushatta people from the start. This is their project, and they call all the shots. When they lack expertise, they seek linguists and anthropological consultants who work well with the community and train tribal members in best practices of language documentation, transcription, archiving, and increasingly, language immersion.[4] Tribal members have conducted nearly one hundred hours of interviews and other speech events, cataloging, transcribing, and translating Koasati texts from numerous speakers, including all the narratives in this collection.[5]

THE STORIES

When the idea for publishing this selection of Koasati literature was presented to the Language Committee members, they listened politely then began discussions in Koasati. They decided to proceed with the effort principally because it provided the opportunity to present a living, vibrant community where Koasati is still spoken daily. Their conditions for participation were the same as those governing all their efforts: that ownership of the texts remain with the tribe, as it has for all the language products produced by the project.[6] The only difficulty was in culling from so many hours of life stories, traditional narratives, and humorous texts to produce a concise and cohesive collection.

We had initially planned to select narratives based on typology, such as *Chokfathihilka* (Rabbit Tales), legends, etc. However, committee members felt that early ethnographers and linguists had focused too much attention on this kind of material, and not enough on the everyday narratives people commonly told at gatherings. For example, text collection at committee meetings usually centered on topics of interest within the community, such as starting school, learning English, treatment in school and on the bus, and employment in the Jim Crow–era South. Gradually, the collection took on the shape of the project itself, beginning with one of the earliest traditional tales obtained, transcribed and translated with permission of an elder, and ending with the first written narrative produced in Koasati by a committee member.

If it had been possible, we would have chosen to include material from each tribal member who contributed to the project in both Koasati and English, but space and stylistic considerations would not permit that. Instead we utilized free translations of recorded texts, sometimes adapting them to include concepts that were understood in Koasati but lost meaning in translation to English or in the transition from oral to written form. The following narratives were selected and edited by the members of the Koasati Language Committee, with great respect for the elders who protected and preserved the community, language, and customs of the people for so many generations. These narratives are presented with the knowledge that *Nihta chafaakap ya oyaak komatlawista immoolaahiskan*, "One day all of this will belong to our children."

NOTES

1. The most humorous example of misidentification occurred at the Smithsonian's Archives, which had filed two 7-inch reel-to-reel tapes of Koasati as "Italian."
2. Language surveys conducted by the Coushatta Heritage Department in 2010 and 2013.
3. The first summer at AILDI was funded by the National Science Foundation,

which has since provided five years of funding for the project (Grants 0804096 and 1065334). Special thanks are due to Dr. Susan Penfield, whose work and support at both AILDI and NSF started and nurtured us along this journey.

4. The Koasati Language Committee is indebted to Dr. Jack Martin from the College of William and Mary, whose contribution of countless hours of his own and his students' work has truly made him "Komokla," our friend.
5. Special thanks are due to Stephanie Hasselbacher Berryhill, a 2015 PhD recipient from William and Mary, for assistance in scheduling, recording, and creating ELAN files for many of these interviews.
6. To date these projects include a talking dictionary, a picture dictionary, a phrase book, a sixth grade textbook, children's books, and an iPhone app, all of which can be accessed at http://koasatiheritage.org/.

Traditional Stories

The Bear Hunter and the Alligator's Gift

Isabel Celestine Robinson, narrator,
Claude Medford, collector (ca. 1960)
Loretta R. Williams, transcriber and translator (February, 2009).
Linda Langley, Jaime Hill, and Crystal Williams, editors.

An Indian man was heading out to hunt for a bear, and kept going until he reached the deep end of the woods.
When he reached the deep woods, he came upon an alligator lying on the ground.
The alligator asked the man, "Can you help me get back to the water?"
"I can help you," the hunter said.
He put the alligator across his back and carried him.
The hunter walked and walked until he came to a big lake, and set the alligator down very gently on the shore.
As the alligator slowly went down the pond, he said,
"Now when I am good and ready I will get out and I will tell you something very precious."
The hunter said, "Then I will wait for you," and the alligator went into the water.
The alligator splashed and splashed and splashed in the muddy water.
He did that for a while and finally came out.
When he finally came out and lay down, the hunter could see that he was really a very, very big alligator.
When the alligator came out, he sang some medicine songs to the hunter, some Indian
medicine songs, so that he would have that knowledge from now on.
So the man sat and listened. He listened and listened to everything the alligator told him.

"Now you will always have that," the alligator told the Indian man.
Therefore, even now, people are getting healed by Indian medicine.
This is not a rabbit tale. This is the real truth. This knowledge is being used
right now. So when we get treated with this medicine, we get better even now.
That is all that I know.

NOTE

This story was originally collected decades before author permission forms were commonly obtained or kept on file by archives. When the Coushatta community first began discussing ideas for the Koasati language project, they asked that we contact every tribal elder to get their permission to proceed with making recordings of songs, stories, words, etc. In March 2007 Bertney and I made a trip to the nursing home where Isabel Robinson was living. Then in her late eighties, Isabel was sharp as a tack and knew exactly when she and her late sister (Irene) Annette Abbey had recorded this story. Bertney asked Isabel if she would support the project, and she thought long and hard before answering. She finally answered that it was time for the Koasati people to take steps to record their language, because their grandchildren were no longer speaking the old language but had mainly switched to English. She gave us permission to use this story, along with traditional songs she and her sister had recorded, in whatever way would be helpful to encourage young people to embrace their language and culture. She also asked that we make a special recording of her talking to her grandchildren, to be kept just for them. She looked at the camcorder case and asked me why I was waiting to turn the camera on. During the entire time we spent with her, not one word was spoken in English until we left her room, when her daughter let out a long breath and said, "Well, you could have knocked me over with a feather when Mom agreed!" In honor of Isabel we selected this narrative as the first story, symbolizing the new era in which the tribe conducted this project themselves, on their own terms. —*Linda Langley*

How the Owl Got Skinny Legs

Ronnie Abbey, narrator (2009)

Bertney and Eli Langley, collectors. Loretta Williams, transcriber and translator. Linda and Bertney Langley, editors.

I remember stories my grandparents used to tell us a long time ago. People today might not have ever heard some of these stories. This is one I remember called "How the Owl Got Skinny Legs":

They use to tell me, if you could ever see the body of an owl with the feathers pulled off, you would realize that the body is really very small, with hardly any thigh, as if anybody ever wanted to eat an owl anyway.

So they used to ask us, "Do you know why the owl's legs got so thin?"

It is said that a long time ago Owl was out flying around, and he looked down and saw Mouse.

And so, Owl flew around, flew down and caught Mouse in his claws, and sat on him.

Then Owl just sat there watching Mouse for a while.

Finally Owl pressed down on Mouse and said, "What do they say my name is?"

But the mouse didn't say anything.

Owl pressed him down harder and again said, "What do they say my name is?"

Still the mouse didn't say anything.

And then again, Owl pressed the mouse down harder, and again he asked, "What do they say my name is?"

And so finally Mouse said, "They say you are the Night's Chief."

Then, again, pinning him down, Owl said, "What do they say my name is?"

And then, again, Mouse would say, "They say you are the Night's Chief."

They did that for a while.

And then the mouse was getting weak and sickly.

Then Owl asked the mouse, "What do they say my name is?"

Mouse said, "They say you are the Night's Chief."

Then Owl got so excited, he jumped up and down and landed on the ground.

Then again Owl would say, "What do they say my name is," and Mouse would say, "They say you are the Night's Chief,"

Owl jumped up and down, ruffling his feathers making an excited noise and landing on the ground again.

And so they did that for a while and then Owl asked Mouse one more time and when he jumped up, the mouse ran into a hole he had been making right there, jumped in and took off, escaping through another outlet and running away while the owl sat waiting on him.

The mouse came out somewhere else and ran away. The owl sat there waiting and waiting for him to come back. As the owl sat there upon the hole, waiting on the mouse that never came back, its legs got skinny. That's how the owl got skinny legs, as they say.

NOTE

Ronnie grew up in the tribal community in Elton, Louisiana, then moved to the Alabama-Coushatta community in Livingston, Texas, where Bertney conducted this interview. Ronnie works for the National Park Service and likes to spend a lot of time outdoors; at his request this interview was conducted outside by a little pond near where he lives. This story about the tiny mouse outsmarting the owl is funny, but also somewhat scary, because the Coushattas are taught that owls can be dangerous creatures, harbingers of death that sometimes are not quite what they seem to be. One of the most interesting aspects of the Koasati project was that many interviews, like this one, were conducted by tribal members, entirely in Koasati, with no outsiders present. When this occurred, Ronnie, like many narrators, seemed to feel more comfortable telling stories he remembered about creatures like Owl, to be recorded but not necessarily translated or shared with outsiders.

Editing Ronnie's story, I gained an understanding of how frustrating it must be for fluent speakers to work with me so patiently day after day, and why they often say that many of their stories have lost their humor or meaning in translation. In part this is due to my progress as a Koasati learner, so that I can now sometimes understand meanings in the original language better than in translation, but in a story like this one it is primarily due to how much context is provided by the oral storytelling devices—the pantomime of the owl swooping down with claws outstretched, the screeching sounds made by the owl, the terrible sense of dread that builds as the owl keeps pressing the mouse for an answer he refuses to give. On the original tape, after hearing Ronnie tell this story, Bertney says, "*Hiichaliimaam* (I can almost see it)." However, when I tried to edit this story to fit into this narrative collection, I had to call Ronnie to ask lots of questions about the ending—I just could not get it without the audiovisual aids. To clarify matters for me, Ronny explained how much it pleased the owl when the mouse finally pronounced him *tamooka-stim-mikko* (chief or king of the night). Each time the mouse used this title, the owl got more excited by his own sense of self-importance, hopping up and down, stomping his feet, and hollering. Ronnie demonstrated Owl's behavior for me over the phone, even mimicking his calls and the sound of his feathers ruffling as he jumped. Thus the smaller creature, the mouse, cleverly used the owl's hubris to trick him into over-exercising and weakening his legs, making him ripe for the mouse's final escape.

Koasati narratives involving Owl and Mouse have been published by John R. Swanton in *Myths and Tales of the Southeastern United States*, Bureau of American Ethnology Bulletin 88 (Washington DC: Government Printing Office, 1929),198, narrated by Selin Langley; and Geoffrey Kimball, translator, in *Koasati Traditional Narratives* (Lincoln: University of Nebraska Press 2010), 157, narrated by Bel Abbey. However, neither of these previous versions contains the element of explaining how Owl came to have skinny legs.—*Linda Langley*

Getting Fire from the Bear

Crystal Williams, narrator and translator (2013)
Adapted from a story told by her grandmother, Mabel Battise

A long time ago, Nita (Bear) was the only animal in the forest to have Tikba (Fire). He guarded it and kept it secret from the other animals, so that he was the only creature to always be warm and able to cook his food. At first, Nita took great care of Tikba, always feeding it and stoking it at night so it wouldn't go out. As time went on, however, Nita began to take Tikba for granted, and after a while he became careless in taking care of Tikba.

One day, Nita woke up to find that Tikba had burned down. He needed to find wood to feed Tikba, but he had used up all of the wood around his den, and he was also very hungry himself. "I will go to get food for us," Nita told Tikba. He went out into the woods, but instead of returning to Tikba right away, he remembered some delicious berries on the other side of the forest and decided he would go get some for himself.

Tikba began to be afraid that he would die before Nita returned, and he began to cry out. "Help me!" he cried, but there was nobody to hear or help him. His flame got lower, and his voice got weaker, but still he kept trying to shout out and cry "Help! I'm going out!"

Just then some Koasati Indians happened by, and they heard the sound of something crying for help. They went into the den, and saw that Tikba had almost gone out. "We will help you," the Koasati said. "What should we bring to feed you, and how shall we take care of you?" So Tikba told them how to find branches and wood to feed him, and how to build a wall around him with stones or dirt so he wouldn't go out at night when they were sleeping. He told them how to carry him safely from place to place, and how to share burning sticks and logs to start another fire without putting his out. After a while, the Koasati Indians asked Tikba if he wanted to go home with them, so that they could always take care of him.

That is how the Koasati people came to have Fire, why all of their dances and special ceremonies are done around the fire, and why, to this day, clan animals are shown as gathered around a fire.

NOTE

Crystal told this story to a group of children at a language immersion camp. The original plan was to have an older tribal member tell the story in Koasati, but it quickly became clear that the children would not be able to understand the story, so Crystal offered to tell it in English. This is the only narrative in the collection originally told in English, and it represents one of the few instances when English was the primary language used in any gathering of Koasati Language Committee members. Perhaps the importance of hearing a traditional tale impressed the children, because the entire multi-generational audience was spellbound, and no one moved a muscle during or for several minutes after she told this story. —*Linda Langley*

Modern Stories and Memoirs

How We Survived Long Ago

Doris Robinson Celestine Battise and Jamison "Jimmy" Poncho, narrators. Claudine Celestine Hasting and Bertney Langley, interviewers (2009). Linda Langley and Jack Martin, collectors. Linda and Bertney Langley, translators and editors.

A long time ago, the bayous were so pretty and the water was so clean that everyone would go swimming in it—not like now when the water is all muddy and full of tree roots and trash. We had one body of water on one side of the community where we would go to swim, and one on the other side where we could walk to go swim. The one on the east side (across from Indian Bible Church) is where people used to get baptized.

It was very hard to get work in those days, and the men had to go wherever the logging crews were working.[1] Sometimes they had to walk a long way, past Basile, close to Bayou Nezpique. Grandmother would cook and pack them a lunch, and they would go camp out all night so they could be there on time to work in the morning. While they were there the men would also chop a lot of swamp cane and they would bring back the swamp cane to make baskets to sell. They used to chop as much cane as they could carry, bring it back, and then start making baskets.

Sometimes several cousins would get together to make baskets, then when they hitched up the wagon they would load the baskets and get on to go sell them. The group would tell us, "You go ask the people if they want baskets." I [Doris] was small so I didn't know any better, so I'd knock on the door (of houses) and ask people if they wanted to buy baskets.[2] If they said yes, they would come to the wagon and pick out the one they wanted, and then trade for items like bacon, rice, sweet potato, and eggs. "Ask for a little bit more," they would tell me, since I was not shy. If they would bring things like rice or sugar, we had our own sack, and they would fill it up. They sewed those sacks out of pieces of clothing in those days. Then, after a while, when they saw our wagon coming, they would wave to us to stop, so my cousin said, "They must really want our baskets, so ask for more!"

The people were very glad to see we brought food home when we got back. That's how we lived and survived back then, we traded our baskets, and got rice, and beans, and potatoes, and live chickens, and so we ate. We'd trade baskets for whatever we could, so we could eat, but we kids were really hoping for syrup too.[3] One of the things we also traded a lot was firewood for cabbage—we got cabbage in trade so often that to this day I [Jimmy] do not like the smell of cabbage cooking!

People had to walk everywhere in those days, because no one in the community had a car. People would pack a lunch and walk to church on Sundays. When they got to church, they would hang their lunch in a tree so nothing could eat it. Sometimes the cows would get to it and eat our lunch! So the older people would say climb higher, and we kids would have to climb the tree higher to put our lunch up even higher.

In those days everyone had to work hard, and even little children had lots of chores around the house. We kids had to help our parents plant the fields, pick the crops, shuck the corn and pound it, everything. Whenever it was time to pound corn, they used to tell us just pound it hard enough to get the skin off, don't pound it so hard you make it shatter—the inside is the good part for making *chawahka* (traditional corn soup). Early in the morning they would get us up and make us pound the corn, before we went to school, so when we got home the *chawahka* would already be cooked.

We also used to help our parents make mounds to store the sweet potatoes. First we would put a big circle of pine straw on the ground, then we put the sweet potatoes on top of that, then we covered them with more pine straw, and put sweet potatoes on top of that, and covered it with more pine straw, and so on—the last layer we put dirt on top.[4] We had several of these mounds in the fields, and we would remember where these mounds were located and which ones were ours—when it was cold and rainy (i.e., during winter months, when there was no food) and our parents needed to cook, they would send us kids out and tell us to get some sweet potatoes, so we would go dig some out. They always told us to be sure to cover the mound back up carefully.

We were very embarrassed to eat at school in front of the white kids, because we didn't have bread to bring to school like they did. We would pack a lunch with the sweet potatoes once they were baked and that's what we would bring to school. We really wanted to have the store-bought bread like the rich kids had. Even though times were so hard, and we were so poor, we always had enough food to eat—but we had to work hard for what we had.

One day my grandfather was working in the fields plowing, and after he got through eating at noon he stopped under a tree to rest. An old French man passing by in a wagon saw him lying there, and called out, "Hey, John, when is it going to rain?" It had been hot, and dry, dry, dry—it hadn't rained for a long time, and everyone was waiting for the drought to end. My grandfather answered, "Tonight—it's going to rain tonight." That night it started to rain a lot, and it sure rained hard! I think he just got lucky, but after that I think a lot of the white people thought he did something.

I [Doris] really wanted to go to school because I was the youngest in my family, so one time I told the older ones I would carry their lunches if they would let me go. In those days the school was on piers, so when I got there the others went inside and I crawled underneath the floor. There were cracks in the floorboards, so I could see the teacher at the blackboard and hear him teaching. I stayed underneath the school until recess, then came out and played with the kids, and when they went back inside I crawled back underneath the school until it was time to go home that afternoon. After that my mother let me start going to school with the other kids.

We didn't have any shoes, so even when it was cold and the ground was frozen we had to walk to school. Boy, did our feet curl up! Even though we didn't have shoes, we were sent to go to school anyway, so we went. We used to snatch the icicles up off the young shoots at the base of the trees and eat them while we walked, almost like young kids today eat [ice cream or snow cones].[5] I guess because we wanted the ice, we would eat it. You don't see that too often anymore because there is no more frost or frozen areas—we had a lot more back then. Some kids got so cold that they turned around and went back home, but Sampson (Robinson) said, "Let's you and me go ahead—jump on my back and I'll carry you like a horseback ride." I don't think we even had coats, but I got on his back and he ran all the way to the old schoolhouse.

In those days the school was located near where the Indian Church is today, and it was just a one-room schoolhouse for first through fourth grades.[6] On cold days they built a fire, but even then we were so cold sometimes we just couldn't get warm.

We kids knew not to complain, so no matter how cold we were we just sat there. When they would call "Primary," the first and second grade would go to the bench by the blackboard and learn, then when they would call the older grades they would go and learn, and so we would rotate. Mr. L. L. Simmons was our teacher, and if you didn't behave he would pinch you hard under your arm and bring you to stand by the window. He was really tall, so when he pinched you like that, you had to walk on your toes to get where you were going or it would really hurt!

There was a brick well located by the church and schoolhouse in those days. At recess and lunch time, we kids would throw the bucket down and pull the rope back up to get water. That water might have been dirty, but it sure tasted good to us! Later when everybody got running water they stopped using that well—they filled in the hole. Most people in the community today don't remember that we ever had a well there—there's a lot of things people today don't remember about life back then.

NOTES

1. Jimmy Poncho and Doris Battise are first cousins, grandchildren of John and Winnie Poncho. Jimmy was born in 1922 and Doris in 1926, so some of their fondest childhood memories occurred during the era of the Great Depression, when jobs were scarce, especially for tribal members whose education, knowledge of English, and access to resources were limited. They very much enjoyed the opportunity this interview gave them to visit

together and reminisce about the olden days. Both being strong supporters of the Koasati Language Project, and of language documentation in general, this was not the first time either person had been interviewed. What made this interview unique was that it covered joint memories involving each other and was conducted entirely in Koasati by Doris's daughter Claudine and Jimmy's cousin Bertney, so that Jimmy and Doris were able to relax and enjoy sharing stories. Many of the stories they told during this interview were translated, edited, and combined to fit into one narrative.

It was interesting to hear them talk about fond memories of a time before tribal families had any modern conveniences. Jimmy remembered the moon being so bright when he was a child—before any bright lights or tall buildings were in the area—that it was almost like daylight at night; he said children wanted to play all night and only went to sleep when their parents fussed at them. Both Jimmy and Doris said that as they got older they realized life had been very hard for their parents and grandparents, because there were no jobs for Indian people and no opportunities to make money. They described detailed survival strategies developed by the older people, like making pine straw mounds to store sweet potatoes, using a metal rod to "fish" for turtles in bayous (the rod was jabbed into the water to find the tail so that the turtle could be picked up without the person being bitten); making slingshots to kill enough birds for a meal; and children crossing the bayou on a *filbacha* (log) to pick blackberries and sell them for fifteen cents a gallon.

Jimmy Poncho passed away at the age of eighty-nine in June 2011, two years after this interview. There are no words to describe the void that his passing left in the lives of his children, grandchildren, extended tribal family, or friends. Those who heard his warm laugh or experienced his rich sense of humor are deeply saddened at his loss but also comforted by the legacy of memories and stories he left behind, such as those in this collection: *Komawiichito̱ stakoyokpa̱a̱hos*—we are so glad that you helped us.—*Linda Langley*

2. Doris mentioned going on several specific basket-selling trips with other renowned basket makers like Rosabel Sylestine, Madeleine Celestine, and Margaret John, saying in classic understated Koasati style, "We really enjoyed it—since we were all kin, we stuck together." Sometimes when they did not have access to a wagon or other transportation, basket-selling trips were done on foot by visiting farms and homes surrounding the community, along the Lauderdale Road.

3. Likely Steen's cane syrup. Older tribal members' narratives include mention of syrup but do not include a specific description of the type of syrup. Follow-on questions generated suggestions of homemade molasses-type dark syrups similar to Steen's, typically eaten on fry bread. This was a real treat for children.
4. Doris used her hands to demonstrate covering the sweet potatoes with four to five inches of pine straw. When she described the final layer covering the mound, she used the Koasati word *sancho*, which is literally translated as "sand." However, we have used editorial license and substituted the Koasati word *okthi*, "dirt," because it is hard to imagine they had large amounts of sand in the fields or would have been able to support pine straw mounds with sand.
5. Doris says these ice treats were called *apakko*, which is the name of the flowers that the ice grew on (literally translated as "passion flower"); however, from their conversation it is clear that they were talking about eating the ice that grew around the cluster of flowers, not the flowers themselves.
6. Coushatta students who wanted to keep going to school past fourth grade could attend public school in Elton. Because of hardships, many could not do so. Both Jimmy and Doris said that continuing school would have meant getting up even earlier to do chores, such as feeding animals and cutting firewood, then walking or running a mile or more each morning to catch a bus that would take them into Elton.

Hunting in the Olden Days, and Tomatoes

Dan Sylestine, narrator (2009 and 2012)
Stephanie Hasselbacher Berryhill and Jack Martin,
collectors. Loretta Williams, transcriber and translator.
Linda Langley, Jaime Hill, and Crystal Williams, editors.

When I was little and growing up, I never hunted deer, only hunted squirrels and rabbits.

There was only one gun in those days, and only one bullet for our gun, so we would take turns hunting with it.

When I was fixing to go into the woods to hunt squirrels, I would get the dogs, and I would tell my mom, "Be ready, when I bring it back, so you can cook it and we can eat it."

After saying that, I'd go hunting, and kill two or three squirrels, and run back with them all the way from the woods.

When I brought the squirrels to my mother, she would clean and cook them then we would eat them.

We used to do that all the time, and she would say, "I must have really believed in you, that you would kill some so we could eat."

I used to wonder, "What would have happened if I came back without killing any?"

Another thing I remember was that I used to run around and play barefoot. When I was small a lot of the Indian kids did that, because most of us didn't have shoes in those days. I used to run barefoot all over the place, and sometimes I would step on something sharp, like broken glass. When that happened, I would be out of commission for up to a month.

The older people used to say that when you get a cut, you are not supposed to eat tomatoes.

That was a saying that was kind of like a rule you were supposed to follow. When I wanted tomatoes, I would sneak off to my grandmother's house, and she would give me some. She used to say, "If it hurts, don't tell anyone, so you don't get in trouble!"

NOTE

Dan Sylestine was one of the first people to volunteer for the Koasati Language Committee; along with his wife Janice, he has faithfully driven from Orange, Texas, to attend committee meetings and working sessions for more than six years. He is often asked to tell a story or relate a memory from his own youth and invariably relates something that makes his audience laugh. Tribal members readily appreciate his knowledge, humor, and straight-faced style of delivery, and the time he introduced himself to visiting scholars as being "from Indonesia" is still laughed about in the tribal communities in Louisiana and Texas. In a second story about tomatoes he refers to *aibachilka*, a term that is difficult to translate but generally understood as "rules governing conduct."—*Linda Langley*

Grandmother and the Nail

Bertney Langley, narrator and translator (2012)
Jack Martin, Collector. Linda Langley, Jaime Hill, and Crystal Williams, editors.

When I hear stories that other people tell, I remember some about my grandmother. I used to stay with her at her house as much as I could.

My grandmother was a medicine lady for the tribe, and people used to come to her for her services when they were sick or hurt.

My story took place when I was playing outside one time and happened to step on a nail. I didn't tell anybody, and the next day or two my foot started to get dark and swollen.

When my grandmother saw me limping around, she asked, "What is wrong with you?" so I had to tell her about the nail. She asked, "How come you didn't tell me right away when it happened?!"

I told her, "I didn't want to get fussed at, so I didn't tell you."

My grandmother sent for my Uncle Bel, and told me to tell him where the nail was. I told him it was on a board, and described where the board was lying. My Uncle went and found the board, and took the nail out, and brought it to her. My grandmother did the medicine, and took some grease, and greased the nail, and told my uncle to go take it to a place where there was running water, like in the bayou. She told him to put the nail into the running water.

He did that, and the next day I was able to walk, and nothing hurt. I still don't know how she did that. I always wondered how she did things like that—I don't know how, but that's how they used to treat us when we got hurt.

NOTE

Bertney's grandmother was Ency Robinson Abbey Abbott (1897–1956), the youngest daughter of Louisa Williams Robinson (1855–1932) and one of the last Coushatta women to practice traditional medicine. Some of Ency

Abbott's medicinal knowledge may have come from her maternal grandfather, August Williams, whom Bureau of American Ethnography photographer M. R. Harrington photographed in 1908. Harrington's plate is labeled with the statement "Old man is a doctor." National Museum of the American Indian, Smithsonian Institution, negative no. 2739. Bertney's uncle (Ency's son) was the famed Coushatta storyteller and artisan Bel Abbey.—*Linda Langley*

Another Story about Grandmother and a Nail

Barbara Langley, narrator (2012)
Jack Martin, collector. Bertney Langley, translator. Linda Langley, Jaime Hill, and Crystal Williams, editors.

I also have a story about my grandmother. My grandmother was also a medicine person. My story is about a nail and a medicine person, too. My story is a lot like Bertney's, but mine is different because my foot didn't heal right away.

One day I was playing outside barefoot, and I stepped on a nail. It hurt so much, and I cried so much, that my grandmother didn't know what to do with me. My grandmother sent somebody to get some pine sap. She put some pine sap on my cut, but it didn't make my foot feel any better. "What did you do with the nail?" my grandmother asked me.

At that time, somebody had built a fire outside, and I was so mad at that nail that I threw the nail in the fire. I told my grandmother that I had thrown the nail in the fire to burn it up.

"That's not what you're supposed to do," Grandmother said.

It took a while for me to get healed, because the medicine did not work right away. I never forgot to ask her first after that.

My grandmother used to really watch over me. If something happened, she was always there for us, and we always used to go to her.

NOTE

When Barbara heard Bertney's story about his grandmother's treatment of his wound, she remembered a similar story that had a different outcome and also shared it with the group. Barbara's grandmother was Suzy Robinson Williams, another daughter of Louisa Robinson, who like her sister Ency was well versed in the family's medicinal knowledge and was one of the last Coushatta women to practice traditional medicine.

Grandmother and the Gift Card

Lorenda Poncho, narrator and translator (2013)

Linda Langley, Jaime Hill, and Crystal Williams, editors

There is a story that we love to tell the kids about their grandmother, my mom. This is something that happened when she was older, already in her eighties. We have a lot of funny stories about things she said or did, especially when she was trying to adapt to things that were new to her, and when she was trying to say things in English.

Mom had gotten a Walmart gift card from her niece. The card came in a pretty little gift tin, with her name and the amount on the inside of the lid. Mom kept asking me to bring her to Walmart so she could spend her gift card, so one day I loaded her up and brought her.

She went around the store selecting what she wanted to buy, then told me to bring her to the cash register to check out. We got into line, and Mom gave me the lid of that little gift tin to give to the girl so she could check us out.

"No, Mom," I tried to explain, "that's just the pretty tin that the gift card came in. You have to give her the card inside the tin."

She began to get angry at me, motioning to me to do as she had said and hand the girl the lid of the tin.

"Mom," I tried to explain again, "that lid is not money. You can't use that lid to buy what is in your cart. Only the card itself is the money."

I could tell she was getting really angry at me, and when I bent down to hear her she told me, "*Matink kahalíį!* (I said, *give* it to her!)."

I knew it was wrong, but I knew Mom was angry and I had no choice, so I handed over that lid to the girl at the cash register.

She looked at the lid, then at me, and finally she said directly to Mom, "I'm sorry, ma'am, but I can't accept this as payment. Even though it has your name, this is just the lid of a gift tin. You need to give me the actual gift card."

Without another word, Mom handed me the gift card to give to the girl.

I knew better than to ever say "I told you so" or anything like that to my Mom, so I didn't say anything at all, just handed over the card.

Mom had a little smile at the corners of her mouth all the way home.

NOTE

Lorenda's mother, Margaret John, was one of the first people to volunteer to be video-taped telling stories and memories of her life. She often told humorous stories at her own expense and laughed along with her son, daughters, granddaughters, and great-granddaughters when they recounted similarly funny stories. The older tribal people particularly enjoyed stories such as this one, about "mistakes" they made in dealing with new products and societal changes in the English-speaking world.—*Linda Langley*

Grandmother and the Turtle

Claudine Celestine Hasting, narrator (2012)
Stephanie Hasselbacher Berryhill, collector. Loretta Williams, transcriber and translator. Linda Langley, Jaime Hill, and Crystal Williams, editors.

One summer, we took our grandmother to the zoo in Houston. She had never been to a big city before, so she was apprehensive but eager to experience the big city. She lived in a small town in Louisiana so this was all new to her.

At the zoo we showed her how they kept the animals that were brought from overseas; the elephants, zebras, giraffes, and the African lions. When we came upon the Galapagos turtles, she stopped and stared in amazement.[1] She stood there for a long time observing the big turtles saying "Mmmmm." She was so surprised that a turtle could grow so big. She stood there rubbing her forehead.

We encouraged her to go see the snakes and salamanders at the next building. She was reluctant to go, but finally she moved on to the next exhibit. After a while, we realized she was missing. We went in all different directions to look for her. We finally found her back at the big turtles. She was so fascinated she did not move. After standing there for a while, she said, "Mmmmm, we could probably feed the whole village with that turtle."

When I told this story to my sister-in-law, she said when she first met my mother and me, she thought we spoke like a beached whale, referring to how the Koasati elders always say "Mmmmm." She said we lost the accent as the years went by.

My husband, Ed, who has been married to me for over forty years, still says "Mmmmm," just like the old people used to say when they saw something new and didn't quite understand what it was.

Akaamos—that's all.

NOTES

Claudine's Louisiana grandmother was Lizzie Poncho Robinson (1892–1970), a woman whose expertise as a basket maker is still represented by numerous granddaughters and great-granddaughters in the tribal communities in Louisiana and Texas. Claudine and her husband Ed are also willing volunteers and intrepid explorers, perhaps also traits passed down from her grandmother.—*Linda Langley*

1. Claudine used the Koasati word *satta* in telling this story because there is no word for "tortoise." We have translated *satta* here as "turtle" with her consent, because that is how it was most commonly translated among the older generation of Koasati speakers.

On My Way to the Meeting (*Ittanahkafa̲ Aayaliis*)

Janice Battise Sylestine, narrator (2010, *Koasati and English*)
Loretta Williams, transcriber and translator. Linda Langley, Jaime Hill, and Crystal Williams, editors.

Today as I was coming to the meeting, I was looking outside through my car window.
What I saw was such beautiful and pleasant scenery.
I was so happy to see that the day was sunny and the sky very blue.
As I was seeing all the scenery, I was telling God how much I appreciated everything He provided.
The trees were blooming in abundance. The leaves of the trees were green, others were red, and others were yellow.
On the other side of the ditch around the swampy area, the mayhaw bushes were blooming in bunches. I realized there was a lot of mayhaw in bloom, but there was a lot of flooding around the bushes.
I thought to myself, "Oh well, by the time it is all ripe and the water dries, someone will gather those berries and make the sweet syrup into jelly."

ORIGINAL KOASATI VERSION, *ITTANAHKAFA̲ AAYALIIS*

Himaayon ittanahhilkafa̲ ontit aayaliik, ammobiilafa̲ paachokkoolit mat-hiichaliis.
Il hiichak kana̲a̲hoosiis.
Nihtak haso̲kbaasin, abak okchakkot naasokkon hiichaliifookok achayoppaas.
Stachayokpaafookok Abachokkooli̲ immankat aayaliis.
Itto tohok bokoplit naasokkos.
Itto hissik okchakkoofookap, miitak homma, miitak laanahchoot naahos.
Hini taththa̲ okthaspi maamiifaap, sattilbik pakaala̲a̲hoosis hasaikahchok.
Hasaika̲hoosit lokkoolihchootoolit aaloliit mantikaap oiwiilasi

The Koasati authors (*front, left to right*): Claudine Hasting, Janice Sylestine, Barbara Langley, Lorenda Poncho; (*back, left to right*): Crystal Williams, Dan Sylestine, Bertney Langley. Not pictured: Ronnie Abney, Doris Celestine, Jamison Poncho.

imatanatliinannaas.

Inkoop hoktit anookaap, okik solotkaahitik ommo̲, kaamip aatoot sattilbi̲ athi imook, sattilbi

Champolokchosi̲talkichaahiskan.

NOTE

This is the first narrative composed and written in Koasati after the Language Committee adopted a practical orthography. While driving to a committee meeting, Janice said she was struck by the beauty of her surroundings and moved to write this lyrical, almost poetic narrative. She wrote each line in Koasati and provided both a word-for-word and a free translation in English. She was surprised when we suggested including it in this collection, saying that she always considered it too hastily written, perhaps even unfinished. To me, however, it has a place of honor as a work that truly bridges the gap between oral and written traditions. As such, it is a stunningly beautiful expression of cultural persistence, a magnificent tribute to the dedication of an amazing group of people, and definitely worthy of being the final narrative in this selection.—*Linda Langley*

SMALLER SOUTHEASTERN TRIBES

Introduction to Atakapa, Catawba, and Houma Stories

William Sconzert-Hall
Interpretations and Stories by Shawn Papillion, Beckee Garris, and MorningDove Verret Hopkins

THE ATAKAPA

Along with larger groups such as the Cherokee, Creek (Muskogee), Choctaw, and Chickasaw, there are smaller nations that have continuously called the southern United States their homeland. Some of these groups were part of a larger confederacy, anchored by larger, more powerful tribes, while others were relatively autonomous.

The Atakapa-Ishak people are native to the swamps, coastal prairies, and bayous of southwestern Louisiana and southeastern Texas. Several places in that region still bear the names descended from the Atakapa-Ishak, places such as Calcasieu Parish, Lacassine, Mermentau, and Carencro. Swanton theorized that the name Atakapa came from the Choctaw term *hatak apa,* "man eaters."[1] The Atakapa prefer to refer to themselves as Ishak, which translates as "the people."

Numerous groups in southeastern Texas and southwestern Louisiana spoke the Atakapa language or very similar languages. The name Atakapa referred specifically to a group that lived around Calcasieu Lake, near the present-day city of Lake Charles, Louisiana. Other groups under the Atakapa grouping included the Akokisa, Bidai, Deadose, Orcoquiza, Patiri, Tlacopsel, and Eastern Atakapa.

The Akokisa may have been the first group to have contact with

Europeans when survivors of Pánfilo de Narváez's expedition washed up on Galveston Island in 1528. These survivors met a group who referred to themselves as the Han. They may have been the Akokisa.

The association of the Atakapa-Ishak with cannibalism has been debated. The Choctaw warned the French about the use of cannibalism by people they called Atakapa. However, just because one group labels another group to be made up of cannibals, that does not necessarily make it so. Furthermore, the historical documents debate this connection. In fact, most of the colonial stories about cannibalism seem to stem from the account of one man, who had been a prisoner of the Atakapa, according to Lauren Post ("Notes," 225).[2] Ultimately this connection could have been a sensationalistic ploy by colonial authorities as a means to create an exotic "other." Since this is a chapter on stories, this will be all that will be said on the subject.

Around 1760 Gabriel Fuselier de la Claire bought all the land between the Vermillion River and Bayou Teche. Afterward, the Appalousa, a rival indigenous group to the Atakapa, forcibly assimilated the Eastern Atakapa into their tribe. Other Atakapa joined the Chitimacha, who had been a trading partner in historical times, and the Houma.

The Atakapa did not consistently rely on agriculture, due to the large population of fish and game animals in the bayous, forests, and marshes. They relied on hunting in wooded areas, where they also were able to gather building supplies and materials. Colonial documents noted that villages were located on riverbanks. The riverbanks often contained those forested areas the Atakapa used for hunting (Post, "Notes," 223).

Many Atakapa went into the cattle industry. In the eighteenth century, Poste des Attakapas, near modern-day Franklin, Louisiana, became a center for cattle branding. The documents for the brandings noted cattle owned by Native Americans and African Americans. The actual number of cattle owned by the tribe or tribal members is unknown. However, it can be inferred that they did have a fairly large number to make it necessary for them to pay the fees and register their brands (Post, "Notes," 233–34).

As of 2015, none of the remaining tribes that use the Atakapa name are federally recognized. They have been working on obtaining recognition, though.

In terms of stories and storytelling, Hugh Singleton was the lead researcher of the tribe and he collected a large number of stories. He also was important in recording the culture and history. His academic research showed that there is still a group of people who are keeping Atakapa traditions and stories alive.

THE ATAKAPA LANGUAGE

The Atakapa language is an isolate, which means that there is no strong evidence that it is related to any other language. However, poorly attested languages from the region may be dialects of Atakapa or very closely related languages. There have been attempts by well-known mid-twentieth-century American linguists, such as Morris Swadesh and Mary Haas, to demonstrate a genetic relationship between the Atakapa language and other languages in the region.[3] None of these attempts has been satisfactory. Any similarities to other languages are usually explained by geographic proximity and contact between language communities.

In particular, Atakapa and nearby languages share similar consonants and vowels. These sounds are *p, t, ts, k, ʃ, h, w, y, m, n, i, a, o*. Furthermore, Atakapa uses an affix agreement system that appears close to the system used by the Muskogean languages. The fact that many languages in the southeastern United States share these features with Atakapa does not mean that they are related to the Atakapa language. These similarities could have been shared through mutual contact and close geographical proximity between groups.

There were three possible dialects of Atakapa have been documented: Eastern, Western, and Akokisa. The Eastern dialect was spoken around Poste des Attakapas (modern-day Franklin, Louisiana). The Western dialect was centered in the area around Lake Charles, Louisiana, where the last speakers were recorded. Akokisa speakers probably lived around Galveston Bay. However, there may be too little evidence of Akokisa to determine its exact connection to Atakapa. It could have been a dialect or it could have been a very closely related language.

THE CATAWBA

The Catawba are native to the uplands of South Carolina and North Carolina and maintain a tribal headquarters at Rock Hill, South Carolina. Their reservation is relatively close to where their territory was located during the eighteenth century. British authorities identified villages along the upper Wateree River as belonging to the Catawba. Major epidemics broke out in the Carolinas in 1698, 1738, and 1759, according to Douglas Brown in *The Catawba Indians*.[4] By 1701 the Native population of the Carolina upcountry was devastated by disease. Many tribes split apart or united with another tribe because of strife caused by disease. Many members of the Saponi tribe (a southeastern Siouan people) moved into the Catawba nation in the 1720s when the relationship between Virginia and the Saponi tribe broke down.

In 1763 the Catawba obtained a 144,000-acre reservation. During the American Revolutionary War many Catawba served as scouts for the colonists against the British. However, by 1800 the dynamic between the tribe and the Americans changed. The larger white population put pressure on the tribe to sell its land, and in 1840 the Catawba signed a treaty with South Carolina that exchanged their reservation lands for five thousand dollars. The South Carolina government promised to assist the tribe in relocating (Brown, *Catawba Indians*).

In 1962 the Catawbas' status as a federally recognized tribe was terminated under the Termination Act. The tribe distributed its remaining territory to tribal members. In 1993 the Catawba gained back their federal recognition and successfully sued the state of South Carolina for $50 million in compensation for the land South Carolina took in the nineteenth century.

THE CATAWBA LANGUAGE

The Catawba language is a member of the Siouan (or Siouan-Catawban, depending on the linguist) language family as part of the Eastern Siouan (or Catawban) languages, along with Woccon. Other Siouan languages include Biloxi (Tanêksąyaa ade), Quapaw, Osage (Wazhazhe ie), Lakota (Lakȟótiyapi), and Winnebago (Hocąk). The last native speaker of Catawba died before 1960. However, there are efforts to revive the language.

Catawba has had a long history of linguistic research. The first recorded documentation of Catawba goes back to 1798. By the late 1880s Catawba had been linked to the Siouan languages. Catawba, along with Woccon, share word innovations not seen in other Siouan tribes, but they do share similarities to other Siouan languages in regard to certain prefixes and suffixes and they do contain numerous cognates with other Siouan languages. In particular, Catawba has instrumental prefixes that convey what caused an action or how an action occurred. These prefixes are very similar to the instrumental prefixes of other Siouan languages.[5]

THE HOUMA

The Houma tribe currently resides in southeastern Louisiana, mainly in Lafourche and Terrebonne parishes. According to oral traditions, they originally lived on the east bank of the Mississippi near St. Francisville. They encountered La Salle's lieutenants there when he went up the lower Mississippi Valley in 1682. After that, they moved down to Bayou St. John, in New Orleans, and then they traveled down Bayou Lafourche to their current location, according to J. Daniel D'Oney ("Houma," 63–64).[6]

Historically, scholars and federal authorities have treated the Houma as a nonexistent tribe. However, early explorers and missionaries noted the existence of the tribe. Famous explorers, such as Pierre Le Moyne d'Iberville, recorded accounts of interacting with the Houma. Jesuit priests also noted meeting the Houma (D'Oney, "Houma," 64–67).

There are further references to a native people in Terrebonne and Lafourche. Newspaper articles from the late nineteenth century acknowledge their presence. However, it was not until around 1975 that there was an increased focused on the Houma, with most of these articles being printed in and around Louisiana (D'Oney, "Houma," 74).

The Houma faced many difficulties with public education. In 1930 Terrebonne Parish implemented a tax so that a school could be built for the "Indians." However, by 1934 the Terrebonne school board started to deny the indigeneity of the Houma by referring to them as the "so-called Indians." By the 1960s all references to "Indians" in the school board minutes disappeared (74–75).

In 1916 a Houma leader tried to enroll his children in a white school, which led to the court case *Billiot v. Terrebonne Parish School Board*. The outcome of the case established that the plaintiff and his tribe were "colored." In the 1950s *Naquin v. Terrebonne Parish School Board* reversed this legal discrimination (75).

In the academic world, ethnographic work with the Houma began in earnest when John Swanton visited in the early twentieth century. Swanton's work in the area was small, probably due to miscommunication between him and his informant. Furthermore, he appears not to have performed much historical inquiry and direct communication with tribal members. He ultimately concluded that the Houma were too mixed to be "Indians" (75–76).

Other ethnohistorians have studied the Houma. Frank Speck and Hiram Gregory are especially celebrated. Speck wrote a review of the tribe's history, while Gregory added to Speck's history and was instrumental in research and college advising for local youths (76). More recent scholarly works have focused on cultural and linguistic issues. The linguistic research has been varied and has looked into both the original language of the Houma and the form of French they use.

As of 2014 the United Houma Nation is not federally recognized. They have spent the last few decades trying to gain recognition. The state of Louisiana has recognized them, but state recognition does not provide much in the way of benefits the way federal recognition does.

THE HOUMA LANGUAGE

The Houma language is an interesting case. There is a debate about what language the Houma originally spoke. Scholars seem to have formed into three camps about the issue. One camp theorizes that the Houma language was a variant of Choctaw. The second camp maintains that it was Mobilian Jargon, a trade language created mostly from Choctaw and Chickasaw. A third camp thinks that it was a distinct Muskogean language related to Choctaw, according to Cecil Brown and Heather Hardy ("Houma," 522).[7]

Interestingly, the language most identified with the contemporary Houma tribe is French. The French spoken by the Houma is distinct from other forms of French spoken in Louisiana, such as Cajun French and Louisiana French Creole. Since the Houma were usually isolated from the other French speakers, their form has maintained many of its distinguishing features (Brown and Hardy, "Houma," 522).

THE STORYTELLERS

Shawn Papillion provided the interpretation of the Atakapa origin story that follows. He is the shaman of the tribe and lives in Louisiana. He described his role in the tribe as being similar to a historian's. Essentially, he is the gatekeeper for the tribe's history, lore, and religious traditions. Featured in this volume is his interpretation as I received it.

Mrs. Beckee Garris provided the interpretation of the Catawba story of how Chipmunk got his stripes. She is a storyteller for her tribe and she currently resides in South Carolina.

The interpretation of the Houma stories is a collaboration between Mrs. MorningDove Verret Hopkins and me. Mrs. Hopkins is a member of the United Houma Tribe of Louisiana and lives in Louisiana. She comes from a line of medicine people and she is the only sundancer for her tribes and participates in traditional Houma dances.

Readers may be interested in other work about the people, history, and languages of the Gulf Coast. I recommend W. L. Ballard "Sa/ša/la: Southeastern Shibboleth?"; William Bright, "Native American Placenames"; Lyle Campbell, "Mary R. Haas and Historical Linguistics"; Albert Gallatin, *A Synopsis of the Indian Tribes* and *Hale's Indians*; Geoffrey Kimball, "A Critique of Muskogean"; Marianne Mithun, *Languages of Native North America*; Lewis H. Morgan, "Indian Migrations"; and Pamela Munro, "Gulf and Yuki-Gulf."[8]

I would like to acknowledge the contributions of Chief Crying Eagle Edward Chretien of the Atakapa-Ishak Nation, Jarred Cole, Hali Dardar, and Corrine Paulk. Without their help, this compilation probably would not have gotten very far. I am forever thankful for their help.

NOTES

1. John R. Swanton, *A Structural and Lexical Comparison of the Tunica, Chitimacha, and Atakapa Languages,* Board of American Ethnology B-68 (Washington DC: U.S. Government Printing Office, 1919); and John R. Swanton, "A Sketch

of the Atakapa Language," *International Journal of American Linguistics* 5 (1929): 121–49.

2. Lauren C. Post, "Some Notes on the Atakapas Indians of Southwest Louisiana," *Journal of the Louisiana Historical Association* 3, no. 3 (1962.): 221–42, esp. 225.
3. Morris Swadesh, "Phonological Formulas for Atakapa-Chitimacha," *International Journal of American Linguistics* 12 (1946.): 113–32; Mary Haas, "The Proto-Gulf Word for *Land* (With a Note on Proto-Siouan)," *International Journal of American Linguistics* 18 (1952): 238–40.
4. Douglas S. Brown, *The Catawba Indians: People of the River* (1966; repr. Columbia: University of South Carolina Press, 1983).
5. Albert Gatschet, "Grammatical Sketch of the Catawba Language," *American Anthropologist* 2 (1900): 527–49; Frank T. Siebert Jr., "Linguistic Classification of Catawba: Part I," *International Journal of American Linguistics* 11, no. 2 (1945): 100–4.
6. J. Daniel D'Oney, "The Houma Nation: A Historiographical Overview," *Journal of the Louisiana Historical Association* 47, no. 1 (2006): 63–90.
7. Cecil H. Brown and Heather K. Hardy, "What Is Houma?" *International Journal of American Linguistics* 66, no. 4 (2000): 521–48.
8. W. L. Ballard "Sa/ša/la: Southeastern Shibboleth?" *International Journal of American Linguistics* 51, no. 4 (1985): 339–41; William Bright, "Native American Placenames in the Louisiana Purchase," *American Speech* 78, no. 4 (2003): 353–62; Lyle Campbell, "Mary R. Haas and Historical Linguistics," *Anthropological Linguistics* 39, no. 4 (1997): 642–67; Albert Gallatin, *A Synopsis of the Indian tribes within the United States East of the Rocky Mountains, and in the British and Russian Possessions in North America*, Transactions and Collections of the American Antiquarian Society 2 (1836); Albert Gallatin, *Hale's Indians of North-West America, and vocabularies of North America*, American Ethnological Society 2 (1848); Geoffrey Kimball, "A Critique of Muskogean, 'Gulf' and Yukian Material in 'Language in the Americas,'" *International Journal of American Linguistics* 58, no. 4 (1992): 447–501; Marianne Mithun, *The Languages of Native North America* (New York: Cambridge University Press, 1999); Lewis H. Morgan, "Indian Migrations," *North American Review* 110 (1870): 54; Pamela Munro, "Gulf and Yuki-Gulf," *Anthropological Linguistics* 36, no. 2 (1994): 125–222.

Atakapa-Ishak

Interpretation of the Creation Myth

Shaman Shawn Papillion

Our creation story is astounding in a comparative relationship to other more established creation myths promoted by the great established religions and beliefs. The Atakapa-Ishak are a prehistoric indigenous tribe of southwestern Louisiana and southeastern Texas that some anthropologists have estimated to have lived in their ancestral home for 10,000 years or more. Our tribe is distinctive in that we have always had a belief in one God, whom we call Otsitat. Our creation myth contains some themes also prevalent in much of human antiquity. Within our myth one finds there is a flood story, the creation of men and women, and the heavens and earth. These same beliefs are held in high regard in many cultures and their holy books. A comparison can be made to the Bhagavad Gita, Gilgamesh Epics, the Egyptian book of coming forth by day and night, the Holy Quran, and the Holy Bible. We believe God was responsible for teaching humanity all we need to know, which brings to mind the forty-two non-confessions of Maat, the Hammurabi code, and the books of the law found in the Bible.

When our people were presented with the beliefs of the European they found no difficulty making a necessary life change toward those beliefs simply because of the familiar themes found within the Bible, such as the flood, people riding in a vessel, God using the earth to make man, the serpent speaking to mankind, breath into the nostrils of man (also prevalent in Egyptian and Sumerian myths), and the sun used as a representation of the power of God, with sun and son becoming easily interchangeable. Medicine bags, which we call *peni*, were replaced by the scapula or medals of the Catholic Church; smudges were, in our eyes, equal to burnt offerings or incense in church. Our ceremonial structures had an opening in the east and west, just as many European cathedrals did, as we watched the course of the sun: so did the light of God shine on our sacred altars just as it did on church altars. Saints were a suitable substitute for the many animal representations of attributes symbolizing aspects of power held by one God and found in every living thing he created.

Our creation myth can be used to explain both the big bang theory presented by scientists and the literal finger of a higher power of creation or creator. The sun represents the old man or God, while his duality is exemplified by the feminine aspect of the moon, and both personages are represented to encompass all. From this dual complex example of personalities both man and woman can be formed and taught what to believe and how they should behave and exist. One can easily identify a familiar theme in the creation myth where a snake plays a vital role in a plot to separate the representations of men and women. The dream of the tree with the white blossoms is the stars, planets not yet fully formed. The uprooting of that tree leads to a great deluge, which represents the formation of other planets, most notably earth. The old man and woman being in the personage of God who comes down from the stars to create people in their image is eerily similar to a trinity of sorts. The seashell is a vehicle of God much like the Hindu Vimana or the Chariots of Fire found in the Bible, while at the same time it served as the ark of Gilgamesh or Noah. The turtle shell sets the stage of the roundness of the earth, while all the animals play a vital role in serving as different creative forces of God. The village in the sky is heaven or the ancestors' final resting place.

The story also explains why the sun governs the day and the moon governs the night, both with equal regularity, yielding that both are needed to promote a full day of twenty-four hours. You also have each animal of our ancestral bands represented in this story playing its vital role. The reader's attention is captured by the fact that God came down and spoke us into being through a song, just as the son of man is said to have been present in the beginning and later was also sent down to earth to engage in co-habitation with mankind for a period of time, only to rise once again into the heavens for all to see, providing the sustaining life force needed for all to survive. Last, "The One That Sits Above All" returns to the sky village, having placed the moon in her own dominion of the sky, then plants a new tree that represents the completion of all the universe, stars, moons, and planets.

Our stories are being used today both to install and to revitalize respect and reverence in our culture. These stories are being told to students in schools, to tribal members, and during pow-wows to promote awareness of our great culture and legacy as a whole. I do not speak the *langue* fluently, but I do mix in some of the words I know in an attempt to generate interest in a serious revitalization of the *langue*. As the shaman, I greatly feel that these stories promote all that identifies us as a people. They connect us to our past, present, and future in such a profound spiritual way that without them mere words could never explain the people as we play our vital role in life. The stories and *langue* paint the entire picture of our identity and cannot continue to exist separate and apart.

Otsitat, the One Who Sits Above All

The Making of the Earth

Shaman Shawn Papillion (2013)

In the beginning there was no earth to live on, but up above, in the Great Blue water where Otsitat sat above all, there was a woman who dreamed dreams.

One night she dreamed about a tree covered with white blossoms, a tree that brightened up the sky when its flowers opened but that brought terrible darkness when they closed again. The dream frightened her, so she went and told it to Otsitat, who lived with her, in their village in the sky. "Pull up this tree," she begged him, but he refused to and tried to explain it was the tree of life and its roots drank so much of the blue water so rain would not fall and flood the sky village. All he did was dig around its roots, to make space for more light thinking that would make her happy. But the tree just fell through the hole that he had made and disappeared.

After that the great blue water began to fall through the hole as rain so Otsitat and the dreaming woman rode the waves of the great blue flood in a large seashell to the top of the highest mountain. The great man grew afraid of the woman and her dreams. It was her fault that the light of the tree had gone away forever. He took dust of the mountain and mixed it with rain of the great blue water and made men and women out of the mud and sang into their nostrils and they lived because he needed help to separate him from the dreaming woman.

There was nothing below them but a heaving waste of water. He called out to the creatures of the deep. "We must find some firm ground to separate me from her," he said anxiously. But there was no ground, only the swirling, endless waters. An alligator went down, down, down to the very bottom of the sea and brought back a little bit of mud in his claws. He found a turtle, smeared the mud onto its back, and dived down again for more. Then the serpents joined in. They loved getting muddy and they too brought mud back from the ocean floor as they spoke to the men and women of mud, telling them to spread it over the turtle's shell. The heron helped also, they smeared the mud off their long black legs onto the turtle, making the shell bigger and bigger. Everybody was very busy now and everybody was excited. This world they were making seemed to be growing enormous!

The eagle and the red bird and the panther and all the animals rushed about building countries, and the continents, until, in the end, they had made the whole round earth. Then the snakes told the people and animals to push the dreaming woman onto the back of the turtle with earth so high it placed her back into the great blue sky. The One That Sits Above All then took the people to a shore in his giant sea shell and taught them how to control the animals and how to talk and hunt and fish and how to build a hut and how to cook and create new life.

Right before the rain stopped falling from the hole in the big blue sky, The One That Sits Above All paddled back up the rain in his giant sea shell and sat on the opposite side from the dreaming woman in the sky. He used a little of the mud from turtle's shell to plug the hole and plant a new tree that blossomed only at night so the woman would not see it as she slept.

Catawba

Interpretation of a Folktale

Beckee Garris

This story is part of a larger genre. We normally say: "A long time ago the Ancient people said, 'This is how the _ (fill in the blank here).'" Native people tell stories not only to entertain children but they are told as a means of teaching them some of life's lessons. They learn how to sit quietly for long periods of time and how not to disturb the person sitting next to them, as there were times when their and the lives of others depended on them being still and quiet. They had to learn this lesson in days gone by due to a wild animal or someone invading their village.

We were always told we only told stories in the wintertime, for if we told stories in the summertime, a snake would wait in the path for you. Today, we think this was another way to impart the wisdom of not being idle as there was much work that needed to be done while preparing for the winter months.

While it is usually left up to the person hearing the story to decide what the lesson may be, I will give you three examples of what the following could mean. "Do unto others," "Am I my brother's keeper?" and last but not least, "You scratch my back, I'll scratch yours."

How the Chipmunk Got Its Stripes

Retold by Beckee Garris (2013)

A long time ago, it is said, the Ancient People told how this is the way the chipmunk came to look the way it does today.

There were two chipmunk brothers that went out to gather nuts and berries to be stored for the winter. While they gathering these things, the younger one turned to the other and said, "My back really itches. Will you please scratch it for me?" The older brother at first refuses to scratch his brother's back. After much pleading the older brother relented and scratched his younger brother's back. The younger chipmunk told his brother, "That feels good." When he grew tired of doing this he stops scratching his back. He asks, "Why did you stop scratching my back because the itch is still there." So his brother once again begins to scratch his back. But because he did not want to be pestered by his brother any longer about scratching his back, he brings out his claws and racks them down his brother's back. His younger brother complains to him about the scratching hurting him. He realizes he really did hurt his brother.

He tells him he is sorry because he really did not mean to hurt him, he just wanted him to stop pestering him about scratching his back. Plus he was afraid his brother would go tell their mother he had hurt him and he did not want to get into trouble for doing so. But once his younger brother is told about the stripes he has put on his back, he does not believe his brother. (Because we all know how older brothers like to tease their younger brothers.) He is told to go down to the stream and look at his reflection in water. When he has done this, he sees he indeed does have stripes on his back. Instead of being angry at his big brother for putting these stripes on his back, he likes the way they make him look. Yet when his older brother realizes how it makes his younger brother look, he wants stripes put on his back also. So of course, his younger brother does this because he wants his brother to look like him.

Houma

Interpretation of Two Traditional Stories

MorningDove Verret Hopkins and William Sconzert-Hall

The two Houma stories showcased in this chapter are centered on the same theme: boastfulness and how it can lead to bad consequences for the bragger. Being a braggart is seen as a particularly bad trait among the Houma. In Houma folklore, Rabbit usually plays the part of a braggart, and by the end of the story he often gets his comeuppance.

The Turtle tale is interesting in that similar stories are told by neighboring people. In particular, it seems the final straw for the animals is Turtle disturbing another animal's offspring. In contrast, especially in comparison to a Chickasaw tale included in this volume, this Houma version has Turtle brought before an animal council and the other animals take turns trying to break his shell. Secondly, the manner in which his shell is broken and who breaks his shell differs between the two accounts.

How Rabbit Lost His Tail

Retold by MorningDove Verret Hopkins (2014)

At one time, the rabbit had this beautiful, beautiful long luscious tail and he used to go brag to all the other animals, "Don't you wish you had a beautiful tail like mine? I have the most beautiful tail in the world." He would wrap it around his head and he made them feel so bad because it was so beautiful.

One day he got hungry and he saw one of his friends fishing in the bayou. He said to himself, "I'll go fish." After a while, he hadn't caught anything. He got tired and he decided to take a little nap. "Oh, I'll just lay here and take a little nap. When I wake up, I'll start fishing again. Then, maybe I'll catch something." He lay down and his big beautiful tail plopped into the water. Instead of a little nap, he slept overnight. It got really cold and ice formed around his tail. He woke and said, "Oh man, I slept for a long time." He tried to get up, but he couldn't get up. He tried to get up again. He jerked on his tail and it wouldn't move; it was frozen to the bayou. He jerked on it again and it still didn't move. "Oh, I'm going to have to take care of this. I can't stay like this all night long. I'm going to freeze to death. I'm going to give it a big old yank and when I give it a yank, my tail will come out." He gave it a big yank and his tail broke right off, leaving a little nub. That's why the rabbit doesn't have a long tail today.

How Turtle Broke His Shell

Retold by MorningDove Verret Hopkins (2014)

Turtle used to brag to all the animals that his shell was so fine and that he could also stay underwater. How many animals could do the things he could do? Can the rabbit or deer breathe under? No, but Turtle could. One day, he came across a nest of baby owls and teased them about the way they looked. They started crying and their mother showed. She was furious and said, "That's it! You have made fun of every animal in this forest! We have to do something! We're going to hold council on you!"

Turtle was sent before the council. The bear said, "I'm going to take him and smash him against a rock. I'm going to break his shell and he'll stop bragging." The bear tried and tried, but couldn't break the shell. The buffalo said, "I'm going to put him the middle of a field and kick him all over the place. If I kick him hard enough, his shell will surely break." The buffalo tried, but couldn't break the shell. The eagle said, "I think I know what I going do. I'm going to take him and fly as high as I can, until the sun is almost burning me. Then, I'm going to let him go and see how hard he's going to fall when he comes down." Eagle grabbed Turtle and flew as far as he could. They were so high that they looked like specks in the sky. Eagle let Turtle go and Turtle hit a rock at the bottom. His shell split into pieces all over the ground around him. He no longer had a shell. Turtle looked around and panicked. "Oh my god, I have no shell! They're going to kill me or eat me! Oh Creator, I need your help! Would you please help me?"

Creator looked down and responded, "You were so bad. You were mean to all the other animals. Now you know how they felt. Now that you have no shell, you have no way to protect yourself." Turtle apologized, "Oh but Creator, help me! I promise that I will never be mean to the other animals. I will respect everybody!" The Creator relented, "Well, everybody needs to be forgiven at least once and I'll only forgive you this one time. I want you gather up all the pieces of your shell in a little pile. I want you to turn the pieces inside out and leave them out in the sun. Then I want you to go to the glue-tree and rub its sap on the pieces and connect them together. Then I want you to let the sun heal it together. However, your shell will never be the same again. It was broken into too many small pieces."

Turtle did everything the Creator told him to do, and he had his shell back. He was never mean to the other animals again.

SOURCE ACKNOWLEDGMENTS

I want to thank all who permitted use or reprinting of the texts that appear here. Greg Bigler, "Rabbit and Turkeys"; Christie Byars, "Chickasaw Creation Story"; Weldon Fulsom, "Why Turtle Has a Cracked Shell"; Beckee Garris, "Interpretation of a Folktale" and "How the Chipmunk Got Its Stripes"; MorningDove Verret Hopkins, "The Importance of Folktales," "How the Turtle Broke His Shell," and "How Rabbit Lost His Tail"; Gloria McCarty, "Estvmvn Estomen Follatskis"; Harry Oosahwee (Adawi Donowelani), "Who Is Cherokee?"; Shawn Papillion, "Interpretation of the Creation Myth" and "Otsitat—The One Who Sits Above All: The Making of the Earth."

Thanks also to the Coushatta Heritage Department for the photograph of the Koasati authors and for the following: "The Bear Hunter and the Alligator's Gift," "How the Owl Got Skinny Legs," "Getting Fire from the Bear," "How We Survived Long Ago," "Hunting in the Olden Days, and Tomatoes," "Grandmother and the Nail," "Another Story about Grandmother and a Nail," "Grandmother and the Gift Card," "Grandmother and the Turtle," "On My Way to the Meeting."

The following appear in *Choctaw Tales*, collected and annotated by Tom Mould. Jackson: The University of Mississippi Press, 2004.

"The Choctaw Creation Legend," 64–65.

"Creation of Three Races" appears untitled, xxxviii–xxxix.

"Why Terrapins Never Get Fat," 208–9.

"The Dog Who Spoke Choctaw," 185–86.

"Running Water," 179.

"The Man and the Turkey," 184–85.

"The Little Man," 133–37.

"Pąš Falaya (Long Hair)," 117–21.

"New Inventions and Lost Traditions" appears as "Electricity, Plumbing, and Social Dancing," 165–67.

"Cars and Changing Values" appears as "Cars, Roads, and Changing Values," 167–68.

"The Third Removal," 170–71.

The following appear at the Sam Noble Museum of Natural History, Native Language Archives, Norman, Oklahoma.

"Boarding School Runaways" appears as Boarding School Runaways. Record number CHA-020

"How I Almost Killed a Hog by Scaring It" appears as Shukha vbi lin aha tuk. Record number CHA-015.

The following appear in *Choctaw Language and Culture: Chahta Anumpa Volume* 2. Norman: University of Oklahoma Press, 2007. Used by permission. © 2007 by the University of Oklahoma Press, Norman, Publishing Division of the University.

"The Miracle," 38–40.

"Neva the Hunter," 80–81.

The following originally appeared in Mary R. Haas, Creek (Muskogee) Texts. Berkeley: University of California Press, 2015.

"The Boy Who Turned into a Snake"

"Autobiography of James Hill"

The following originally appeared in Earnest Gouge. *Totkv Mocvse/New Fire: Creek Folktales*. Translated by Jack B. Martin, Margaret McKane Mauldin, and Juanita McGirt. Norman: University of Oklahoma Press, 2004.

"Rabbit Steals Fire," 29–31.

"Girl Abducted by Lion." 125–130.

Portions of "How Poison Came to the Chickasaw and Choctaw," originally appeared in *Chikasha Stories Volume One: Shared Spirit* by Glenda Galvan and illustrated by Jeannie Barbour, "How Poison Came to the Chicksaw and Choctaw." Courtesy of the Chickasaw Press. All rights reserved. For permissions and other rights under this copyright, contact the Chicaksaw Press.

The following are from Jack F. Kilpatrick and Anna G. Kilpatrick. *Friends of Thunder: Folktales of the Oklahoma Cherokees*, Dallas: Southern Methodist University, 1964. Reprinted with a foreword by Robert J. Conley. Norman: University of Oklahoma Press, 1995.

"The Rabbit and the Image" 35–37.

"Thunder and the Uk'ten" 53–56.

The following are from *Cherokee Stories of the Turtle Island Liars' Club* by Christopher B. Teuton. Copyright © 2012 by Christopher B. Teuton. Used by permission of the University of North Carolina Press. www.uncpress.edu.

"Rabbit and Possum Look for Wives," 162–68.

"How the Possum Lost His Beautiful Tail," 51–53.

"How the White Man Was Made," 198–99.

"The Owl in the Window," 218–20.

"Crossing Safely," 169–70.

"Santeetlah Ghost Story," 132–35.

"The Little People and the Nunnehi," 183–87.

"The Spirit of an Ancestor" 89–93.

"The Language and the Fire," 53–55.

"The Cherokee Migration Story," 68–76.

Selections from *A Cherokee Vision of Eloh'*, edited by Howard L. Meredith and Virginia E. Milan, translated by Wesley Proctor. 15–17, 21–27, 29. Muskogee, Oklahoma: Indian University Press, Bacone College, 1981. Reproduced with permission.

"The Trail of Tears" from *Living Stories of the Cherokee*, edited by Barbara R. Duncan. 221–26. Copyright © 1998 by the University of North Carolina Press. Used by permission of the publisher. www.uncpress.edu.

Selections from *Mankiller: A Chief and Her People.* © 1993 by Wilma Mankiller and Michael Wallis. 97–116. Reprinted by permission of St. Martin's Press. All Rights Reserved.

CONTRIBUTORS

Marcia Haag is professor of linguistics at the University of Oklahoma. She studies Native American languages, particularly Choctaw and Cherokee. She has published three books with longtime collaborator Henry Willis: *Choctaw Language and Culture: Chahta Anumpa Volumes 1 and 2* (2001 and 2007), and *A Gathering of Statesmen: Records of the Choctaw Council Meetings 1826–1828* (2013), all with University of Oklahoma Press.

Linda Langley recently retired from McNeese State University as a professor of anthropology and currently serves as the Coushatta Tribe's historic preservation officer. Together with her husband, Bertney Langley, a member of the Coushatta Tribe and native speaker of Koasati, Dr. Langley served as co-principal investigator of the original Documenting Endangered Languages grant that provided the impetus for organizing the Koasati Language Committee in 2007.

Mary Linn is curator of cultural and linguistic revitalization at the Center for Folklife and Cultural Heritage, Smithsonian Institution. Her primary research is in the Euchee and Oklahoma languages, and she has worked in effective strategies in grassroots language and cultural sustainability, language policy, and community-based language documentation and archiving worldwide.

Lokosh (Joshua D. Hinson) is of Chickasaw, Choctaw, Muskogee (Creek), Cherokee, and Euro-American ancestry and is a citizen of the Chickasaw Nation. He is currently the director of the Chickasaw

Nation's Chickasaw Language Revitalization Program in the Division of History and Culture.

A conversational speaker of the Chickasaw language and an award-winning artist, he holds a master's degree in Native American art history from the University of New Mexico and is a doctoral student in Native Language Revitalization at the University of Oklahoma. His research interests include Chickasaw stickball and stickball regalia, Chickasaw cultural history, and Chickasaw language revitalization.

Lokosh's edited publications include the *Chikasha Stories* series (2011–13), *Ilimpa'chi' (We're Gonna Eat!): A Chickasaw Cookbook* (2011), and *Anompilbashsha' Asilhha' Holisso: Chickasaw Prayer Book* (2012), and he authored *Chikasha: The Chickasaw Collection at the National Museum of the American Indian* in 2014. Hinson, whose Chickasaw name Lokosh translates as "Gourd," descends from the *Imatapo* (Their Tent People) house group and *Kowishto'* (Panther) clan. He and his family live in the Chickasaw Nation, just outside Ada, Oklahoma.

Jack B. Martin is professor of English and linguistics at the College of William and Mary. He specializes in language documentation and the Muskogean family of languages. His books include *A Dictionary of Creek / Muskogee* (with Margaret McKane Mauldin, University of Nebraska Press, 2000) and *A Grammar of Creek (Muskogee)* (University of Nebraska Press, 2011). Working with elders Margaret McKane Mauldin and Juanita McGirt, he also edited Earnest Gouge's *Totkv Mocvse / New Fire* (University of Oklahoma Press, 2004) and Mary R. Haas and James H. Hill's *Creek (Muskogee) Texts* (University of California Press, 2015).

Phillip Carroll Morgan is a Choctaw/Chickasaw poet, historian, biographer, and novelist. Four of the six books he has authored or co-authored since 2006 have won regional, national, or international awards. His most recent work, a novel titled *Anompolichi the Wordmaster*, a story set in 1399 in America, was published in October 2014 by White Dog Press. He holds three degrees in English, including an MA and PhD from the University of Oklahoma, where his primary concentration was in Native American literature.

Tom Mould is professor of anthropology and folklore at Elon University and director of the honors program. He is the author of three books—*Choctaw Prophecy: A Legacy of the Future* (University of Alabama Press, 2003), *Choctaw Tales* (University Press of Mississippi, 2004), and *Still, the Small Voice* (Utah State University Press, 2011)—and co-editor of two others. His research areas include oral narrative, sacred narrative, contemporary legend, American Indian studies, Mormon studies, performance studies, and ethnography.

William Sconzert-Hall has an MA in applied linguistic anthropology from the University of Oklahoma. His master's thesis is titled *The Effects of State-Sponsored Bilingual Legislation and Promotion of Minority Languages on Native Languages*. He presently lives in Louisiana and works on documentation and preservation of endangered languages in the Gulf region.

Christopher B. Teuton (Cherokee Nation) is professor of American Indian Studies at the University of Washington–Seattle. His most recent book is *Cherokee Stories of the Turtle Island Liars' Club* (University of North Carolina Press, 2012), a collection of forty interwoven stories, conversations, and teachings about Western Cherokee life, beliefs, history, and the art of storytelling. In 2013 *Cherokee Stories of the Turtle Island Liars' Club* received an American Book Award by the Before Columbus Foundation.

Kimberly G. Wieser is an assistant professor of English and an affiliated faculty member with Native American Studies at the University of Oklahoma. Her areas of interest are American Indian critical theories, contemporary American Indian literatures (particularly women's literatures), American Indian rhetorics, and American Indian creative writing.

INDEX

Page numbers in italics indicate illustrations.

IN THE NATIVE LITERATURES OF THE AMERICAS SERIES

A Listening Wind: Native Literature from the Southeast
Edited and with an introduction by Marcia Haag

Inside Dazzling Mountains: Southwest Native Verbal Arts
Edited by David L. Kozak

Pitch Woman and Other Stories: The Oral Traditions of Coquelle Thompson, Upper Coquille Athabaskan Indian
Edited and with an introduction by William R. Seaburg
Collected by Elizabeth D. Jacobs

Algonquian Spirit: Contemporary Translations of the Algonquian Literatures of North America
Edited by Brian Swann

Born in the Blood: On Native American Translation
Edited and with an introduction by Brian Swann

Sky Loom: Native American Myth, Story, and Song
Edited and with an introduction by Brian Swann

Voices from Four Directions: Contemporary Translations of the Native Literatures of North America
Edited by Brian Swann

Salish Myths and Legends: One People's Stories
Edited by M. Terry Thompson and Steven M. Egesdal

www.ingramcontent.com/pod-product-compliance
Lightning Source LLC
Chambersburg PA
CBHW020935310726
48980CB00007B/781/J
* 9 7 8 0 8 0 3 2 6 2 8 7 4 *